Missing Foxx

When you least expect it…

By
Lisa Mackay

Sexy M.F. Series - Book II

Published by Lisa Mackay

Version 0.2

*****~*|*~*****

lisamackayuk@gmail.com

@lisamackayuk

www.lisamackay.uk

www.facebook.com/lisamackayauthor1/

ISBN-10: 1523841257 - ISBN-13: 978-1523841257

Front cover artwork: www.saxonoak.co.uk

THANK YOU

To all my amazing readers who have not only read my first novel **M.F.** but were kind enough to tell me how much they enjoyed following Max and Vivienne's story
My deepest gratitude.
X:-)
To my wonderful friends and family who suddenly realised I was serious about writing these stories and offered me their undying support throughout.
Love you more.
Xx:-)
To Shiralee Swan of Saxonoak Photography for giving me exactly what I was looking for on the front cover of
Missing Foxx
You're a Star! Thank You.
X:-)
To Nathan Sykes - Over & Over Again
Beautiful song, perfect lyrics
X:-)
And finally, to our own imagination, may it never fail us!
May we all find our Sexy M.F. But if not…
May we always have books.
X;-)

CONTENTS

BAD FEELING
(MAX)

Our bond cannot be broken, lest you wish it or forget.
Our bond defies the burden of lamentable regret.
And if your heart's reflected in another lover's eyes,
when you least expect it, I will come to claim my prize.
So break it not, nor fracture it, this bond holds strong and true.
For when you least expect it…
My prize, my love, is you.

"She could be anywhere by now, Guv'. With all that cash she could have chartered a boat to Timbuktu."

"She can run all she wants. I will find her, and when I do…."

"Are you okay, Guv'?"

Hardly. I've just attended the funeral of my four year old nephew, poisoned to death by his psycho-bitch of a mother. How can anyone be okay after that? "I will be when we find that fucking bitch." *I've got a bad feeling about this.*

I've thought of little else since we left F1. Just a few hours ago, I was carrying Charlie's tiny little coffin into the church. God knows I've known pain in my life, but the pain of losing Charlie has cut me deep. I should have protected him. I should have saved him. I'll never forgive myself for failing him like that. Never.

Raising my hand to a woman is not my style but right

now, I'd gladly wrap my hands around Monica's throat and squeeze until the life drained from her treacherous eyes. She killed her own son and took him away from me, she'll pay for that.

"Trencher has sent me a text, Guv', there's a car waiting for us at the airfield."

"Okay, good. We're almost there, is Steve's ID still sending out a signal?"

Parker checks the iPad. "Yep, still at the same location too. What about the Police? If Monica's here, you're going to have to involve them sooner or later."

I shoot Parker an angry frown. "They've come up with fuck all so far. She's had more than enough time to find a way out of the country, she's long gone by now. But I'll find her."

I land at the airfield and power down the helicopter. Parker heads off to the small office building to retrieve the car keys. I'm feeling edgy and agitated so I decide to drive, I need to be doing something.

Parker navigates, following the signal transmitting from Steve's ID card, to an address near the seafront. It's a hotel, but as we pull into the road we have to stop when we're faced with a road block. "What the fuck?" Two police cars with flashing lights are parked across the road, and further down I can see the entrance to the hotel is littered with people, police cars, and ambulances. "Are you sure this is the right location?" I ask, reversing into a parking space.

Parker checks the iPad again. "Yep. Hundred percent. Looks like a bit of a shithole, though." We stare at each other for a moment. "What are you thinking Guv'?"

"I think Steve's dead."

We get out of the car and walk up the road toward the hotel. Every building in the street looks run down and neglected, it's obviously been a long time since any of them have seen a fresh lick of paint. As we pass several news crews crowding the pavement outside the hotel, I can hear them reporting about a shooting. *My bad feeling was right.* It has to be Monica they're talking about. I'm guessing Steve had finally exhausted his usefulness to her.

Parker and I exchange a look, and as I lift the police barrier tape to enter the hotel grounds, a young officer rushes over and stops me. "You can't cross the line, Sir. Please, step back. Only police personnel past this point."

"Who's in charge?" I ask impatiently.

The officer frowns at my abruptness. "D.I. Mills, but you can't see him, he's busy."

"I need to speak with him. Right now," I demand.

"I'm sorry, Sir, but—"

"My name is Maxwell Foxx. I need to speak with him right away, it's very important." I reach into my inside pocket for my business card then I hand it to him. The young officer looks down at it, then up at my stony glare. After a moment, when he realises I'm not going anywhere until I get what I want, he reluctantly radio's his Detective Inspector.

"Sorry, Sir, but I've got a Mr. Foxx at the front of the hotel. He says he wants to speak with you and that it's very important."

"Did you say, Foxx?" the voice on the radio asks.

"Er…yes, Sir. Maxwell Foxx," he replies reading from the card.

"Okay, send him up."

The young man warily eyes me then Parker before lifting the barrier tape. "He's up on the sixth floor, just ask for D.I. Mills."

We enter the dark, shabby lobby of the hotel and find the elevator with a handwritten note taped to the door, 'out of order', so we take the stairs. As we reach the sixth floor, a female officer stands in our way. "I'm sorry, Sir, this floor is closed to the public, you'll have to—"

"I'm looking for D.I. Mills, he's expecting us," I interrupt, handing her one of my cards.

The young officer blushes. "Oh, okay, follow me." She

leads us down a dark, tatty corridor toward a room buzzing with activity. Stopping a few feet away from the open door, she asks us to wait while she goes to find D.I. Mills.

There's a heavy smell of iron in the air. *Blood.* My stomach rolls. I've never been able to handle the smell, and it takes all my willpower to banish the flashbacks of my parents' death from my mind.

Parker's hand lightly rests on my shoulder. "You okay, Guv'?" I nod and swallow the bile that's forcing its way up my throat. Parker and I exchange a knowing look, we're both thinking the same thing. Monica's killed Steve and by now, she's probably miles away. *Shit. I knew I had a bad feeling about this.*

After a few moments, a slim, bearded man comes out of the room and walks toward us. "Mr. Foxx?" he asks, glancing between Parker and I.

"That's me," I answer, reaching forward to shake his hand, "And this is Parker." I don't bother to elaborate any more than that.

"D.I. Mills." His enquiring eyes swing back to mine. Opening his notepad, he retrieves a pen from his breast pocket. "Are you a relation of the deceased, Mr. Foxx? You have the same name."

What? "Monica's dead?" My wide eyes travel past him to the open doorway.

"I'm sorry, I thought you knew. I thought that's why you were here… Was she your wife?" he asks, waiting for me to focus on him again.

"What? ….No… She's… She was my sister-in-law." *Monica's dead?*

"What about Steve?" Parker asks.

D.I. Mills looks down at his notepad, flicking through the pages. "Steve Lombard?"

"Yes, he was with Monica when she went missing last week."

The detective pauses for a moment, mulling something

over in his head, then he checks his notes again before swinging his narrowed eyes back up to mine. "He was an employee of yours wasn't he, Mr. Foxx?"

"Yes, he works for Treadstone Security. My company, Foxx-Tech Global, employ Treadstone for all our security needs… What the hell happened here?"

D.I. Mills writes something down in his notepad before swinging his eyes back up to mine. "There appears to have been some kind of altercation between the two of them. Mr. Lombard was shot in the thigh and the neck. The neck wound hit an artery and unfortunately, he bled out."

"And what happened to Monica?"

He scratches his beard and looks over to Parker then back to me. "She was shot in the face three times at close range, but I'm sure she wouldn't have known much about it. The paramedics said she would have died almost instantly." He checks my reaction with sympathetic eyes.

Jesus! "Who shot her, Steve?"

"It would appear so, yes… We've got an approximate time of death at around eleven a.m. this morning. The town's annual parade along the beach front would have been well underway by then. Loud music, boat horns blasting out, thousands of people wandering around, nobody heard a thing. And as there's nobody else staying in this dump, the bodies weren't discovered until late afternoon. We got the call a couple of hours ago from the manager." I rub my forehead then I drag my hand through my hair. This has all come as a bit of a shock. "I'd like you to come down to the station to give me a statement, if you will, Mr. Foxx? We're pretty much finished here, I'm on my way back to the station now if you have the time?"

"What? …Yes, of course. Where is it?"

"Do you have a car? It's not far from here."

"We're parked just down the road, we'll follow you," Parker answers.

My mind is all over the place, I can't think straight. I can't believe Monica's dead. But what strikes me the most, is how unemotional I feel about it. *That bitch deserved to die.*

The smell of blood churns my stomach. A wave of nausea hits me and I suddenly feel light headed. Parker nudges my shoulder. "Come on, Guv'. Let's get some fresh air."

When we reach the front of the hotel, Parker indicates to D.I. Mills where we're parked, then he strides off to the car. I stand on the steps and take a couple of deep breaths to clear my head. I need to call Vivienne, I need to hear her voice.

"Max? Are you okay?" The sound of her beautiful voice warms my heart and calms my restless mind.

God, I miss this woman. "Yeah," I answer, struggling to hear her above the cacophony from the crowds gathered on the pavement. The reporters are jostling forward shouting questions at me as I walk away from the hotel, it's very distracting, I can't hear myself think.

"What's wrong? Did you find her?" Vivienne's voice sounds anxious, but I'm struggling to hear her as I fend off half a dozen microphones being shoved into my face by the press. I ignore them as I always do and just keep walking. "Max?"

"Sorry, baby. It's very noisy here. I can hardly hear you."

"Did you find Monica?" she asks, with a tremble in her voice.

"Yeah, Steve too! They're both dead. Looks like Steve shot her before he died from his wounds." *I still can't believe she's dead.*

I reach the car and stand at the passenger door resting my elbow on the roof. I suddenly feel a sense of relief, like a pressure has been lifted. I'd wanted to hunt Monica down and make her pay for what she did, but now she's gone and I didn't have to lift a finger.

"Are you coming home?" Her simple question swells my heart. Home is wherever she is, and I want to go home, right now. I just want to hold her, gaze into her beautiful brown eyes and never let her go.

"I've got to give a statement at the police station but we should be home in a few hours. Are you okay, baby?"

"Yes, I'm fine. I just… I want you home. And Max? …I want you to ask me that question."

What? She's completely surprised me. I've asked her to marry me so many times, but I never thought I'd be lucky enough for her to say yes. I ache for this woman. I've loved her since the very first moment I ever laid eyes on her. I had longed for someone like her before I even met her. She's everything I could wish for. Everything.

"Max? Are you still—"

"You make me so happy, baby. I'll be home as soon as I can, and Vivienne… I *will* ask you that question. I love you."

"I love you too, with all my heart."

Her words ring in my ears and fill me with pride and longing. *I can't believe I'm the guy she wants to marry. How could I be so lucky?*

As I get in the car, Parker starts her up and D.I. Mills waves at us to follow him as he emerges through the road block.

"Everything okay?" Parker asks, pulling away from the kerb.

I can't help the silly smile creeping across my lips. "S'all good."

"Aye-aye. What's brought that cheesy grin on?"

I let out a long, contented sigh while my grin gets bigger and bigger. "She makes me so happy."

Parker throws me a knowing look. "I can see that Guv'. She's a diamond that girl. She's got a beautiful heart."

"Yes," I smile. "She certainly has." *And it's all mine.* Butterflies fill my stomach. I feel so lucky to have the love of such an amazing woman, my woman. And I can't wait to see her. "She's the one, Parker. She's the one I've been waiting for my whole life. I'm going to propose to her." Parker's smiling face is fixed on the car in front as we follow it to the police station. "And I'm going to need a best man," I add grinning.

Parker does a double take. "What? …Me?"

I smile at his stunned face. "Of course you. You've been like a brother to me. I'll never forget what you've done for me and my family."

Parker's eyes blink, he looks a little choked up, and then he just smiles his big cheesy grin. "It would be an honour, Guv'. A real honour." He looks back to the road ahead, but his smile slowly slides from his face and a concerned frown slips into his brow. "It's good to see you happy, Guv'. I know Charlie's death has knocked you sideways, it's been hard for all of us, but… I'm really proud of you for not…you know, for not—"

"Yeah, I know," I interrupt softly. Everyone's been watching me like a hawk since Charlie's death. I know they're all worried that I'll slip back into my darkness. I can't blame them, it's been my solution for dealing with my emotions since I was a young boy. But I feel much stronger now. Vivienne's brought about a change in me. Everything makes sense with her, everything feels right. "You don't have to worry about me anymore Parker, I'm okay. Really. I'm more than okay. The bitch is dead and I'm going to marry the woman of my dreams."

Parker gives me a look, a mixture of pride and concern. He's always looked after me, he really *is* like a brother to me.

"Well!" he grins. "I'd better take Jan shopping for a new hat then!"

IDENTIFY

As we pull into the car park of the police station, I leave Parker in the car and follow D.I. Mills into the building. He walks me through a myriad of corridors until we finally end up in a small, sparse room with just a table and four chairs. D.I. Mills leaves the door open and sits in the seat opposite me, then he calls out to one of the officers passing the doorway.

"Eric? Could you bring me a couple of coffees? Cheers." The young man pokes his head around the doorway, nods, and then disappears. Another officer arrives with a folder.

"Sir, G-seven and G-eight are being transferred now, and Doctor Mendez is doing the P.M.'s tonight," she says, handing the folder to D.I. Mills. "Anything else, Sir?"

"No. Thanks, Sally, that's all." She glances at me shyly, then leaves the room.

D.I. Mills takes his time to sift through the papers in the folder, and then he takes his notepad from his coat pocket. After asking me to state my name, date of birth, and home address, he proceeds to ask me questions about Monica and Steve.

"Okay, I just need to clarify a few points with you, if I may?" he says, glancing over a document in his hand. "I've just learnt that Monica Foxx was in fact wanted for the murder of her four year old son Charlie, is that correct?"

"Yes, she poisoned him to death," I answer bluntly,

clenching my jaw. Charlie's death still feels so raw and painful. "His funeral was this afternoon."

"I see," he nods. "I assume you have witnesses for your whereabouts today, Mr. Foxx?"

I wait for him to stop writing and look up at me, my irritation clearly showing on my face. "Of course."

"And what brought you down to the south coast today, Mr. Foxx?" His eyes are shrewd and assessing. I shift in my seat and clasp my hands in front of me, leaning my arms on the table.

"I only found out this afternoon, that Steve Lombard had been assisting Monica in her escape. He carries an ID card that Foxx-Tech provide to all our personnel. The ID transmits a signal, I followed the signal and wound up here."

He raises his eyebrows. "Wow, technology really is great, isn't it?"

I frown at his glib remark. "It's my company's field of expertise." I'm starting to lose my patience, this line of questioning feels like a total waste of my time. "Is there something more specific you wanted to ask me?" I sigh angrily.

"Actually, yes." He pulls out another sheet of paper from the folder. "Your statement to the Met Police after Charlie's death, says that on the day Monica went missing you believe she stole five hundred thousand pounds and a handgun from your safe, is that correct?" He folds his arms across his chest and rests back in his seat.

"Yes! Look, you know everything. I've already given a full statement about that, what more can I tell you?"

As the D.I. stares at me for a few moments, Eric returns with two plastic cups of coffee and some sachets of sugar and milk. "There you go." He leaves, closing the door behind him.

D.I. Mills pours the milk into his cup, takes a sip, and pulls a face. "Euww, don't bother it tastes like shit," he mutters, placing it back down on the table and sliding it away. "The thing is, Mr. Foxx. I'm a bit confused. You see, between them, we only found eighty-nine pounds and some loose change. Do you know what could have happened to the rest of the money?"

I lean forward in my seat and look him straight in the eyes. "I don't care about the money. What difference does it make?"

He seems surprised at my answer. "I'm just trying to figure out what they did with half a million pounds? They certainly didn't spend any of it on their hotel accommodation."

His comment snags me for a moment. *Fair point.* "As I said, I don't care about the money… What about my gun?"

His eyebrows raise then he looks down at the files on the table. Pulling out a photograph of a black handgun, he places it in the centre of the table. "Is this yours?" I slide the photograph toward me, it looks like my gun. I check the handwritten serial number in the top left-hand corner.

"Yes. That's mine." I slide the photograph back to the centre of the table, tapping my fingers impatiently. D.I. Mills places it back in the folder.

"We'll have to wait for forensics to match up the bullets found in the victims, but as Mr. Lombard was still holding your gun when we arrived, I think we can safely assume that he used it to shoot Mrs. Foxx." He leans back in his chair. "However, we've checked with Treadstone Security and they confirm that Steve Lombard was issued with a firearm when he started with the company five months ago. The funny thing is, his holster was empty and we haven't, as yet, found his gun at the scene. Do you have any idea where his gun may be?"

"I don't know, maybe he left it back in his apartment."

"Then why wear the holster?"

Yeah …That does seem strange.

The D.I. stares at me for a moment, then he gathers all the papers together and closes the folder. "Do you have any objections to being fingerprinted and DNA tested, Mr. Foxx? It's just for elimination."

"No. Whatever you need, just get on with it," I snap, impatiently tapping my fingers on the table. I just want to go home.

"Okay, I'll send someone in to take your prints and a swab. Oh, and before you go, Mr. Foxx, would you be able to formally identify the bodies?" he asks, rising from his seat.

"Er, yes. Of course," I reply hesitantly.

"Okay, good. If you could wait here, I'll be back in a minute."

Identifying the bodies is not something I really want to do, but the sooner I get everything cleared up down here, the sooner I can go home to Vivienne. I miss her, and right now after the shitty day I've just had, I really need to be with her. I check my phone, no messages or missed calls. I'm just about to dial Vivienne's number when the door opens and a man enters carrying a metal briefcase.

"I'm Terry," he smiles, "I'm just going to take your prints and a swab for DNA," he says, removing all the required items from his case.

Shortly after Terry has finished, D.I. Mills returns and asks me to follow him. We leave the main building of the police station and walk through a small courtyard to another more modern building. He presses a button on the intercom and looks up at a small camera above the panel. Shortly after, the doors click open and I follow him inside.

The small lobby is stark and bright with only a reception desk. A young woman behind the desk looks up, acknowledging D.I. Mills with a smile, and me with a blush and a bat of her lashes. Her eyes roam over my face and linger a little too long for my liking.

I'm taken sweetheart, just get on with it.

"Personal effects for G-seven and G-eight?" D.I. Mills asks, drawing her attention away from me.

"Oh, yes, if you could just wait a moment, I'll get them

for you." The girl throws me a coy smile, batting her lashes and smoothing her skirt before disappearing into another room behind her desk.

Yeah, yeah, just do your job so we can all go home!

After a short while, she returns with two clear plastic bags, and a large opaque yellow bag. She opens the large yellow bag and shows us the contents. I recognise some of Monica's clothing. A green coat, black dress, shoes, and a handbag. The yellow bag also contains some men's clothing which I assume are Steve's. All of them are drenched in blood.

"Because of their condition, if you don't want to keep these items we can dispose of them here, if you would prefer?" the girl asks, smiling at me seductively.

"Yes, just get rid of them, thank you."

She places the two clear bags on the counter along with two forms. "And these are the personal effects of Mrs. Monica Foxx and Mr. Stephen Lombard. If you could check the items and then sign for them here," she says, leaning closer to me.

Take the hint sweetheart! I ignore her, and take a look in the bag containing Monica's effects. I see her passport, credit cards, a photograph of Charlie as a baby, her wedding ring, some cash, and the delicate silver necklace with entwined hearts that I gave to her when we first met. "These are definitely Monica's things," I mumble, staring down at the necklace. I hadn't realised she'd kept it.

Steve's bag only contains a watch, his ID card, a wallet with thirty pounds, a driving licence, a silver lighter, and his empty gun holster.

Once we've dealt with all the formalities, we carry on down a short corridor into a larger area with a glass wall on the left, and open plan offices on the right. D.I. Mills walks over to a metal panel set in the glass wall and presses one of the buttons, creating a loud buzzing noise inside the bright, white and stainless steel room beyond.

"Hi, Sam, have you started the post-mortem yet?"

An attractive, middle-aged woman, wearing the full forensics kit, white gown, rubber gloves, hairnet, and short wellies turns to face us. "Oh, hello, Oscar. Nice to see you again," she says, before glancing over at her computer screen. "Er, yes, I've just started the post-mortem on G-seven. She's a white female, a hundred and twenty-five pounds, five feet nine, green eyes, red hair, small tattoo on right ankle, and a c-section scar on lower abdomen."

Her voice drones on, but my eyes are drawn down to the pale skinned, red haired body lying on the metal trolley behind her. *Monica.* My stomach knots and a wave of nausea makes me feel light headed. The smell in here is very strong, very clinical, it burns in my nose.

"Well, before you continue, Sam, I've got someone here who can formally identify the bodies for us, is there any chance we can do that now?"

Sam lowers her head and gives the D.I. a steely glare over the top of her glasses. "Oscar! You know full well that I cannot allow anyone to contaminate the room during a post-mortem."

"Yeah, I know Sam, but it would really help me out if we can clear this up tonight."

She huffs out an exaggerated sigh. "No. Oscar, you know the rules. However, if you look at the screen behind you, I can relay the image from my head-cam, will that suffice?" she asks, obviously irritated at our intrusion.

"That would be perfect, I owe you one," he says, cheekily.

She raises an eyebrow. "You owe me several, D.I. Mills. I shall call in my favours one day so you'd better be prepared."

He rolls his eyes then he nods for me to follow him to the office behind us. We sit at one of the desks and wait for the monitor screen to display the image.

Mentally, I brace myself. D.I. Mills had spared no details when he told me what to expect when I saw Monica's face. She'd been shot three times at close range, it wasn't a pretty sight. He explained to me how one of the bullets had ripped almost all of the skin away from the bone on her right cheek. Her left eye was completely gone, and the bones in her left cheek and jawbone had been shattered. As detailed as his warning was, it still hadn't prepared me for the stark reality of what finally flashed up on the screen, and yet, I couldn't take my eyes off it. The image was both macabre and compelling.

Jesus! Monica's usually voluminous red hair is matted with blood around her almost unblemished alabaster forehead. The rest of her face is horribly disfigured and swollen. Bone and teeth are easily visible through the torn and bloodied flesh. As I stare wide-eyed at the screen, the doctor raises Monica's swollen right eyelid, revealing a dead and lifeless green eye staring out from her ruined face. As the doctor's head cam lingers on what was once such a beautiful face, she manoeuvres a flap of skin back into place over her cheek bone, I look away. A flashback to my mother's ruined face on the day she died, floods my mind and wrenches at my gut. *Shit.* I need some fresh air. "It's her. It's Monica," I mumble, suddenly rising to my feet and trying to ignore the bile rising in my throat.

D.I. Mills walks over to the intercom. "Okay, Sam, we're done here, thanks. Is G-eight in the fridge?"

Sam turns to face him then she looks over at me with sympathetic eyes. "Yes, and he's in a much better condition."

"You okay to carry on?" he asks me. I nod impatiently, I just want to get this over with and go home.

We leave, and walk a short distance to another room. D.I. Mills punches in the code and we enter the grey tiled room. The temperature is freezing in here. Either side of the room are more glass-walled partitions with stainless steel trolleys in each. Steve's body lies on one of the trolleys, covered up to his chest in a black plastic sheet. I recognise him instantly. His pale grey face is relaxed, almost serene, and the small reddish-black circle on his neck looks innocuous enough, and yet here he lays, in the mortuary.

"Yes, it's him, Steve Lombard," I say, looking away.

"Good, thanks for doing that. Will you notify the next of kin, Mr. Foxx?" I nod, unable to voice anything. "Okay, good. I just need you to sign a couple of forms before you leave."

We walk back out to the reception desk to collect the personal effects and to sign the required documentation.

"If I need to reach you, can I contact you at Foxx-Tech?" D.I Mills asks, walking me to the exit.

"Of course. I assume you'll let me know when the bodies can be released for burial?"

"Yes, of course, we'll contact you as soon as possible." He smiles, opening the door.

"What about my gun?"

"We'll need to let forensics finish with it, but we'll notify you as soon as it's released." We shake hands and then I quickly march out of the building, desperate to breathe in some clean, fresh air.

Parker's leaning against the car and walks around to open my door as I approach. "Alright, Guv'?"

"Let's get out of here," I grumble, throwing the bags into the rear seat.

"What are they, Guv', personal effects?"

"Yeah, make sure Steve's family get his things, and tell his parents that I'll pay for all their funeral expenses."

"Will do. What about Monica's stuff?"

"Apart from the photograph of Charlie, I couldn't give a fuck. Toss it all in the trash."

As Parker makes quick work of getting us back to the airfield, I take my phone out and dial Vivienne. The phone rings and rings. I start to wonder if she's in the shower, or maybe she's asleep. It's been a very long emotional day for all of us. Just as I'm about to end the call, it answers.

"Vivienne? ...Baby?"

The line suddenly goes dead. I check the signal strength

and redial. This time, it goes straight to answer-phone. Vivienne's giggly answer-phone message makes me smile. I remember while she was trying to record the message I was kissing her neck, which of course led on to much more distracting activities. I guess she never got around to re-recording it. "Baby, we're on our way home. See you soon, I can't wait. I love you."

Once I've left my message, I stare down at the image of Vivienne on my screen. I'm so looking forward to seeing her tonight. It's been a really shitty day, one of the worst in many respects. Burying my beloved nephew was one of the most painful experiences of my life, but knowing I'm going home to Vivienne, and knowing she's going to be my wife, nothing could spoil how I feel right now.

"Oh, by the way, Guv', John called while you were in the police station. He dropped Jan home after the wake and he was going to take your mum home too, but she wanted to go and see your dad in the hospital, so he's going to wait with her until she's ready to leave. I told him what happened, but I told him not to mention it to your mum yet."

"Okay, good."

Since the day they adopted us, it was clear Sylvie and William were inseparable. It's been hard for Mom since Dad's been in the hospital. She doesn't like to go a day without visiting him, but with the funeral this afternoon, I guess she's missed him. I've always respected the love they have for each other, it's a rare thing these days. I never thought I'd ever find a love like that, until I met Vivienne.

"How are things working out with you and Jan? You seem very happy together," I ask smirking.

Parker throws me his cheeky smile. "That woman melts my heart, Guv'. But what she sees in me, I'll never know."

"Admit it, Parker, under that hard exterior you're just a big old softy." We both laugh at ourselves, two powerful men besotted and bewitched by two beautiful women.

Once we're back at the airfield I fire up the helicopter

and we head off home. Parker spends most of the flight talking to Trencher, filling him in on all the latest developments. Then he has a long and giggly conversation with Jan. The man's besotted. Fifty minutes later, we land on the roof of the Foxx-Tech building.

I SHOULD HAVE PROTECTED HER

The elevator arrives at F1. Parker's heading down to his car in the basement and then he's off to see Jan, and I can't wait to see Vivienne. It's been an exhausting day, and all I want to do is hold her in my arms and gaze into her beautiful brown eyes.

"Well, good luck, Guv'," Parker smirks, throwing me a cheeky wink and waggly eyebrows as we shake hands. The elevator doors glide open, and suddenly his smirk disappears and his eyes widen as he looks past me. "Something's wrong."

I turn to see there are no lights on in the foyer. The light from the elevator hits the penthouse doors, which are open and the penthouse is dark inside.

"What the fuck?" *Vivienne!* I dart across the foyer.

"Guv! Wait!" Parker yells, but I can't wait. I need to find Vivienne. I need to know she's alright.

Please God… Don't let anything have happened to her.

I run into the penthouse and try the switches in the hallway, but it remains dark. The moon is blanketed by clouds so there's hardly any light coming in through the windows, it's too dark to see anything. My eyes fiercely try to adjust as I frantically call out to her, "Vivienne? …baby, where are you?"

"I'll go and check the fuse box," Parker says, from behind me. "Here, take this." He hands me a small flashlight and then he rushes back out to the foyer, to try and get the lights back on. I stand there listening for a moment. There's no sound at all, it's eerily quiet, just the sound of my heart beating out of my chest.

What the fuck happened here? Feeling uneasy, I take out the gun Trencher had given me and I disengage the safety. I shine the flashlight around the hallway, then I check the dining room and the kitchen. Everything looks normal. I slowly make my way into the living room, trying not to bump into the furniture. Shining my flashlight around the room, it lands on the study door. There's a long smear of blood on it. My heart stops and the blood in my veins suddenly feels ice cold. *Oh, my God. No.* I quickly move toward the study. The heavy, metallic smell of blood hits my nose, churning my stomach. The door is open about four inches. I stop again to listen, but there's nothing, not a sound. I tentatively push the door open a little further, then a little more, and then finally all the way, but there's no one here.

Shining my flashlight around the room, I see the desk lamp is on its side and the fragments of the shattered bulb twinkle in the beam of light. Everything else in here looks normal until the flashlight lands on the wall behind the door. My eyes widen in horror at the blood spatters and smears on the cream coloured wall. My stomach rolls. *So much blood …What the fuck happened here?*

As I follow the trail of blood down the wall, the beam of light lands on a glistening pool of red on the marble floor. I feel sick. My heart pounds in my chest, and I can't breathe. *No. Not Vivienne.*

As I move back to the doorway, I stand on something hard so I quickly shine the light down on it. The smashed remains of Vivienne's phone lie on the floor. It's then that I notice a trail of blood spots and a bloody footprint leading out of the doorway. I follow the trail back out into the living room. "Vivienne? …Please! Where are you, baby?" *Please be okay. Please.*

Suddenly, all the lights come on at once. Parker must

have reset the system. I quickly look around me, there's more blood out here too and the trail leads me to an open door to the terrace. "Vivienne!" I run for the door but my heart sinks as I skid to a stop when I find Vivienne's lifeless body lying in a pool of blood out on the terrace.

"Jesus! Vivienne." I sink to my knees and immediately feel for a pulse on her neck with trembling fingers and an anxious heart. "Parker! She's here!" I yell. "Call an ambulance. Hurry!" *Please don't leave me, baby …Please be okay, I can't lose you now.* "I'm here, baby. You're going to be okay," I whisper, choking back the tightening lump in my throat. My wide eyes scan over her body checking for any signs of life. Suddenly, I feel a very weak pulse. Relief washes over me knowing that she's still alive. "Thank God," I whisper, closing my tear filled eyes.

Her skin is freezing so I quickly remove my jacket and cover her half naked body. She's only dressed in a short, silk, blood-drenched nightgown, she needs more warmth. "Parker! I need a blanket and something to stop the bleeding. Hurry!" I yell over my shoulder.

Parker suddenly appears beside me. He throws me a blanket and some towels as he ends his call to the hospital. "They're on their way Guv'. Is she breathing?" he asks nervously.

"Yes, but it's very shallow. I'm frightened to move her, she's got a terrible head wound and she's lost such a lot of blood." I cover her with the blanket and quickly press a towel into the wound to try and stem the blood flow. Her skin is pale and her lips are grey. The gash on the side of her head is still pouring with blood. I press as hard as I can to stop the bleeding.

"I can't lose her, Parker. Not her." The words catch in my throat, and the tears spill down my cheeks as I look up to Parker for reassurance, but the look on his face tells me he's as scared as I am.

The thought of losing Vivienne slowly crushes my heart. There is no me without her. With a trembling, blood stained hand, I caress her cheek and lean down to kiss her tenderly on her cold lips. "I love you, baby. Please, please don't leave me."

Parker's phone rings. "Yeah! …F-one, three, zero, zero, three. Hurry! …They're here, Guv'. I'll meet them at the lift, and I'll call John and Trencher to give them the heads up." He quickly marches off.

For fifty-five paralysing minutes, I anxiously watch the paramedics as they try to stabilise Vivienne for transfer to the hospital. Her pulse is incredibly weak, her blood pressure is dangerously low, and she hasn't regained consciousness. I feel so lost and useless. The ache inside is unbearable. If anything happens to her… *I should never have left her. I should have been here to protect her. What if…?* I can't even think about losing her.

When the paramedics finally manage to stabilise her, they take her down to the ambulance and blue-light it all the way. A knot of dread sits in the pit of my stomach and my chest feels tight as Parker drives like a bat out of hell following the ambulance.

"What do you think happened, Guv'? I checked all the locks on the doors and windows, none of them were forced or damaged, and nothing appears to have been stolen either. Although, I don't know about the safe. But I don't get it? Could she have fallen or something?" Parker asks, running a red light.

"No!… It was no accident. She was definitely attacked." My hands clench into tight, white knuckled fists against my thighs. "The paramedics showed me the finger marks on her neck and shoulders. Somehow, someone got inside and…" My stomach churns at the thought that she must have felt so scared and helpless.

"But who? And how the fuck did they get inside?" Parker asks angrily, pulling into the car park. "Unless… Unless she let them in…" He looks over at me waiting for me to comment, but I haven't got time to worry about that now. I get out of the car and run into the hospital. My main focus is Vivienne, she's all I can think about right now. I just need to know she's going to be okay. I just need to be with her.

Since I found her lying half dead in a pool of blood, I've asked myself those very same questions over and over. Who?… Why?…But nothing makes any sense. Vivienne wouldn't let anyone into the penthouse she didn't know, she's way too cautious for that. *Unless… Mike?*

I have to endure another agonising wait while Doctor Alexander and his team examine Vivienne. She's then rushed straight into surgery after the scan revealed a skull fracture. I'm scared shit-less, and they won't let me see her until she comes out of surgery.

Parker joins me in the waiting room as I pace up and down like a caged lion. "Any news?" he asks, handing me a clean shirt. The one I'm wearing is covered in Vivienne's blood. I just shake my head, I can't speak and the wait is killing me. "She'll be okay," he says, softly.

I take a long, deep breath. I really hope he's right. *I can't lose her.*

My mind keeps flipping over all the possible scenarios for what could have happened at the penthouse tonight. When I spoke to Vivienne earlier, she sounded fine. *What the fuck happened? Did she let someone in? Did Mike turn up?*

As I'm buttoning up my clean shirt, Parker hits me with a question like he's just been tuning into my thoughts.

"You don't think Mike could've had anything to do with this, do you?"

She would have told me if he'd been pestering her again…wouldn't she? My heart sinks when I suddenly recall the night she ran away from me. She'd found out that I'd slapped Mike around a little because I'd thought he was responsible for trashing her apartment. I know Mike's still in love with her, he told me so himself. And he made no attempt to conceal his feelings toward me that night I showed up at his apartment. *Maybe Vivienne has spoken to him recently?*

Anger boils to the surface at the thought that maybe Vivienne had told him we were getting married, and maybe he'd turned up at the penthouse to try to talk her out of it. To try to get her back.

Maybe they'd had a fight? Maybe it all escalated out of control and… Rage courses through my blood. "I'm going to kill that son-of-a-bitch!"

Parker watches me closely as I continue to pace, grumbling under my breath, then he moves into my path, stopping me in my tracks. "Don't go getting your knickers in a twist over Mike," he frowns, staring me out. "Yeah, he's a bully, but he isn't the kind of bloke to have the balls to rattle *your* cage. Especially not after your last visit!"

I scowl at him and grit my teeth. "Maybe he was looking for revenge?"

Parker shakes his head still frowning and staring me out. "He loves the girl, why would he want to hurt her? …You? Yeah! But not her… If it'll make you feel better, I'll speak to Miles to find out who came into the building last night, and I'll get Trencher to check the c.c.t.v."

I walk around him and continue to pace. It's the only way I can keep myself from freaking out. *Why are they taking so long?* Parker huffs out an irritated sigh then he starts to walk out of the room. "And tell Trencher to check out her mother too!" I call out, dragging my hands through my hair.

Parker stops in the doorway. "Her mother?…Why?"

I stop pacing and turn to face him. "Vivienne's mother is an alcoholic drug addict. When she found out from the newspapers that Vivienne was dating me, she contacted me asking for money. Vivienne doesn't know," I say, looking down at the floor. I hate keeping secrets from her. "I refused to give her any money unless she went into rehab... She wasn't interested."

Parker walks back into the room. "So, you think she might have come to ask Vivienne for money?"

"I'm not ruling anything out at the moment."

"But you don't think she'd hurt her own child, do you?" he asks sceptically.

"It didn't seem to bother Monica," I grate, clenching my jaw. A long sigh of frustration huffs out of me. "Oh, I don't know. But it had to be someone Vivienne knew. Why else would she let them up to the penthouse and open the door?" Parker stands there for a while processing the idea before leaving me on my own.

After what felt like an eternity, Doctor Alexander's soft voice draws my attention. I stare at him trying to read his face, he looks worried. My stomach churns as I anxiously wait for him to speak. *Please, let it be good news.*

"The surgery went very well," he says, offering me a reassuring smile. "We've moved Vivienne to the critical care unit and put her into a medically-induced coma, for the time being."

"Oh, my God no." Suddenly every breath feels toxic.

"It's just a temporary measure while we assess her. The scans indicate a linear fracture in the skull and a swelling of the brain at the point of impact. It's not severe, but we'd like to keep her sedated while we monitor the swelling."

I can't lose her. My knees buckle and I have to sit down before I fall down.

"Mr. Foxx please don't upset yourself, it's not like Charlie's coma, it's fully reversible," he says, reassuringly, almost as if he's just read my thoughts. "We administer a controlled dose of anaesthetic to create a deep state of unconsciousness, which helps to protect the brain by reducing the metabolic rate of the brain tissue, as well as the cerebral blood flow. She'll be closely monitored and once the swelling decreases we will bring her out of the coma."

"Can I see her?"

"Of course, just let me check with Matron," he says, patting my shoulder.

My head is spinning. She's not out of the woods yet and

that scares the fuck out of me. I take my phone out of my pocket and stare at Vivienne's image on the screen, her beautiful face smiles back at me. My heart aches, and for the first time in a long time, I pray.

"Mr. Foxx?" I look up and see a nurse standing in the doorway. "If you'd like to follow me, I'll take you to see Vivienne." She leads me down the corridor to a set of double doors. Swiping her card through the scanner, the doors click open. "When you're visiting just use the intercom and someone will let you in," she says, leading me past a small reception desk and then onward to a bay containing six beds. "Vivienne's in the first bed on the right," she smiles, then she walks away.

I hesitantly walk over to Vivienne's bed which is surrounded by high tech machines and monitor screens. A male nurse stands at her side drawing blood from an intravenous line in her arm. He glances up at me. "Hello, I'm Rashid, I'll be looking after Vivienne tonight. Please, take a seat. I just need to check her arterial blood gasses and then I'll talk you through what we're doing." I nod at him, but I can't take my eyes off Vivienne's face. She has a much better colour in her cheeks than she had earlier, and her lips are no longer grey, but she has a breathing tube in her mouth, IV lines coming out of her neck and arms, and a row of stitches closing the wound in her head which runs vertically for about four inches from just below her temple, up into her hairline. My eyes linger on the small faint scar just above her right eyebrow. The memory of how she got that scar comes flooding into my mind.

She'd received a blow to the head after drinking herself into oblivion and passing out in the gent's toilets at Jamie's Gallery launch night. Ironically, the memory makes me smile. That was the night I introduced myself. Up until that point, I'd only previously seen Vivienne from a distance. The first time was while she was working at Great Ormond Street hospital. Her smile lit up the room and her giggle just blew me away. I was hooked at first sight. I desperately wanted to get to know her, but annoyingly at the time, she had a boyfriend.

After that, I'd seen her again on the red carpet at my gala ball. I couldn't believe my luck, she was standing right in front of me with those beautiful brown eyes. All I wanted to do was walk right up to her and confess my feelings, but of course, she'd have just laughed in my face. After that, I'm ashamed to say that I stalked her a little.

She was so intriguing, and when I found out she visited Java Mama's almost daily, I made Parker stop there every time we passed, just so I could catch a glimpse of her. She was mesmerising, the most enchanting woman I'd ever seen. I couldn't get her out of my head. I've known many beautiful women in my life, but none like her. She had the face and the body no man could resist, but her eyes were something else, one look and I was lost inside them.

I didn't even know she was going to be at Jamie's launch that night, so I was delighted to find her sitting alone at the bar. I'd wandered over to talk to her, I just had to meet her. I remember feeling drawn to her like a moth to the flame, she was captivating. Even drunk she was stunning. And, as I recall, she was hilariously funny and really put me in my place.

I was fascinated by her, and it was then that I found out that she and her boyfriend had split up. I couldn't have been more pleased to hear it. And that's when I knew. I had to have her. The timing, as usual, wasn't good. I had to fly out the next day and I wasn't sure if she was still in love with Mike, so after she'd fallen and I'd taken her to the hospital, I did the gentlemanly thing and I gave her some space…until I couldn't wait any longer.

A harsh alarm sounds from one of the monitors beside her bed, startling me out of my thoughts. I anxiously watch Rashid with wide eyes as he calmly looks up and then walks over to the monitor, pressing a button to silence it. After looking at the various screens for a few seconds, he checks the small round pads attached to Vivienne's chest.

"What was that?" I ask nervously.

"Don't worry," he smiles, "one of her monitors became unattached." He returns to his position at the end of her bed. "As you're probably aware, Mr. Foxx, Vivienne lost a lot of blood. She has a small linear fracture in the skull, and as you can see, her consultant has decided to keep her in deep sedation to help alleviate the intra-cranial pressure. The breathing tube is only there to assist her breathing while she's in sedation, she is, in fact, breathing on her own," he says, cheerily.

I reach for Vivienne's hand and give it a gentle squeeze. "What happens next?"

"We'll monitor her for the next few days, she'll have another scan tomorrow morning of course, and we'll see how she goes."

"Can she hear me?"

"There's no harm in trying," he smiles.

I gaze at Vivienne's inanimate body, watching the slow rise and fall of her chest. Her face is relaxed and her hair is lying in a halo of chocolate brown waves around her beautiful face. "Please come back to me, baby." I squeeze her hand a little tighter and rub the back of it with my thumb. I hate to see her like this, but just to be near her, holding her hand, makes me feel a little better.

The hours pass so slowly and in spite of everyone trying to get me to go home, or to eat something, or to sleep, all I want to do is watch her and hold on to her. I've sat with her for hours. Talking to her, sometimes just staring at her willing her to get better, to come back to me. I miss her so much. She's the most precious thing in my life, and I can't bear to see her like this. She must have been so frightened and I wasn't there to protect her. I should have been there. I should have protected her.

WHO DID THIS TO YOU?

"Sweetheart? …Max?"

"Vivienne." Waking with a start, I lift my head from the edge of the bed and stare at Vivienne's face with blurry eyes. I feel like shit. Blinking the sleep away I try to focus. Her eyes are closed, one hand resting at her side, one hand in mine.

"Sweetheart?"

I suddenly realise it's my mom's voice I can hear, she's standing beside me. I kiss Vivienne's hand and lay it on the bed and then I rise to give my mother a hug.

"Any change?"

"No," I sigh wearily.

"Oh, Max. I'm so sorry, sweetheart," she says, hugging me tightly.

"They're doing another scan this morning, so I guess we'll know more then?"

Giving her my chair, I pull over another one and sit next to her. As I glance at my watch, I notice it's seven-thirty in the morning. Another day has passed without Vivienne. I miss her so much.

"Vinnie told me that Monica and Steve are both dead. I'm shocked, but I can't say I'll mourn that woman. Not after what she did to my poor grandson," she grates, shaking her head. "So, who do you think could have done this to Vivienne?"

"I don't know yet," I sigh, looking back at Vivienne.

"Hopefully she can tell us when she wakes up." I stroke her hand and stare down at her beautiful, bruised face. I feel so lost without her and so angry that someone could harm her like this. *I'm so sorry. Please come back to me, baby.*

"I've been in to see your father, he's doing very well. They're hoping that if he keeps improving like this, he'll be able to come home soon. We'll have to think about a full time nurse, at least for the first few months, but it'll be good to have him home again." Mom's eyes glisten, she's been through hell since my father became ill. "What is it with us and hospitals?" she huffs. "Haven't we had enough already?" she adds frowning and tutting. She squeezes my arm. "Sweetheart, I'm going to sit with Vivienne for a while, why don't you go home and get some rest. You haven't been home for two days, you must be exhausted."

"No, I don't want to leave her."

She smiles at me affectionately. "Max, I promise, I'll call you if anything changes. And you should bring in some of Vivienne's things for when she wakes up."

I don't want to leave Vivienne, but I do want to speak to Trencher to see if he has any more information about that night. I've already given a statement to the police, but I haven't heard anything from them yet. They must have something to report by now. Maybe I will go? Just for an hour.

I lean over and gently kiss Vivienne on the forehead, then I smooth my fingers down her cheek. "I won't be long, baby. I love you." I kiss my mom on the cheek. "I'll be back soon, Mom. Call me if—"

"I will. I promise… And don't forget to eat something," she smiles.

As I leave the ward, I call Parker. He picks me up from the front entrance and takes me back to F1. On the way, he fills me in on Trencher's progress.

"The c.c.t.v. footage in the lift came up with a big fat zero. No Mike, and no one else that shouldn't have been there. The only people shown on the footage entering the lift, were your guests at Charlie's funeral and the staff at Foxx-Tech. He's even tracked all the staff ID cards, but they all checkout."

"What about the stairwell?"

Parker's eyebrows lower to a frown. "There aren't any cameras in the stairwell. Only the lobby and the lift."

What?...For fuck's sake. "Are you telling me that the company that builds the most advanced, hi-tech equipment in the world, doesn't have eyes on every corner of its own building?" I ask incredulously.

"Yeah, pretty much," he shrugs. I can't believe I didn't already know that? Treadstone are the best of the best. My father holds Trencher and his team in the highest regard. I naturally assumed my security would be watertight.

"What about the lobby footage? What about Miles, or whoever was on the night watch that night?" Parker eyes me warily like the bad news isn't over yet. I can feel my frustration building to the point where I'm going to go ape-shit on somebody's ass.

"Miles was on duty Thursday night. He said that he left the main door unattended for about five minutes when he heard music coming from inside the ladies toilets in the lobby. He went in to have a look, and he found an iPod lying on the floor blaring out Chaka Khan's greatest hits."

"And he didn't think that was odd?" I'm stunned at Miles' incompetence.

Vinnie cringes. "Apparently not."

"So, what about the footage from the lobby? There must be something on that." I can't believe we wouldn't have captured this fucker somewhere on the security cameras.

"He's checking it now. He said he'll call you when he's got something to report."

Jesus!

As I enter the penthouse, Jan greets me with sad eyes. "Mr. Foxx, I can't believe what's happened to poor Vivienne. If there is anything, anything at all that I can do, please just ask." I offer her a weak smile, she's always so thoughtful and kind. "How is she?" she asks tentatively.

My heart sinks. "No change yet."

"Oh, that's a shame. By the way, Sir, the police have telephoned. They just wanted to go over your statement again. Vincent's also given them a statement, but they still want to talk to you." Jan's voice blurs into the background as my eyes slowly wander toward the study door. There's a strong smell of bleach in the air, and I notice that Jan has cleaned all the blood away. "I've organised a team to redecorate the study, Sir. Unfortunately, there are some stains that just won't clean off," she says, softly. "And I've laid some items out on your bed, just a few things that Vivienne may need."

"Thank you."

I head toward the study and take a deep breath before I enter. My eyes immediately swing around to the wall behind the door. Harsh sunlight highlights the faint blood stains marking the wall. I feel hollow inside. I can't imagine how frightened Vivienne must have felt that night. As I glance around the room, I notice the false panel covering the safe is still in place. I open it and check the safe door. It's locked. I punch in the code, but as I knew it would be, the safe is empty. The five hundred thousand that I had replaced after Monica had stolen the money the last time, is gone. Whoever it was, knew the code. *Jesus! I'd have given them the fucking money if it meant Vivienne could have been spared all this.*

I leave the study and drag my weary body up to my room. I need to take a quick shower and get back to the hospital, I hate being away from her.

As I enter the bedroom, my eyes fill with tears as they land on Vivienne's clothes and toiletries lying on the bed. I can smell her in here. My heart clenches and the room starts to spin so I sit on the edge of the bed and hang my head in my hands. *Oh baby, I can't lose you now. Please, please don't leave me.*

My phone rings, making me jump. I spring up and grab my jacket, fumbling in the pockets trying to find it. My heart stops when I see that it's Mom calling. *Shit. I should have stayed with Vivienne.* "Yeah! What is it? What's happened?" I yell anxiously.

"Sweetheart, calm down, it's good news," she says, softly. I collapse down onto the bed, my hands are trembling. "She's just had a scan, and the doctor said the swelling has reduced quite significantly. They're talking about maybe waking her up tomorrow or the next day, but they're very hopeful."

I lie back on the bed and close my watery eyes. "Thank God." Swallowing the lump in my throat I try to steady my voice. "I'll be back soon."

"Okay sweetheart. But please, eat some breakfast before you leave. I can't have you making yourself ill as well," she says, as only a mother can.

My emotions are all over the place. I lay on the bed, our bed, with tears in my eyes and the most awful sense of dread in the pit of my stomach. Vivienne is the most precious thing in my life, she has to pull through this. It scares me to think of the alternative. The news that she's improving is wonderful, but I need to see her beautiful eyes smiling back at me, I need to feel her lips against mine, I need to hold her in my arms, or none of it is real. She's only just come into my life, I can't lose her now. *There is no me without you, baby.*

I dry off after a quick, refreshing shower and I walk over to the sink to brush my teeth. I don't want to waste any time shaving so I don't bother. Once I'm dressed, I run downstairs and grab a sandwich that Jan had thoughtfully prepared, along with a small flask of coffee, and then I head down to the office to speak to Grace.

We clear my schedule for the rest of the week. Once I know Vivienne's out of the woods, I'll be able to think straight. Until then, all this other shit can wait.

Parker's busy organising a complete new overhaul of the

building's security systems so while he's busy doing that, I drive myself back to the hospital.

Just as I park up and get out of the car, my phone rings. I don't recognise the number. "Foxx," I snap, walking toward the entrance.

"Hi, Max, it's Lucy." Her chirpy voice stops me in my tracks. "I'm sorry to call you on your mobile, but I haven't heard from Viv, and I've been trying to contact her but it keeps going to answer-phone, is she with you?"

I suddenly realise no one has told her what happened. "Oh. …I'm sorry, Lucy. Ah…She's in the hospital. She—"

"What? Oh, my God. She didn't face plant another toilet bowl did she?" she giggles.

"No, she's… she's been attacked."

"Fuck! When? What happened?"

I feel awful telling her over the phone. She's been a good friend to Vivienne. I should have gone to see her. "I don't know. Sometime after Charlie's wake, someone got into the penthouse and hit her on the head. She lost a lot of blood and… she's in a coma, or at least, they've put her in a coma to help her heal. I'm at the hospital now. Look, I'm just about to go and speak to her doctor, I'll know more after that, okay?"

"Can I come and see her?" she asks in a small, fragile voice.

"Of course. She's in the critical care unit at the Limberton."

"Okay, I'm on my way."

I race into the hospital. As none of the elevators are on the ground floor, I run up the five flights of stairs to the ward. One of the staff grants me access via the intercom and I march straight through to Vivienne's bed.

As my eyes find her, she looks so serene, even though the bruise forming along the side of her face, and the dark, bloodied stitches in her skin look horrific.

Even though Vivienne's unconscious, Mom is merrily

chatting away to her, disclosing all my foibles as a teenager. She abruptly stops talking and turns to face me. "Max? Is that you?" I marvel at how aware she is of her surroundings even though she can't see.

"Yeah, it's me. Any more news?"

"No, not yet, son. But they did seem very pleased with her scan."

I lean over to kiss Vivienne. "I'm here, baby," I whisper against her forehead. Then I take her hand in mine and sit next to my mother.

Mom lets out a long sigh, resting her hand on my arm as a small smile curls her lips. "I spoke with Jan. She said Vinnie told her you were going to propose to Vivienne."

My heart clenches. "Yeah, I was." I turn back to look at Vivienne, squeezing her hand a little tighter. "I'd asked her like a million times before, but this time… I know she was going to say yes." Mom lets out a little giggle. "What?" I ask confused.

"No, it's nothing," she smiles, "you just remind me so much of William, that's all. I may be blind sweetheart, but I can still see how good you two are for each other. I think you and Vivienne will have a wonderful life together, just like me and your father."

I hope so… I really hope so.

While we wait for Doctor Alexander to arrive and to give me an update on Vivienne's progress, Mom decides to go home for a while, she looks tired. These last couple of weeks have really taken a toll on her. I call John, and then I walk her down to meet him at the entrance. When I return, Doctor Alexander is having a chat with the nurse by Vivienne's bed. They're discussing her chart, and although I don't understand half of what they're saying, it does sound positive.

"Mr. Foxx. Good to see you," Doctor Alexander says, shaking my hand. "We're very pleased with Vivienne's progress. The swelling has significantly reduced, and if it continues at this rate, it's fairly likely that we may be able to bring her out of deep sedation sometime tomorrow."

I let out the breath I was holding and I finally relax. "That's great news."

"Do you have any questions, Mr. Foxx?"

I do. One, in particular has been bothering me for a while now. I don't want to ask this question, but I fear I must. "What about her head injury, is there any chance that she may have suffered any brain damage?"

His sympathetic expression doesn't change, but the pause before he speaks puts me on edge. "It's difficult to say at this stage. Physically, Vivienne is fine, and healing very well. When we bring her out of the coma she may take a while to wake up, everybody's different, but once she's fully awake we'll be able to conduct some neurological assessments in order to evaluate her cognitive function, as well as her basic, sensory motor processes. So, in answer to your question, I'm afraid we will just have to wait for the time being."

My stomach churns, that wasn't the answer I was hoping for.

An overwhelming sense of guilt churns my insides. I knew Monica had become dangerous. After she'd killed Charlie, I realised pretty quickly that she was a danger to us all, but I'd been so focused on finding her that I didn't protect Vivienne from Mike, or her mother, or whoever it was who threatened her life that night. Whatever the outcome of this, whatever she needs, I will never leave Vivienne unprotected again.

Several loud, argumentative voices suddenly break the peaceful quiet of the ward. I recognise one of them to be Lucy's voice, she's swearing like a trooper. I rise and quickly walk toward the commotion.

Lucy is standing at the entrance to the ward. She's trying to push a skinny woman with black hair back out the door, but the skinny woman is hanging on to Lucy's jacket for dear life. Both of them are shouting and calling each other names. A male nurse tries to break them up, but fails miserably.

"What the fuck is going on?" I yell, striding toward them. Both women stop and stare at me open mouthed.

"Max, don't let her in. She's never given a shit about Viv before!" Lucy yells angrily. "She's only after more money for her fucking drugs," she adds, scowling and pushing against the woman who's still clinging to her jacket.

This is Vivienne's mother?

The skinny woman bites back with a string of expletives.

"Shut the fuck up!" I yell, silencing them both. The male nurse stares at me for a moment and then he walks away. He obviously knows better than to get involved in the middle of two angry women. I swing my eyes between the two of them and lower my voice. "People in here are fighting for their lives, have some fucking respect," I spit out angrily.

"But Max, she's only here for money, she's—" I hold my hand up to silence Lucy. Her concern is commendable, but I want to speak to this woman. For starters, I want to know how the hell she knew Vivienne was here. It seems highly unlikely that Lucy would have told her.

"What's your name?"

She stands there twitching and sniffing, looking all around her with wide eyes and a sallow, haggard face. She looks much older than her probable years. "Carol," she eventually answers, glaring up at me.

"We've spoken before, haven't we?" I ask, in a sarcastic tone. She just shrugs in response. "I told you then that I wouldn't give you any money for drugs or alcohol, and I meant it. If you want help to get clean, that's different."

She nervously shifts from one foot to the other.

"How did you know Vivienne was here?"

"Sharon told me," she says, defiantly, like it's none of my business. She looks all around her like she's going to run any minute.

Shit. She's high… Jesus, what a role model. "Sharon who?" I ask impatiently.

"Daly. She's my mate. She's a cleaner here at the hospital. She rang me."

"Where were you last Thursday night?" I ask bluntly.

She frowns for a moment, confused at my interrogation. "Down at the Duke with Sharon, Bill, and Spider."

"What is that, a pub?"

"Yeah," she nods stiffly.

"Wait here." I turn away from Carol and grab Lucy's arm walking her a few feet up the corridor. "Take her in to see Vivienne. I'm going to go and find this Sharon, I need to check out her story." Lucy looks at me all wide-eyed and confused. "Don't worry, I'll explain everything when I come back." I turn back to Carol, who's still nervously fidgeting from one foot to the other. "Go with Lucy, I'll be back in a minute." She stares up at me with wary eyes then she darts past me.

I head down to reception and ask to speak to the ward manager. After a few minutes, I'm shown into a small office where I'm greeted by a man who introduces himself as Mr. Brown. His reticence to give me any information on Sharon, is immediately replaced with enthusiasm once I remind him of whom I am, and my contribution to this hospital. He searches on the computer and informs me that Sharon will be on her break, probably outside having a cigarette. I take a good look at her ID, committing it to memory, and then I head off to the area commonly known as, 'smoker's corner.'

Sure enough, I find Sharon sitting on a bench near the front entrance, cigarette in hand, coughing her lungs up. She's a short, round woman with spiky hair, thick glasses, and a nose ring. I walk over and stand right in front of her.

"Can I help you?" she asks, looking up at me indignantly.

"Yes, I wonder if you could tell me where Carol Banks was last Thursday night?"

She frowns at me, and then looks all around her. "Who are you?" she asks warily. I reach into my pocket and pull out my wallet, then I take out a twenty and hold it up between my first and second finger. I'm guessing Sharon shares the same habits as her friend. Sure enough, Sharon's eyes eagerly land on the money and then slide up to mine. "She was with me and the lads in The Duke. Thursday night's bingo night," she says reaching for the money, but I pull it away.

"The lads?" I ask impatiently.

"Yeah, Bill and Spider, well his name's Pete, but we call him Spider 'cuz he sleeps in the bath and can never get out of it on his own," she grins, displaying her rotten, nicotine stained teeth, then she begins another round of wheezing and coughing.

"And what time did she leave?" I ask offering her the money. She snatches it out of my fingers, her eyes darting all around her.

"We all left at closing time and then we went down to the kebab shop, then back to my place. She slept on the sofa with Bill," she says, folding the money and sliding it into her pocket. "Why do you want to know?"

I don't bother to explain. I walk away from her and dial Trencher, asking him to check out Sharon's story and to get back to me as soon as possible. Although, having now met Carol in person, I doubt whether she would have the strength to overpower anyone.

Trencher informs me that Mike has a watertight alibi for that night. His credit card puts him in a hotel in Portugal on the night that it happened, and he's booked on the return flight later on today. *Shit.* Vivienne had to have known the person well enough to have let them in, but if it wasn't Mike or Carol? Then who the hell was it?

Trencher finally gives me some good news. He's found something interesting in the footage from the c.c.t.v. in the lobby, and he'll send it to my phone as soon as he can.

When I return to the ward, I see Lucy and Carol on opposite sides of Vivienne's bed. I hang back and study Carol for a moment. She looks like shit. It's easy to see that she would have once been a striking woman, her perfect bone structure is still there, but the ravages of chemicals and neglect have robbed her of her beauty. Her long, straggly black hair hangs limply around her aged and haggard face. Her brown eyes are sunken and lifeless, and she looks like she could do with a good wash and a decent meal. She's twitching in her seat like a little bird, but she's stroking Vivienne's hand like a mother should at times like these.

I'm conflicted about letting her near Vivienne. From what I know of her, Carol's parenting skills are non-existent. She's led a selfish, drug and alcohol inspired life, neglecting Vivienne and at times, putting her in great danger. How Vivienne ever became such a grounded and caring individual defies her upbringing. I'm at odds at what to do about her. I can't imagine Carol would be sitting here now if she had done this to Vivienne. It's more likely that she would be hiding away somewhere, drowning in a bottle of Vodka. Even though she and Vivienne don't have a close mother and daughter relationship, I know Vivienne still protects her by bailing her out financially, and, as I recently found out, she pays for a monthly delivery of food from the local supermarket, so her mother will always have food in the cupboard.

My phone vibrates in my pocket. Trencher has sent me the footage from the c.c.t.v., so I quickly walk back outside to take a look. The clip shows a tall, thin man with dark shoulder length hair. He's wearing dark, baggy jeans, a hoodie, sunglasses, and a black baseball cap. He would have stood out like a sore thumb if the lobby hadn't been so busy. He enters the building and walks with his head down toward the bank of elevators at the back of the lobby. I check the time and date stamp, it was around about the time that we were holding Charlie's wake in the penthouse, just before I left to fly to Portsmouth. The guy walks straight past the elevators and on toward the door leading to the stairs, then he disappears from sight.

Why the fuck were there no cameras in the stairwell?

That video clip stops and then another one begins. It's much later in the evening, almost an hour before Parker and I made it home. Except for a few illuminated sculptures scattered around the lobby, it's empty and dark. Miles is sitting at his desk drinking a mug of coffee and reading the paper by the small desk lamp. He's not even bothering to check the security monitors beside him. *For fuck's sake.*

My eyes are suddenly drawn to the stairwell door at the back of the lobby behind Miles. The same guy from the previous clip slowly walks out from the stairwell and then moves quickly into the ladies toilets. He reappears a few seconds later and moves across the lobby, hiding behind the pillars and sculptures, until he makes it all the way to the other side. A few moments later, Miles looks up from his paper and then he looks around sharply, standing abruptly. *He must have heard something.* He puts his paper down on the desk and moves toward the ladies toilets. As he walks, he takes out his flashlight and shines it around the lobby but he keeps heading for the toilets, then he disappears into the ladies room.

The guy in black races for the glass doors at the front of the building. He's carrying a black bag, which he wasn't carrying when he entered the building earlier. Without hesitating he reaches up to release the top lock, then down to the bottom lock and then he pushes them and they fly open. Unfortunately, all the camera picks up is the top of his head. No facial features at all. *He knows this building. Fuck!* In the blink of an eye, he's out and gone. The doors close behind him, and then moments later, Miles saunters out of the ladies toilets carrying something in his hand. *The iPod.* He's completely oblivious to what just happened and he moves back to his desk, then he carries on reading his paper.

Jesus! Fucking hell. I'm incensed by what I've just seen. The incompetence of my night watchman boils my blood. *Heads will fucking roll for this!* I dial Trencher immediately.

"Sir?"

"I assume you've watched the footage?" I growl, angrily.

"Yes, Sir. I'm sorry, Sir. I've relieved Miles of his duties and Vincent and I have organised a full and thorough overhaul of the security for Foxx-Tech. An installation team is already working on the new security measures as we speak, Sir."

I can sense him trying to ward off my anger, but it's not working. "Why the fuck was our security in such a goddamn mess?" I know yelling doesn't help but I'm so fucking angry.

"Sir, your father was never a fan of closed circuit surveillance. He designed the security for Foxx-Tech and I'm afraid we were just following orders, Sir."

I shake my head in disbelief. But maybe it's my own fault for not even asking the question when I first took over from my dad. He's old school. He would think it an invasion of someone's privacy to watch them on security cameras.

I take a deep breath to calm my anger. "Any lead on the guy?"

"No, I'm afraid not," he sighs. "We didn't find any prints either, you can see in the clip that he's wearing gloves and he kept his face hidden the whole time, so I'm afraid there's no way to identify him visually. He's clever though, only the rear exit is alarmed at night, and he used the iPod to distract Miles away from the front doors. We also think he may have hidden in the utility cupboard in the foyer of the penthouse for a while, probably waiting for everyone to leave. According to Parker, the fuses for all the downstairs rooms in the penthouse, except for the study, were disengaged. He knew the safe was in the study. A forensic team is checking out the cupboard now."

Shit! Fuck! Goddammit! I walked right past the fucker. "And what about the penthouse? Did he override the locking system?"

"No, Sir. I called out the company who installed the

scanner, and they said it doesn't appear to have been tampered with at all."

Then she must have opened the door.

"Sir, this guy seemed to be pretty sure of what he was doing, and he seemed to know exactly where all the cameras were. I'm checking into anyone and everyone that could have had any access to the penthouse entry system. It may take a while, but I'll get back to you as soon as possible."

"You do that." I drag my hand through my hair in exasperation. "Somehow this fucker got in. I want to know who it is, and how the *fuck* he did it!"

"Yes, Sir."

I make my way back upstairs to see Vivienne. I'm angry and frustrated. Everything is going to shit. If Vivienne were awake, she'd be smiling up at me with her beautiful, kind, loving eyes, telling me to calm down. *God, I miss her.*

IRONCLAD ALIBI

When I return to the ward, Carol is gone. I'm not surprised, she knows I'm no easy touch, and until Vivienne is awake she's got no way of getting any money from her. Lucy is still sitting at Vivienne's bedside with tears rolling down her cheeks. I walk over and give her shoulder a gentle squeeze, then I lean over to Vivienne and kiss her forehead. "I'm here, baby."

"Max! What the fuck is going on? And why did you let that fucking troll anywhere near her? She hasn't given a shit about Viv for years," Lucy huffs, wiping her eyes.

"Look…I don't really know what happened that night. I left Vivienne to follow a lead on Monica, and all I know is some guy entered the building, waited until everyone else had left the penthouse, and then somehow he managed to get inside and…" The words catch in my throat. Mental images of Vivienne fighting off her attacker make it hard for me to breathe. "But I promise you, Lucy. I'm going to do everything I can to find him."

Lucy suddenly sits bolt upright. "What about Mike? Maybe he—"

"No," I interrupt on a sigh. "He was the first person I thought of. But he seems to have an ironclad alibi."

"Oh," she sighs, then she slumps back in her seat. I know how she feels. Suddenly she sits up again. "What about Monica? Viv told me all about her. That psycho-bitch probably wants Viv out of the way because of you.

She's obviously capable, I mean, she killed her own kid for fuck's sake."

"She's dead."

"What?" Her confused eyes land on mine. "When?"

"When I left the wake to follow a lead on her and Steve, I found them both dead in a hotel in Portsmouth."

Lucy's eyebrows shoot up. "Jesus. …Well, if it wasn't Mike and it wasn't Monica, who the hell was it?"

I sag with fatigue and frustration. I wish I knew. "I don't know, Lucy," I sigh wearily. "Her mom has an alibi too."

She gives me a strange look. "Her mum? No. She wouldn't do that. But if it was money she was after, she knows some pretty shitty people on the estate." We exchange a look, both of us contemplating the idea, but neither of us speaks. I stroke Vivienne's hand and gaze down at her, willing her to get through this.

"I guess she'll tell us when she wakes up."

Lucy stares at Vivienne for a moment, I can tell exactly what she's thinking by her expression. "Do you think she might have…?"

"I don't know…we'll just have to wait and see." I don't really want to have a conversation on the possibilities that Vivienne may have suffered brain damage. It's unthinkable. *Please, baby. Please be okay. I'll never forgive myself if… No. She has to be okay.*

Dan arrives to take Lucy home. She leaves in tears, devastated by what's happened to her friend. It's nice to know she cares so much about her. During the many hours of waiting, and praying, and willing Vivienne to be okay, my mind drifts over our brief but amazing time together.

Everything changed when Vivienne came into my life. Before that, although I'd cleaned up my act and I'd stopped the drugs and excessive drinking by then, I was still dead inside. After rehab, I'd thrown myself into my work and I was functioning pretty well on that level, but I felt like I was just going through the motions. My beloved nephew Charlie, and the charity work that he inspired kept me sane, but it wasn't until I met Vivienne that I truly felt alive again.

I'll always remember that first time I saw her. I'd brought Charlie with me to visit the directors at Great Ormond Street Hospital, to discuss a new fund-raising idea. He was bored by it all and he could hear the other kids having fun at a birthday party further down the corridor, so I let him wander away to join them. When our meeting ended, I found him sitting down in front of Vivienne, and just like Charlie, I couldn't take my eyes off her. She was making the kids laugh, and she was just so natural, so warm. She was stunning, so beautiful, and her laugh made me smile. It was crazy. I had butterflies in my stomach, and I suddenly felt nervous, it was strange how she affected me. She was intoxicating.

I'd never felt this way about a woman before, not even Monica. She literally took my breath away. I wanted her. I wanted her so badly.

I watched her from a distance, planning what I would say to her when I'd built up the courage to ask her out, but the little girl whose birthday it was, asked Vivienne if she had a boyfriend and she answered 'yes'. I was devastated. What a cruel twist of fate. But thankfully fate, and a large amount of alcohol at Jamie's Gallery launch, finally brought us back together. And now, I can't imagine my life without her.

ACRYLIC HAIR

"Mr. Foxx?"

My eyes spring open and land on a nurse's face smiling down at me.

"Sorry, Mr. Foxx, we're taking Vivienne down for a scan, it'll be about thirty minutes or so. Maybe you should go and get something to eat while you're waiting, you haven't left her side for hours." She smiles warmly.

"What day is it?" I mumble, rubbing my eyes.

"It's Sunday."

Sunday? I stand and stretch out all the kinks in my body, my ass is numb from sitting in that chair all night. I lean over and kiss Vivienne on her cheek. "I'll be here when you come back, baby."

When I walk into the canteen, Parker is sitting reading a newspaper. I grab us a couple of coffees and then I walk over to his table.

"Alright, Guv'? I'm just waiting for your mum, she's visiting your dad. How's Vivienne doing?"

"She's going down for another scan so I guess we'll know pretty soon," I sigh, rubbing my eyes and scratching my stubbly chin.

Parker rakes his eyes all over me, then he smirks. "You look like dope on a rope."

I frown at him, dragging my hands through my dishevelled hair. "I feel like dope on a rope," I mutter, yawning. The muddy coffee does nothing for my taste buds, but it does help to wake me up. "Any more news from Trencher?" I ask, hoping he's come up with something new.

Parker folds his paper and throws it on the table. "Not on the guy, no. But both Mike and Vivienne's mum's alibis check out, so we can strike them off the list. And we've made a good start with the new security system, it should be fully installed and ready in a couple of days," he says, reaching for his coffee.

"Good." I can always rely on Parker.

"I forgot to ask you whether or not you'd checked your safe?" he asks, slurping his coffee with his pinkie sticking straight out.

"Yeah, it was cleaned out. Whoever it was knew the code too."

"So it was a burglary then?" Parker asks, scratching his head.

"Looks that way." I spin my coffee cup around and around on the table. "But I can't worry about any of that shit until I know Vivienne's going to be okay."

Parker nods with a sympathetic smile, then he leans down and picks up a small bag at his feet, placing it on the table. "Jan packed you some clean undies, jeans, and a shirt. And I think there's a toothbrush and some other bits in there too," he says, tapping the bag. "And your mum told me to make sure you eat something," he adds, on an arched brow.

I don't feel hungry, I'm too anxious to eat. "I'm going to go back up. I'll talk to you later. Oh, and tell Jan I said thank you," I say, picking up the bag.

He smiles. "Will do, Guv'. Call me if you need anything, and…keep your chin up."

"Yeah, thanks."

As I walk to the stairs, someone calls out my name so I turn around.

"Mr. Foxx?" A tall black guy walks up to me and extends his hand. "Hi, I'm D.I. Langford." I stare blankly at him for a moment, the name does ring a bell but I can't place him. "We've met before…When your nephew was—"

"Oh! Yes of course." I shake his hand and keep on walking toward the stairs. I want to get back up to Vivienne.

"How's Miss Banks doing?"

I stop and turn sharply to face him. "She's in a coma in the critical care unit, which is where I need to be right now." *I haven't got time for this.* I carry on walking, but he's right behind me.

"Yes, I'm sorry. It's just that, I wanted to let you know that forensics found an acrylic hair in the cupboard in the foyer of F1, and also in the study."

I stop in my tracks, then I turn to face him. "A wig?" I ask, confused.

"Yes, it would seem so. And the fuses had definitely been tampered with but unfortunately, we found no prints." I stare at him, pondering the new information. He looks at me with a questioning frown. "On your instruction, Mr. Foxx, we've not been allowed any access to Vivienne since she was brought in here, but we'd really like to take some samples of any tissue that may be lodged under her fingernails. It may help with our investigation."

Shit. Why didn't I think of that? I briefly close my eyes and drag my hand through my hair. For a smart guy, I really dropped the ball on this one. "Goddammit!" I'm angry with myself for being such an idiot. I look at the guy, clenching my jaw. "I cleaned her up," I say, shaking my head. "I've been sitting with her for days waiting for her to wake up, she was covered in blood, I didn't even think. I'm sorry."

He nods and looks a little pissed off at my stupidity. "Okay, well, if Miss Banks remembers anything when she wakes up, anything that could help the investigation, I'd be grateful if you'd call me." He hands me his card.

"I will. Now, if you don't mind, I'd like to get back up there."

He gives me a tight smile. “Yes, of course.”

I turn and quickly climb the stairs back to the ward. When I walk back into the critical care unit, I see that the curtain is pulled around Vivienne’s bed. My heart drops to the pit of my stomach. *Shit. What’s happened?* I race toward her bed, but as I pass the reception desk a nurse quickly jumps up.

“Mr. Foxx. It’s okay! Really. There’s nothing to worry about. Vivienne’s had her scan and her consultant has instructed us to bring her out of sedation, they just need a minute or two to remove the breathing tube,” she says, calmly. “Are you okay? You look a little pale.”

I feel light headed. I should have eaten something. “No. I’m fine.” I murmur, pacing up and down. This is excellent news, but I need to be with her, I want to be there when she opens her eyes. I’ve missed her so much.

Fifteen excruciatingly long minutes tick by while I wait for them to finally open the curtains. I move to her bedside and reach for her hand, squeezing it gently and lifting it up to my lips. “I’ve missed you, baby. You’re going to be okay.” I choke up, trying to hold back the tears threatening my eyes.

“Mr. Foxx?” I look up and see a man I haven’t met before. “Hi. I’m Ted. I’m the head of neurology here.” I stand and shake his hand. I’m worried about what he’s going to tell me, and I still feel a bit dizzy so I sit down again. “I’m very pleased with the scan we took this morning. As you can see, we are bringing Vivienne out of sedation,” he smiles. “All her vital signs are stable and she’s breathing very well on her own now so we’ll be moving her to a private room on Worthing ward, which is one floor down. She may take a while to come round, but that’s to be expected after deep sedation,” he shrugs. “We like to let them come round in their own time. She’ll be able to hear you and may try to respond, but her throat may be a little sore and dry because of the tube, so try to be patient, okay?” His warm smile calms me. I briefly close my eyes and nod in response. It's like a massive weight has been lifted.

She can have all the time she needs, as long as she comes back to me.

"I'm sure Doctor Alexander has already explained," he continues, "but we'll give her some time to recover and then we'll carry out some neurological tests to evaluate her sensory, neuron, and motor responses. These tests will show us whether or not Vivienne has sustained any impairments to her nervous system from the brain trauma." I know I'm looking at him with a worried expression when he offers me a sympathetic smile. I've had nothing but sympathetic smiles since Vivienne came in here. "Try not to worry, Mr. Foxx. She's doing very well, and she's in good hands." He smiles, then he turns and walks away.

I sit in a daze for a moment, relieved and exhausted. As tired as I am, I can't leave her. I don't want to leave her. I want to be here when she opens her eyes.

A couple of hours later, Vivienne is moved downstairs to a private room. I haven't been home for over twenty-four hours, so I take advantage of the en-suite and I have a quick shower to freshen myself up. I lay Vivienne's toiletries out in the bathroom and hang her clothes in the closet, then I brush her hair, avoiding the stitches on the left side of her head. As I carefully untangle her hair near the scar, I take a closer look at it. A shiver runs down my spine. She must have been so frightened. It looks pretty awful, but it seems to be healing very well. I gently wipe her face with a cool, damp cloth and then I sit with her, squeezing and stroking her hand.

"I'm so sorry, baby, this is all my fault. I never should have left you alone." I watch her eyes for any sign that she can hear me, but her face is motionless. She looks perfectly relaxed. Her lips are pink, and her cheeks are rosy. "You take all the time you need. I'm right here, baby. I'm not going to leave you ever again, I promise." I bring her hand up to my lips and gently kiss her fingers. "I love you, so much." As I hold her hand in mine, I feel her giving me a gentle squeeze. *Thank God.* My eyes dart up to her face, searching for a flicker of awareness but she remains still, motionless. Tears prick my eyes and all my emotions surge up to the surface. The thought that I might lose her has been killing me. I've waited so long for this beautiful woman to come into my life, I don't know what I'd do if I lost her.

Please come back to me, baby.

PROTECT YOU (VIVIENNE)

The distant sound of my phone's ringtone has me bounding down the stairs with delight. I don't want to miss his call, but the ringing stops. Running into the dimly lit room, my feet skid to a shuddering stop. My heart beats wildly in my chest as adrenaline courses through my chilled veins.

I see my phone face up on Max's desk.

"Vivienne?…Baby?" His beautiful voice calls out to me. I want to answer him but I can't. I can't move. I can't speak. I can't breathe. Everything seems to slow down, like a slow motion effect has been triggered by the crippling fear paralysing my body. My own heartbeat is now the only sound I hear, beating a frantic rhythm inside my chest.

The dark figure steps out from the shadows. Reaching out with a gloved hand he repeatedly smashes the screen with a hard black object and then flings my phone away. I watch as it bounces off the wall and slides across the marble floor. As my wide, terrified eyes drift up from the shattered remains of my lifeline, the figure moves into the dim light of the desk lamp and quietly sits down in Max's leather chair. Raising his head, he lifts the hard black object and points it straight at me…

"You!"

"Lucy… Look… Her eyes are moving. She looks agitated by something."

"She's dreaming. That's a good sign, Max. That means she's out of the coma."

"Thank God… It's been seven hours since they brought her out of sedation, I thought she'd be awake long before now."

"Well, the doctors don't seem to be worried, they said it could take some time. Besides, she always did enjoy a lie in. Talking of which, Max, you need to sleep, you look like shit."

"I don't want to leave her. I need to know she's going to be okay."

"She will be… Viv's a fighter."

~

"It's ironic, isn't it?… All his wealth, charm, and power and yet he still can't protect you. But that's the thing about Max, he never could protect his women. It's pathetic. You're pathetic."

"Here, I brought you a coffee. It tastes like shit, but it's wet and warm."

"Thanks… How much longer do you think it will take for her to wake up?"

"I don't know but I must admit, it's taking longer than I'd expected. What did the doc say?"

"Nothing really, just that we have to be patient."

"Has she opened her eyes since the last time?"

"No."

"Max, I know you said Monica was dead, but you didn't tell me what happened to her? How did she die?"

"Well, we think she recruited Steve to help her escape after she'd killed Charlie. She took half a million in cash from my safe, and I think her plan was to charter a boat from the south coast over to Europe, or maybe even back to the States. She couldn't risk using her passport by then. I don't know the details, but something must have gone drastically wrong between the two of them. She shot Steve, fatally wounding him, and somehow he must have managed to take the gun from her, and he shot her in the face. They were already dead by the time Parker and I got there that night."

"Jesus... Well, I can't say I'm sorry. I know you had history with Monica but from what Viv told me, she was a fucked up nut-job."

"Yeah, apparently so."

"And what about the guy who did this to Viv, did you find out who it was?"

"Not yet... But whoever it was, they knew the layout of the building. They also knew the safe was in the study, and they had the code for it too. At first, I thought Vivienne had known whoever it was and let them in, but now I'm not so sure. They'd obviously come to steal the money, and I think Vivienne just got caught up in it by accident."

"Shit. Poor mare. She must have been so scared. ...Oh. No. Max, I'm sorry. Come on. She's going to be okay. If I know anything about Viv, she'll pull through this. She's made of strong stuff that girl."

"I hope so, Lucy. I don't know what I'd do without her. I can't lose her, I can't."

"I know... Come on, dry your eyes. You don't want Viv to wake up and see you like this."

"I'm okay. I just need her to come back to me."

"Max! Look ... Is she crying?"

"Vivienne? Baby? Can you hear me? ...I'm right here, baby, and so is Lucy. Can you hear me?"

"Maybe she just needs a little more time."

~~

"Surprised to see me, Vivienne?"

"...and if we get the venue we want on the date we want, it'll be a bloody miracle. But there's so much to plan and organise. I hadn't realised how stressful organising a wedding would be. And of course Dan's no help, he'd be happy to marry me in a registry office."

"Well, if I had my way, it would be just the two of us on the beach of a secluded tropical island so that I could have Vivienne all to myself. But if she wants a big wedding with a million people and a marching band, she can have it. Whatever she wants. I don't care, as long as she's happy."

"You really do love her, don't you?"

"With all my heart."

~~~

"All. Your. Fault."

I wake with a start and blink my eyes to focus. *Oh, my God.* I feel disoriented. My heart is racing in my chest, my mouth is dry, my throat is sore, and I feel incredibly fragile. A dull throbbing headache beats against my skull.

My eyes land on a picture on the wall at the foot of my bed. It's a watercolour of a meadow with a pony grazing in the sunlight. I remember seeing it before, the last time I had opened my eyes. The room was quiet then. I'd seen Lucy resting her head on the side of my bed, sleeping. Poor Lucy, she looked so uncomfortable.

My constant and terrifyingly vivid dreams had intermittently woken me from my deep sleep. Each time I'd woken from my nightmares, I'd heard voices talking in hushed tones, but I wasn't ready to wake up. My eyes were unwilling to stay open so I had drifted back into the darkness. But this time, the thought of closing my eyes and being subjected to those frighteningly vivid images again forces me to keep my eyes open. I take a deep breath.

"Vivienne. You're awake. Thank God."

My eyes slowly drift across the room. My right hand is being squeezed. I look down at it, watching as he lifts it to his lips and kisses my palm. The look on his handsome face is pure and utter relief. I stare into his beautiful blue eyes. "Who? …Who are you?" I ask with a raspy voice. I
~~~

desperately need some water, I'm so dry.

The look on his face becomes anxious and scared. He quickly glances over at Lucy. I feel her lifting my other hand and rubbing it between hers. His worried watery eyes return to mine. "Vivienne? It's me, baby. I'm right here," he says, softly, searching my face.

I turn away from him and look over at Lucy in confusion. "Who is he, Luce?" I croak.

She stares at me with a look of utter surprise. "Viv, it's Max. …your, erm, your boyfriend."

I frown and shake my head. "Mike," I say, struggling to speak. "Where's Mike?" Lucy stares down at me for a moment, then she looks away, shaking her head with a worried frown.

I feel him tugging on my hand again. "Vivienne, it's me, Max. …Don't you remember, baby? We live together… We love each other. We're going to be married." His voice is shaky and his eyes are wide with concern.

I blink up at him, searching his face. "I… I'm sorry… I don't know you," I whisper, pulling my hand out of his. His wide eyes glisten with tears, he looks completely devastated. Lucy quickly rises and walks over to him putting her hands on his shoulders. He doesn't take his eyes off mine.

"It's alright, Max… Just give her some—"

"Vivienne. What's the last thing you remember?" he interrupts. His fearful eyes penetrate mine as he reaches out and grips my hand. His intensity is alarming.

I blink a few times and stare past him to the wall behind. "I don't… I don't know?"

"Think, baby, think!" he urges, squeezing my hand so tight that the bones rub together. I swallow and blink a few times as I try desperately hard to put everything in order.

"I remember being at work, and… Clive caught me reading a poem…my dad's favourite, Fractured Heart by Plomme DeNoome, and then I… I spoke to Mike about the film, and…that's right, we were going to the cinema. And then… I don't know? What's happened to me? Where am I?" My confused watery eyes flick between him and Lucy. He closes his eyes and his whole body sags. He looks up at Lucy with such a painful expression on his face, it's hard to watch.

Lucy gently rubs his shoulders. "Max, it must be something to do with the head injury. I've heard of people losing their memory, but then it can suddenly come back. I'm sure it's only a temporary thing… Look, why don't you go and speak to the doctor?" she urges.

He sits there in shock for a moment, shaking his head and looking at me with such disbelief and sorrow in his eyes. "But you love me, Vivienne." His voice quivers with emotion, and everything he's feeling is right there in his eyes. I look away from him, it's just too intense.

"How can I love you, if I don't know you?" I murmur, glancing up at him as he slowly rises, swaying on his feet. He looks exhausted, devastated, and completely destroyed. Reluctantly, he backs away from me and then he turns and leaves the room. I watch the door silently closing behind him.

Lucy, clearly upset, tries to compose herself before moving back to the bedside. She sits and takes my hand, and then with a false happy face she smiles down at me. My throat tightens, choking me, and hot tears flood my eyes as I begin to sob uncontrollably.

"Oh, Viv. Please don't cry. You're going to be okay, I promise! You've had a terrible head injury and your memory must have been affected because—"

"I remember everything," I blurt in a croaky voice, trying to pull myself together.

"What?" she asks in a confused, high pitched voice.

"I need water." Lucy's stunned face stares back at me. "Water, please," I repeat anxiously. "There's no time, Luce. I need to tell you before he comes back."

Lucy quickly grabs the beaker and hands it to me. I sip a

couple of mouthfuls then I rest my head back on the pillow. My headache is pounding aggressively.

"What do you mean you remember everything? What the fuck's going on?" Lucy asks angrily.

I look her straight in the eye. "Luce, Monica isn't dead. She did this to me. She tried to kill me. It's only because the gun wouldn't fire that I'm still alive." I speak so fast, I'm afraid he'll come back any minute. I need to tell her.

"What?" she gasps. "But… I don't understand? What the fuck are you saying?"

"She threatened to kill Max if I didn't leave him." My adrenaline is spiking like crazy, I'm so dry, and I feel sick. "More water."

Lucy hands me the beaker again with shaking hands. "But… I don't understand? Max saw her. She was dead. He identified her body for fuck's sake."

"No. That wasn't Monica. I'm telling you, Luce, she's still alive."

I finish the water and hand it back to her. She leans into me with a deeply concerned frown on her face and anger brewing in her eyes. "Viv, you're not thinking straight. If she did this to you, you've got to tell Max."

"No! Promise me Lucy. You can't tell him. You can't tell anyone. She's dangerous. She said she'd kill him if I didn't leave him. I can't take that chance. It's the only way. If Max knew she'd done this to me, he'd go after her. She's fucking crazy. And I won't let him put himself in danger over me." I grab hold of her hand, imploring her. "Please, Lucy. Please! If anything happened to him, I'd—" The tightening lump in my throat chokes off my words.

Her soft, sad eyes gaze down at me. "But Viv…this will kill him anyway," she murmurs, shaking her head. "He won't let you go. He loves you too much." Her voice is so sad, and her soft hazel eyes fill with tears. Something inside me breaks.

I lay back and close my eyes as the tears begin to roll down the sides of my face. "I know. And I love him.

Which is why I have to protect him… Promise me, Lucy. Please."

Her nervous eyes trail over my face, then she takes a deep breath and releases a long weary sigh. "…Okay."

This is going to test my strength in every way possible. I've gone over and over my plan time and time again during the moments that I had woken up. I'd woken many times, sometimes Max and Lucy were sleeping, sometimes I'd hear them talking and I would pretend I was still asleep. I wasn't ready to look into his eyes. I wasn't strong enough to see the pain I was about to inflict. It took every ounce of willpower not to reach out and run my fingers through his hair as he rested his head uncomfortably on the side of my bed. But I knew what I had to do. I'd considered all the options and this was the only one that would keep Max safe.

As far as he's concerned, my memory of him, and anyone or anything associated with him, has been totally erased. Jan, Vinnie, his mum and dad, this place, and especially Monica. It all has to appear to be wiped clean from my memory. I can't give Max even the slightest glimmer of hope that I would remember him or my plan will fail, and God knows what Monica will do to him. She's capable of anything. I have to do as she says. I have to leave him.

But I love him so much. It hurts like a physical pain gnawing away at my heart. Walking away from Max will be the hardest thing I'll ever do. I just hope I'm strong enough to do it. But Monica's given me no choice. If I stay with him and she does what she's threatened to do? I'll lose him. If he finds out it was Monica who did this to me, he'll track her down to seek his revenge, and in all probability, I could still lose him. At least this way, as painful as it is, I'll know he's safe. It's a sacrifice I'm willing to make.

My heart jumps in my chest as the door opens. Max walks in with Doctor Alexander. I recognise him from my last visit to this hospital but I mustn't let him, or Max know that I remember. *Come on, Viv. You can do this. You have to do this.*

I swing my eyes up to Lucy, silently pleading with her to help me. *Please don't let me down.*

"Vivienne, how are you feeling today?" Doctor Alexander asks. I slowly turn to face him, but Max is standing right beside him and his tortured face breaks my heart. My words just won't come out.

"Erm…Doctor, she doesn't seem to remember what happened to her," Lucy chips in. "We've talked, and it seems she's lost the last few weeks of her life. She doesn't remember the last time she was here. And…" Lucy's eyes swing over to Max, "she doesn't remember you, or anything since the morning of your gala ball," she shrugs nervously.

Thanks, Luce. Perfect answer.

The doctor's eyes return to mine and then they nervously swing over to Max, who looks completely destroyed. I almost weep at the sight of his tortured face. Max's anxious eyes swing up to Lucy. "But… the morning? That was before we met…" he says, in barely a whispered voice. "And she was there at the gala. She saw me I know she did. She took my photograph."

"Yes, I know," Lucy sighs. "But I'm afraid she has no memory of you at all."

I can't look at him, it's too painful. This is much harder than I thought. It kills me to see him like this. *I love you, Max…I'll always love you.* I struggle to keep the lump in my throat from choking me.

Doctor Alexander looks uneasy for a moment, then he directs his attention to Max. "This can happen to patients who have suffered brain injury, it's not uncommon," he says, trying to reassure him. "Often patients will regain their memory, but I'm afraid there's no way of knowing if, or when, that will happen. Maintaining a normal routine can often trigger the memories," he adds, reassuringly. A glimmer of hope flashes across Max's face.

Oh, no. He's going to want me to go home with him to the penthouse. I can't do that.

I can't look at Max, he reads me too well, and I can't stand to see him so sad, so I take the easy option and feign exhaustion. I close my eyes and try to calm my breathing, even though every nerve ending is screaming out. All I want to do is run into his arms and never let him go, but the reality that I'll never do that again hits me like a wrecking ball. I turn my face away from him as the tears begin to seep from my eyes. I can't hold them back any longer, and I've lost the will to try.

"We should let her rest," the doctor suggests. "We'll carry out a thorough evaluation when she's had some time to recover."

I hear the door opening and then I hear the doctor's voice, "Mr. Foxx, if I could have a word with you in private?" he asks softly. A few moments later, I hear the door closing again.

I feel Lucy shaking my arm. "Viv… He's gone," she whispers. My teary eyes spring open. "Bloody hell. We both deserve an Oscar for that performance!" Lucy says, shaking her head. "I thought I was going to pass out. You know what a shit liar I am."

"Thank you," I sniffle, wiping my eyes. "Do you think he believes me?"

"Well if he doesn't, maybe *he* should get the bloody Oscar," she smirks.

The look on Max's face will haunt me forever. I've hurt him more deeply than any bullet ever could. If only I could tell him why I must leave him. If only I could tell him how much I love him. But I know he'd never let me go. I don't want him to let me go. But I need to keep him safe.

I've relived every terrifying moment of Monica's attack through my dreams and nightmares. Monica had come to the penthouse to kill me. She would have, if the gun she'd held at my head had actually gone off as intended. Luckily for me, something had jammed and my life was spared. But a bullet to the brain? A quick death compared to a lifetime without Max? Maybe I'm not so lucky after all.

"Are you sure you want to do this, Viv? I mean, don't you think you should at least tell the police or something? That mad bitch is still out there somewhere. She's tried to kill you once already, what makes you think she won't try it again?"

That terrifying thought has crossed my mind about a million times. "Yeah, I know." My stomach rolls every time I think about her. That woman scares me to death. "I can't go to the police. She warned me that she'd be watching me. I can't do anything that will set her off… Not yet."

Lucy looks nervously between me and the door. "So, what's your plan? I assume you have a plan? I mean, Max isn't going to just let you walk out of his life, the man's besotted with you."

I try to sit up. Lucy helps by propping my pillows up behind me.

"Luce, you need to help me get out of here. I need to go home."

Her eyebrows shoot upward. "Are you fucking crazy?" she yells angrily. "You've got a four inch gash on the side of your head—"

"Ssshhh. Keep your voice down," I hiss. "Look, Max can wander in here whenever he wants. You heard the doctor, he's going to want me to carry on with a normal routine, that means Max will want me to stay with him. He's going to try and make me remember. I don't know how long I can keep this up, Luce. It's killing me." Tears well up in my eyes and the lump in my throat tightens like a vise. "I can't bear hurting him like this, but if Monica sees me living at the penthouse, it's game over. I need to get away from him. Please, Lucy. Please!"

Lucy grabs my hand and squeezes it for all she's worth as I sob my heart out.

"Oh, Viv. I'm so sorry. Please don't cry, come on. You know I'll help you any way I can."

A light knocking at the door has both our heads whipping up. The rapid movement makes my head pound with an aggressive pain making me flinch. We quickly dry our tears as a nurse opens the door and pokes her head in.

"Hello, sorry to disturb you but you've got a visitor," she smiles.

Lucy and I exchange a glance, both of us trying to compose ourselves. Butterflies invade my belly. I can't let Max see me like this. The nurse pushes the door open all the way and stands to the side as William enters my room in a wheelchair. *Oh.* He looks so much better than the last time I'd seen him. It's good to know he's doing well. Max will have his father back, and right now, he'll need the support of all his family.

I glance up at Lucy, she hasn't met William before. She looks at him quizzically then she looks over at me in that, *sort-yourself-out,* way. I suddenly remember that I can't let William know that I recognise him either or he'll tell Max. *Shit.* I quickly arrange my expression to match Lucy's as William wheels himself into the room and parks next to my bed. He looks over to Lucy and nods a smile at her. She tentatively smiles back.

"Hi, I'm Lucy, Vivienne's friend."

The nurse pats William on the shoulder. "I'll come back for you in a few minutes," she smiles, then she leaves the room.

The concern in William's eyes betrays the smile on his face as he looks at me with fondness. "Vivienne, I can't tell you how sorry I was to hear about what happened to you." The sadness in his voice chokes me. I know he'll be worrying about how this will affect Max. He really doesn't need this right now, the poor man has his own problems to deal with.

While I try to keep my expression to a minimum, and nervously figure out what I'm going to say, he spares me having to lie to him with his next sentence, "I had hoped my snazzy pyjamas and my rugged good looks would have triggered your memory, Vivienne. But alas, judging by your face, I guess I'm just not that memorable," he smiles. "I'm William. I'm Max's father." He leans over to pat the back of my hand. "We've met before. You kindly visited me when I wasn't feeling so great. I'm very sorry that you've lost your memory, it must be very frightening, but I hope only the good things come back to you. And don't worry about a thing, you just look after yourself and get better soon." He smiles warmly.

My heart aches at his loving words. The fact that he's made the effort to find me is very touching. I smile back at him, trying really hard not to give myself away.

"Have you been in here long?" Lucy asks.

William gives her a wry smile. "Yeah, it's been kind of like my second home recently."

"Oh, that's a shame," I say, trying not to blush. I feel like such a fraud.

"No, it's okay. The nurses here are very sweet, and I've been here so long the food's starting to taste pretty good."

The door opens, and the nurse reappears. "Mr. Foxx, it's time for your physio." William nods me a wink as the nurse wheels him away.

As he reaches the door, he turns back. "If you want a game of scrabble, or you just need to talk, I'm only down the hall. Take care of yourself, Vivienne. Nice to meet you, Lucy." He smiles, and then he's gone.

Resting my head back on the pillows, I close my eyes and take a deep breath. *How did I ever think this was going to be easy?* I open my eyes and see Lucy refilling my water beaker.

"He's nice," she says, offering me the water.

"Thanks… Yeah, they're all lovely," I sigh. *I'll miss them… All of them.*

My headache has got decidedly worse, probably because of all the tension of having to lie through my teeth to everybody I care about.

"Luce, how bad is my head?" I ask, suddenly realising I have no idea what it looks like.

She pulls a face. "Well, this time, it's more Frankenstein than Rocky! But I'm sure once the stitches come out and you can wash your hair, it'll be fine," she smirks. "How bad does it hurt?"

"On a scale of one to ten? …Twelve." I grumble.

"I'll get the nurse, you should have some pain killers for that," she says, rising from her seat. I don't want her to leave me alone, but my headache is getting worse. I watch her leave the room, then I rest my head back and close my eyes trying to erase the painful memory of Max's tortured face.

"Vivienne?"

My heart stops. *Please, Max. Please don't make this any harder than it is.*

"Baby?" I keep my eyes closed as he enters the room. I know if I take one look he'll melt my heart and I'll succumb to his beautiful blue eyes. He picks my hand up and kisses my fingers, the feeling of his soft lips brings a flutter of butterflies to my belly. "Baby, I… I don't know if you can hear me? …And I know you don't remember me right now, but… I need you to know that I love you. So much." The catch in his throat pulls at my heart. It's all I can do to stop myself from leaping out of bed and throwing my arms around him, but I remain as still as I can and I try desperately hard not to cry.

I love you too, Max. With all my heart.

"Baby, I've loved you from the very first moment I saw you. I'll never stop loving you. If it takes forever… I'll be waiting."

I hear someone enter the room. "Oh! Max. Erm, I think she's sleeping. It's been a very confusing day for her."

I hear Lucy walk around to the side of my bed, then I feel Max's warm lips pressing gently into mine. My heart aches. His lingering kiss is soft and loving. I want to kiss him back so badly. As he pulls away, a tear drips onto my cheek as he whispers, "I'll be waiting." And then he's gone. I want to scream out his name. I want to run after him, but all I can do is cry my heart out.

"Viv, just tell him the truth. This is no good for either of you."

"No! I… I just need to go home… Get some space."

Lucy hands me a small white pot containing two tablets. "Here. Take these, you need to rest." My brain feels like it's banging against my skull like a farrier's hammer, so I take the tablets and settle back into the pillows while they take effect on the headache from hell.

APPEASE HER WRATH

"You!"

"Surprised to see me, Vivienne?… I think I look pretty good for a dead person. What do you think?" She removes her hood, cap, and glasses, then she drags the black wig from her head and shakes her red hair loose. Her smug green eyes bore into mine with contempt, then they trail down my trembling body. The look on her face is pure hatred and disgust.

I'm rooted to the spot, although every instinct tells me to run for my life. The gun in her gloved hand is pointed straight at me. I'm trapped and acutely aware that no one will be coming to my rescue. No one knows she's still alive. No one knows I'm in danger. Tears spring into my eyes.

"How did you get in here?" I try not to show fear, but my voice betrays me.

She reaches into her pocket and throws a black, plastic key-card onto the desk. "You left this behind when you ran off," she gloats.

"What do you want?" I whisper nervously. My heart is pounding in my chest, and my body trembles with fear. She throws her head back and laughs, loud and strong, but then almost as suddenly, she stops and hits me with hate filled eyes as a snarling smile slinks across her lips.

Pulling the gloves from her hands with her teeth, she spits them onto the desk. "I want what you stole from me, you bitch. I want Max… But you've got him wrapped around your little finger, and now he thinks he's in love with you." Suddenly, Monica stands and moves so fast that I panic and stumble backwards. My body hits the wall, and

I've got nowhere left to go. Fear knots my stomach and chills my blood. In an instant, her tall, threatening frame bears down on me. I scream as she grabs me by the hair and smashes my head back against the wall. She presses the gun to the side of my head and her face into mine, until we're almost touching. I screw my eyes shut and brace myself for the inevitable. I don't want to die.

"He doesn't love you, you stupid bitch," she hisses, spitting all over my face. "He loves me. He's always loved me. And he always will. We've got an unbreakable bond that even you couldn't break.... He needs me."

I don't know how or why I think it a good idea to antagonise her right now, but something inside me snaps and makes me open my eyes and grit my teeth. "You took the life of your own son. He'll never forgive you for that. Even if you kill me, especially if you kill me, Max will never love you."

Fury darkens her eyes as she screams with rage and pushes the gun harder into my skull. "Fuck you!" she shouts venomously. I scream and flinch, expecting the worst. I don't want to die. But the metallic click that follows does nothing. Then another click...again nothing.

"Fuck!" She screams as she keeps pulling the trigger over and over again, but nothing happens. There's no big bang, there's no pain, other than the pressure of the hard, cold steel pressed against my skin.

The pressure suddenly disappears, my eyes spring open, then a sudden blinding pain sears through the side of my head as Monica screams and strikes me with the gun. I hear the loud clatter as the gun hits the marble floor and then immediately I feel the pressure of Monica's bare hands around my throat. I'm pinned against the wall as I desperately gasp for air, reaching out with my hands to try and push her off of me.

My head feels like it's splitting with the pain, and a warm wetness flows down my cheek. The blood stings my eyes and everything becomes blurry and hazy. She wrestles me to the floor, choking the life out of me with a maniacal look on her face as I frantically kick and claw at her, but it makes no difference, she's freakishly strong.

Her deranged eyes are wide and wild. "It's your fault Charlie's dead," she seethes. "If you hadn't come along and fucked everything up we'd be a happy little family right now. But no. You had to go and spoil it all, didn't you?" she hisses, gritting her teeth. "You think you're so fucking clever." I hopelessly scratch and claw as her hands tighten around my throat. I can't breathe. I desperately need air! "You think you can just take him from me and get away with it? You stupid fucking bitch!"

The unrelenting pressure of her bony fingers wrapped around my throat, feels like a vise. I feel the life draining out of me. I can't breathe. I need help. "No… Please… Don't," I gurgle, struggling for air. But suddenly the pressure of her fingers crushing my windpipe, releases. My body convulses in a reflex as I frantically gasp for air pulling my hands up to my throat. The oxygen burns in my lungs.

She sits on top of me, pinning me to the floor, glaring down at me with fury in her wild green eyes. "You're right… Killing you would only martyr you. And we can't have that… No… I know a much better way." I flinch as she softly trails a finger down my cheek and then raises her hand to look at the blood on her fingertip. She stares at it, tilting her head, while she silently contemplates my fate. Her eyes suddenly dart to mine, making me shrink in fear. "You have to leave him… You have to hurt him," she snarls. "Then he'll see how much he needs me." I stare up at her in shock. She's fucking crazy!

I flinch and whimper when she leans down into my face, hovering above me she tilts her head and smiles wickedly. My eyelids are getting heavy, they begin to droop involuntarily. I'm fading. I've lost too much blood. I can feel myself slipping away as a wave of exhaustion takes over my body.

"Wake up!" she yells, slapping my face hard. The sting in my cheek snaps my eyes open. Trailing her deranged eyes all over me, she prods her fingers over the painful wound on my head. "Oh, dear," she grins. "That's going to leave a mark."

My skull feels like it's going to explode. The strong smell of blood fills my nostrils and makes me feel sick. She grips my jaw tightly in her bony fingers and wrenches my face around, her eyes boring into mine with hate. "It's very simple, Vivienne," she says, with a menacing smile. "If you don't leave Max, I will kill him… If you tell him I was here, I will kill him." She leans in even closer, her lips twitching into a snarl. "If you do anything to piss me off, I will kill him… And it will be all. Your. Fault!"

I lie there trembling from head to toe, drenched in my own blood, and struggling to breathe. I don't want to pass out, but I have no energy left at all. I have to force my eyes to stay open. I desperately need help. Please, somebody, help me!

She quickly moves off of me and over to the desk. She bends down and picks up a black bag from the floor and throws it on the chair, then she puts the wig, cap, gloves, and glasses back on. I nervously look around me. I feel strange like I'm floating. I'm so cold. I can't focus on anything very well, and the pain in my head is unbearable. I flinch as she smashes the desk lamp throwing the room into darkness. Her shadowy figure walks toward me, then she bends down to pick up the gun. Squatting down beside me, she grabs my throat in one hand. I panic, maybe this is it? Maybe she's going to kill me after all.

"Remember what I said, Vivienne… I'll be watching."

"No!… No!"

"Jesus! Viv, it's okay. It's me. Wake up."

I wake with a jolt. My lungs are gasping for air as my eyes ping open. I'm batting my hands out in front of me, but it's Lucy staring down at me. I nervously look around the room until I realise I'm not where I thought I was. *Oh, my God.* It seems that every time I close my eyes I have to endure the attack over and over again. Each time feels so real, it's terrifying.

"Viv. You're alright, it was just a dream," she soothes, stroking my arm. "You're lucky. Max left just before you starting babbling. If he'd heard any of that, he would have been able to guess that it was Monica who had done this to you. It sounded awful. You've got to tell someone about this." I rest back on the pillows and take a couple of deep calming breaths, grateful to be somewhere safe. "There's something else," Lucy says, eyeing me warily.

"What?"

"You've been sleeping for ages so I went out to phone Dan… When I came back this was lying on your chest. There was no envelope." She holds up a small, 'get well' card, with a picture of a teddy bear holding some flowers.

"Who's it from?"

Lucy hands it to me. "It's not signed."

It looks cheery enough on the outside, but as I open it, all it says inside, in scribbled blue ink is, *'Hope you'll be well enough to LEAVE soon. The sooner the better!'*

My stomach churns. "It's a message from Monica," I mumble, staring down at the card. I pull my shaking hand up to my throat. "She's been here!"

"What? No!" Lucy gasps. "Why would she come here? What if Max had seen her? Come to think of it, I don't even know what she looks like." Lucy snatches the card out of my hand and pops it into her bag. "I'm keeping this as evidence, for when you have the fucking sense to call the police," she snaps. "She's taking an awful risk coming in here."

I look up at her pale, angry face and shake my head. "I told you, Luce, she's watching me. She's fucking crazy and I don't think she'd stop at anything right now. That's why I have to go home. I need to get away from Max."

Lucy tuts and huffs at me, clearly feeling the pressure. "Well, you're not going anywhere until they discharge you from the hospital. I don't care if I have to sit here all week keeping watch. You can't even think about going home yet." she frowns.

"How long have I been here?"

"Five days."

Shit. It worries me that Monica may be growing impatient. If she is watching me she'll know Max has still been visiting. I don't want her to think I'm defying her, God knows what she'll do. I look down at myself. *I feel okay, I think?* I've only got an IV line in the back of my hand, which hasn't even got anything attached to it anymore. They took the catheter out this morning, and the last time the nurse checked my blood pressure and vitals, she said everything was fine.

"I need my clothes, I'm going home." I pull the IV line out of the back of my hand, quickly putting pressure on the needle mark to stop the bleeding. Once it's stopped, I throw my sheets back and swing my legs over the side of the bed.

"Viv, for fuck's sake, what are you doing?" The pain in my head is just about bearable but as I stand up, my knees buckle and I collapse back down to the bed. I feel very fragile. "Viv, you're not ready to leave the hospital yet. Look at you! You've just had major surgery for fuck's sake."

I try to stand again and this time I manage to stay upright, although I do feel very queasy and unsteady on my feet. "Luce… Please, help me."

"And what happens if something goes wrong?" she asks, dragging a hand through her loose hair.

"Then I'll come back to the hospital. I promise."

Reluctantly she moves to the closet, grabs my clothes, and helps me dress. I need a wee before I go anywhere so I slowly move into the en-suite, closing the door behind me. When I enter the bathroom, I'm shocked when I see my reflection in the mirror. I look thin, pale, and drawn. I run my hand over the purple bruises on my neck. A chill shivers up my spine remembering Monica's bony hands crushing my throat. The bruising on my face is dark, and the bloodied scar on the side of my head looks horrific. It doesn't help that my hair is still matted with dried blood in that area. I look awful. No wonder my head hurts so much.

As I start to pee, I hear a male voice talking to Lucy, it's Doctor Alexander. I start to panic, but Lucy does a great job of fobbing him off and manages to get rid of him before I come out of the bathroom.

"That was close. We haven't got much time," Lucy huffs. "He's doing his rounds and he'll be back soon so we'd better hurry. I told him you were having number two's."

I blink up at her. "…Thanks."

"What?" she frowns. "I had to say something." I smile and shuffle over to her, grabbing onto her arm for support. She engages my eyes with a nervous look on her face. "Are you sure about this?"

"I'm sure."

Lucy checks outside the door before we edge out of my room. The area is quiet, so we continue down the corridor. I have no idea where we're going so I let Lucy lead me. She'd given me a knitted hat which covers my scar and most of my hair, once she'd finished tucking it up inside, and I'm wearing Lucy's jacket over my t-shirt and jeans. I could be anyone, a regular visitor. Nobody would expect to see me walking about, but if Max sees Lucy we're done for. My stomach churns and I wonder if Monica is watching me now?

Thankfully, everyone we pass doesn't pay us any attention. We take the stairs so that we don't have to wait for the lift, and we slowly make our way down to the exit. Once outside, I have to stop for a second to catch my breath, I'm exhausted.

"Viv, we need to move," Lucy says, looking all around her. "Oh, shit!" she grates, looking across the car park. I follow her line of sight. The press are gathered at the exit on the boundary of the hospital and they're looking at us with interest. I instantly notice Derek, the fat faced journalist I'd had to run from before. Lucy grabs my arm. "Quick, let's get out of here."

I pull back. "No! This is just what I need. If we drive really slowly out of the gates and let them ask me about Max, I can at least pacify Monica with an official quote." Lucy shakes her head and mumbles something about me losing my marbles under her breath, then she takes my arm.

We make it to the car and I'm grateful to be sitting down again. I feel like a little old lady.

"Are you okay?" Lucy asks nervously.

"Yeah, fine." I don't feel so good, but I don't want her to worry so I say nothing.

"I'll stop at the chemist on the way home and get you

some painkillers," she says, pulling my seatbelt across me. She starts the car and heads for the exit. I quickly pull my hat off so they can get a clear view that it's me.

As we reach the press pack, who are eagerly waiting on the pavement just beyond the hospital gates, Derek pushes to the front and leans forward trying to take my photo. They crowd around the front of the car almost blocking our path.

"Stop the car. Luce! Stop the car."

"You're friggin' bonkers," she mutters, but she does as I ask.

I roll my window down. "What do you want?" I ask in a fake annoyed tone.

Derek looks flabbergasted that we've stopped to talk to them, as he, and everyone else crowds around my door. "Vivienne, what happened to you at Mr. Foxx's residence? And why isn't he with you now?"

"Who?" I ask, knowing I've got to answer these questions without getting myself caught out.

"Maxwell Foxx, your boyfriend. Why isn't he with you? And what happened to you at his home? Did he hit you, Vivienne?"

Oh, no. They surely can't think he's responsible? I stare up at Derek, I know he works for a daily tabloid paper, and I know he'll get this story into the next edition. It's just what I need to appease Monica.

"Look. I have no memory of what happened to me. All I know is that I received a blow to the head and I've lost all memory of the last few weeks. As I understand it, I was attacked by a burglar while Mr. Foxx was away… And, for the record, Mr. Foxx and I are no longer together. I have no memory of him either. Now if you don't mind, I'd like to be left alone to recover." As I roll my window back up, I can hear them firing more questions at me, but Lucy edges forward then floors it out onto the main street, and we drive away.

I lean my aching head against the window and stare out

at the world. My world as I know it, will be different from now on. The thought of never waking up with Max's arms around me, or never being able to gaze into his beautiful blue eyes, creates an ache in my heart that just won't quit, and I don't think will ever go away. *I love you, Max. Always remember, I love you.* Picturing his sad face, I close my eyes to keep the tears from falling.

I'LL BE WAITING

"We're home." Lucy softly pats my hand. I blink my eyes to focus. Looking down, I see a white bag on my lap. I hadn't even noticed that Lucy had stopped to get the painkillers. "Come on, I'll help you in, and then you need to rest, lady. You look like shit. And I'm going to stay with you tonight," she says, squeezing my hand. "And tomorrow, I'm taking you to your doctor. She needs to know what's happened to you, just in case. You're probably going to need antibiotics, and those stitches will have to come out in a few days."

Lucy does a good job of fussing over me like a mother hen. She settles me in on the sofa and then brings a bowl of warm water to clean up the dried blood in my hair. Very tenderly, she manages to clean off most of it, and then orders some food.

"Once we've had something to eat, I'll pop along to the corner shop and get you some essentials, you've got bugger all in the fridge," she frowns.

"Thanks, erm, I'll also need you to get the rest of my stuff from Max's place at some point," I mumble sheepishly.

"Great," she huffs. "I'm really looking forward to that!" She folds her arms across her chest, I can tell she's still not happy about my decision to handle this on my own.

"You do realise he's going to hate this? Especially now you've publicly told the world that you're not together anymore." Suddenly her expression softens, she looks sad. "Viv, when you were in the coma, and he thought he might lose you…he cried. I mean, he really cried. He really does love you, you know. Are you sure you know what you're doing?"

No… But I don't know what else to do. "Luce, if I thought the police could do anything, I'd tell them. But they couldn't find her after she'd killed Charlie and whoever that poor woman was that Max thinks was Monica, she must have killed her too. She's gone to a lot of trouble to throw him and the police, off her scent, and she's already murdered three people that we know of. I'd be stupid to underestimate her after all that."

Lucy nods and lets out a long sigh. "But she must realise that Max wouldn't want anything to do with her now. I mean, for fuck's sake, Viv, the woman's mad." I shudder. I don't think I will ever forget the look in that woman's eyes. And I know she'll stop at nothing.

A sudden scary thought comes into my mind. If I leave Max as she asks, and then she tries to make contact with him thinking he would fall in love with her again, because that's just how crazy and fucked-up she really is. What would happen?

The doorbell interrupts my thoughts. Lucy grabs her purse. "That'll be the pizza," she says, leaping up to answer the door. I rest my head back and continue to mull over the possibility that Max is in danger whichever way you look at it.

"No, Max. She's fine, she just needs to rest."

Oh, no. He's here!

I sit up and wince as a sharp pain stabs in my head. As I look up at the doorway, Max is standing there looking back at me with confused, angry eyes.

"What the hell are you doing, Vivienne? Why did you leave the hospital?" The rawness of his emotion clouding his eyes, and the pain in his voice, makes my heart ache. Lucy tries to pull him out of the room by his arm, but he doesn't budge and he doesn't take his eyes off mine.

"It's okay, Lucy," I say, softly, "Let him in." Her eyes dart to mine, then reluctantly she releases him and comes to stand behind me. Max walks over to me and sits on the edge of my sofa. Taking my hand in his, he looks at me for the longest time, searching my face with his sad eyes. His scent wafts into my nose. His soft, warm hands caressing mine, sends a tingling sensation through my skin. It takes all my strength not to throw my arms around him, but I know if I do, I'd never want to let him go.

"Why did you leave the hospital?" he repeats in a velvety rasp, the emotion colouring his voice.

"I'm feeling much better," I lie. "It's been a very confusing time for me, and I just wanted to be somewhere familiar," I add, thinking that it sounds like a reasonable excuse. Lame, but reasonable.

He lifts his chin, a defiant expression creases his brow. "But you don't live here anymore, you live with me."

I look away, his stare is too intense and he reads me too well.

"Max, maybe going back to the place where…you know, where it happened, might not be the wisest move at the moment," Lucy says.

He suddenly has hope in his eyes. "But maybe it could help her remember?"

"And maybe it could set her back. Max, she's been through so much, she needs time to heal, and then we'll see."

His sad eyes travel back to mine. "You don't remember me… at all?" The hurt pours out of him, crushing me inside.

I shake my head. "I'm sorry, but…no." I look away. This is so hard. He's suffering and I hate that I've done that to him.

"Look at me." His velvety rasp sounds so inviting, but I can't look. I don't dare look at him. He'll see everything. "Vivienne, please. Look at me." The gentle squeeze of my hand and his soft, pleading voice, nearly does me in. I brace myself, then I slowly bring my eyes up to his. He softly shakes his head as his eyes narrow on me. "I know you know me." His eyes search mine with an assured intensity like he's seen right through me. I suddenly feel hot and anxious.

Oh shit! Don't blush, don't blush!

"I can see it in your eyes, Vivienne." And that's my downfall, he probably can.

Lucy clears her throat and shifts into my line of sight. "Max…why don't you just give her a few days to at least get over the injury, and then maybe you two could talk?" she says, slipping me a shifty glance. "I'll look after her, I promise. Just give her some time."

His confused eyes swing up to her, and thankfully, he seems to be at least considering what she's saying. He slowly drags his eyes back to mine, so I look down at my blanket nervously picking at a loose thread.

"You fell in love with me once before, Vivienne… It's only a matter of time." He reaches up to smooth my cheek with his fingers as a tiny smile plays on his lips. I'm glad to see him smile. The last thing I need is for Max to lose his ability to cope. He's come so far, but the more I think about it, the more it worries me that I could hurt him so much that he'd return to using the vicious coping mechanisms he'd always relied on before. I don't think I could live with that. He reaches into his pocket and pulls out a white box and a phone. "Doctor Alexander gave me these," he says, placing the box on the table. "They're antibiotics, you need to take the whole course," he frowns. "Make sure she does," he adds, looking up at Lucy with an arched brow. "Your old phone was smashed up so I bought you a new one. It's the same number. I managed to recover all your content so I put it on this phone…maybe some of the pictures will help you to remember?" he says, handing it to me.

"Erm, thanks," I stutter. A mental image of Monica

smashing my phone to pieces suddenly flies into my mind. As I press the home button, the screen illuminates with a photograph of me and Charlie in our painted faces. His cute little Tigger face, and my silly Meerkat face. *Poor Charlie.*

I remember when this picture was taken. We'd had a wonderful day at the zoo. I miss him so much, his cute little face, and his squeaky little voice. My heart twists knowing that I'll never hear him calling me 'Auntie Viniven' again. I suddenly realise that Max is carefully studying me as I look at the photo. He's done this on purpose, to try and jog my memory of him. "Who's the little boy?" I ask, cringing inside. I raise my eyes to Max waiting for his answer. He looks utterly deflated at my question.

His eyes fall down to the photo, a small frown wrinkling his brow. "He was my nephew, Charlie. We buried him six days ago."

My heart breaks. I feel like such a shit. Max has been through so much and now I'm just adding to it. "I'm sorry to hear that," I murmur. *What am I doing? Maybe I should just tell—*

"Hey! What about I pop round and get a few of Vivienne's things, would that be okay?" Lucy asks, interrupting my thoughts and obviously trying to lighten up the moment and move the conversation away from Charlie.

"Sure. Anytime," he sighs wearily. He suddenly stands up. I miss the contact of his hand on mine immediately.

Don't go!

"Call me if you need anything," he says, to Lucy. His expression is tight and I know he's trying very hard not to show his feelings. But I know him well enough to know that he's hurting inside, and I'm the one causing it.

I suddenly feel a sense of dread. I don't want him to go, but I also know that Monica could be watching us right now, and she has to think that it's over between us. She has to think I've left him. *He* has to think I've left him. *Come on, Viv. You know what you have to do.*

"Thanks for the phone, but… please don't try to call me. It's all been very confusing, but I just need to be left alone for a while, to figure things out for myself. I hope you understand."

His brow creases and his eyes begin to water. The look on his face stabs me in the heart, twisting and wrenching until I can't breathe. As much as it hurts, I hold my expression and fight against the tears threatening my eyes.

"If it takes forever… I'll be waiting," he murmurs.

Lucy walks to his side and gently pats him on the shoulder. "Just give her some time," she soothes. He slowly turns away and walks out of my life.

What have I done?

Closing the door behind him, Lucy runs over to the window and watches him leave.

"Viv, he's crying… Oh fuck! He's just punched the bloody car!… I hope you know what you're doing, lady?" she says, still staring out the window. "Oh. Pizza guy's here." As she turns to face me, she sees me crying and comes running over to give me a cuddle. I hold on to her for dear life and sob uncontrollably into her shoulder. "Viv. This is all wrong," she sniffles. "You've just found the man of your dreams, and now you're going to let some fucked up, psycho-bitch, nut-job split you up? I don't understand you. I don't understand you at all."

She's right. I'm scared, and I'm running away. I've never run away from all the other things I've had to deal with in my life. Why am I starting now?

I haven't got much of an appetite so I nibble a small piece of Pizza and rest back on the sofa. When Lucy's finished eating, she makes a list of essentials and then she heads out to the corner shop.

I close my tired eyes for a while and try to switch off for a minute or two. Of course, that doesn't happen, there's way too much floating around in my head to switch off, so

I reach for my phone and I stare at the picture of Charlie and I. Tears prick my eyes. He was such a lovely little boy, but now he's gone and it hurts so much.

How could Monica have killed her own son? A mother's love is supposed to be deep, nurturing, and unconditional. But Monica's love is tainted by obsession and revenge. She's created such a shit-storm. She could have had it all with Max. She did have it all. But she threw it all away, and when Max fell in love with me, she couldn't bear it. Monica's so obsessed she'd kill Max just to stop me from having him. She's crazy alright, but she must have a weakness somewhere? She's supposedly dead. How will she manage without an identity? Where will she live? Nothing makes any sense.

A text alert pops up on my screen;

```
You made him cry. Good start.
But if he visits you again, he's dead!
Remember what I said.
BTW, your friend is very pretty…
It's up to you whether or not
she stays that way.
```

Fuck!

I feel sick as I stare at the message while my mind races with questions. How could she know he had been here? How could she know he had cried when he left? *She must be close. She really is watching me. And now she's threatening Lucy.*

"I'm back!" Lucy calls out, startling me. She walks in with a bag of shopping and two bottles of wine in her hand. "You okay?" she asks, with a worried frown.

"Er, yeah. Fine," I stutter. I'm far from fine, but I don't want to scare Lucy with Monica's threat. As long as I do what she wants, Monica will have no reason to harm Max or Lucy.

"You sure?" she asks, with a confused look on her face.

"Yeah. Want some help?"

Her wary eyes travel all over me. "No, you're alright." She wanders into the kitchen which gives me time to compose myself, although the butterflies in my stomach are starting to make me feel sick. I can hear her opening cupboard doors and then the fridge. "Where are your wine glasses?" she yells.

"In the oven," I answer automatically.

"Jeez, Viv," she giggles, "you're worse than I am about cooking."

The familiar sound of clinking glasses as she walks back into the living room and then plonks herself down on the floor, makes me smile. Wine is the solution to everything as far as Lucy's concerned. "Fancy one?" she asks, holding the bottle up.

"Don't suppose it'll hurt any more than a blow to the head by a crazed psychopath," I smirk.

"You know it makes sense." She pours us both a glass. "Well, I'm glad she didn't ruin your sense of humour," she smirks, stretching her legs out and leaning back against the sofa.

My eyes trail over Lucy's pretty face. How do I warn her to be careful without scaring the life out of her.

"I've been talking to Dan—"

"You didn't tell him anything, did you?" I blurt. She gives me that, *as-if* , look which makes me feel bad for doubting her. "Sorry."

"Dan and I are going to the South of France on Saturday, just for a week to check out some wedding venues, and we both think it would do you good to come with us and spend a little time in the sunshine. You know, a bit of convalescence, some time away from you know who? And maybe just some time to think about what you're doing," she says, slipping me a sideways glance. "Besides, I don't really want to leave you on your own, not yet anyway."

Hmm…Get away from Max for a few days? That sounds like a very good idea. I need to heal, and then I need to figure out a plan to get rid of Monica once and for all.

"Well, what do think?" she asks hesitantly.

"I think that's a great idea. But it's a bit short notice, isn't it? Will you be able to book me in?" Her eyebrows raise and she looks all shifty all of a sudden. "What?" I ask on a frown.

She just shrugs and fails to suppress a smirk. "I told Dan to just go ahead and book it, so it's already done."

I lean forward and clink her glass. "That's the first bit of good news I've heard all day."

"We'll have to check with your doctor that you're okay to fly, and it will still depend on how you're feeling. There's no point in going anywhere unless you're up to it," she says, arching her brow.

"Thanks, Luce."

My headaches are pretty bad, but I'm sure all the added tension of lying to Max, and having to deal with threatening messages from Monica have made things much worse than they really are.

"What are you going to do about Mike?" Lucy asks out of the blue.

I hadn't even thought about him. "Why? What do you mean?"

"Well, he's bound to find out that you've left Max sooner or later, and he's going to use that opportunity to try to get you back so you'd better be prepared."

There's so much I hadn't thought of. "What about work, did you tell Clive what happened?"

"Yeah, they know you were attacked. Clive and Ed wanted to visit you at the hospital, but Max didn't want lots of people turning up until you were well enough. The newspapers have been running a story too," she says, rolling her eyes. "They're calling it a 'burglary'," she says, using her fingers to invert the commas. "As far as I know, Max hasn't made any public comments yet, so it's all just hear-say at the moment. Hopefully, after giving them your story today, they should leave you alone. But it makes sense for you to get away for a week. You know how persistent they can be."

"Yeah, I remember." I hated them chasing me. They

made me feel like a hunted animal.

"They came into my salon the other day trying to get a story, but I pointed my scissors at them and told them all to piss off. I think they got the point!" She laughs but suddenly her expression changes.

"What is it?" I ask hesitantly.

Her eyes stay lowered to her glass. "Your mum came to the hospital to see you, when you were still in the coma."

Oh?

"Apparently, one of her friends works at the hospital and they called her."

"Pff, I'm surprised she made the effort to come at all. Did she ask you for money?" I wouldn't want Lucy to be out of pocket.

"No. She knows better than to ask me," she scowls. "But apparently, she has asked Max for money."

I'm shocked. "When? He never said anything." I had wondered why I hadn't heard from my mother after the newspapers had plastered us all over their front pages.

"Apparently, she contacted him shortly after you moved in, but he refused to give her any money unless it was for rehab. And I'm sure you know what she said to that," she smirks, rolling her eyes.

She wouldn't agree to that. Why didn't he tell me? "How did she look?"

Lucy shakes her head, frowning. "Viv. You're too kind to that woman."

"Yeah, I know. I can't help it," I shrug. "I worry about her."

"Well, she always looks like she could do with a bath and a hot meal but she seemed okay. And I have to say, she actually did look quite concerned about you."

I raise my eyebrows. "There's hope for her yet." A niggling thought crosses my mind. "Luce… Monica said she'd be watching me, but where do you think she could be?"

Lucy turns to face me with an arched and angry brow.

"Rotting in hell with any luck." A sudden loud noise above our heads has us both looking up at the ceiling. "Oh, I forgot to tell you," Lucy says, pouring another glass of wine, "the flat upstairs has been rented out. I haven't met them yet."

"Not for me, thanks." I place my empty glass on the coffee table. My headache is getting worse. "What about George? I didn't think he wanted to move out of his flat?"

"He didn't," she shrugs, "but his daughter was worried about the stairs since he had the hip operation, so he's staying with her for a few months."

"Oh, well, that'll be nice for him. I like George, he's a nice old fellow." I yawn, I'm exhausted and the wine has finished me off.

"Come on, sleepy head. Let's get you into bed."

Lucy helps me undress and get into my PJ's, then she leaves me to have a wee and brush my teeth. As I snuggle under my duvet, she brings me some water, my medication, and leaves my phone beside the bed. Lucy strokes my hair and gives me a loving smile. "Dan should be over soon, he's going to stay here tonight so don't worry if you hear him, okay?" I nod and smile up at her. "How's your head?"

"Not great. But I don't suppose I should have had the wine," I smirk.

"Just yell if you need me," she says, bending down to kiss me on the forehead.

I watch her leave my room then I close my eyes, I'm so tired.

WARNING

"Hey. Wake up sleepy head, I've brought you some coffee."

I peel my eyes open and blink the sleep away. "What time is it?" I croak.

"It's eleven-thirty. I thought I'd let you have a lie in."

I stretch and yawn. I feel thoroughly rested and I realise it's because I've had a completely dreamless sleep. No night terrors. It's comforting to know that I may not have to endure them every time I close my eyes.

"How do you feel?" Lucy asks, helping me to sit up, propping my pillows behind me. I think about it for minute. I actually feel okay, and my headache is there but hardly noticeable this morning.

"Yeah, I feel good." But then I get a sudden pang of dread. Everything is different now. I'm back in my own flat and for all intents and purposes, I'm no longer with Max. I yearn for him. This whole scenario is depressing.

"That arrived for you this morning," Lucy smirks, nodding at the single white rose in a glass tube vase on my bedside table. I know it's from Max. He gave me a single white rose every morning after I'd moved in with him. It brings a big smile to my face and brightens my mood, a lot.

He's so romantic.

"You've had calls, cards and deliveries all morning. Everyone is wishing you a speedy recovery," she smiles.

"You've had some lovely flowers from Sylvie and William. Jan has sent over some cookies, and I can tell you, Viv, they're the best cookies I've ever tasted," she smirks. "Everyone at your office has sent a huge card and a massive box of chocolates. Oh, and Vinnie called this morning, he said that Max is driving him nuts. But he said to tell you that both he and Jan send their love and best wishes."

Oh, that's so sweet. I know they'll be worrying about me, and I wish I could tell Vinnie what happened. Maybe I should?… Something Jan had said to me on the day of Charlie's funeral about Vinnie not being just a driver, has been playing on my mind. She didn't elaborate at the time, but the night he and Max went to Portsmouth in pursuit of Monica, she hinted that he had special skills and could handle himself in a dangerous situation. *I wonder what she meant?* Maybe Vinnie could be useful in finding Monica? I know he'd trust me enough to help me without involving Max. *Hmm…. Maybe…*

"Viv …Viv. Oi! Are you listening to me?"

I suddenly refocus my attention to Lucy's raised eyebrow. "Oh, sorry. I zoned out. What were you saying?"

"I was saying that your doctor's appointment is booked for two o'clock, and I've run you a bath, so drink your coffee then I'll give you a hand getting ready."

As I drink my coffee, I pick up my phone and have a look through the texts. Max has sent a message;

```
Good morning, beautiful.
You said not to call, but you
didn't say I couldn't text.
I know you need time and
I'll give you whatever you
need to get you back where
you belong.
If it takes forever… I'll be
waiting. I love you.
Max X;-)
```

Tears fill my eyes blurring his message. He's used the little smiley face kiss at the end which was always how I signed my texts to him. I start to text him back, but then I stop myself. It's ridiculous. What the hell am I going to say? I can't encourage him to keep contacting me. I need to nip this in the bud, right now.

Thank you for the flower,
I know you mean well.
You say you'll give me whatever
I need...
I just need some space.
Please don't contact me again.
If and when I'm ready, I'll
contact you.
Vivienne.

My finger hovers over the send. That's not what I want to say at all. I want to tell him that he's the love of my life, and that I can't live without him. That I love him with all my heart and always will. In a sudden movement I hit the send and my text is delivered. *Oh, no… What have I done?*

I sift through the many texts and voicemails that I've received since last Thursday night. Most of them are from well-wishers, some are from Lucy asking me to call her back when she couldn't reach me, and one is from an unknown number. It was received very late last night after I'd gone to sleep. My wide eyes stare at the words;

Remember what I said.
I'm watching you.
No-one is safe.

Where are you? How can you—

"You ready for your bath?" Lucy startles me and I drop the phone.

"Er, yeah." I swing my legs over the side of the bed and stand up, a little too quickly. The room spins and I sway on my feet.

"Take your time. Here, let me help you," Lucy says, wrapping her arm around my shoulders. I'm going to have to respect the fact that I'm still not well enough to do anything on my own. I'm so grateful Lucy's here to help me. She walks me through to the bathroom and helps me to undress and get into the bath. "Ooh, those still look sore," she says, running her eyes over the fading purple finger marks on my neck and shoulders. "What the hell did she do to you?" I haven't given her a blow by blow account of what happened yet. I don't think I'm ready to relive any of it just yet.

She helps me bathe and carefully washes my hair, without getting my stitches wet. The skin around my head wound is starting to feel tight and itchy. With any luck, I can have the stitches removed in another three or four days, hopefully before we go away.

"Mike rang," Lucy says, not even trying to disguise her sarcasm. She wraps me in a big fluffy towel and starts to dry me off.

"Really?" I sigh. "What did he want?"

"He read your story in the newspaper this morning, and he thinks that you dumped Max because you're still in love with him." She launches the eyebrow. That says it all.

"What? Oh, no." My belly churns. I don't need him thinking there is any chance of us getting back together, especially not now.

"Don't worry, I told him not to hold his breath," she smirks. "And I told him not to pester you either. But you know what he's like, he'll probably try to call you sooner or later."

Lucy helps me to dress and settles me into the sofa while she pops down to the lobby to pick up the mail. I sit back and open all the lovely cards and letters from all my friends. Even my long suffering boss, Frank, has written a special message inside the card. 'Get well soon, I need you back at work!' It makes me smile. I'm grateful to know I still have a job to go back to.

Lucy wanders in and sits beside me. "I'm going to have to work tomorrow and Friday, will you be okay on your own?"

"Yeah, I'll be fine. You're only down the road, if I have any problems I can call you. I'm feeling okay, really." I give her my most reassuring smile. I don't want her worrying about me, she's got a business to run. Besides, I do feel okay, as long as I take my time and don't do anything silly, I'm sure I can manage.

"I had a call from Max," she says, slipping me a sideways glance. "He just wanted to know how you were," she shrugs.

Butterflies invade my belly. "How did he sound?"

"Oh, you know, like a man with a broken heart." I feel awful, this must be so hard for him to understand. Lucy purses her lips together and arches her brow. "He told me that you'd asked him not to contact you, which didn't go down very well as you can imagine," she huffs. "But he did say that he'd do whatever it takes to get you back… I told him about our trip to France—"

"You told him?" I blurt in a high pitched voice.

"Yeah. He actually thinks it's a good idea for you to get away and have some relaxation in the sun while you recover. But he wanted to know where, when, and for how long? I told him that he had to respect your wishes and give you some space."

"Good," I sigh. Lucy's forehead wrinkles with a frown and for some reason, she looks a little dejected and hurt. "What's up?"

She huffs out a sigh and shakes her head. "He offered us his chateau and the private jet."

"He's got a chateau in the South of France?" I don't know why I'm so surprised, he'd once promised to show me, or rather christen, all his beautiful houses, one surface at a time.

"Yep! And a yacht in the marina," she huffs. "I'm telling you, Viv, I was very tempted. And if Dan finds out I said no to all that, he's going to disown me," she scowls. "You owe me, lady! Big time!"

I reach over and squeeze her hand. "Sorry," I mumble sheepishly.

Lucy clasps my hand in both of hers and suddenly her face is sad and concerned. "Viv, I know you think you've got this all worked out, but I think you're going about this all wrong. We don't know what that mad fucker will do next. Surely Max is in danger whether you're with him or not?" My belly churns. She's right. But now Monica has upped the stakes and threatened Lucy too. Until I can figure out a decent plan that doesn't prompt her to do anything stupid, I'm going to let Monica think she's frightened me off. That's my only hope at the moment otherwise, God only knows what she'll do next.

My phone beeps with a text from an unknown number. I know it's Monica. My blood chills;

```
Clever girl.
Your story in the paper
was very convincing but
if your pretty little
friend continues to talk
to Max, she'll pay the price.
No one is safe!
Acid can do such terrible
damage to such beautiful skin.
This isn't a game, Vivienne.
You've been warned.
```

"Who's that?" Lucy asks, rising from the sofa.

"Oh, just someone from work," I lie. My stomach churns into an anxious knot. *Why did I lie?*

"I'm going to make some lunch, you hungry?" she asks, wandering toward the kitchen.

"Yeah, great," I mumble, not really listening. *She's never going to stop. And now Lucy… Jesus! I can't let her hurt Lucy.*

My phone rings, making me jump. I'm so relieved when I see it's Clive calling. For a moment I'd feared it could be Monica. "Clive! Hi, how are you?"

"Oh sweetie, I'm fine but more to the point, how are you? We were all so worried about you."

"I'm okay. Lucy's taking great care of me. How's everything at work?"

"Oh, you know, chaos as usual," he laughs. A beat of uneasy silence stretches out between us. "Sweetie… I read in the newspaper that you've lost your memory and you don't remember what happened that night. You remember me, though, right? You're not just bullshittin' me here, are you?"

I laugh out loud. "No. How could anyone forget you or your taste in fashion," I giggle.

"But you don't remember being with Max? Like, at all?"

"No." My belly churns. Another beat of silence prompts us both to speak at the same time, then we both apologise at the same time.

"I was just going to say that if you need anything, Vivienne, just call, anytime. And we all miss you here, sweetie. And Luke sends his love too." The affection in his voice makes me smile. "Thanks."

"You've been through hell, just take as much time off as you need. Frank told me to tell you, that if you still want your job it's going to be waiting for you when you're ready, okay?"

"Oh, I'll definitely be coming back, probably in a couple of weeks or so."

"Great. Well, take care of yourself and I'll speak to you soon, okay? Bye, sweetie."

"You too. Bye."

Lucy brings me an omelette and some orange juice, then she sits and eats with me. The new neighbours upstairs break the peaceful calm by starting up a power tool. It sounds like they're going to drill straight through the ceiling. By the time it stops my headache is thudding relentlessly against my skull so I ask Lucy to get me some more painkillers. While she's gone, I notice her phone on the table so I grab it and send Max a text;

```
Vivienne doesn't want us to
talk anymore. Please don't
call me and please respect
Vivienne's wishes.
Lucy
```

I send the text then I quickly block his number and return her phone to the table before she comes back.

"Here," she hands me the pills and some water. A light

knocking at the front door draws both our heads up.

"If that's Mike, tell him I'm asleep," I whisper. Lucy rolls her eyes and heads to the door.

"Miss Banks?" I don't recognise the voice.

"No. I'm Lucy, her friend."

"I'm Officer Wilson. I need to take a statement from Miss Banks regarding the incident at Mr. Foxx's residence last Thursday evening. I went to the Limberton hospital, but they said that she'd discharged herself yesterday."

"Er. Yes. She's here, but—"

"It's okay, Luce, let him in." I knew I'd get a visit sooner or later, and I've rehearsed my speech, so now is as good a time as any to get it over and done with. The uniformed officer enters the room and Lucy directs him to the seat opposite me.

"Would you like some tea or coffee?" she asks politely.

"No thanks." He smiles, fumbling for his notebook in his top pocket. "How are you feeling, Miss Banks?"

Oh, you know, scared, heartbroken, depressed! "I'm okay."

"Good… Erm, I just need to take your statement for—"

"I'm sorry," I interrupt. "I don't actually have any memories of what happened that night," I lie, pulling my hand up to my neck. I can still feel the crush of her bony fingers wrapped tightly around my throat every time I think about it.

The officer eyes me with confusion. "Nothing at all?"

I shake my head and look down. "No. I seem to have lost the last few weeks of my life. I don't even remember being in a relationship with Mr. Foxx." I glance up at him, he's holding his pen above his notebook poised for action, but he has nothing to write.

"So, you can't tell me anything about the burglary? Or who attacked you?"

I shrug and shake my head. "No. I'm afraid not."

"Oh. Er…this has never happened before." He frowns, glancing up at Lucy. "Well, I don't know what else we can do at the moment, but if you do recall anything, Miss

Banks, this is Detective Inspector Langford's number, he's dealing with the case, just call him if you remember anything, okay?" He hands me a card. The young officer gathers his things and stands up, smiling awkwardly. "I hope you feel better soon, Miss Banks."

"I'll see you out," Lucy says, giving me the death stare behind his back.

Once he's gone, she stands there glaring at me with her hands on her hips. "I hope you know it's against the law to withhold evidence and pervert the course of justice."

"Please, Lucy. I just need to handle this in my own way." She just continues to stare at me, shaking her head with a face on.

Doctor Tracy is very nice, thankfully I've not had the need to visit her very often in the past. She's reading something on her computer as I enter the room, then she looks up at me above the rim of her tortoiseshell glasses.

"Hello, Vivienne. Please, take a seat," she says, casting her eyes all over my injuries. She returns to her screen reading intently then she turns to face me and removes her glasses. "I've just been reading your notes sent over by Doctor Alexander at the Limberton. Your last scan looks normal, no swelling." she smiles.

How did they know where to send them?…Max.

"Firstly, Vivienne, why on earth did you discharge yourself so early?" I look down and fidget in my seat. "You've had quite a serious head injury and you should have remained in the hospital for at least another week," she sighs.

My hands fidget in my lap. "I felt fine. I just wanted to go home."

She waits for me to engage eye contact, then she stands and walks around her desk to have a closer look at my head wound. "You seem to be healing okay," she says, gently pressing around the wound. "And there doesn't appear to be any infection. Are you still taking the antibiotics they gave you?" she asks, walking back to her chair.

"Yes. And I feel okay, really."

She sits behind her desk and types something into the computer. "Any dizziness, nausea, or pain?" she asks, still typing.

"No. Just a light headache, but I haven't needed the strong painkillers since yesterday evening. I just take paracetamol when it gets too much."

She looks up at me, resting her elbows on the desk. "And what about your memory, have you regained anything yet?"

I look her straight in the eyes. "No." I suddenly realise I'm getting much better at lying without having to look away.

"It's fairly likely that your memories will return in time, however, in some cases those memories can be lost forever. I know counselling and hypnotherapy have been useful for some patients suffering with memory loss, but unfortunately, there are no guaranteed solutions to effectively restore those losses."

"I know."

"Have you had any flashbacks, blackouts, or nightmares since the incident?"

"No, none," I lie. The all too vivid images are still very present in my mind whether I'm awake or asleep since Monica threatened to harm Lucy too.

"I'd like to see you next week—"

"Oh, actually," I interrupt, "I'm going away for a week, this Saturday in fact. I was wondering if the stitches could come out before I go?" Her surprised expression worries me for a moment. Maybe I should be acting more upset and concerned about my fake memory loss. "Yeah, erm, I just need to get away for a while," I add quickly, "it's been so confusing. I just need some space to try and process everything that's happened to me. And I need to get away from the press too. They've been hounding me for a story on something I just can't remember."

She smiles sympathetically. "Yes, of course. It will probably do you the world of good Vivienne."

"So, is it okay for me to fly?" I ask nervously.

She stands and walks around the desk to take another look at my scar. "That would be nine days since the accident… hmm," she mumbles, inspecting my head. "But it is healing very nicely, so maybe if you come back in on Friday we can take the stitches out then, okay?"

She takes my blood pressure then she checks my eyes, ears, and temperature. "You seem to be in very good health, but you must contact the surgery if you have any pressure or pain in the eyes, head, or the neck, and please finish your course of antibiotics," she says, walking back to her chair.

"I will."

I'm relieved that she's given me the thumbs up. We make an appointment for Friday, and I walk out to find Lucy.

On our way home, we stop at Java Mama's for a hot chocolate. Estelle is beside herself with concern over me and she fusses over us like a mother hen. She refuses to let us pay for anything and she gives us extra-large drinks and a couple of chocolate eclairs, with extra cream. I gaze out of the window secretly hoping that Max will pull up outside in his limo. I miss him so much, but strangely, the sooner I get away from him, the better I will feel. My eyes dart around the street outside. I feel like I'm being watched. Or am I just being paranoid.

Where are you?

A flash of red draws my attention and quickens my heart rate, but the young girl with bouncing red curls isn't Monica. And why would I think that she would just be wandering around the streets without some form of disguise? The woman's crazy, not stupid.

NO ONE IS SAFE

Lucy's making breakfast as I wander into the kitchen.

"Will you be okay on your own?" she asks warily, serving my scrambled egg on toast. I sit and pour a glass of orange juice.

"Yeah, I'm fine. No headache today," I lie. My head is pounding like a bastard. "I'm going to make a list of what I'll need to pack for France."

"Okay, good. I'll get your things later," she says, glancing down at her watch. "I'd better go, call me if you need anything."

Once Lucy's gone, I relax. I feel like shit and I'm exhausted, but I don't want Lucy to worry. I'd woken up several times during the night, always with the same dream. Monica's distorted smile leering down at me as she chokes the life out of me. I'd woken up gasping for air. I could literally feel the pressure of her fingers around my throat, but of course, it was just a dream.

Having lost my appetite, I scrape the food into the bin and tidy up the kitchen then I start to make my packing list. *Shit! My passport.*

I quickly search through all my bags, pockets, and drawers, but I already know where it is. I left it at F1. I can't call Max, and I'm afraid for Lucy to call him. If she makes contact with Max again it could trigger Monica to do something stupid. *What the hell am I going to do?* Maybe I should call Vinnie, but what if he's with Max? I decide to call Jan, that seems the safest option. I rehearse what I'm going to say to her then I dial her number with trembling fingers.

Please don't be with Max. Please don't be with—

"Hello?"

"Erm. Hi. Are you Jan? It's Vivienne. Lucy told me you could help me," I say, shakily, trying to keep up the pretence.

There's a short pause followed by a deep sigh. "Oh, Vivienne. How nice to hear your voice," she says, affectionately. "How are you?"

"Oh, erm, I'm good thanks." This is awkward. The poor woman is worried about me, I can hear it in her voice.

"Have you regained any—"

"No. I'm afraid not," I interrupt quickly.

"Oh…that's such a shame. What can I do for you, dear?" she asks warmly.

"I'm going away for a while, and I think my passport must be at Mr. Foxx's house but I don't remember where?"

"Oh, yes, of course. Don't worry, Vivienne, I'll find it and get it sent over to you." I'm so relieved, my eyes tear up a little. I really miss Jan and Vinnie, they've been so kind to me and I know they care a great deal about me, as I do them.

"Thank you." I quickly end the call and breathe deeply to calm myself.

Wandering back to the living room I stare out of the window. *Where are you, Monica?* A familiar car pulls up outside. My shoulders sag, he's the last person I want to see right now. Mike strides up to the main entrance and out of my view. I really don't want to see him yet. The doorbell sounds and makes my belly churn, but I brace myself and walk to the door, opening it a few inches only.

"Hi. Can I come in?" he asks hesitantly. The look on his face is apologetic. Begrudgingly I open the door and let him in.

We sit on opposite sides of the coffee table. He looks all tanned and handsome from his holiday, but he also looks worried and concerned as his eyes trail across my bruises and scar.

"Viv, what the hell happened to you? Lucy wouldn't tell me anything, but I read in the papers that you were attacked during a burglary and you've lost your memory."

I don't really want to talk about it. Everything still feels so raw, but in a way, I think I need to talk about it, even though I can't tell him exactly what happened.

"Yeah, I woke up in the hospital with this," I point at the scar, "and all I know is the last few weeks of my life have totally disappeared."

He winces slightly and sits forward resting his arms on his knees. "Do you remember us?" he asks tentatively.

That's the trouble with lying. You have to have an excellent memory. *How ironic.* I know I have to be careful with my timeline here. As far as Max is concerned, I lost everything from the morning of his gala ball, which means I hadn't even seen Max by this point, and Mike's fling with Michelle had yet to be discovered. A moment of inspiration dawns on me.

"Mike, Lucy told me all about your relationship with Michelle. I don't remember what happened between us, and quite frankly, I really don't care anymore."

"I still love you," he says, softly. "I want you back."

I shake my head and stand up, swaying a little on my feet. A dull thumping headache pounds against my skull. "Please, Mike… I can't do this right now. Please, just leave." To my surprise, he looks apologetic and stands up placing his hands in his pockets.

"I'm so sorry. I never meant to hurt you. Please, Viv. Please give me another chance, or at least think about it?" He looks so dejected and hurt. I look down and shake my head. "I'm here for you, whenever you need me," he says, quietly. With a sad smile, he walks out the door, closing it softly behind him.

A small part of me still cares about him, but even though Mike is the safe and easy option for me, I know I could never love him the way I love Max. Underneath all his insecurities, Mike is a good man who will inevitably survive this. But, will I?

I walk over to the window and watch him walk back to his car. He doesn't look up, and in a few moments, he's gone.

Lucy, Dan and I have dinner together down at Lucy's flat. Dan made a delicious chicken curry with all the extras, and we polished off a few drinks too. Even though I probably shouldn't be drinking at all. At my request, Lucy had warned Dan to stay away from asking me any probing questions about the attack or Max. As far as he's concerned, the subject is just too distressing for me.

"So, what time are we leaving on Saturday?" I ask, polishing off my wine.

"The flight's at eleven-thirty in the morning, so we need to be off by seven," Dan answers, filling the glasses again.

I cover my glass. "No more for me, thanks." I'm pooped, and the wine isn't helping my headache.

"What about those?" Dan asks nodding up at my stitches. "Will we have to take you to a hospital in France to get them taken out?"

"No, hopefully they're coming out tomorrow," I shrug.

"Well, you look pretty good, Viv, but how do you feel?" I know he's worried that I'll have a setback while we're away so I smile to reassure him.

"I feel fine. I promise." He doesn't seem entirely convinced.

"So, what venues are you looking at while we're out there?" I ask, trying to move the subject away from me.

Lucy bounces excitedly in her seat. "We've seen a couple of nice hotels with beautiful gardens, and there's even a castle too."

"And don't forget the marina," Dan chips in. "There are

some really amazing yachts out there. I've always wanted to have a look around one of the really big ones. I saw Spielberg's yacht on the internet. Man, it was awesome!" Lucy catches my eye and gives me the death stare. I blush, she'll never let me live that one down.

After a satisfying meal and a very pleasant evening, I decide to head back upstairs to bed. Lucy wouldn't let me help with the dishes and I'm struggling to keep my eyes open. I'm exhausted.

"I'm off you guys. Thanks for dinner."

"I'll walk you upstairs," Dan says, rising from his seat.

I push him back down and kiss him on the cheek. "Don't be silly, I'm okay. I'll call you if I need anything."

When I open my door, the whole place is dark. It was still daylight when I left and I forgot to leave any lights on. I quickly put the lamp on by the door and throw my keys on the small table. The room is cold, making me shiver. *I thought I'd left the heating on?*

I check the thermostat which looks okay, then I go and check the boiler in case it's broken down, but it all looks fine. *I must have left a window open.* I check the living room window, the bathroom and bedroom windows, but they're all locked up tight. I'm just about to check the kitchen window when my phone startles me.

"Everything okay?" Lucy asks. "I just wanted to make sure you got home alright."

"Yeah," I giggle, rolling my eyes, "I live like twenty feet away, Luce."

"I know," she giggles. "See you tomorrow, Viv."

I yawn and shuffle through to the bathroom to brush my teeth. Too tired to even bother changing out of my comfies, I kick my shoes off and crawl into bed, snuggling under my duvet.

My eyes ping open and I sit bolt upright in bed, gasping for air. The room is dark. As my eyes adjust, something doesn't feel right. It feels like the air around me has shifted, almost like someone is in my room. I reach for the bedside lamp and switch it on. Looking around my room, everything looks normal but it's freezing in here. I get out of bed and head to the living room to turn the thermostat up. I check the locks on the front door and then shuffle wearily back to bed.

INTRUDER

The morning sunshine flows in through the curtains and lands directly over my eyes. I move, but annoyingly it's still there, blazing in through my closed eyelids. I groan and pull the covers up over my head. I'm not ready to get up yet.

A tapping at the front door focuses my attention and gets my eyes open. *Who the hell is that?* I drag myself out of bed and quickly check myself out in the mirror. *Eeuuww!* I look awful. My hair is all over the place, and the yellowing bruises across my cheek and throat make me look dirty. Looks aside, I actually feel much better today, and I'm perfectly steady on my feet.

The tapping repeats, louder this time. "Just a minute!" I call out, on my way to the door. I open it a couple of inches and see John's smiling face. "Oh." I almost greet him with a smile, but then I suddenly realise I can't. "Er, can I help you?" I croak, clearing my throat.

He smiles down at me and holds up a large suit-bag in one hand, and a big holdall in the other. "I've brought your belongings, Ma'am."

Thinking on my feet, I frown at him and throw him a questioning look. "My belongings?"

His smile drops a little. "From F1…the penthouse... Mr. Foxx?… Jan asked me to bring your passport and all your belongings over." His astute eyes search mine. I try hard not to look away, it's like he's looking right into me.

"Oh, right. Thanks." I reach out to take them from him. His eyes are checking me out the whole time. I need to keep my cool.

"Still nothing, Ma'am?" he asks, with a sad expression.

"I'm sorry?"

"Never mind." He smiles, but it doesn't quite reach his eyes. "Take care, Ma'am." I watch him walk away, wishing he had been Vinnie.

Everything I had taken with me to Max's home, is now here. Everything except two things. The first is the eye scan image Max had acquired from Doctor Alexander. He knew I wanted a copy, and not only did he get it for me, but once I'd moved in with him, he'd had it framed and mounted on his study wall as a piece of, what he called, 'beautiful living art.' The second is my bike. My crash helmet has been returned, but not my bike. I know why he wouldn't want me to have it. He'd always refused to let me ride it on my own for fear I could have an accident. He's hardly likely to let me loose on it while he's not around to protect me.

I can't ask for either of those things because they both happened after I met Max. My suspicious brain starts to wonder if these missing items are some kind of test.

Once I've put away all my stuff, I notice that it's nearly time for my appointment with Doctor Tracy so I quickly take a shower and get ready.

Doctor Tracy gives me another blood pressure check and asks me all the same questions as before, then she inspects my head wound. After getting a second opinion from Doctor Walton, they both decide the stitches can come out. My head actually feels a lot better once the stitches are gone, it doesn't feel so tight anymore.

After a pep talk from Doctor Tracy about the dangers of UV sun rays on a fresh scalp wound, I'm on my way home. I stop at the post office to pick up some euros, and then I pop into one of my favourite shops to buy a straw Stetson.

When I return home at around five, I finish packing my case and head to the bathroom to shower, de-fuzz and paint my nails. As I walk into the bathroom, I stumble to a shuddering stop. My eyes widen in shock and disbelief as a cold shiver rattles up my spine. Right in front of me on the bathroom mirror are the words, 'No One Is Safe' written in lipstick in big scrawling letters.

Monica! The blood drains from my head and I stumble backward, the backs of my legs hitting the edge of the tub. *How the fuck did she get in here?* Panic grips my stomach. Is she still here? My wide eyes dart everywhere. If I actually see her, I think I'd die from the shock alone.

I edge out of the bathroom looking all around me. I quickly find my baseball bat and I hold it up ready to swing, but after checking all the rooms and cupboards, I realise there's no one here. *What the fuck is she playing at?*

I clean the mirror, then I anxiously pace up and down the living room trying to figure out how the hell she could have got into my flat in the first place.

My heart jumps when I hear the lock on the front door clicking open and Lucy bursts in with an armful of shopping bags.

"Bonjour!" she yells, giggling. She marches in and throws the bags down on the sofa. "Oh, I'm so excited about tomorrow, Viv. I've bought us some French wine and cheese to get us in the mood," she giggles, rummaging around in one of the bags. "And look! I couldn't resist it, I bought these for us." She hands me a beret. She puts her one on, and then she stops moving and stares at me warily. "What's the matter?"

In that split second I decide not to tell her. I can't spoil her mood, she's so happy. And what would I say that wouldn't scare her to death.

"Nothing." I force a smile and put my beret on. "Stitches are out, case is packed, I've got my euros, my passport, and I'm all ready," I add, trying to match her enthusiasm.

"Great. Do you want to have dinner here?" she asks,

collecting all her bags.

"Yeah, why not? Maybe you and Dan should stay here tonight too." I say it as nonchalantly as possible but inside I'm praying that they do stay. I don't want to be by myself tonight, not now I know that Monica has been here. Safety in numbers.

Lucy agrees, then heads off downstairs to finish her packing.

We meet up at eight for wine and cheese, then we head off to bed at a reasonable hour for the early morning train ride to the airport. I feel safer knowing Lucy and Dan are here, but it doesn't help me sleep. Every creek and groan of the building keeps me on tenterhooks.

NEED SOME SPACE

We leave in a rush, not an unusual scenario for us, Lucy's never on time for anything. We do, however, arrive at the airport in plenty time. Dan helps me with my case, and we're all very excited to be going to the South of France. I've never been there so I'm really looking forward to it.

When we hand our passports over at the check-in desk, the orange-faced lady at the counter informs us that our flight has been upgraded and we are now flying first class.

"But, there must be some mistake," Lucy says. Dan is trying to shush her up, but she bats him away and stares at the lady with raised eyebrows.

"No, your flight was upgraded yesterday," she says, with a corporate smile and overly enthusiastic voice. She checks our luggage in, then returns our passports and boarding passes. "Your flight will begin boarding in forty-three minutes, please make your way to the V.I.P lounge. Enjoy your flight."

We all stare at each other with raised eyebrows. "It has to have been Max," I say, shaking my head.

Dan's face beams with a big cheesy grin. "Well, let's not insult the poor man by refusing his generous gift."

Lucy throws her arms around Dan's neck. "Woo-hoo! First class. I can't believe it." After twirling around and giggling at each other, Dan stops and cocks an eyebrow at me.

"Viv, are you sure you don't remember him? And even if

you don't, shouldn't you at least pretend that you do. If this is how he looks after you, you should grab it with both hands."

I feel uncomfortable at Dan's remark. Max's wealth was never the attraction for me, in fact, meeting his twin brother proved that. They have totally different personalities. Beneath all his looks and charm it was Max's warmth and vulnerability that drew me to him. It's what I love about him. His outward playboy persona is arrogant and businesslike, typical of the mogul he's become. But because of his looks and the way he fiercely protects his privacy, copious amounts of speculation, driven by the gossip hungry media, has enforced a public perception that just isn't him. To me he's kind, caring, and sensitive. The way Max makes me feel about myself is what makes him special to me. All this extravagance is nice, but ultimately, it's the man that counts.

"Viv… Viv! Are you okay? You look kind of pale," Lucy asks, frowning at me.

"What?… No, I'm fine,"

We make our way into the V.I.P lounge, where we are waited on hand and foot. After a short wait, we board the flight and turn left. It's the first time I've ever flown first class. The cabin attendant shows us to our seats and after noticing my head wound, she seems to pay extra special attention to me.

Knowing Monica had somehow managed to get into my flat yesterday had ruined any chance of a good night's sleep, so once we take off, I recline and close my eyes.

He doesn't love you, you stupid bitch!

I wake with a start, my heart is pounding in my chest, my lungs gasping for air.

"Viv, are you okay?" Lucy's face comes into focus, her concerned eyes stare down at me. "You were dreaming," she says, softly.

"Oh, I'm sorry," I mumble. Her soft, caring eyes search

my face. She turns to look over her shoulder at Dan, who's engrossed in the in-flight entertainment. With his earphones in, he's completely oblivious. I move my seat to the upright position.

"Was it another dream about…you know?" Lucy whispers. I just nod. She who must not be named, is a constant visitor in my dreams. The dreams always feel so real, they're terrifying.

An announcement that we are coming in to land, makes me look out of the window. I'll be glad to get to the hotel, my head is pounding. A cool, dark room and some rest feels long overdue.

Lucy turns back to Dan, nudging him to get his attention. "What are you listening to?"

"Muse," he answers loudly, over the noise in his earphones, "live in Rome. Excellent band," he grins.

"Alright. No need to shout."

We walk straight through the first class arrivals lounge, which is just as well, the queue for the economy passengers winds back for ages. Once we're through customs, we head for the exit. The first thing my eyes land on as we walk through the doors, is a guy in a grey suit holding a board with my name on it. He looks straight at me.

"Miss Banks?" he asks, with a French accent and a smiling face. He strides toward us.

How the…? I nod, a little bemused. How did he know it was me? I look over at Dan and Lucy, but they're as surprised as I am. *Max!* How did I ever think he would just let me swan off to another country without somehow remaining under his protective wing?

"Mesdames et Monsieur, Je suis Renard. Welcome to France," he smiles. "Please, follow me." He reaches down and takes my case, then he walks us out to an enormous white stretch limo. It makes me smile. Max is so kind and generous, and always a little over the top. I miss him so much.

"I told you he wouldn't let you go," Lucy whispers as we climb into the plush, red velvet interior of the limo. A chilled bottle of Champagne and three glasses are set out in front of us. Lucy reaches forward and picks up the small white card lying against the bottle on the silver tray, then she hands it to me, with waggling eyebrows. The handwriting is instantly recognisable.

Bonnes Vacances,

Don't forget to wear sunscreen.

X;-)

He hasn't signed the card, but the smiley face that he seems to have adopted from me, makes me smile.

We sip our Champagne, and as we travel along in the glorious sunshine, Lucy and I gaze out of the windows. Dan suddenly sits forward and taps Renard on the shoulder.

"Erm, mate. I think you're going the wrong way, our hotel is back that way." He points over his shoulder.

Renard smiles into the rear-view mirror. "Monsieur, I have been instructed to take you to ze Grand Hyatt Hotel Martinez, in Cannes," he shrugs, still smiling.

We all stare at each other, then Lucy clinks Dan's glass. "Well, cheers to that, Mr. Foxx." She clinks mine too, but I feel uneasy. Butterflies invade my stomach and I put my glass down as my hands begin to shake. He's taking over, controlling everything, and as much as Lucy and Dan are delighted by it, I start to worry that Monica may find out and think that I'm trying to deceive her.

But how could she possibly know? Besides, it's not like he's here.

We pull into the entrance of the magnificent Hotel Martinez. Renard hands me his card and tells me to call him if we need his services during our stay. I'm happy to see Dan offering him a tip, but Renard graciously declines. He removes all our luggage from the boot and then a porter stacks them onto a trolley. Renard bids us all a very pleasant day, then he leaves us in the capable hands of the receptionist.

"Welcome to the Grand Hyatt. You'll be staying in the deluxe sea view suite on the sixth floor," she says, handing us our keys.

"What, no penthouse?" Dan giggles.

"No, Sir. I'm afraid that's already booked," she says, as if answering a legitimate question. I give Dan the stink-eye, and Lucy digs him in the ribs.

We're shown to our amazing suite, and after a brief tour of the bedrooms, bathroom, and our own lounge and bar area, we rush out to the huge balcony to take in the magnificent view.

"Friggin' hell!" Lucy grins. "This is unbelievable. I should call Max and thank him."

Oh, shit. "No!" I blurt. Dan and Lucy stare at me for a moment. That sounded rude and ungrateful, but that's not what I meant. I don't want Lucy contacting Max. Monica knew she was speaking to him before and if we antagonise her any more than we already have, I'm scared of what she might do. "Erm… I mean, I'll thank him," I smile, blushing.

Dan claps his hands together. "Right! Come on, you two. Let's get our swimmies on and go and check out the pool, it's boiling and I need a beer!" Dan marches off dragging their cases to one of the bedrooms and Lucy follows giggling with excitement.

I change into my red bikini and wrap a sarong around my hips, then I grab my new Stetson and flip flops. I pop my book and sunscreen into my bag and then we go in search of the pool.

The hotel is gorgeous, and the pool area is simply stunning. The bar is well stocked, and there's a steel band playing at the poolside. We wander over to a table with comfy chairs and a huge parasol. Within a few moments, a friendly waiter arrives to take our order. I forgot to take a painkiller before I left the room, so I decide to stay away from the alcohol for a while, until my headache from hell subsides. Instead, I order a coffee.

A few moments later the waiter returns with our drinks and places a small vase with a white rose in the centre of the table. I look around at the other tables, but none of them have any flowers. The waiter says nothing, then he leaves. My eyes slowly scan the area, surely Max wouldn't follow me out here? *Oh, God I hope not.*

"What's the matter?" Lucy asks, drawing my attention.

"Oh, nothing… It's lovely here isn't it?"

"It's amazing. The hotel we'd booked was nothing like this," she smirks. Lucy and Dan snuggle together, kissing like a couple of lovesick fools.

"Get a room you two," I giggle.

"Well, we couldn't have afforded the one we've got," Dan smirks. "It was really nice of Max to do this for us," he adds, reaching for his beer. "Especially now that you've effectively dumped the poor guy." Lucy gives him one of her glares, but he doesn't notice. "He must think a lot of you, Viv. Do you still not have any memories of him?"

I glance down at my hands. "No. None."

"Do you fancy a walk out to the beach?" Lucy asks as we finish our drinks.

"Actually, I've got a bit of a headache. I'm going to take some painkillers then I think I'll lie in the shade for a while, but you two go, I don't want you worrying about me, I'm quite happy to sit around the pool and read my book."

"Are you sure you're okay, you look a little pale?" Lucy asks, eyeing me with concern.

"Yeah, I'm just tired. Go and enjoy yourselves." I smile, shooing them away.

After they leave, I head back up to the room to take something for my throbbing head. I wander through to the bathroom to find my tablets and fill a glass with water. As I inspect my face in the bathroom mirror, I suddenly get a flashback to the night Monica attacked me. I remember staring into the bathroom mirror when I'd thought I'd heard a noise as I was drying my hair. *She must have been in the house by then.* I remember I couldn't find my phone, which I know I left on the bed. She must have crept into the bedroom and taken it. She was in the next room, and I was totally oblivious. *She* was the sound I'd heard. It creeps me out thinking about it.

Lucy's right, I do look pale and tired. It's only four days since I was lying in the hospital. Maybe this week will do me good. I feel like I need to recharge my batteries, but I need to use this time wisely. I need to formulate a plan of action. I don't want to live the rest of my life without Max, why should I? I love him. I need him. This separation is all wrong. Lucy was right about Monica too. It's not like she can live a normal life now. She's wanted for the murder of God knows how many people.

I don't know why it hadn't occurred to me sooner, but when Monica realises there's no way Max would ever take her back, she's going to flip! And then what? She'll probably kill the pair of us out of spite.

"Shit!" I've been so completely and utterly stupid. I should have reported Monica to the police straight away. *What the hell was I thinking?* I lean on the edge of the basin and stare at my frowning face. "You're a bloody idiot." I say, to my reflection. "You've got to get a hold of yourself and sort this fucking mess out."

I suddenly feel emboldened and strong. I've never been a quitter, a little cautious maybe, but I've never run from all the other problems in my life. If my poor excuse for a mother was good for anything, it was that she made me learn how to cope under pressure.

The afternoon sun is still strong so I grab my bag and head back to the poolside to find a nice shady spot to sit in. Making myself comfortable on one of the sun-loungers under a palm tree by the pool, I pop my sunglasses on so I can read my book without squinting.

The waiter arrives with a tall glass of iced water and asks me if I'd care for a beverage, but I decline. I still have a terrible headache so alcohol is off the menu until it goes.

As I get a few pages into my book, my phone rings. It's Dan's number.

"Hey, Viv, it's me. How are you feeling?" Lucy asks.

"Yeah, I'm fine, the headache's going and I'm just lazing by the pool reading my book. Where are you?"

"We're having a look around the shops at the moment, but Dan wants to go to the marina later on to have a look at the yachts. If you feel like it, we'll come back to the hotel and pick you up in a couple of hours."

"Yeah, okay. Sounds like fun."

"Max never could protect his women."

I wake with a start, batting my eyes to focus. I relax when I realise I'm not where I thought I was. *When will these dreams ever stop?* My book is still in my hand, I must have drifted off. I sit up and place it on the small table beside my lounger. My eyes instantly land on the white rose in the small glass vase. *That thing is following me around.*

I check my watch, then I quickly gather my things together. I'd slept for ages. I need to shake a leg and get changed to meet Lucy and Dan, they're probably back already.

When I reach our suite, Lucy and Dan are sitting on the balcony enjoying a glass of wine. "I'm sorry guy's, I fell asleep by the pool."

"Don't worry," Lucy smiles. "You needed to rest. We thought we'd go and look at the yachts and then maybe have dinner at the marina, there's usually a live band on somewhere, what do you think?"

"Sounds great. I'll go and change."

I take a quick shower and change into my short, strapless, yellow sundress and sandals. I don't bother with any makeup, and I pile my hair up in a messy up-do. Dan looks very Mediterranean in his cream jeans, black, short sleeve shirt, and black loafers. And Lucy looks gorgeous in her beige shorts and white halter neck top. I grab my camera and we wander out of the hotel and head off toward the marina.

"So, what did you buy?" I know how much Lucy loves to shop.

"Not much, some of the stores are quite expensive here, but we found a great little street full of tourist shops and I bought these." She shows me her new bangles. "And Dan bought me this." She points at the pretty, and very delicate, heart pendant necklace.

"Oh, that's lovely."

Dan is beaming with pride. He really loves her.

When we arrive at the marina, Dan walks ahead to inspect all the yachts. Some even larger ones are moored together against a larger concrete pier. It must be the tycoon section, you can almost smell the affluence. Dan is positively drooling. The elegant vessels bob gently in the calm waters, and even I'm impressed by some of them. I take a few photos of Dan pretending to board one. And some of him and Lucy walking hand in hand, they're so in love. A little pang of jealousy hits me and I start to think about Max, I miss him.

After about an hour of wandering around the marina, Lucy manages to drag Dan away and we find a nice little restaurant with outdoor seating to have dinner. The menu is varied, and I'm starving. I haven't eaten since last night and even then, I'd lost my appetite after Monica's warning on my bathroom mirror.

"So, what are your plans for tomorrow?" Lucy asks, finishing her dessert.

"I don't have any really. I'm happy to sit by the pool, or maybe I'll go down to the beach. But you two don't have to worry about me, just go and do whatever you want and we'll meet up for dinner."

"Maybe we should find Mike's cousin's bar and pop in for a drink," Lucy says, pouring another glass of wine.

Dan scrunches his face up. "No, I don't think so. I don't get on with his cousin Daryl."

Dan surprises me. He gets on with everyone. I was just going to ask him why they don't get on, when he interrupts me. "Are you sure you won't be lonely stuck on your own?" he asks with a caring frown.

"No, of course not. I'm going to veg out in the sun for a bit. God knows I could use a tan!" I giggle.

We stay at the restaurant all night, drinking and talking, mostly about the wedding. I hadn't asked Lucy why they were thinking about getting married in France, but it turns out that Dan's grandmother lives in Nice and this was where Lucy and Dan had spent their first holiday as a couple so it holds great significance for them. Plus the weather is amazing.

As the live entertainment begins, Dan drags Lucy up from her chair and pulls her onto the dance floor. I watch them for a moment, they're so happy, so in love. My heart twists. A little over a week ago I was about to tell Lucy that I was also going to be married, but then all hell broke loose and now I can't even acknowledge the man I love, let alone marry him. Tears prick my eyes so I turn away to stare out at the bustling crowd passing the restaurant on the promenade. *Oh. …Is that John?* I strain to see through the crowds of people meandering past. I'm sure I just saw him. I stand up to get a better view but there are just too many people and I can't see him anymore. It suddenly falls into place. I've cut off all communication with Max so he must have sent John to watch over me like he did the last time I ran away from him. I smile to myself. It's quite comforting to know that Max is still protecting me. I keep looking, but I don't see John anywhere now. *Maybe I was wrong?*

"Are you okay, you look worried?" Lucy asks, sitting down next to me, trying to see what I'm looking at. Her face is flushed and she's out of breath. I turn and stare at her with a humorous frown.

"What the hell have you two been up to?" Dan looks like he's going to pass out from heat exhaustion.

"Didn't you see us? We've been trying to do the jive, Dan was chucking me about all over the place," Lucy grins, fanning her face.

I stare at them both for a moment, then it suddenly dawns on me. "Don't tell me you two are planning to do a show dance for the wedding?" They both look very sheepish. "Oh, my God, you are, aren't you?"

They both burst out laughing. "Yeah! We've been having secret lessons but at the rate we're learning, we'll have to postpone the wedding for at least another five years," Dan smirks, still trying to catch his breath.

"Oh, no you don't," Lucy chides. "We're getting married even if we have to do the Okey-Cokey." We all burst out laughing. Knowing Lucy as I do, that's a very likely possibility.

As we wander back to the hotel, I keep looking around me for any sign of John, but then I convince myself that I must have been mistaken.

Lucy and Dan decide to go and hit the bar for a night-cap, and I head upstairs to our room. It's been a long, tiring day and I'm ready for my bed.

YOU MEAN NOTHING TO ME

I wake fairly late to another beautiful day. The sunshine streams into my room as a gentle sea breeze billows the net curtains at the windows. I've had such a pleasant week tanning myself on the beach, wandering around the local markets, and taking photos of all the stunning sights that the South of France has to offer.

As this is our last day before we fly home, Lucy and Dan are cramming in as much as they can. They've already visited many places of interest, and several venues for their wedding. They also took me along to meet Dan's grandmother, who was very charming and delighted to see us.

Today they've booked a boat trip. They wanted me to join them, but I didn't want to be a gooseberry on their last day so I declined. Besides, I want to finish my book before we go home.

I've still been suffering from flashbacks and nightmares about the attack, but as the week went on, I'd begun to realise that the more I drank, the less I would dream, so Lucy, Dan and I have hit the bar every evening in true party style. My headaches are now only hangovers. The bruising has almost completely gone, and the scar has healed very well, it's hardly noticeable now.

Since we've been out here, Monica has gone silent. I haven't received any more threats from her, which has been a blessing, but she's been unnervingly absent. I've bought an English newspaper every day in the hope that I may read that she's been found and arrested. Sadly, those headlines have not materialised but I'm ever hopeful.

I haven't seen John again, even though I've looked. It was probably just my fertile imagination playing tricks on me, but I've had a weird sense that someone was watching me. My initial instinct was that it could be Monica, but then again, I do have a tendency to over think everything so it could just be my paranoia.

I've had no contact at all from Max. It's what I'd asked for, but it hurts. Although, every day the hotel have presented me with a white rose, either at our table at dinner, or at the bar. No one has mentioned it, but I did notice we were the only ones to receive such a thing.

As I lie in my bed staring up at the ceiling, I wonder if Max has finally given up on me and decided to move on. I couldn't blame him. But the thought puts an ache in my heart and butterflies in my stomach. I've thought about Max every waking moment of every single day, I miss him so much. With a heavy heart I drag myself out of bed and take a shower.

As Lucy and Dan are on their boat trip today, I decide to go down to the pool and finish my book. I remove my sarong and slip my sandals off, then I settle into one of the sun-loungers. *Ahh, this is the life.*

As I finish the last line of my book, I stare down at the page and almost gasp out loud. It was a very satisfying read, but the cliffhanger ending has left me with my mouth open.

As I slip my book into my bag, my phone rings. It's Lucy's number.

"Hey, Luce, how's it going? Have you thrown up over the side yet?" I giggle.

"What do you think you're doing?" The harsh, bitter tone in Monica's voice chills me to the bone. The blood drains from my head and I sit up in a panic.

"What? What do you mean? Wh…Where's Lucy?" My

heart lurches in my chest as a wave of fear puts a tremble in my voice. I quickly scan the area around me.

"Don't play fucking innocent with me, you bitch."

"I'm not! I promise… Where's Lucy? What do you want?"

"You know what I want," she hisses.

"And I've done everything you've asked me to, I—"

"Oh, really? Then why has he followed you to France?"

"What?" My wide eyes search around me again. My heart pounds in my chest and I feel sick. "No! I… I didn't know? I didn't ask him to come here, I swear." I'm speaking so fast and I can't catch my breath. A cold sweat creeps across the back of my neck like a frost.

"End it! Now! Or so help me I'll—"

"I will! I promise. Please don't hurt Lucy, please! I promise I'll… Monica?… Monica." The line goes dead. I stare down at my phone in shock as Lucy's smiling face fades to black on the screen. *She's got Lucy… Fuck! It's all my fault.* My eyes well up with panicked tears and I quickly stand up and wrap my sarong around me with fumbling fingers. I grab my stuff and shove it into my bag as quickly as I can. *What do I do?… What do I do?*

I'm shaking with adrenaline, so much that I can't get my sandals on so I pick them up and run barefoot around the pool into the hotel. As I run through the lobby, I look all around me. If Max is here, I need to find him and tell him to leave me alone. He's going to ruin everything. *Oh, Lucy I'm so sorry... What have I done?*

I run straight up to the reception desk and push in front of the two elderly people already talking to the girl behind the desk. I'm so out of breath, I can hardly get the words out. "I need you to tell me if Mr. Maxwell Foxx has checked in?" I ask in a panic.

The girl smiles, but it doesn't hide her disapproval. "I'm sorry Madam, if you could wait until I have finished serving these people."

I blow out an exasperated sigh and slam my hand down

onto the counter. "Look! This is an emergency. Please, just tell me!" I yell. I look over at the couple who are tutting and staring at me in disgust. "I'm sorry," I mumble, fidgeting.

The girl throws me an irritated glare, apologises to the couple, and then checks her computer screen. "No, he hasn't," she says, curtly.

Oh! I turn away from the desk completely confused. Why would Monica think he was here? And how would she even know? And what has she done with Lucy? *What the fuck is going on?*

I quickly run to the lift and make my way back to our room. My mind is racing with a million questions. How the hell did Monica get close to Lucy in the first place? And what about Dan? Where the fuck is he? I've got no choice, I'm going to have to call the police and report them as missing. God knows what Monica's done to them. An icy shudder ripples up my spine, remembering her threat of using acid. *She wouldn't…would she?* I'll never forgive myself if anything happens to her or Dan.

I enter the room in a panic and run to my bedroom to throw on my jeans, a t-shirt, and my converse. As I run back out to the living room, the main door suddenly flies open and Lucy and Dan barge into the room pulling each other's clothes off, giggling and kissing. Lucy stops abruptly when she sees me standing in the living room open mouthed just staring at them in shock. "Oh!… Shit… Sorry," Lucy blurts, blushing and pulling her top back into place. "We thought you were still down at the pool."

Dan is leaning back against the wall trying to cover his erection with his hands. His shirt is open, as well as his fly, and his cheeks are bright red with embarrassment. "We were just…" He blushes and trails off. They both look at me like naughty children, then they burst into laughter.

Oh, for fuck's sake, Lucy's here! They're alright. What the fuck's going on? "Where's your phone?" I ask, a little too harshly.

"I didn't bring it," Lucy shrugs. "We were in such a rush to leave, I left it on charge in your kitchen by mistake," she says, frowning.

Oh… Good.

"Why? What's the matter?"

I feel relieved that Monica isn't here. And over the moon that Lucy hasn't been harmed, but somehow Monica's managed to break into my flat, again. *How the hell is she getting in?*

"Viv?" Lucy repeats.

"Nothing… I… I just wondered where you were, that's all." I say it as nonchalantly as possible, trying not to sound worried, but they're both looking at me like I've got two heads or something.

"Is there a problem?" Dan asks. I look down and fidget with my bag. I can't say anything about Monica with Dan listening.

"No. No, not at all. I just, well I just wondered where we were going to eat tonight?" I blush at my not very convincing answer. Thankfully they doesn't seem to notice, or pretend not to anyway. Suddenly I feel like a spare part. They've obviously come back to the room for sex, and I'm standing here discussing our plans for dinner.

I glance down at my watch. "Erm, I'm going to walk around the shops for a bit, how about we meet in the bar at say… five?" They both shrug and nod as I awkwardly squeeze past them and head out the door.

"Are you sure you're okay?" Lucy asks.

I turn and smile. "Fine… As you were," I grin, then I turn and walk down the corridor muttering under my breath. I hear the door close and the pair of them giggling.

As the lift travels down to the lobby, I try to make sense of it all in my head. I was so frightened when I thought Monica had kidnapped Lucy. I had visions of her being horribly disfigured and left for dead. The thought makes me shudder. I haven't told Lucy about Monica's threats. Should I? But if Dan finds out he'll go straight to the police. And rightly so. That's what I should have done at the very beginning. *I don't know what I'm doing.*

As I exit the lift and walk through the lobby, my eyes dart everywhere. Monica said Max has followed me out here, but if so, where is he?

I walk out of the hotel and wander along the seafront for a while, then I turn into one of the side roads to find the shops I'd been to before. I'm not really interested in buying anything, I just need to clear my head and figure out what I'm going to do.

After a good hour of browsing the various trinket stores and clothes shops, I come across a nice little café and take a seat out on the pavement. A handsome waiter comes up to me with a big smile on his face.

"Pretty lady, why you all alone?" he asks, chatting me up.

Good question. I just order my coffee, smile back at him, then I look away, hoping he'll take the hint and leave. I'm not in the mood for randy French waiters at the moment. I shouldn't be on my own anyway, I should be with Max. I've let this whole sorry mess get way out of control and now I don't know what to do to put it right. I can't protect Max, Lucy, Dan, and everyone else I care about, and I'm sure the police can't either. And why should they? I've lied to them. I've given Monica a massive head start, and all I actually know for certain is that she's crazy enough to do everything she's threatened to do. If she's so far gone that she's willing to risk everything for a man she'll never have, I can't take any chances.

Suddenly, I can't wait to go home. I can't do anything out here. I need to talk to Vinnie, he'll know what to do.

I leave some cash on the table and make my way back to the hotel. It's after five, and as I enter the lobby and walk over to the bar, I hear Lucy's raucous laughter before I see her. As soon as I round the corner, I stumble to a halt as my eyes land on Max. The sight of him stirs the butterflies in my belly and evokes a painful longing in my heart. Casually dressed in black jeans and an open neck black shirt, he looks absolutely gorgeous. I rake my eyes over his flawless face. He's a welcome sight, it's been too long since I've laid eyes on him.

Sitting at the bar beside Lucy, he laughs along with her until his eyes lift from her face and land on mine. His expression changes instantly. He looks nervous, but he never takes his eyes from mine as he rises to his feet. My heart pounds in my chest, and in a split second, I choose my course. Whether it's the right one or not, I haven't got time to analyse it. All I know is that I need to protect him. As tears prick my eyes, I turn and walk in the opposite direction.

"Vivienne! Please! …Wait!" I feel Max closing the distance behind me, but I keep walking. "Vivienne!"

His hand clasps around my arm, halting me in my tracks. He moves in front of me, still holding my arm and searching my face with his bemused, beautiful eyes. His familiar, intoxicating scent invades my nose, and it takes all my strength not to throw myself into his arms. I look past him, I can't look at his face anymore. My steely resolve has no defence when he looks at me that way, and I fear he'll see straight through me, he reads me too well.

"Please, Vivienne. Why won't you talk to me? I've tried to stay away from you but I'm going crazy here! Why can't we just talk?"

All of my hatred for Monica, all the pent up frustrations and anxiety that she's caused me suddenly give me the strength I need to deliver my lines. I can almost feel myself switching off inside. He's the most precious thing in my life. I will protect him. *Please, Max. …Please forgive me.* I steel myself and look him straight in the eyes.

"Why can't you get it through your thick skull!" I yell, glaring up at him. "I don't remember you. I don't love you. And I don't want to see you, or talk to you, ever again. You mean nothing to me. Nothing!" I can hear myself yelling the words in his face, but I'm on some kind of crazy, emotional auto-pilot. I can see the shock and pain in his eyes and yet, all I can feel is…nothing. I'm totally numb. Empty. Lost.

I hate myself for causing the look on his face, but I'd hate myself even more if anything happened to him because of me. My yelling has made everyone in the lobby stand still, watching us. The whole place falls silent.

I can't stop the tears, God knows I've tried, so I let them flow. I watch his sad eyes continue to search my face for a shred of hope. I make sure he doesn't find any, and then I feel his fingers slowly releasing my arm. I say nothing more. I don't need to. I've done my worst. I just walk away from him.

I walk to the lift on shaky legs, not daring to look back. I hear Lucy calling out my name but like a zombie, I just keep walking. As I enter the lift, I let the doors close behind me before I collapse to the floor in floods of tears and regret. I don't know who I've hurt the most, him or me.

I hear the lift doors opening. "Oh!…Are you okay?" I look up with tear blurred eyes and I see a young couple staring down at me. The man kindly helps me up to my feet and hands me my bag. "Are you alright?" In a daze I just walk between them out of the lift, I don't even say thanks.

I'm on the roof terrace. The bar stands right in front of me, the perfect place to drown my sorrows. I sit at the bar and order two double vodkas. I knock the first one straight back and wince at the way it burns in my throat, then I do the same with the second, and then I order a bottle of Grey Goose to save faffing about. I'm in this for the long haul.

Each drink does little to assuage the way I feel inside, but it helps to reinforce my Teflon exterior. I'm hurting inside like never before, but I think at this point, even if I was set on fire, I wouldn't feel a thing. Just empty. Dead.

"Oh, shit. Not again, Viv." I feel someone pulling the empty bottle of Vodka out of my hand. "What do you think you're doing? We've been looking for you everywhere."

I slowly drag my focus up to the nagging voice beside me. "Leave me alone," I slur angrily.

"Why? So you can drink yourself into oblivion and smash your face against the urinals?" Lucy huffs. "Been there, done that." I burst out laughing. I don't know why, but I'm so pissed, that her stern, angry face just makes me laugh. "Viv, you're shit-faced."

"Yes. I am," I giggle. "And thank you for noticing." I reach out for the bottle of Vodka but Lucy pulls it away from me.

"It's empty… Don't you think you've had enough?" she sighs wearily.

"Nope," I giggle. "Come on Loosh, less-hava-nother-drink." I try to whistle at the bartender but my lips won't pucker properly so I wave at him instead. "Nother vottle o' bodka an-another glass for Mrs. Grumpy-drawers please, Mishter Barman," I slur, still giggling at Lucy's scowling face.

"Viv. You've had enough," she chides, folding her arms across her chest. I swing around to face her, tears blurring my eyes. Suddenly all the humour has left me now, I just feel so utterly sad and depressed.

"Lu, if I don't drink, I think." My teary eyes wander back to my glass. "Hey!" I giggle at myself. "That rhymes."

Lucy sits beside me, her teary eyes trailing all over my face. "Okay, one more drink and then you're going to bed, lady." She nods at the waiter, who pours us both a drink. I knock mine straight back, while Lucy sips at hers. Staring into the bottom of my empty glass I feel Lucy squeezing my arm. "Viv… He's gone… He's gone back home," she says, softly. Her words hurt. I close my eyes and take in a deep breath, then I let out a long painful sigh. All I can see are his sad, blue eyes pleading with me to stop hurting him. "If it was your intention to destroy the man, you did a great job," Lucy sighs. Her words cut me like a knife. I had no choice. It's not just him I have to protect now.

"You don't know," I slur angrily.

"Don't know what?"

"You just… don't know."

I can't see straight, and suddenly I feel really sick.

"Oh, no you don't." Lucy grabs me around the shoulders and pulls me from the bar stool. I lurch along beside her leaning all my weight against her, my legs just won't work. We barge through a doorway and she pushes me into the ladies toilets. I stagger into the cubicle, my knees buckle, and I slump down retching and gagging as I heave a bottle of Grey Goose into the toilet.

"You could see that coming a mile off," Lucy says, sarcastically, as she holds my hair back and rubs my shoulders.

When there's nothing left to evacuate, I sit on the floor and rest my back against the wall. Lucy wipes my face with a damp tissue and then takes my phone from my bag and calls Dan.

"Hi, babe, I found her… No, upstairs at the bar on the roof terrace… Yeah, she's fucked! I'm going to need your help to get her back to the room… Okay, see you in a minute."

"Come on. It's time to get up."

I struggle to peel my eyes open and gradually focus on the smiling, hazel eyes staring down at me. As I lift my face off the pillow, my head pounds like a drum, I have an awful taste in my mouth, and I could drink a gallon of water.

"How's the piss-head?" Dan calls out as he pokes his grinning face around the door.

"Not so good," Lucy giggles. "But she did a fantastic impression of her mother last night," she says, cocking an eyebrow.

Oh, no. What have I done now? "What did I break this time?" I croak, checking my teeth with my tongue. I know I'm a clumsy drunk, and the last time I got shit-faced, I ended up in the hospital.

"Only Max's heart," Dan chips in. I wince as the memories come flooding back. Lucy turns to glare at him as he sheepishly ducks back out of the room. The harsh memory of Max's face as I told him he meant nothing to me, and then walking away from him, floods my brain and churns my stomach. Even a bottle of Grey Goose hasn't been able to erase that memory.

Lucy checks that Dan isn't in earshot, then she walks back to my bed and sits on the edge. "Viv, when we get home, you and I need to talk," she says, nervously. "I need to know everything." She looks worried, and suddenly I'm wide awake.

What did I tell her last night? I wrack my brain, but all I can remember is Max's sad eyes and me yelling at him in the lobby. I know I got drunk after that, but for the life of me, I can't remember what I said. I nod sheepishly. I don't know what to say.

She offers me a weak smile then rises from the bed. "I've packed your case, you just need to shower. If you hurry up, we can grab a coffee before Renard picks us up," she says, walking out of the room.

After a quick, refreshing shower, I get dressed and pack

the last few items into my case. Lucy and Dan are waiting for me on the balcony. I have to slip my shades on to block out the intense sunlight, even my eyes have a headache.

We take all our cases down to the lobby and walk over to the reception desk to check-out. The gentleman informs us that Mr. Foxx has settled our bill and there's nothing to pay. I feel awful. He's been so generous and kind, and all I've done is broken his heart and trampled all over his feelings. If only I could explain it to him? I just hope that someday soon I can explain it all, and that he'll understand.

We head to the poolside to grab a coffee. Our usual waiter brings our drinks, but this time I notice there's no white rose. This is the first day since I've been here that I haven't seen a white rose. My heart twists and the weight of his loss crushes me.

We meet Renard at the front entrance and he drives us back to the airport. I can't wait to get home, although, I'm nervous of finding out what condition my flat may be in, knowing Monica's been in there at least once since we left.

Dan is the only one making any conversation as we head back to the airport. Lucy is unusually quiet, and that just worries me even more. I must have said something to her last night when I was drunk. *Shit! I hope I didn't tell her what Monica had threatened to do to her?* That would freak anyone out!

WHAT DON'T I KNOW?

Once we've collected our baggage and been fortunate enough to whizz through passport control and customs, we make our way to the exit. John is standing at the arrivals area and smiles at me as we approach. I'm surprised to see him, I'd have thought after my behaviour toward him last night, that Max would have cancelled all his generous acts of kindness. But no, Max isn't like that. He's quite possibly the nicest person I've ever known. It just makes everything so much harder.

"Oh, look!" Lucy says, looking at me in a weird, over the top way. "It's John, *Max's* bodyguard." She does it again. I give her a questioning frown until I suddenly realise, I'm not supposed to remember who he is. Dan looks at us confused for a moment, then he walks up to John and shakes his hand. I keep my eyes down and quietly thank Lucy for averting a complete cock-up on my part.

John walks us to the car. He doesn't say much, other than to ask us if we've had a pleasant holiday, then he drives us home with the glass partition closed. I notice him looking at me a few times in the rear-view mirror, like he's checking me out, but every time our eyes meet, I look away.

As we pull up to our apartment building, I see the white Volvo with my number plate, VF1 parked up at the kerb. I remember the day Max had given it to me. I'd only just bought my bike but he was adamant that I shouldn't ride it. He thought it was too dangerous so he'd bought me the car and hidden my bike keys. I was a bit miffed at the time, but it was just another kind and caring gesture on his part. *I need to send that back.*

As we get out of the car, I tentatively glance around wondering if Monica is watching us. If she's seen the car and now John bringing us home, she'll think I'm still with Max so I try to hurry Lucy and Dan up so he can leave.

I reach down for my case but John beats me to it. I feel uncomfortable at the way he's looking at me, and I start to wonder if he saw my initial reaction to him at the airport as recognition.

"You saw me at the marina," he says, quietly. "You recognised me didn't you?" he adds, searching my eyes.

Shit. I blush. I wish I could control that response, but I can't. "What?" I stand there blinking up at him. "I'm sorry, but I don't know what you're talking about." I pull my case out of his hand and smile. "Thanks for the lift home." Then I briskly walk away from him. *Shit! Shit! Shit!*

As I anxiously walk toward my building, I hear John get into his car and drive away, then I let out the breath I was holding. I can only hope he won't jump the gun and say anything to Max.

I meet Lucy and Dan on the stairs and hug them before they go into their flat.

"Thanks, guys, I've had a great week."

"Do you want any help with your case?" Dan asks, reaching forward for it.

"No!… I mean, I'll be fine," I smile. I don't know what to expect when I get home. If Monica's trashed my place, I don't want Dan to see it, not yet. I need to figure out what I'm going to do first.

My stomach churns as I put my key in the door, but I'm pleasantly surprised to see everything just as I left it. I dump my bags in the bedroom, check my bathroom, then I walk through to the kitchen. Everything looks normal.

Even Lucy's phone is still sitting on the side attached to the charger.

Once the laptop is up and running, I Google locksmith's in the area and I call one out. They'll be here in an hour so I make a quick cup of coffee, make the call I've been dreading, then I go and unpack my case.

Lucy arrives shortly after the locksmith. As he's busy changing the lock on the front door, she retrieves her phone from the kitchen and nods at me to follow her through to my bedroom so we can talk in private.

She sits on my bed checking her phone and then she waits for me to join her. Her face is set with a serious frown and I feel a lecture coming on.

"Viv, I understand why you blocked Max's number from my phone. I also understand why you would want to leave him after the things Monica threatened you with, but I think it's about time that you told me everything," she says, with a deadpan expression. My belly churns. I'm frightened to tell her what Monica threatened to do to her.

"I told you what happened that night," I answer sheepishly, looking down at my hands.

Lucy sighs in exasperation. "Viv, don't treat me like a fool. When you were steaming drunk last night, you said to me, 'You don't know,' you said it more than once and then later on, when I put you to bed, you were mumbling, 'leave her alone! Don't hurt her.'

Oh, shit.

"So, tell me… What don't I know?" she asks angrily. "Because what I *do* know is that you're in love with a guy that you're willing to just walk away from, and, incidentally, break his heart, all because his psychotic ex-girlfriend, Miss Crazy-pants, has told you to leave him." I can see she's really losing her patience with me, but I don't know what to say. I don't know how to tell her. She glares at me shaking her head, annoyed at my reluctance.

"Viv, I don't get it. You're letting someone who's not only tried to kill you, but who is also wanted for the murder of at least three other people we know of, tell you what to do. I just don't get it! In my book, that's enough to go to the police. But you won't do that one, sane, simple, sensible thing! So, tell me, Vivienne. What don't I know?"

My hesitation fuels her frustration. "Viv! For fuck's sake!" She narrows her eyes on me as I hesitantly reach for my bag and find my phone. I reluctantly show Lucy the texts I'd received from Monica threatening to harm her with acid, and then I tell her everything I'd been keeping from her.

She looks at me with incredulity, then the fear sets into her eyes. She quickly checks her calls log. "Shit! She really did call you from my phone yesterday. But how did she know Max had gone to France?... Come to think of it…how did she know *we* had gone to France?"

I have no idea. But that question triggers my brain. Since I'd received a sharp blow to the head, my usually overactive, suspicious brain cogs have been decidedly sluggish. *How could she have known?* Her ability to know our movements, and the fact that she's been able to get into my flat on more than one occasion, makes me wonder if Monica has help. But who?

Lucy's eyes are wide and scared. "I knew something was wrong with you yesterday. That's why you're changing the locks, isn't it?"

I nod again then I take her hand in mine. "Luce, I won't let anything happen to you. I promise. I know I've fucked this up, but she won't do anything if I do exactly what she wants."

Lucy wrenches her hand out of mine, she stands quickly and then paces the floor.

"Can you hear yourself?" she says, angrily. "Do you really think she's going to leave you alone? Or me, for that matter!" She stops pacing to hit me with the death stare then she continues pacing again with her arms folded across her chest. "Even if you leave Max for good, do you really think she'll just walk off into the sunset and send you a nice little thank-you card!... *You're* the reason he left her." She stops pacing and stares at me shaking her head. "It's not like he's ever going to take her back. I'm sorry, Viv, but I think crazy-lady's going to wake up and smell the coffee pretty soon and then we're all going to suffer."

A soft voice draws our attention. Lucy and I look up at the locksmith hovering at my bedroom doorway. "Erm, I've finished," he shrugs.

I quickly grab my purse and pay him. Once he leaves, I turn back to Lucy handing her the spare set of keys. She snatches them out of my hand and walks over to the bed collapsing down on the edge with a long, exasperated sigh.

"Luce, the first thing I did when we got back was to call the locksmith," I say, quietly, taking a seat next to her. "The second call I made was to Vinnie."

Lucy's eyebrows fly up to her hairline. "Good! Finally! You're talking sense. When's he coming?"

I take a deep breath. "He was on his way to New York with Max," I sigh. "I couldn't say anything with Max in earshot so I made out that I wanted to return the Volvo, he said he would come and collect it when they return in a few days. I'll talk to him then."

Lucy's frown reappears as she searches my face. "When?... When are they back?" She asks impatiently.

"I didn't ask," I shrug. "But he'll call me."

She huffs out a long, angry sigh, folding her arms tightly across her chest. "Then we'll just have to keep looking over our shoulders until they get back, won't we?" Her voice carries a certain amount of contempt. I feel terrible. Lucy's scared, and rightly so. But with Max out of the country, at least Monica can see that we're not together anymore.

Lucy's expression softens as she reaches over and squeezes my hand. "Viv. I don't want to see anything happen to Max any more than you do, but until that woman's found, we're all in danger." Her eyes glisten, and she pulls me in for a hug. I squeeze her tightly. She's my best friend, and she's right, I've put everyone I care about in danger.

"As soon as Vinnie gets back, I'll sort this mess out, Luce. I promise. He'll know what to do."

She pulls away and gives me a sad smile. "You can stay with us if you like," she says, squeezing my hands.

"No, I'll be fine." I give her a reassuring smile, even though inside I'm petrified.

I feel much better now the locks have been changed, and after I've sorted out my laundry, I decide to go and get some shopping to re-stock the fridge.

When I return, I make some lunch and call Clive. I've decided to go back to work on Monday. I can't sit around here worrying about Monica's next move anymore, it's driving me crazy. And I need something to distract me from the aching loss I feel every time I think about Max.

When I'd made the call to Vinnie this morning, I was hoping I could tell him everything and ask for his help. But he took ages to answer and then when he spoke, his voice was very soft and quiet, almost a whisper. I realised Max must have been close by so I used the pretence of returning the Volvo as an excuse to call.

Vinnie seemed saddened by my request and he asked me if I'd recovered any of my missing memories. Of course, I had to lie. I couldn't take the chance that Max would overhear the conversation. After a short pause, it sounded like Vinnie was on the move, he then told me that Max had returned from France earlier than expected in a terrible depression, but he had refused to talk about it.

I'll never forget the look on Max's face when I'd told him he meant nothing to me. It scared me knowing how much he'd been affected. He doesn't handle emotional loss very well, if at all.

Vinnie tentatively asked me what had happened in France, so I told him. It choked me up to repeat it and I could hear the sadness in Vinnie's voice, but I had to stick fast with my story. By this point, my emotions were frayed. Unable to continue the pretence any longer I quickly asked Vinnie to contact me when they return from New York to arrange the collection of the car, and then I ended the call.

YOU SAID YOU'D WAIT

By Sunday evening the weekend has dragged by without much to talk about. Thankfully, Monica hasn't made any contact since we left France. And I assume as Vinnie hasn't called yet, that he and Max are still in New York.

Lucy and Dan popped in to see me earlier, but they had to dash off to a family commitment so I've spent most of the time on my own. I'm actually glad of the solitude. I feel so depressed.

Meeting Max has been a roller coaster of emotions from the very beginning. We had a shaky start to say the least. And our short-lived relationship now lies in tatters. Whatever the outcome, I'll always be glad to have known him, to have been loved by him. But it saddens me to know that I'll never find that kind of love again.

Clive calls, startling me out of my thoughts. He's spoken to Frank, who said that there's nothing for me to do until Wednesday. I offered to go in and just make the tea, but he laughed and told me to make the most of my time off. We're coming up to the busy season of balls, galas, and parties so there will be plenty of work coming up.

My assignment for Wednesday is a charity ball in London. Apparently, it's a black tie evening event which Frank wants me to cover, so I don't need to go into the office until four o'clock for my briefing. He's arranged a car to take me there and bring me home, and as it's a late night, I don't have to go in until eleven the next morning.

What will I do with myself until Wednesday? As usual, there's bugger all on the telly so I ramp up the volume on my iPod and set it to shuffle, then I make a start cleaning out all the crap I've collected in my drawers and cupboards.

By midnight, I'm pooped. I've got a large pile of old clothes, books, and knick-knacks to take down to the charity shop so that will keep me busy tomorrow. I drag my exhausted body into the bathroom and take a quick shower, then I go to bed and hope I don't dream.

The room is dark. Glancing at the bedside clock, I see that it's only 04:06am. I'm wide awake. I lie there staring at the clock until it changes to 04:07am. With a deep sigh, I roll onto my back and stare at the ceiling. A creaking noise at the door draws my attention making me jump. Lifting my head off the pillow, I look over at the door, but I can't see anything. My eyes strain to see in the darkness as my heart pounds in my chest and rings in my ears.

"You've put us all in danger." Lucy's voice at my right hand side startles me and has my head whipping around. She's lying beside me on the bed, her head on the pillow next to mine, the flesh on her face, melting and smoking from the acid. Her milky eyes stare up at me in anguish and pain.

Sitting bolt upright in bed, I gasp as my arms and legs flail around wildly. *Oh, fuck!* Of all the dreams I've been having lately, that one is by far the worst. Since we came home from France, I've had the same dream for the last four nights. It's exhausting. I've found it hard to sleep, and when I finally do drop off, I only sleep for a few hours before I wake up drenched in sweat and screaming from the terrors that feel so real. *This has got to stop!* I try to catch my breath as I reach up to turn my bedside light on. I can't sleep now, and I don't want to if I'm going to see things like that in my dreams. I leave the light on and rest my head back down to the pillow, staring up at the ceiling.

A sharp, shrill beeping noise wakes me up. I feel like shit. I fling my arm out and hit the snooze on the alarm clock then I roll over to look at it. 07:00am.

The vivid dream that woke me earlier of Lucy's disfigured face, is still at the forefront of my mind. It makes me shiver. *Christ. When will these nightmares ever end?*

I throw the covers back and haul myself out of bed. I take a quick look at my scar, which is throbbing but looks okay, tie my hair up, and throw my running gear on. I need to clear my head, and a run usually works.

For the first time ever, I remembered to bring a bottle of water with me. I get half way around the park and I have to stop for a drink. I haven't run since the attack, and I'm ridiculously unfit. While I lean against a tree and guzzle most of the water, I realise I'm never going to be able to run the rest of the way so I cut across the middle of the park and walk back.

My legs are trembling from exhaustion as I climb the stairs to my flat, and although the sofa looks enticing, I head straight to the bathroom to take a shower.

When I'm dressed, I call Lucy to check that she can still fit me in today. I'm working at the swanky Marchand Du Volpino Hotel tonight and Frank told me to dress appropriately. It's a black tie event and I will be mingling with the guests.

Lucy's very kindly let me borrow her long, red, halter neck dress, and after she and Maggie have glammed me up, I expect to be looking like a million dollars. Lucy wants me to come down to the salon at two-thirty, so after I've been to the doctors for my check up, I'll still have time to run the Hoover round and clean my camera equipment before I head off to the salon.

Taking a taxi, I arrive at the office just before four. Lucy and Maggie have done a wonderful job of making me look fabulous and as I walk in, Sandra our receptionist, greets me with enthusiasm and runs around her desk to give me a big welcome back hug.

"Vivienne, you look great," she gushes. "How do you feel?" Her genuine concern is very touching.

"Yeah, I'm good." We have a quick catch up, then I make my way up to my floor. As I walk to my desk with my suit bag over my shoulder, everyone turns to look at me. I hang my dress up so it doesn't crease, dump my bag and jacket on my desk, and then I go to Frank's office for my briefing on tonight's assignment.

"Yeah!" Frank barks, as I tap lightly on his door. "Oh! Vivienne, come in," he smiles, as I poke my head around the door. "Wow! You scrub up well," he adds, making me blush.

"Thanks. I've brought an evening gown," I smirk, just in case he thinks I'm going to go in my jeans.

"You look great, but how are you feeling? Are you sure you're ready to get back to work?" Concern softens his voice. I'm not sure whether he's referring to my physical, or mental health considering I'm supposed to have lost my memory, so I slap a big smile across my face and engage my chirpiest voice before I answer.

"Completely. I've had the all clear from my doctor today, and I'm raring to go."

"Good!" he smiles. "Well then, your contact tonight is Mrs. Savchenko. She asked for you personally so I'm glad you're back otherwise we'd have lost it."

Really?

"It's a glitzy fundraiser, you know, the usual," he shrugs.

"Is Ed coming with me?"

"Er, no," he says, shuffling the papers on his desk. "He's still at a fashion show at the Hexagon, but you can handle it, right?"

"Yes… Of course I can."

"You'll have a car to take you there and take you home, and the client has very kindly given you a seat at dinner."

That's unusual. "Will you need the memory cards back tonight?" I ask, checking I have some spares with me.

"No, tomorrow will be fine. Now, the room is going to be full of celebrities and I don't need to tell you that I want photographs of everyone. We're the only magazine invited so do what you do best," he grins.

"So there are no other photographers at all?" I ask, a little surprised. Usually the big fundraisers like to have as much commercial coverage as possible.

"No, just us," he shrugs, pushing his glasses up to rest on the top of his head.

I wish Ed was coming.

"So, here's your list of who is attending, and as you can see the guest list is pure gold." Frank loves the big celebrity events. His magazine sales go through the roof when it's crammed with hot celebrity photos. I quickly scan the list, Max's name isn't on it which is a relief. "Ed's left you these," he says, handing me some extra memory cards. "And your transport will be here at five-thirty," he adds, smiling up at me.

"Thanks, Frank. I really appreciate you keeping my job open for me. I know I've been off quite a bit lately."

"I'm glad to have you back," he smiles, it's genuine too. His smile soon fades, and his expression changes to that of a concerned parent. "Ah, from what Clive's told me, it was pretty awful what happened to you… Did anything come back to you yet? Any memories?" he asks hesitantly.

I look down and fidget. "No. Not yet."

Frank clears his throat then he smirks. "Well, go get 'em, kid. I expect nothing but the best from my top photographer."

I walk back to my desk and check my watch, I've still got another forty-five minutes until I have to leave so I walk over to the coffee machine and get myself a latte. Clive comes bounding over clapping his hands and squealing like a small child. "Sweetie! Oh, my God. You look fabulous darling." Clive's quintessential gay man's greeting has me smiling at him. We hug, almost spilling my coffee, then he holds me at arm's length by the shoulders.

"Vivienne, you really do look amazing," he gushes.

"Wait till you see the dress," I grin, waggling my eyebrows.

He walks me back to my desk and sits on the edge, beaming down at me. "I can't believe you came back to work so early, but I have to say, you look very well," he grins, eyeing me up and down.

I tap my head. "No sense, no feeling."

"So, how was France?" he asks, grinning like an idiot.

"It was nice," I shrug. It was nice, but unfortunately, every time I think about it I remember Max's face when I told him he meant nothing to me. My stomach churns. He's not contacted me at all since I told him I never wanted to see or hear from him again. He's given me exactly what I asked for. I hate it.

"Sweetie? Are you okay?" Clive asks.

Oh, crap. I relax my frown. "Er, yeah."

Clive's concerned eyes linger on mine. "Vivienne, do you still not remember anything before the accident?"

Accident? Attempted murder you mean. As much as I love him, Clive is the last person I'd confide with at the moment. He's a gossip magnet and he can't keep his lip-glossed mouth shut. "Nope. Nothing."

I steer the conversation away from me, and I ask him about what's been going on in my absence. Clive delights in being able to tell me all the office gossip, starting each snippet of information with the words, 'I shouldn't say anything, but,' which just proves my case. Everyone seems happy to confide in Clive, but I don't think he's ever managed to keep a secret in all the years I've known him.

My eyebrows shoot up when he tells me that Sandra is dating a woman. Apparently, it's another secret that Clive was supposed to keep so I've been sworn to secrecy. I never knew she was a lesbian, not that it makes any difference to me, but we've never spoken about her personal life in that way before. She's never been much of a talker. She always seemed so shy and she hardly ever came out for a drink with us, and even on the rare occasions that she did, she never brought a partner with her.

When I first started dating Max she reacted as every other woman does when she saw his picture. Either he has that effect on every female no matter what their persuasion, or she was trying to cover up the fact that she was gay.

Clive's biggest revelation is his announcement that he and Luke are getting engaged. I'm so happy for them, they're a great couple, and I know Luke makes Clive very happy. They haven't decided on a date yet, but he promised to let me know as soon as they do. He also reminded me that it's Luke's birthday on Friday, and when they decide where they're going to celebrate it, he'll let me and the others know.

By the time he's divulged all the office secrets, it's time for me to change into my party frock so I grab my dress and head off to the ladies room. The floor length, fire engine red evening gown is beautiful. It hugs my figure in all the right places and makes me look stunning. Once I've checked my hair and makeup, I make my way back to my desk to collect my equipment.

"Oh, Sweetie. You look absolutely gorgeous!" Clive gasps. I blush and smile back. I really do feel amazing in this dress.

A black Mercedes is waiting for me when I exit the building, and the driver opens my door for me. I feel like a celebrity. When we arrive at the venue, the driver carries the equipment inside. There are security guys in evening dress at the doors, and after they have checked my credentials and my bags, they let me through.

I walk in and find the ballroom where the event is taking place. At the entrance, I see a line of waiters with trays of drinks awaiting the arrival of the guests. I walk over and ask one of them where I might find Mrs. Savchenko, but they just shake their heads, none of them seem to know. After a moment, a young lady in a dark suit approaches me with a smile.

"Vivienne? I'm Rosie, you can leave your bags in here." She shows me to a small room just off the hallway. "Mrs. Savchenko has asked that you photograph all the arrivals here," she points toward the alcove where a fairly boring background has been transformed into a beautiful setting of pale pastel colours, dressed with soft crystal encrusted fabrics. "Then you can take some informal shots at the Champagne reception in the ballroom, and then, of course, you have been invited for dinner," she smiles. "There will be speeches after dinner and then an auction which she would also like you to photograph."

"Okay, fine. Is Mrs. Savchenko here?"

"She'll be here soon, but if you need anything just ask for me."

"Okay, thanks."

I set up my tripods, lighting, and the laptop with projection monitor so that the photos can be viewed later on by the guests, then I take a few test shots. Once I'm all set up, I realise I'm quite excited about tonight. I've missed my job and this is the perfect setting. No outdoor weather conditions to worry about, I've already been offered two glasses of Champagne, which I declined, I don't want to get drunk and cut everyone's head off in the photos, Frank would kill me! And I'm looking forward to a lovely meal too. What could be better?

At exactly six forty-five the four piece orchestra begin to play and the lighting is dimmed to a more flattering tone. I check my camera and await my first couple who are ushered over to me before being handed a drink in the reception room.

I take a full-length shot of each couple followed by a tight shot of their head and shoulders. Some of them need a little direction, but on the whole, they seem to know what is expected of them which makes my job so much easier. The women have obviously gone to a lot of trouble to look glamorous for this evening. Some of the jewellery looks priceless, and I've seen so many of my idols from the movies and the music industry that I'm having a thoroughly fantastic evening.

The couple I've just photographed smile at me as they walk away, then I quickly look down at my camera to check my settings. As I look up to the next couple, I freeze. Suddenly it feels like all the air has been sucked out of the room. Max is standing right in front of me looking drop dead gorgeous in his tux. The sight of him makes my heart stutter. He literally takes my breath away. My stomach fills with butterflies and I can't take my eyes off him.

I don't know how long I was just staring at him, but then my focus is drawn to the beautiful young woman standing beside him. He has his arm curled around her waist, like he used to do with me. My heart twists in my chest, my breath catches in my throat, and I suddenly feel hot, nervous, and sick to my stomach. He stares at me with a totally serious expression. A small, angry frown creasing his brow. His hard rancorous eyes search mine. I wonder if maybe he hadn't expected to see me here tonight. I know I hadn't expected to see him, I thought he was still in New York.

I look away to catch my breath and quickly gather myself together, then I lift the camera to my eye. I can't stop my hands from shaking, my mouth is dry as a Martini, and my breathing is very short and shallow. I take a calming breath and try to steady my hands or this photograph is going to be awful. As I look through the lens his eyes penetrate mine, his jaw clenches repeatedly, and he doesn't even attempt to smile. His lovely escort drapes her hand on his shoulder and leans into him, pouting into the camera with a sultry supermodel pose. I feel jealous and hurt. He's moved on. *How could you?*

Once I've taken their photographs, I look down at my camera as they leave, his scent infiltrates my nose as he sweeps past me. He doesn't say a word and that really hurts.

I try to catch my breath and calm my shaking hands. Seeing him with another woman has hurt me more than I thought possible. I feel so humiliated, angry, and jealous. I try not to, but I can't help myself from turning to watch him walk away. *You said you'd wait!*

His confident, predatory walk stirs my butterflies. He doesn't look back, he just tightens his grip around her waist and hands her a glass of Champagne before walking out of sight into the reception room.

How could he just move on so quickly? He said he'd wait. He said if it takes forever, he'll be waiting. Tears prick my eyes. I want to run away, as far away as possible. I want to find a private corner and cry my heart out. But I can't, I have another couple patiently waiting for me to take their photo so I steel myself, plaster a big fake smile across my face, and force myself to get on with it.

The rest of the arrivals filter through at an achingly slow pace. I've wanted to leave, to go home and cry my eyes out since I saw Max with another woman. But I'm the one who shouted in his face. I'm the one who told him he meant nothing to me! I pushed him away, and now he's gone. He's found someone else, and it's all my own stupid fault.

As I finish photographing the last couple, I march over to the waiter and take a glass of Champagne. I can't get through this evening without something to numb the pain.

I see Rosie walking toward me. "Everything okay?"

I quickly put the glass down. "I'm sorry, I just wanted one drink." I blush, realising how unprofessional it is to be drinking on the job.

"Don't be silly," she smiles. "You're welcome to drink, eat, and dance," she adds, picking up a glass and taking a sip.

"Really? Won't the host mind?" I ask, a little surprised.

Rosie looks at me with a wry smile. "She'd mind if you

didn't!" She smirks at me, takes another sip of her Champagne, then she wanders off.

Once I've finished my drink, I go to the ladies room to check my makeup and to give myself a little pep talk. Luckily the bathroom is empty so I get to do it out loud. "Just breathe, Vivienne. He's obviously not worth it if he can't wait five fucking minutes." I check my eyes, they're not too puffy, but they sting a little from the tears that keep threatening to appear. I reapply my lip gloss and check myself out in the full-length mirror. I look pretty good in spite of how I feel inside. I give myself one last inspection in the mirror, then I walk back to my equipment.

Dismantling the tripods, I pack them away before heading off to the reception room. I slowly make my way through the guests, taking informal shots and eavesdropping on some of their conversations. I find myself occasionally casting my eyes around the room looking for Max. I know if I see him it's going to hurt, especially if he's got his arm wrapped around that woman again, but I just can't seem to stop myself. I don't see him anywhere and then I start to wonder if he's left, with her! My blood starts to boil at the thought. *How could you move on so quickly? I thought you loved me? You said you'd wait.*

The Maître d' announces dinner and everyone starts to wander through to the dining tables. I have no idea where I'm supposed to sit, not that I have an appetite anymore. I still haven't met the host and Rosie is nowhere to be seen.

I watch everyone walking through to their tables, but I hang back at the bar. I feel awkward all by myself. Someone taps me on the shoulder, as I turn around Grace, Max's p.a., is standing there smiling at me in a stunning blue gown.

"Hello, Vivienne."

Before I engage brain to mouth, I almost put my foot in it. "Gra…ah, Great party," I stutter. My face flushes with heat as I realise how close I came to almost saying her name. She'd know that I recognise her. Big mistake. Her shrewd, assessing eyes narrow on me as if she's seen right through me. *Think, Viv. Think!* "Mrs. Savchenko," I blurt. "Lovely to meet you." I reach out to shake her hand.

Confusion flits across her face. "Oh, no dear," she chuckles. "Mrs. Savchenko is my mother. I'm Grace Harmon, Max's personal assistant." Tilting her head in sympathy and with a warm smile, she holds my hand in both of hers. "I heard about your accident, Vivienne. I'm sorry, you probably don't remember me, but we've met before."

"Oh. We have?" I ask, trying to keep up the pretence.

"Don't worry, dear. You're on my table, why don't we go through."

I let her lead the way, and I follow on behind. As we walk to our table I start to panic, she's probably going to ask me all sorts of questions, and I'm going to have to come up with all the right answers.

She leads me to a large round table. Four people are already seated, they all greet Grace with affection and nod a polite hello to me. As we sit, Grace introduces me to her husband Tom, then she informs me that the lady at the top table with silver hair, is her mother Mrs. Savchenko, and patron of the charity they are supporting tonight. Grace has her mother's eyes and her engaging smile, and I recognise the lady from the red carpet I did at Max's Foxx-Glove gala ball. Grace seats us together, opposite a couple of empty chairs then she leans toward me. "These events can be quite stuffy," she whispers, arching a brow. "But they serve great wine and the food's not bad either," she smiles. "Oh, excuse me a moment, I think my mother needs me."

"Oh, of course." I smile, watching her walk away. As I turn back, I suddenly feel like I've been punched in the stomach when I see Max pulling a chair out for his beautiful companion. He takes his seat right opposite mine and rests his elbows on the table. His eyes burn into me with a hard, unyielding glare. He looks pissed off, and who could blame him? But I'm not the one dating again. Suddenly breathless, I look down and fidget with my napkin. My butterflies return with a vengeance.

"Miss Banks, would you care for some wine?"

I look up. Max is holding the wine bottle aloft and looking straight at me. His expression is cold as his eyes search mine waiting for my answer. I've missed those eyes, even though right now they look at me with utter contempt. I've hurt him, and he's letting me know it. I nod shyly, I'm desperate for a drink.

He stands and reaches over the table to pour the wine for me and Grace, and then he sits and pours one for his girlfriend and himself. Every time I glance up at him, his stormy eyes are fixed firmly on mine. I watch his girlfriend gazing up at him with admiration, although he doesn't look at her. Seeing them together makes me feel incredibly uncomfortable and outrageously jealous. I've got no hope of eating anything now, with all the butterflies in my stomach, I don't think I could keep anything down. I notice he hasn't bothered to introduce me to his new girlfriend either, but I imagine he's hoping we'll never have to meet again after tonight.

I should make my excuses and leave the table. I should…but I can't. I've missed him so much, I don't want to leave. To have him here, within touching distance, is like an unbearable pain that I just can't survive without. *Don't be a fool! Just get up and walk away.*

Grace returns to the table. I push my seat back and rise quickly. "I'll be back in a minute," I mumble to Grace. She looks up at me with confusion at my abrupt departure. I don't look at Max, but I feel him watching me as I walk away. Tears prick my eyes as I make my way to the ladies room.

Barging through the door, I stop suddenly when I see it's full of chattering women so I double back and head to the exit. When I get outside, I take a few deep breaths. The cold night air clears my head and chills my skin.

"I know you remember me. I can see it in your eyes." His velvety rasp caresses my ears and sends butterflies to my stomach. I don't dare turn around. "You look beautiful, by the way," he adds, softly. I close my eyes and compose myself with one last deep breath before I turn to face him. His now gentle eyes search mine, delving deep into my soul. "Why are you lying to me, Vivienne?" His eyes pull me in, and his pleading, soft voice breaks down my steely resolve with ease.

Oh, no. Please don't. I know she can't possibly be here, or hear what we're saying, but I get a terrible sense of dread that Monica will somehow see us together. I need Vinnie. I can't trip at the last hurdle. "I'm not. Why would I?" I answer, trying to maintain eye contact.

"I know you are, Vivienne. I just don't know why?" he says, clenching his jaw and narrowing his eyes on me. He straightens his back and shoves his hands deep in his pockets. Lifting his chin, his wary eyes search mine. "Is it Mike?...Are you still in love with Mike?"

No! How could you even think that? His question takes me by surprise, and the hurt look on his face crushes me inside. I instinctively want to run into his arms to take away all his doubts and fears, but I don't. I know what I need to do. I take a deep breath and level my eyes on his. "Yes... I am."

I helplessly watch as those three little words destroy him right in front of my eyes. I have to look away, I can't bear to see the hurt on his face anymore. I need to change the subject before I cave in. These barefaced lies are killing me.

"Vinnie said he'd contact me to collect the Volvo, but he hasn't called yet." The curt edge to my voice wasn't intentional, but my emotions are playing havoc with my control, and I'm confused that I haven't heard from Vinnie yet. Surely they came back from New York together?

His head bows and he exhales a deep sigh. "He had to

take Jan to Scotland for a few days, her mother's been very ill."

Oh God. Poor Jan.

He drags his hand through his hair on an exasperated sigh, then he shoves it back in his pocket. I know he hates the fact that I'm returning his gift. "If it means that much to you I can send John to—"

"No! There's no rush," I blurt. I need to speak to Vinnie. I wish he was here. He eyes me warily then steps toward me taking his hands from his pockets, but I back up, which makes him stop. *Please, Max. Please don't, I can't do this for much longer.* If he touches me or takes me in his arms, it's game over.

His stormy eyes become soft. "You said you loved me," he whispers, sadly. "You said…" He stops speaking, but the emotion is etched all over his face. I have to look away. I swallow the tightening lump in my throat and look past him, avoiding his eyes at all costs.

"You should get back to your table." *Back to your girlfriend!*

With the saddest eyes, he gives me one last questioning look then he turns and walks back inside the hotel. I watch him walk away. I want to run after him, but I don't. I just stare at him until he walks out of sight, taking my broken heart with him.

Once I've dried my tears, I can't face going back to the table so I decide to hang around the bar until I'm needed after dinner. This was supposed to be a great first day back at work, but it's turned out to be one of the shittiest gigs of my life.

Rosie calls me to action after the dinner and speeches. I was sorely tempted to drink myself into oblivion at the bar, but in the state I'm in emotionally, I had the good sense not to.

I photograph the auction prizes and the happy winners. Max and I trade the occasional moment of eye contact as I move around the room. I can feel his eyes on me the whole time. I'm sure his girlfriend must have been delighted.

When he bids heavily on the last auction item, which is a holiday for two in Tahiti, and then wins it, I have no choice but to move in close and take his photograph as he receives the tickets. He smiles straight down the lens, but it doesn't reflect in his eyes. When he walks back to his table and hands the tickets to his girlfriend, I get a pang of jealousy when she throws her arms around his neck and kisses him on the cheek.

How could you? My heart twists and I have to leave the room before I burst into tears. I quickly throw my camera into the bag and then I dismantle the laptop and monitor and bag them up as quickly as possible.

"Leaving already?" I turn to see Mrs. Savchenko walking toward me, with her carved silver handled walking cane. "The band will be starting soon, you're very welcome to stay for the dancing," she says, with a kind smile.

"Thank you, but I need to be up early tomorrow."

"Well, thank you for all your hard work, Vivienne. You've done a great job," she smiles. "Tell Frank I'll call him tomorrow with the total of the funds raised."

"Yes, I'll tell him."

I make a hasty exit and find my driver waiting in the car park. As I climb in and wait for him to load the equipment into the boot, I see Max striding out of the hotel. His anxious eyes search the car park and then he finds me as we start to pull away. I quickly look down, I can't let him see me cry.

When I get home, I kick off my shoes and grab a bottle of wine from the fridge. Sitting on the sofa, I curl my legs underneath me. I pour myself a large glass of wine and I sit in silence reliving every heart-breaking moment of this evening.

Max looked incredible, he always does. He's the sexiest man I've ever met, and he melts my bones when he looks at me with those gorgeous blue eyes. I miss him so much.

An image of him with that woman flies into my mind and pisses me off. How could he date another woman so soon? Why didn't he wait for me like he said he would? But then, why would he? He thinks I'm still in love with Mike.

I laugh and cry at the same time. I've really fucked everything up this time. As the tears roll down my cheeks, I pour myself another glass of wine.

Max picks me up in his strong arms and carries me to the bedroom. He slowly peels my dress from my body and stares down at me with hooded, seductive eyes.

"You're so beautiful," he murmurs, kissing my neck and shoulders. "I've missed you, so much." His raspy voice sends heat through my exposed skin as he caresses me with his eyes. Pulling his shirt from his waistband, he unbuttons it slowly, teasingly, never taking his eyes from mine. Then he shrugs it off and lets it fall to the floor.

My eager eyes trail over his lean, hard, perfect body as he strips naked and lays me down on the bed. He lies beside me running his hand up my thigh and across my belly. The warm contact sparks my nerve endings with delicious tingles, then he sinks his hand into my knickers and gently strokes my aching sex. I shudder and close my eyes, arching my back. Running my hand through his silky hair I moan with pleasure.

He leans down and kisses my breast, rolling his hot tongue over my erect nipple, then his luscious lips travel up my throat nipping and lapping until his lips find mine and he devours me in a passionate, hungry kiss. I've needed this for so long. As he breaks the kiss and pulls back, he nuzzles my ear as the intense sensations build in my core from his expert fingers.

"I love you, baby," he whispers against my ear. My heart flutters. I love those words coming out of his mouth.

"I love you, too."

"Open your eyes," he murmurs softly. I open my eyes and see Monica standing at the side of the bed with a sickening grimace on her face and a glinting blade in her hands held high above her head. I scream in horror as she brings the blade down and plunges it into Max's back over and over again…

"Max!" My garbled yell wakes me up as I lurch forward in my seat gripping the armrest. *What the…?*

As I try to make sense of my surroundings, I realise I'm still wearing my red dress and I'm on the sofa in the living room. I look all around me, then I relax my tense muscles and sink back into the sofa on a long, ragged sigh. My hands are still shaking with adrenaline, and I can't get rid of the terrifying images still swirling around in my brain. My sex is still throbbing with arousal. "Wow." I gasp, still trying to catch my breath. "That felt so real."

I glance at my phone to check the time. It's five-thirty-nine in the morning. *Crap*. I drag myself out of the sofa and head to the bedroom. Stripping off, I hang Lucy's dress up and dive under the covers.

WHY DID YOU LIE?

I wake at nine thirty and haul my tired body out of bed to go and take a shower. Once I'm dressed and ready, I head off to work with all my equipment.

As I make my way into the building, I say hi to Sandra, who looks decidedly chipper this morning. I'm wondering if it has anything to do with her new girlfriend.

Clive wanders over and perches on the edge of my desk. "How was your gig last night?" he asks with a cheeky smirk.

"Yeah, it was okay," I sigh, throwing my bag on the desk and my jacket on the back of my chair.

"Oh! Before I forget, you know it's Luke's birthday tomorrow? Well, we're all going out to celebrate at Chymeira. Lucy and Dan are coming, so is Ed and Sandra. I expect to see you there too." Leaning closer he lowers his voice. "Maybe we'll get to meet Sandra's new girlfriend," he grins. My phone interrupts us before I have a chance to comment. I don't recognise the number so I let it go to answer-phone.

"Yeah, sounds great." I don't know if I'm really in the mood for celebrations, but if I tell him what he wants to hear, he won't bombard me with a ton of awkward questions about Max. My phone rings again. It's another unknown number but this time, I pick up.

"Hello. Vivienne Banks."

"Do you really think a new lock will keep me out?"

Monica! Shit. My eyes flip up to Clive, who's watching me intently. 'Could you get me a coffee?" I mouth to him while covering the phone. He nods and walks over to the coffee machine. "What do you want?" I ask brusquely. I'm getting really pissed off with her now.

"You had a cosy little chat with Max last night, didn't you?"

How the fuck does she know? "Look! It wasn't my fault. I was working, he just happened to be there." I quickly glance around the room and lower my voice. "I'm doing everything you asked—" An idea suddenly pops into my head. "Why don't we meet up and talk about this properly?"

"Oh, we will, Vivienne. You can count on it." The line goes dead.

Shit. What does that mean?

Clive returns with two coffees. "What's the matter?" he frowns. "You look a little peeved."

"I am," I huff, folding my arms across my chest. "But not for long if I have anything to do with it."

Clive leans forward, his gossip radar is fully engaged. "Why? What's happened?"

I stare up at him with an arched brow and an angry frown. "Clive. If I told you, you'd never believe me."

He shrugs and almost raises a Botox'd eyebrow. "Try me."

Yeah. Nice try, Mr. Smalls.

Frank arrives at my desk interrupting Clive's probing glare, and hands him a folder. "Send these up for Saturday's print, I've marked the ones I want to use." Frank says, slipping me a cautious sideways glance. Clive opens the folder and gives me the same look. I realise Frank must have handed Clive the photographs I took last night. No doubt he's using a photo of Max for the front cover. He sells more magazines for Frank than all the beautiful models put together.

"Vivienne. I, ah…I didn't know Mr. Foxx was going to

be at the gig last night. I wouldn't have…you know, I hope it wasn't awkward for you," he says, cringing slightly.

I force myself to shrug with cool indifference. "That's okay. I don't know why everyone's making such a big fuss about it. I don't remember the guy. How could it bother me?" I say, glibly, shrugging my shoulders. It isn't okay at all. And it bothers me a lot. Seeing Max with another woman stung like a bastard. I know I pushed him away, but he said he'd wait. He said if it takes forever, he'd wait for me. But he didn't. And last night I had to suffer the pain of seeing him with his arm curled around another woman. *Gah!*

"Vivienne?…Vivienne. Did you hear what I said?"

I look up at Frank's questioning frown. *Shit! Pay attention, Viv.* "Sorry?"

"I said that's good. It's excellent in fact, because I've got another assignment for you this afternoon."

"Oh… Great… Where is it?"

Frank shifts on his feet and puffs his cheeks out on a big exhale while scratching his beard. "Foxx-Tech Global."

There's a beat of silence as I digest the information.

Are you fucking kidding me? "Great. Is Ed coming with me?" I say, as nonchalantly as possible under the circumstances.

"Ah, no. Are you sure you don't mind doing it?" he asks, nervously.

Yes! Of course I fucking mind. "No. Not at all." I should have said no. But now I've confirmed to Frank that Max means nothing to me, what possible excuse could I give for not wanting to do the job? *Shit! Fuck! Bollocks!* I'm going to take myself to the ladies room and kick myself up the arse. I'm such an idiot!

Frank looks relieved and hands me a small piece of paper with the details of the assignment. I almost snatch it out of his hand in anger, but I manage to calm myself down just in time.

"It's just some corporate shots for their website and

marketing. They asked for you personally, and paid very handsomely for it, so I'll have a bonus cheque ready for you on Friday," he smiles. "Oh. And unless something comes in, you might as well take the rest of the week off. I'll see you bright and early on Monday, okay?"

I mumble an acknowledgement as I stare down at the paper. *Max is doing this on purpose.*

As soon as Frank leaves, Clive perches on the edge of my desk. He's all fidgety and twitchy, and his eyes are burning into me. "O.M.G! You're still in love with him," he squeals, grinning like an idiot.

Think, Viv, think! I flick my eyes up to Clive's trying to maintain my poker face, but he's seen right through me. "I've never loved Frank," I huff, internally praising myself for the quick response.

"Huh? No, silly. Not Frank, Max." He lays the photograph of Max right in front of me. "You remember him now, don't you?" he says, narrowing his wise eyes on me. I look down at the photo. I know I can't show anything in my expression or Clive will do a back flip, a cartwheel, and shout it from the rooftops. So I just pull a face with a shrug and slide the photo back to Clive.

"He's very nice to look at, but no. I don't remember him, at all." I rise and put my jacket on. If I don't get out of here right now, I'm going to give the biggest mouth in London the worst possible gossip. I know he's still staring at me waiting for confirmation, but I avoid any eye contact while gathering my equipment together, then I quickly kiss him on the cheek and leave.

"But—"

"See you later, Clive," I call out, over my shoulder.

When I pass Sandra at the front desk, she's having what seems like a heated conversation on the phone. She nervously looks up at me so I wave and smile as usual, but she quickly turns away. I don't want to intrude in what could be her and her girlfriend's first argument, so I carry on walking.

I decide to walk to Foxx-Tech. I've left way too early but I needed to get away from Clive, he's almost as good at reading me as Max is. I'm angry at myself for not being able to control my emotions earlier. Clive is the last person I should show my feelings to, and I've only got myself to blame for this mess. I need to work out a strategy so that if I bump into Max today, I can control the situation with a little more finesse. I'll just have to maintain a professional approach and get the job done as quickly as possible.

My stomach rolls. I keep seeing Max's sad eyes pleading with me to stop hurting him. I don't think I'll ever forget the look on his face. But then my niggling brain starts to wonder if he took his new girlfriend back to his place last night? *No! Stop it Vivienne. Stop winding yourself up.*

I arrive outside the Foxx-Tech building with almost an hour to spare so I decide to pop into the Starbucks next door to grab a coffee. It's fairly empty so I place my order and find a comfy seat in the window so I can stare out at the world.

As I sip my coffee, I notice a car pulling up outside the Foxx-Tech building. I recognise the number plate immediately. It's Max's Bentley. I grab the menu and hold it up to block my face, I don't want Max to see me. I'm so glad when I see Vinnie get out of the car. *He's back.*

Vinnie opens the passenger door and Max steps out looking dreamy as ever. Butterflies fill my belly as my eyes trawl over his gorgeous, million dollar face. He runs his hand through his hair then straightens his tie. He looks so sexy and handsome, exuding a vibrant, unrelenting power with his magnificent maleness.

Suddenly, my heart sinks as he turns back to the open door and holds his hand out for the young woman he was with last night. She looks stunning. Smiling up at him, they link arms and walk toward the entrance. My stomach knots with jealousy and sadness as they disappear into the building.

I need to talk to Vinnie but I can't speak to him yet, not

while he's still with Max so I sit back and drink my coffee, feeling totally depressed.

A few minutes later, I see Vinnie on his own leaving the Foxx-Tech building. I quickly stand and bang on the window but he doesn't hear me so I run to the door. I check the Foxx-Tech entrance but Max has definitely gone inside, so I call out to Vinnie.

He turns and looks the wrong way so I shove my fingers in my mouth and whistle. He finally turns to face me with a confused expression. As soon as he realises it's me, he glances over at the Foxx-Tech building then he quickly walks toward me.

"Alright, Miss?" he frowns.

I beckon him inside while still checking the entrance to Max's building. I'm nervous that he'll walk out any minute and see us. "Vinnie, I'm so glad you're back. Can we talk, in private?"

He eyes me with uncertainty for a moment, then his face morphs into a big cheesy grin. He quickly looks over his shoulder at the car. "Yeah, come on. I need to move the motor or he'll wonder why it's still sitting outside."

I grab my bags and follow him out. He opens the passenger door and I quickly slide in. I feel nervous and excited. It feels like a huge weight has been lifted now that I can finally talk to Vinnie and tell him what happened.

"How's Jan?" I ask. "Max said her mother has been ill."

Vinnie eyes me sceptically. I know he's wondering if my memory has come back. His eyes lower for a moment. "Her mum passed away, Jan's still up in Scotland," he sighs, returning his eyes to the road ahead.

"Oh, I'm sorry to hear that." I feel bad for Jan. I've wanted to call her since I heard the news that her mother was ill, but I'm still trapped in this awful situation.

Vinnie drives us to the basement of the Foxx-Tech building and parks up. Turning to face me with his eyebrows raised, he smiles at me with a cheeky grin. "I'm all ears, Miss."

I suddenly don't know where to start. He doesn't prompt me or fidget, he just calmly waits for me to begin. My mind is racing. I take a deep breath and swallow. My hands begin to shake with adrenaline. I end up wringing them in my lap, suddenly feeling very nervous. "Vinnie…I've done a really stupid thing." His eyebrows lower but he doesn't say anything so I continue. "Oh, God… Where do I begin?"

"Just take your time," he says, softly.

I raise my eyes to his and take another deep breath. "…Monica isn't dead." I watch Vinnie's shocked reaction. His eyes widen and blink, his mouth opens, but he says nothing. "She's very much alive, Vinnie. I don't know who that poor woman was who Max identified in Portsmouth, but I can assure you, it definitely wasn't Monica. She was there that night at the penthouse. She had a gun. For some reason, God only knows why, it wouldn't fire so she beat me with it and tried to strangle me to death." Tears start to roll down my cheeks and my bottom lip quivers as the memories of that night flash through my mind. Vinnie's wary eyes narrow on me.

"I thought you couldn't remember?"

I hang my head in shame and regret. "I was lying."

"Bleedin' hell. I knew something wasn't right." Vinnie reaches into his pocket and hands me his handkerchief. "Here, dry your eyes," he says, softly, still eyeing me warily. I dry my cheeks and try to compose myself. "Why did you lie?" he asks softly.

"I had no choice, Vinnie. She threatened me. She said she wanted me out of the way. She told me I had to leave Max. She thinks he's going to fall in love with her again… I… I know it sounds crazy, but the woman's fucking insane!" I'm yelling. My voice is trembling with nerves and frustration. I can still feel Monica's bony fingers wrapped around my throat, and I'll never forget the wild, hateful look in her eyes.

Vinnie searches my face with concern, quietly absorbing

the information.

"She's dangerous, Vinnie. Crazy and dangerous. She thinks if I'm out of the way, he'll take her back." I begin to sob, almost laughing too. It sounds so ridiculous. I look up at Vinnie's angry face then he offers me an anxious smile and puffs out a long sigh.

"You were lucky. She must have been using Steve's gun. The Governor said they couldn't find it at the murder scene so she must have had it." He suddenly looks very pale, rubbing his face. "Fuck me! That really was lucky," he sighs, shaking his head with a deep frown. "Steve's gun is a ZX-Nyro which has a palm print identification built into the hand grip. It won't fire unless it recognises the user."

I stare at his incredulous face with wide eyes. *That gun saved my life.*

Vinnie looks at me with cautious eyes and a deep frown still etched in his brow. "Why didn't you tell us when you woke up?"

"Because she threatened to kill Max!" I blurt. "She's been threatening me ever since. I couldn't tell anyone." I can't stop crying, but I want to tell him everything. For my own sanity, I need to tell him. "She let me live because she's got some sick idea that if I hurt him badly enough, he'd realise how much he needs her. She told me if I didn't leave him, she'd kill him." The words get stuck in my throat.

"You're alright, come on," he soothes, gently rubbing my shoulder.

I dry my cheeks and look up at him. "She's watching me, Vinnie. I know she is."

"Has she given you any clue as to where she might be?"

"No, but she's close. She's been inside my flat too. She left a message on my bathroom mirror for fuck's sake. I don't know how, but she knows about every visit, every phone call. She even knew Max had come out to France. She probably even knows I'm talking to you right now." I nervously glance out of the windows. "I've done everything she's asked me to, but I realise now, that I can't protect Max on my own. I need help."

He smiles at me with kind eyes. "You've come to the right place," he says, softly.

"What are we going to do?" I sniffle.

He throws me an arched brow. "You. Are going to do exactly what she says. Leave the rest to me."

I reach out and grab his arm in panic. "You can't tell Max, he can't—"

"Don't worry," he smiles. "He can't know yet, he'll just go steaming in and fuck it up." Vinnie looks thoughtful for a moment. "How did she get into the penthouse?"

I cringe slightly. "The night I ran away, the night she killed Charlie, I'd left my key-card behind. I didn't think I was coming back.… After that, I was always with Max, so I hadn't noticed it was missing."

He nods thoughtfully and stares out of the windscreen tapping his fingers on the steering wheel.

"There's something else," I say, waiting for Vinnie's eyes to swing back to mine. He gives me his full attention. "Monica's threatened to hurt Lucy too. And the way she was that night," I shudder at the memory, "I think she's capable of anything." My stomach churns.

Suddenly Vinnie's phone rings making us both jump. His frown deepens when he checks the screen. "Bugger. It's the Governor. I'd better take this. Not a word," he says to me before answering the call. "Yes, Guv'… Yeah… No, I went for a cuppa… I'm on my way there now… Alright." He raises his eyebrows as he ends the call and lets out a sarcastic huff. "He's always such a pleasure to be around when he's got a mood on," he smirks.

"How is he?" I ask hesitantly.

Vinnie shakes his head then shoots me a nervous look. "Not good, Miss. It's like he's grieving."

"He hasn't…" I can't say it. I'm so frightened that he'll revert to his coping mechanism of self-harming.

Vinnie shakes his head and lowers his eyes. "Not that I know of, but he's a mess. Me and Jan have tried to keep him off the bottle, but he's suffering," he sighs. His eyes suddenly become very sad. "When he thought he'd lost you that night we came home and found you in a pool of blood, it was painful to watch. And now…he thinks he's lost you all over again."

My heart clenches. "He hasn't lost me, Vinnie. He just has to be patient." But he hasn't been patient. My heart twists as the image of him and that woman flies into my mind. *Why didn't you wait?*

Vinnie takes my hand in his and gives it a squeeze. "I knew you hadn't forgotten us, Miss."

Tears spring into my eyes. "Oh, Vinnie. I've missed you all so much. I realise now how stupid I've been, but I thought I was doing the right thing. I had to protect him. I couldn't bear to have anything happen to him, or any of you." Tears flow down my cheeks as all my pent up emotion finally breaks free.

"I wish you'd come to me right at the start, Miss. But she can't hide away forever. And as long as you keep your eyes peeled and do what she says, we may have enough time to catch her out."

"How do we do that?" I ask nervously.

"I'm working on it!" he frowns. "I need to talk to D.I. Mills in Portsmouth. It's going to be tricky keeping this from Max, but he's been so depressed lately, he's cancelled a lot of his meetings so I should be able to sneak off tonight or tomorrow." He suddenly looks at me like a concerned parent. "I'd prefer it if you were back at the penthouse, Miss. At least I'd have you and Max in one place. It's easier to protect you that way."

I shake my head. "No. I can't put Lucy in danger. I need more time."

He nods and offers me a weak smile. "Alright," he sighs. "I'll get you a new phone so we can talk, Monica may be tracking yours. How can I get it to you?"

My mind races. "I'm actually taking some publicity shots at Foxx-Tech today, what about leaving it at the reception desk, I can pick it up when I leave."

"Great," he smiles. The smile fades, and he looks me straight in the eyes. "By the way, John told me he thought you'd recognised him in France. If he says anything, just deny it. Let's just keep this between you and me for now. I want to make sure I know who's on our team before we let the cat out the bag."

I slowly nod in response. I'd never thought about it before. John was so kind and helpful to me when I'd found out about Max's room of guilt, but Vinnie's right, Monica could have recruited him too.

I glance down at my watch. "Shit. I'm late, I'd better go."

Vinnie starts the car. "I'll drop you off just down the street so you can walk in the front entrance. We've got new surveillance cameras now so we'd better be careful."

I suddenly panic. "What do I do if Monica finds out we've met?"

Vinnie shrugs. "From what you've told me, she probably knows you're working here anyway, there's not much we can do about that now. Maybe the best thing for you to do, is to be really cold towards Max, because if she has eyes on him that will get back to her." My heart sinks. I hate this. I hate hurting Max, but if it keeps him and Lucy safe then that's what I'll do.

AERIAL

Vinnie drops me off in a side road and I walk to the entrance of the Foxx-Tech building.

The girl at reception is expecting me and sends me up to the offices. As I exit the lift and walk through the plush lobby, I get a sense of Deja-vu. Charlie and I came here the day we went to the zoo. That was such a lovely day. A day I'll cherish forever.

I wander over to the desk and speak to one of the receptionists. "Hi, I'm Vivienne Banks. Star-Biz Magazine. I'm here to do the publicity shots."

"Oh, yes, Miss Banks, one moment," she says, tapping something on her keyboard.

"You're late!" Max's stern voice makes me jump. I turn to face him, trying to settle my breathing and calm my fluttering heart. Butterflies invade my belly as soon as my eyes land on his gorgeous, angry face.

"I'm sorry, I—" He gives me a filthy look, then he abruptly turns away and starts walking. *How rude.* I suddenly realise I should follow him, so I try to keep up as he strides down the corridor to a large board room.

He points at a chair on the end of a very long table. "Sit!" he snaps. I do as instructed, but his attitude is starting to piss me off. I may have been the one who pushed him away, but he's the one who found it so easy to start dating again. *You said you'd wait… Why didn't you wait?*

He walks to the middle of the long table and takes a seat.

We're miles apart. I lay my bags on the table then I fold my hands in front of me. He just sits there glaring at me with hard, stormy eyes and a clenched jaw, making me feel very uncomfortable. Without taking his eyes off mine, he takes a deep breath as if he's going to say something, then he lets out a long, exasperated sigh and drags his hands through his hair. He looks deeply annoyed.

"Why did you ask me to come here?" I ask, breaking the silence.

His eyes narrow on me. "To take pictures. That's what you do isn't it?" he says, angrily, clenching his jaw. We stare at each other until I blush and look away.

Suddenly he rises from his chair. I watch him walk to the vast window where he stands with his back to me, staring out at the metropolis below. He shoves his hands in his pockets and huffs out an aggravated sigh. "Why couldn't you just tell me, Vivienne?" His voice is strained and raspy.

I wait for him to turn and face me, but he doesn't. "Tell you what?" I ask hesitantly.

"That you were still in love with Mike. Why couldn't you have been honest with me?" My heart sinks. I can see his jaw clenching as he straightens his back. How do I answer that? I look down at my knotted fingers. Trying to say the words without any emotion is impossible, but I have to try.

"Max, I don't remember you... I don't remember us. Whatever we had, it's gone." I almost choke on the words and I feel sick to my stomach.

"Then why do I see it in your eyes?" he says, turning to face me. The look on his face is almost my undoing.

I quickly rise and sling my bags over my shoulder. "You don't… It's only what you want to see."

Max's watery eyes suddenly dart above my head. I realise someone has walked into the room behind me. Max turns away from me again to face the window. Even from this distance I can feel the heat of his emotion rippling through him.

"Hello, Miss Banks, I'm Scott." I turn to face the voice.

A young man in a blue suit extends his hand to me. "If you'll follow me." I look back at Max, wishing I could tell him everything, but he's too wrapped up in his pain to turn and face me, and my hands are still tied. I can see the crease in his brow and the ferocious ticking in his jaw. I've hurt him, deeply. But what he doesn't know, is how much it hurts me too.

As Scott ushers me from the room, Max speaks in a clipped, monotone voice. "Aerial. Save it till last." We both turn to face him, but he stands with his back to us both. I look up at Scott who smiles down at me and then leads me from the room.

Aerial?

Scott has me photographing the staff, the lobby, the lifts, the front reception desk, the sculptures, the water feature out front, and finally he takes me up in the lift. I've been here for hours and I'm knackered.

When the lift doors open, I realise we're on the roof. *Aerial?...Oh shit.* The helicopter stands ready and waiting for me. It's bigger than the last one I was in. The wind whips my hair in all directions as Scott leads me to the rear passenger door. My stomach churns like a washing machine as I climb in. It's not my favourite mode of transport, as Max knows only too well. *He's done this on purpose.*

I pull my hair from my eyes and tie it back in a ponytail as Scott buckles me into my harness and then slides the door closed.

"We wouldn't want you to fall out."

Max? His voice comes at me through the speakers in the headrest behind me, I whip my head up and stare at the back of his head.

"London control, Golf-Foxtrot-Oscar-X-ray-X-ray requesting left orbit in my present position....departing zone to a three-hundred-sixty degree at present position.... Confirmed, thank you London control, Golf-Foxtrot-

Oscar-X-ray-X-ray out." He doesn't turn to look at me and before I have a chance to say anything he takes off, hovers for a moment, and then swoops off to the left. I feel like I've left my stomach back on the roof as it churns relentlessly.

He leans back and hands me a headset without looking at me. I snatch it from his hand and shove it on my head. I'm fuming.

"You'd better get your camera ready. It's not a joy ride, Miss Banks. You've got a job to do!" he snaps angrily.

You pig!

I wrestle with my camera bag to get my lenses out without dropping them, and then I prep my camera while my stomach feels like it's being jostled around like a lonely sock in a tumble dryer. I've got very little window area to shoot through so I try to find a clear point of focus on the building he's circling. At this angle, I do feel slightly sick.

He reaches up to a button on the panel above his head, as soon as he presses it my door clicks, moves out, and slides back. The wind rushes in and takes my breath away making me panic. "Oh, my God! The door!" I yell, in a high pitched voice. I hang onto my harness with white knuckles, and I push myself back into my seat. My right leg is now firmly wedged against the back of his seat. I'm terrified and he knows it.

"Are you getting this?" he smirks, looking out of his window at the Foxx-Tech building below.

What a bastard! "You won't be so smug when I vomit all over the back of your head. You want pictures? I'll give you fucking pictures." I grumble under my breath.

It takes all my strength not to freak out. The only thing keeping me from falling out, is a harness that I can only hope has been regularly checked and serviced by health and safety. But I try not to think about it, and I do what he's paying me to do. I'll be damned if he thinks he can bully me.

I don't know how I managed it, but I got tons of photographs at various heights and angles. Max had swooped and dove all over the place, it can't be legal this close to the buildings. He didn't even bother to speak to me which really pissed me off. He arrogantly threw me around so much, and made me so angry, that I think I got over my fear. He's probably done me a favour without knowing it. *Yeah…Fuck you!*

As he finally levels the helicopter and closes my door, I realise my hands are freezing from the cold wind, but I'm glad I didn't give up. If he wants to take his frustrations out on me, fine. Maybe I deserve it. But I won't be a victim. Not anymore.

Max lands the helicopter and I quickly unbuckle myself from the harness and pull the handle to open my door. Grabbing my bags, I march off to the lift.

"Vivienne!" he calls out behind me, but I keep on walking. I'm glad to see the lift is waiting so I get in and quickly press the lobby button. He's striding toward me as the doors begin to glide shut.

"Vivienne, I'm sorry!"

"Goodbye, Max."

The lift doors close before he reaches me, and then it descends. I suddenly want to cry. I'm angry, frustrated and depressed all at once. And that's even before I see the state of my hair in the mirrored walls. *Jesus!* I quickly sort out my wind ravaged hair and then I run my hand along the mirror. This lift holds so many wonderful memories for me. On our first date, after dinner in Rome, this was where he kissed me for the first time, but now…

He's angry with me because he thinks I've chosen Mike over him. He couldn't be more wrong but I can't tell him. Not yet anyway.

The doors open and I head to the reception desk. "Hi, Vivienne Banks. Do you have a package for me?"

"Oh, yes, Miss Banks." She hands me the small plastic

bag. "Have a nice day." I march out of the building and walk to the tube station.

When I get home, I open the bag that Vinnie left for me and I set up my new mobile phone. He's already programmed his number into it, and I notice it's not the same number that he previously had. Vinnie's obviously being extra cautious. The bag also contains a taser and a can of pepper spray. He's also left me a voice message;

"I'm going down to Portsmouth tomorrow evening. I can't sneak off before then or the Governor will get suspicious. I'm going to speak with D.I. Mills about re-opening the case. Call me if you have any problems, and don't trust anyone until we know who's helping her. Keep your minces peeled. If she approaches you, use the taser and call the police, then me. Stay safe."

I run down to Lucy's flat to let her know that I've contacted Vinnie and that, with any luck, he can help us put this sorry mess to bed once and for all. As I knock on the door, I can hear her and Dan yelling at each other. I don't want to intrude, they're obviously in the middle of a row so I turn to leave but the door suddenly flies open and Dan walks through with a face on. He's mumbling under his breath and he throws me a moody glare when he sees me. "See if you can talk some bloody sense into her will you," he grumbles as he walks past me and down the stairs.

"Um, yeah, okay. Bye, Dan." I watch him walk away in a huff. I know things have been a bit stressful between them lately, the wedding has sparked all sorts of arguments.

I tentatively push the door open. "Luce, it's me. Can I come in?" I walk through to the kitchen and find Lucy leaning against the counter pouring herself a glass of wine. She opens the cupboard and grabs another glass for me so I sit down at the table and wait for her to join me.

"That man drives me nuts." she huffs, plonking herself down on the chair opposite me then sliding my glass toward me.

"Cheers." I raise my glass and smile at her moody face. "What's the matter?"

She takes a sip of her wine, I can see by her expression that she's trying to diffuse her anger before she speaks. "We finally agreed on a date for the wedding, but then Dan's brother Josh, tells us that he can't do that date." she huffs, gulping down another mouthful.

"And that's a problem because….?"

"He's Dan's best man!"

"Oh." Lucy drains her glass and pours another. "Why can't he do your date?" I ask, feebly trying to see if there is anything to work around.

She pulls a face and looks me right in the eye. "Because there's an important rugby match on that date. Fucking rugby," she huffs.

I smile at her sympathetically, trying to calm her down. I know Dan wouldn't let something like that bother him, he's always put Lucy first in his life, and I can't imagine he would cause a row over something like that. "So, what did Dan say about it?"

Lucy's expression starts to soften. I can tell she now feels bad about their argument. "He said stuff him. He'll ask Jamie to do it instead."

I smile. I was right. "So, what's your problem?"

"That's not the point, Viv. Dan should have his brother by his side on his wedding day. It shouldn't just be all about me. It's his special day too." Her eyes begin to water so I get up and walk around to give her a cuddle. "Oh, Viv. We've had more rows about this bloody wedding than we've ever had before. I'm starting to think we should just elope," she sniffles.

"What? And make me miss out on being your bridesmaid. Not bloody likely!" I chuckle. "Besides, your mum would never forgive you." I give her a cuddle until she stops sniffling and then I take my seat again.

"I've got some news," I say, changing the subject. "I saw Vinnie today. I told him everything." I actually feel relieved to be able to say that.

Lucy's head whips up. "Does Max know?"

"No, Vinnie wants to keep him out of it for a bit longer, at least until he's spoken to the police in Portsmouth. He's going to try and get them to reopen the case. He thinks Monica may be tracking our phones and if Max knows, it could alert Monica too early."

Lucy looks worried. "So what are we supposed to do in the meantime?"

"Just wait," I shrug. "Wait and see what he comes up with."

She shudders. "Well I hope he comes up with something soon, that woman scares the crap out of me."

"Yeah…me too."

Lucy scowls and gives me the eyebrow, you know, the one that seems to tell you off without words. "Have you had any more threats from the psycho-bitch from hell?"

I sag and release a long sigh. "She called me this morning while I was at work. She knew I'd seen Max last night."

"You didn't tell me you'd seen him," she says, indignantly.

"I was working. I didn't know he was going to be there. I wish I hadn't seen him." The image of him and that woman suddenly comes into my mind. It really pisses me off.

"Why? What happened?"

"You know I borrowed your dress for that charity gig last night? Well, I didn't know Max was back from New York, but he turned up as one of the guests." I take a sip of wine to calm my frustration.

"And?"

I frown and rest my elbows on the table. "He arrived with another woman."

"What? No… Are you sure it wasn't just a colleague or something?"

"Pff, didn't look like it. He had his arm around her, and when he won some tickets to Tahiti in the auction, and then gave them to her, she was all over him." *Why didn't you wait?*

Lucy huffs angrily and tops up my glass. "Bastard."

"It gets worse," I say, rolling my eyes. "Frank gave me an assignment at Foxx-Tech today."

"Oh, shit. You didn't go did you?" she asks incredulously.

"I had no choice. I've been banging on about not remembering him so Frank thought it wouldn't be a problem. Although, Clive almost caught me out."

"So, what happened? Did you see Max?"

I take another sip. I'm still angry about how the day went. "I did… He thinks I'm still in love with Mike. He thinks I've chosen Mike over him and I couldn't deny it because I'm not supposed to remember our relationship." I sag against the back of my chair. My intricate web of lies is beginning to close in around me.

Lucy leans across the table and squeezes my hand. "Now you've got Vinnie on side, I'm sure it'll all get sorted out soon enough. Then you and Max can get back together and put all this behind you," she smiles.

My eyes begin to water, I feel so sad. "How can I, Luce? That woman was with him again today. No matter what he says, he's obviously moved on. He said he'd wait, but he didn't." I cover my face with my hands and begin to sob. *How could you?*

Lucy stands and walks behind me wrapping her arms around my shoulders. "Oh, Viv. What did you expect?…He must have women throwing themselves at him all the time, and you've been pushing him away and told him in no uncertain terms that he means nothing to you… You broke his heart. He's probably just trying to make you jealous. Trying to get you to remember him, that's all."

Neither of us speaks for a moment. I can't talk past the lump in my throat, and I think Lucy has run out of excuses for him betraying me.

"Hey, why don't you come to the salon tomorrow and we'll get Trevor and Maggie to give us the works for our night out on the town, what do say?"

I nod and dry my tears. Maybe a good night out is what I need to drown my sorrows.

After another couple of glasses, I say goodbye and head up to my flat to take a bath and give myself a good pampering. I'm feeling sorry for myself, and I need to keep busy.

Wrapped only in a towel, I walk through to the kitchen to make a coffee. I stumble and yelp when I tread on something sharp. Hopping around the kitchen issuing a string of expletives, I lean against the table to take a look at my foot. There's a shard of glass poking into my skin so I gingerly pull it out and throw it in the sink. *Where the hell did that come from?*

I see more shards glinting on the floor tiles so I grab the dustpan and brush and sweep them up, then I notice some more tiny shards on the counter top by the sink. I look up at the window but it's still intact.

When I open the bin to throw the pieces inside, I see a broken wine glass lying on the top. *I don't remember doing that?* I remember putting one on the draining board yesterday, but for the life of me, I can't remember knocking it over.

The draining board is directly underneath the kitchen window so I lean over and check the lock. It's loose, and the window opens with ease! The metal fire escape is directly outside the window. *That's how she's been getting in.*

I grab my toolbox from the cupboard in the hall and I hammer some nails into the frame to secure it. That night I'd come home and felt cold, even though the heating had been on, she must have just left by the window. I shudder. How many more times has she come and gone? *Fuck you, Monica!*

Before I go to bed, I check my new phone for any

messages from Vinnie but there are none, and I've no more messages from Monica on my old phone either. I'm glad, but I have to admit I had been expecting something from her, considering I've seen Max twice in the last twenty-four hours.

~

I'm woken from a dreamless sleep by a loud bang from overhead. My eyes pop open and I sit up in a rush, checking all around me. I glance at the clock to see that it's only 03:16am. My nerves are frazzled and my eyes widen, trying to adjust to the darkness. But then I hear distant voices shouting at each other from the flat above. I stop breathing to listen, but their words are indecipherable. *Great! Noisy neighbours. Just what I need.*

Shoving my head under my pillow, I go back to sleep.

HORNET'S NEST

I get up at nine and force myself to put on my running gear. It's been a while but I really need to get fit again, I've been lounging around too much lately, and I don't feel any better for it. I take a bottle of water, some cash, and my new phone, then I head off to the park.

I can't make my usual full circuit of the park, it's too exhausting and my muscles are screaming out for me to stop. I'd drunk all the water after only ten minutes, so I slowly wander my way toward Java Mama's for a drink and a sit down.

Java's is busy and noisy with shoppers taking coffee with their friends. After I've spoken to Estelle and placed my order, I take the last table right next to the door. I check my phone for the millionth time, but Vinnie still hasn't contacted me yet so I slide it onto the table.

A cool breeze wafts up my back from the open door as a customer walks in behind me. A lady with long brown hair, wearing a green Parka, pulls out the seat opposite me and sits down. I look up and smile, then look away, but I can feel her staring at me so I look up again and do a double take. She looks familiar, but I can't quite… *Monica!* Now I'm staring at her in shock as her cat-like smile creeps across her lips sending an icy shudder up my spine.

"Do you like my new look?" Twirling a lock of brown hair in her fingers, she glances around the room. Everyone is busy chatting and laughing. Her dark brown eyes land back on mine. "I found a bag of these in your apartment. Lucy makes a very nice wig."

I stare at her in stunned silence, she looks so different. And then I notice her brown eyes, she's wearing contacts.

"I think he'll like it, don't you?"

Shit. I suddenly realise the taser and pepper spray that Vinnie gave to me are still at home. I feel utterly exposed and completely defenceless. I look down at my phone but she quickly places her hand over it and slides it to the far side of the table. Blinking up at her, I try to read her expression. "What do you want?" I ask, trying to control the fear in my voice.

She sits back in her chair, smiling at me in that smug way of hers. "Oh, Vivienne. Do we really have to go around the same inane questions? You really are beginning to bore me now."

"But—"

She holds her hand up to silence me. "Don't speak. You have nothing to say that could hold the slightest interest for me." She leans forward and clasps her hands together on the table in front of her. Her dead brown eyes glare at me intently. "I've been very patient with you, Vivienne. But I'm growing tired of your pathetic lies and silly games," she says, in a low, threatening voice. "I know you went to see Max yesterday. Even after I'd warned you of the consequences, you still won't do what you're told. So, I'm just going to have to punish you."

"I was working," I blurt "It wasn't my—"

"Don't fuck with me," she spits out. Her eyes glare at me with utter hatred. Almost immediately, she composes herself and smiles her cat-like smile. To anyone watching us, we just look like two friends chatting. My heart races in my chest, my breathing is quick and shallow, and my hands tremble with fear.

"I can hurt you in so many ways, Vivienne," she gloats.

I'm all too aware of her capabilities, but something inside tells me to fight back. "Why are you doing this? You can't honestly think that Max would have anything to do with you now?"

Rage replaces her confident smile. I can see her fighting with herself to contain it. "You don't know him like I do," she hisses. "You don't know what he needs. He loves me. He needs me. And—"

"No. He doesn't," I interrupt, sitting forward to drive my point home. Her eyes widen at my outburst as a snarl twists her lips. "And he doesn't beat himself anymore, did you know that?" I add, smugly. I don't know where my sudden burst of bravery comes from, and I'm still shaking like a leaf, but I vowed to myself yesterday that I would no longer be the victim, especially not for her. "I helped him overcome his misplaced guilt over the death of his parents. That was what you revelled in, wasn't it? His weakness. His pain. You don't love him, Monica. You want to control him. But you can't. Not anymore… He chose me."

She looks at me with hate and contempt boiling in her eyes.

"You're playing a very dangerous game, Vivienne. Are you really sure you understand the rules?" I don't respond, other than to lift my chin a little higher, and to try not to blink first. "Don't fuck with me you stupid bitch. Your friend Lucy may never forgive you." Her smug eyes trail all over my face. "It was a mistake to let you live. I won't make that mistake again."

Estelle suddenly appears and starts jabbering away to me in broken English. Monica smiles and swiftly rises from her seat, walking past me toward the door. I turn to watch her but Estelle is blocking my view and I lose sight of her as more people enter the café. I quickly move and push past Estelle, but as I stand on the pavement outside looking left and right and then across the street, I can't see her anywhere. She's vanished.

"Fuck it."

I retrieve my phone from Java's and I send a quick message to Vinnie, then I apologise to Estelle and make my exit. Dread lurks in the pit of my stomach as my eyes search every doorway and side street as I make my way home. I need to warn Lucy about Monica's change of appearance. I'd given her a photograph of Monica, but now she looks totally different.

I run up to my flat and take a quick shower, then I check the kitchen window again. It's still secure. I feel better knowing she can't get in here anymore. I check my phones once more, but I still have no messages, from anyone.

When I arrive at Lucy's salon, she's bursting with joy as she babbles on about her wedding. The fight she'd had with Dan, obviously long forgotten. She's so happy and carefree that I choose not to burden her with the details of my unexpected meeting with Monica earlier. My stomach churns. I was proud of myself for standing up to her, but now I'm worried that I may have just stirred the hornet's nest.

DID I LOSE YOU?

Trevor and Maggie use their incredible skills to transform Lucy and I for our evening out. My hair is full with bouncing waves and shining like glass. The scar on my head is practically invisible now. Maggie has given me a very sultry evening makeup which really makes my eyes stand out. I look amazing, but I don't feel it.

When we arrive home, I'm glad to see Dan's already there. I'm relieved that Lucy's not on her own. We say goodbye, and I wander up to my flat. As I put my key in the lock I hear feet on the stairs above so I walk back to the landing to look up, so I can introduce myself to the new tenants.

"Hello!" I call out, but no one replies and I can't hear them anymore. "Hello…" Nothing.

I have a fairly lazy afternoon. I've been checking my phones regularly but there are still no messages from Vinnie. I sent him a message to call me, but he hasn't, and I don't know what else to do until he does.

I wrap Luke's birthday present and write his card, then I go and get dressed for tonight. After debating whether to wear the short pink dress or the knee length black dress, I decide on the pink one. It's sexy and short and fits the best. I pair it up with my black heels, which aren't the most comfortable of shoes, but they do look nice.

I grab my coat and bag, then I pick up my keys from the drawer in the hall table. The taser and pepper spray are also in the drawer, but I'm going out in a crowd tonight so I shouldn't need either. Besides, I'm sure the club will only confiscate them at the door.

As I make my way down to Lucy's flat, I can hear them arguing again through the door. *Oh, no. Not again.* I knock loudly and wait. Dan opens the door and gives me that, she's-driving-me-mad look, so I smile and walk through to her bedroom.

Poking my head around the door, I watch her huffing and grumbling to herself as she steps into her dress. "Here, let me give you a hand." I do the zip up, and the little hook and eye at the top and then I sit on her bed. "Everything okay?" She stands in front of the mirror and smooths her long blonde hair then she shoots me a death stare through the mirror. *Enough said!*

"Could you find my navy heels. There in the bottom of the wardrobe," she snaps, applying her lip gloss with a scowl.

I find them and place them by the bed. "Anything else?" I ask, smirking.

"No… Sorry… We've had another row about the sodding wedding," she sighs, rolling her eyes.

"Luce, just forget about it for a while. It's stressing you out too much, and it's supposed to be the most wonderful day of your life Just chuck it in the fuck-it bucket for now. At this rate, you're going to break up with Dan and give yourself an ulcer."

She laughs. "Yeah, you're right."

We find Dan patiently waiting for us on the sofa. He looks up at Lucy with an edge of wariness then he stands up shoving his hands in his pockets. She walks up to him and gives him a kiss on the lips. "I'm sorry," she mumbles.

Dan's face lights up with a big grin. "Yeah, me too."

"Okay, people," I giggle, ushering them out the door. "Let's go before you end up having make-up sex and make me feel like a right gooseberry."

As we make our way downstairs to the waiting cab, I

turn to Lucy. "Hey, have you met the new tenants yet?"

"No. You?"

"No, but I heard them making a racket early this morning. Sounded like they were having a bit of a ding-dong."

Lucy rolls her eyes and looks at the back of Dan's head. "Yeah. I know the feeling," she smirks.

When I walk outside, the first thing I see is my motorbike parked up on the pavement. The Volvo is gone. I stop in my tracks and stare at it as my heart sinks. *He's sent it back… I've lost him.* Max would never let me have the bike back unless he's finally let me go. My heart twists in my chest as I stare at it with tears pricking my eyes.

Lucy suddenly realises why I've stopped walking and pulls at my arm. "Come on, Viv. It doesn't mean what you think," she says, softly.

"Doesn't it?" Why would he send it back if he still wanted me? He hates me riding that thing.

We meet up with Clive and Luke at the bar in the club. Ed has come with one of his previous girlfriends, which is unusual for him. He's rarely seen with the same girl twice.

"Viv, you look amazing," he says, giving me a hug. He asks me about the attack and how I feel since I broke it off with Max. I knew I would have to deal with everyone asking me about that tonight. I haven't seen most of my friends for ages, so I knew I would be the topic of conversation. The good thing about pretending to lose your memory is that when they hit you with a question you don't want to answer, you can tell everyone the same thing. 'I don't remember.' But what I hadn't bargained for was the amount of sympathy my break up with Max has generated. Everyone seems genuinely concerned for me, which actually makes it harder.

Luke has the good grace not to bombard me with a ton of questions when he gives me a kiss on the cheek and hands me a glass of Champagne.

"Thanks, everyone. First of all, thanks for coming tonight, it means a lot to me that you're all here to celebrate my birthday. But I'd also like to make an announcement." Luke pulls Clive into his side and wraps his arm around his shoulders. "This beautiful man has agreed to marry me!" Clive and Luke beam with pride as we cheer and whistle our approval at their happy news.

After a few drinks at the bar, Lucy and I take a seat at one of the tall tables, both of us are suffering from aching feet already. We haven't even had a dance yet. Dan disappears to the bar to get us some more wine so I take the opportunity to have a quick chat with Lucy. She still looks a bit pissed off with Dan.

"I heard you arguing again tonight. Have you not managed to sort out the problem with Dan's brother yet?"

She scowls at me. "No. And you know what Dan's like, he just tries to please everybody else, but it pisses me off that Josh can't see how important this is to Dan and I."

"I know, but it's not really Dan's fault, is it?"

She shoots me a withering glare. "Well, it's not mine either." I decide to drop the conversation. Lucy's definitely got a bee in her bonnet and when she's like that, it's always best to keep out of her way.

I open my bag and check my phone. Still no reply from Vinnie. *Where the hell is he?*

Dan comes back with the wine then Lucy drags me off to the dance floor. We join the others and carve a little space on the packed floor. My feet hurt, but I decide to let my hair down and enjoy myself regardless. As we grind and twerk, I see Sandra from the office standing at our table talking to Dan.

"Hey, Lucy. Sandra's here." She looks over at her and then huffs like a jealous girlfriend when she sees Sandra giggling with Dan. "Don't go getting your knickers in a bunch, lady," I chide, laughing. "She's a lesbian. She's got a girlfriend."

Her eyebrows shoot up. "Really? I didn't know she was

gay."

"No, me neither. I'm surprised to see her here, she rarely bothers to come out when we ask her."

"Yeah, she's very quiet, isn't she."

We stare over at Sandra who's wearing a very nice fitted dress with killer heels, and her hair and makeup is lovely. I don't think I've ever seen her look so good. At work she's normally dressed in plain, ill-fitting clothes, with her hair tied back and not much makeup. Tonight though, she's a babe.

Clive makes me yelp when he pinches my bum and spins me around on the dance floor.

"Did you know Sandra was here?" I yell, above the music.

"Yeah, she looks great," he nods, twirling me under his arm. "Did you know Max was here?"

I stop twirling and bump into Clive's chest. "Where?" I ask automatically. *Shit!*

Clive's eyes widen. "I knew it," he grins. I quickly look away, blushing. "You remember him now, don't you? I knew it. I could see it in your face." He looks a bit surprised at my reaction. "What's the problem?"

I look him right in the eyes. "It's complicated, Clive. Please don't say anything, to anyone. I mean it, Clive. Not anyone."

He manages a small frown with his Botox'd brow. "Sure, sweetie," he shrugs.

I know he doesn't understand, and I know he's going to tell someone, I just hope it's only Luke that he blabs to. I know Luke can keep a secret.

I leave Clive on the dance floor and I walk over to our table, looking around the club as nonchalantly as possible, but I don't see Max anywhere. I scoot up onto the high stool to rest my feet and pour myself a glass of wine. Lucy and Dan are now standing over by the bar. I can tell by their body language that they're still arguing so I turn away to leave them to it.

Sandra wanders past with her head down. "Hey, Sandra! Come and have a glass of wine," I say, leaning out to catch her arm. She was just going to walk straight past me. She nervously looks up and then sidles over to the other stool. "I didn't know you were coming? Who are you with?" I ask, pouring her a glass of wine.

"Oh, no one. I'm on my own," she mumbles shyly.

I want to ask her about her new girlfriend, but we don't really know each other that well. Maybe I shouldn't pry? "Cheers." I clink glasses with her and take a sip. "So, tell me about yourself, Sandra. I mean, I've known you for a while now, but we haven't really spoken much have we?" I stare at her, expecting her to rattle off her life story, but she just smiles nervously and takes a drink. *Jeez, it's like pulling teeth.* "Where do you live?" I ask, trying to get the ball rolling.

"Erm, actually, I just moved into your building," she mumbles.

My eyebrows ping up. "What, you mean George's flat? The one above me?" She nods. "You're kidding me? Why didn't you say so? I didn't realise we were neighbours?" I laugh. She just shrugs and blushes shyly. "So, did you move in with your girlfriend, or did she move in with you?"

She looks surprised that I know she has a girlfriend. Her body tenses up, and she blinks a lot before answering. "Erm, well, I moved in with her, but I'm not sure how long I'll be there."

I remember hearing a row in the early hours, and I also remember her having a heated discussion on the phone the other day. Obviously their relationship isn't running as smoothly as it could. I feel sorry for her.

"Well, if you ever need to borrow a cup of sugar, just give me a knock."

Lucy wanders back to our table. "Hi, Sandra," she says, before launching into a weary dialogue about her and Dan's argument. I look over at Dan who looks like he's doing the same thing with Ed at the bar. I hate seeing these two fighting, they've always had such a loving relationship. It's all because of this damn wedding.

Sandra looks up at me apologetically as she slides off her stool and prepares to make a getaway from Lucy's rant. "It's too late for me, Sandra. Save yourself!" I smirk. She smiles and sidles off. Lucy doesn't notice and doesn't miss a beat as she whinges on about Dan, so I fill our glasses and prepare myself for an hour's worth of relationship woes.

As Lucy explains all the painstaking efforts she's put into creating the wedding of her dreams that Dan apparently doesn't seem to appreciate, my mind wanders a bit, and I find myself looking around the room for Max. Clive said he was here, but I haven't spotted him anywhere. Trust me, I've looked.

Suddenly, I see him, dead ahead. He's on the far side of the club in the V.I.P Section, and he's sitting with that woman. *Give me a break!* That's three times I've seen them together. His arm is draped behind her on the top of the sofa, and he looks drunk as a sack. *Oh, Max. What are you doing?*

In spite of his drunkenness, he looks mouth-wateringly gorgeous, as ever. His unruly hair framing his ridiculously handsome face makes me sigh. He hasn't shaved, and the stubble just adds to his sexiness. His stunning girlfriend is sitting close beside him, chatting with another woman. I can't take my eyes off him. My butterflies return and I've stopped hearing Lucy's voice altogether.

His girlfriend places her hand on his knee and whispers something into his ear, this makes him turn his head and his eyes land on mine. I stiffen as our eyes meet, but I can't look away. He's clearly drunk, but he's obviously seen me as he sits forward in his seat and frowns right at me. I quickly look away and slide off my stool. "Sorry, Luce. I need to go to the loo. I'll be back in a minute." She just shrugs and pours herself another glass.

I walk to the ladies and open the door. Three girls are chatting at the basins, fixing their hair and makeup so I walk into a cubicle and lock the door. Pulling the toilet lid down, I take a seat and silently cry. He's been with that woman every time I've seen him since France, and it hurts so much. *You said you'd wait.*

The giggling women at the basins gasp as the main door bangs open against the tiled wall. "Oi. You can't come in here! This is the ladies toilets," one of them yells.

"Oh, I don't know? Hello handsome, are you looking for me?" one of them giggles.

"Vivienne!"

Max?

"Vivienne, I want to talk to you," he slurs. "Why won't you talk to me?"

I jump as he bangs loudly on my door. "Go away!" I yell, sniffling. I grab some tissue off the roll and dry my tears.

"Did I lose you, baby? Did I really lose you?" he slurs, in a soft, raspy voice.

My heart clenches and fresh tears burn in my eyes. *If you'd just waited…like you said you would.*

"Baby?"

"Max, just go away and leave me alone."

I see his hand holding the top of the door then I hear him pushing against it. The lock pings off and he falls in, almost right on top of me. I hear the girls gasping and giggling to themselves outside.

I push him back and stand up, backing myself up against the wall. He squeezes past the door, closes it, then places both hands on the wall either side of my head. Leaning into me he breathes over my face, the strong smell of alcohol hits me as he stares down at me with semi-focused eyes. He leans in and tries to kiss me so I turn my head and try to push him away. "What do think you're doing?" I snap.

"I love you, Vivienne. I need you. You're driving me crazy…crazy-good," he smiles. His smile disintegrates and a frown creases his brow as his sad eyes search mine. "Why are you trying to break my heart?" he slurs, in a broken voice.

I look away. "That was never my intention," I mumble, choking on the lump in my throat.

He gently pulls my face around, searching my eyes. "But you did," he whispers, leaning closer, pressing his forehead into mine. My heart leaps in my chest. I've missed him so much. I want to wrap my arms around his neck and hold him. But instead, I close my eyes and take a deep breath. His scent invades my nose, powerful, familiar, and oh, so intoxicating.

"Why are you lying to me?... Why are you lying to yourself?" His voice becomes louder. He pulls back and staggers on his feet. Removing his hands from the wall he holds my face in his palms, lifting my gaze to his, then he searches my eyes for the longest time. I feel myself being drawn into the bluest, saddest eyes I've ever seen. The force of his will, an undeniable attraction, drawing me toward him like a magnet. "You love me, I can see it. I can feel it. I know you, Vivienne." His eyes do their worst and draw me in until I'm almost lost inside them. I almost rise up onto my toes and throw my arms around his neck.

"Max! Max, are you in here?" The soft voice of his girlfriend breaks the spell, and I pull back and look away. "Max!... John, I think he's in there."

I pull Max's hands from my face and push him back so I can get the door open. I'm shaking like a leaf and any moment I'm going to burst into tears.

John drags Max out by the arm then he gives me an awkward smile before dragging him away. "Wait! I need to talk to her," Max mumbles as John removes him from the room.

I come face to face with his girlfriend. She smiles at me apologetically. "Are you okay?" she asks softly. I'm surprised she even cares. I ignore her and move to the mirror to sort myself out.

She's still standing there like she's waiting for me to speak. I quickly glance up at her through the mirror. "I'm sorry, I didn't encourage him."

She looks at me in confusion then she moves closer and places her hand on my shoulder. My eyes fly up to hers through the mirror. "He hasn't stopped talking about you," she smiles.

And that doesn't bother you? I frown and stare at her warily.

"He's waiting for you to remember him, but I'm afraid he's the least patient person I know!" she laughs.

Are you for real? I turn sharply to face her. "But he didn't wait, did he?" I snap. "He found you!"

Her eyes widen, her mouth opens, and then she stifles a smile. "Vivienne, I'm not his girlfriend. My mother is Max's p.a. and he's just looking after me while my fiancé is in New York. Max wouldn't do that to you, he loves you." She smiles, rubbing my shoulder.

…*Oh* I stare at her with wide eyes and an open mouth.

"I'd better go, John will be waiting for me. Nice to meet you, Vivienne. I hope your memories come back quickly. Max needs you." She smiles again and walks out.

I turn back to the mirror, my expression is priceless. Tears fill my eyes, and I feel such a sense of relief.

Suddenly, the door opens again and Dan sheepishly pokes his head in. "Is Lucy in here?" he asks with a worried frown.

"No. I haven't seen her." I smooth my dress and follow him out. "Why? What's happened now? Have you two had another fight?"

He rolls his eyes and sighs deeply. "We did. She told me the wedding's off. One minute she was talking to Sandra, the next minute she'd disappeared."

"What? Oh, don't listen to her, Dan. She's just stressed out by the whole thing and she's taking it out on you. She doesn't mean it," I say, squeezing his arm. "She's probably just gone to get some fresh air. Have you checked outside on the terrace?"

"Yeah, but I'll have another look." Dan marches off looking for Lucy. I wander around the club but I can't see her anywhere. As I walk back to our table, I see Sandra walking quickly to the exit with her coat over her arm.

"Hey, Sandra? Have you seen Lucy?" Again, I have to reach out to stop her or she would have walked right past me. I'm beginning to wonder if she's deaf. "Sandra?… Have you seen Lucy?" I repeat. Her cheeks blush, and her eyes dart all over the place.

"Erm….yes. She looked upset, she said something about going to her mum and dad's for the night."

"Oh. Okay, thanks."

"Bye, then." Sandra turns to leave.

"Hey, do you want a ride home with us?" I ask.

"Oh! No… I'm er, I've got a lift home, but thanks."

"Okay, I'll see you at work." She smiles nervously and leaves quickly. *She's a weird one.*

When I find Dan, I tell him what Sandra had said, and he finally relaxes.

"Don't worry, Dan. Her mum will talk some sense into her." He looks pensive, but now he knows where she is, he's not so stressed out. He sits down to finish his drink.

"I wish I'd never proposed," he huffs. "All we've done is argue." I suddenly realise their rows only really started when I'd burdened Lucy with all my problems with Monica. The threats Monica had made toward Lucy must have worried her immensely.

That's why she's been so tetchy. "Dan, please don't worry. Just give her some time to cool down, I'm sure she'll be fine."

He nods and smiles and pours another glass of wine for us both. I check my phone. Still nothing! I'm starting to wonder if Vinnie's okay. If I haven't heard from him by tomorrow morning, I'll call him again.

WHERE IS SHE?

An unusual ringing sound alerts my brain and wakes me up. The sun is streaming into my bedroom through the curtains and hurts my eyes when I try to open them. I realise the annoying sound is the ringtone of my new phone. *Vinnie!*

"Alright, Miss? I didn't wake you did I?"

"No! No, not at all," I say, rubbing my eyes and trying not to sound half asleep.

"I'm still in Portsmouth, and you were right, Miss. The body Max identified is a dead ringer even down to the c-section scar, and the small rose tattoo on her ankle, but it's not her."

"Monica doesn't have a rose tattoo, she's got a bumble bee. Max must have known that, surely?" I blurt, sitting up in bed.

"Yeah I know, but apparently they didn't show him the tattoo when he identified the body. Everything else seemed to fit. And I must admit, even though her face was pretty mangled from the gun shots, she does look like Monica."

"So, who was the poor woman?"

"Her name was Elena Rihanov. She was a lap dancer at a local club run by the Romanian mafia. She was an illegal immigrant, that's why no one reported her missing. One of her friends at the club said that Steve had come in splashing the cash, he was looking for false identities, fake passports, that sort of thing, and this girl went off with Steve one night and didn't come back. In hindsight, I reckon Monica must have had it all planned. To kill the girl to make it look like she was dead, and then to shoot Steve to tie up a loose end. Then she must have taken Steve's weapon to come gunning for you. And I'm glad she did use Steve's gun, because if it had been Max's gun… you'd be dead."

Fucking hell. My fuzzy brain tries to absorb the enormity of what he's saying. "Did you get my message about her turning up yesterday?"

"Yeah, but the signal's shit down here. I'm in the black hole of Calcutta, I only got it an hour ago," he grumbles. "John told me he saw you last night at the Chymeira club. He said you had a bit of a problem with grumpy," he chuckles.

I roll my eyes. "Yeah, you could say that! So what happens now?"

"I'll be coming home soon, I just need to talk to the Romanians to try and find out what identity Monica's using now. Go to my house and stay there until I get back. I'll text you the address and where to find the key. And Vivienne, don't trust anyone. Not even John, okay?"

"But what about Lucy? I can't leave her unprotected."

"Take her with you. I'll be back as quick as I can."

"Yeah, okay. And Vinnie…thanks."

"No worries, Miss."

I call Lucy and leave a message for her to call me straight away, then I take a quick shower and start to pack a bag.

Dan calls, he sounds worried. "Viv! Have you heard from Lucy?"

I glance at my watch, it's almost lunchtime. "No, but she'll be at work now won't she?"

"I've just been there, she hasn't shown up for work today, and her mum and dad haven't seen her. She didn't go there last night."

"Have you spoken to Jamie? Maybe she went there

instead?"

"I'll give him a call… If she gets in touch with you can you please get her to call me?"

"Yes, of course I will." I suddenly remember Lucy telling me about the empty flat above the salon. If she's trying to make Dan squirm, that would be an ideal place to sneak off to. I grab my phone and race downstairs to her flat to find the keys.

When I reach the salon, I go around to the back. The flat smells musty and has nothing in it except boxes of hair products and towels. I check in all the rooms, but she's not here.

Dan calls me as I'm leaving. "Viv. Jamie hasn't seen or heard from her either, and I'm starting to panic. Where the hell has she gone?"

"Look, don't worry, we'll find her. Go and check the gym, I'll check Java's, and I'll meet you back at mine, okay?"

"Yeah, okay," he sighs. "But if we don't find her I'm going to the police. She could have got into a dodgy cab last night and—"

"Dan, try not to worry, we'll find her." My stomach churns. This isn't like Lucy at all. She'd rather have a stand-up fight than run away from anything.

Monica's face pops into my mind. Remembering the look in her eyes when she said she was going to punish me, stirs my fear. *Not Lucy. Please God, not Lucy.*

I race to Java Mama's and burst through the door. Estelle greets me as usual, but I haven't got time for chit-chat. "Estelle, have you seen Lucy?" I'm out of breath from running so I lean on the back of a chair to catch my breath.

"No, not today. You wanna—"

"No. Sorry Estelle, I'm in a rush. See you later." I make a quick exit and head home. All the while my mind is racing with the possibility that Monica has somehow managed to abduct her. She said she could hurt me in many ways, this would definitely count.

I arrive home and check Lucy's flat, but there's still no sign of her, and I can see that she hasn't taken any of her stuff. The navy shoes and dress she had on last night are not here either. *Where the fuck are you?*

Dan calls as I walk back up to my flat. "Anything?" he blurts.

"No, I'm afraid not," I sigh, pacing my living room. I'm starting to feel really anxious. I was hoping Lucy was just trying to make Dan squirm, but now I'm convinced something has happened to her. It's just not like her to go missing.

"I'm going to the police. I'm going to report her missing." Dan's distressed voice breaks my heart.

"Okay, but she's only been gone twelve hours, they probably won't even do anything yet." I don't know if that's true, but I'm sure I heard it somewhere.

"I don't care, I'm going there now. Call me if you hear anything."

"I will."

I know I'm going to have to tell Dan everything. If I'd just told everyone at the beginning, maybe we could have protected each other. Maybe then, Monica wouldn't be in such a powerful position. If she's taken Lucy to punish me and anything happens to her, it'll be all my fault. *Jesus! What have I done?*

I check my phone again, and I see the text message from Vinnie with his address, but I can't think of going anywhere until I know where Lucy is. I quickly dial Sandra, in case she can remember anything else from last night. The call goes straight to answer-phone.

Shit… "Hi, Sandra, it's me, Viv. Look, can you give me a call when you get this message, thanks, bye." A loud thud draws my attention to the ceiling. *She's in.*

I run up the stairs to Sandra's flat and knock on the door. There's no answer so I knock a little louder. She still doesn't answer. *Come on. I know you're in there.* Just as I'm about to knock again, I hear a noise from behind the door. "Sandra? Sandra, it's me. Can I talk to you for a minute?" After a long pause, I'm just about to knock again when I hear the lock turning. The door only opens a couple of inches and I can see the chain has been engaged. The flat looks dark behind her as Sandra looks up at me through the gap. She's wearing a short nightie, her hair is all over the place, and her face and chest are covered in sweat. *Oh, my God! I've interrupted them having sex.* I blush and fidget on my feet. "I'm sorry to disturb you, Sandra, but have you seen or heard from Lucy? She's gone missing and no one's heard from her since last night. In fact, you were the last person to see her," I ask, moving closer.

"No. I'm sorry I haven't," she smiles at me, but it looks forced. I get the distinct impression that she wishes I'd just hurry up and leave. I can't blame her. I'm sure I'd be annoyed if someone interrupted me during sex.

"What about your girlfriend, maybe she's seen her?"

"No," she shrugs. "She doesn't even know Lucy."

"Okay, well if you do see her, can you ask her to call me?"

"Yes, of course." Sandra begins to close the door even before I've turned to leave.

That girl certainly is a dark horse.

I go back to my flat and wait for Dan. I can't sit still so I send Lucy another text and then I pace my rug wracking my brain for any ideas on where she could have gone. If Monica has taken her, where would I start looking for her? She could be anywhere?

After about an hour, Dan arrives. He's distraught that the police didn't seem to be very interested. I sit him down and make him a coffee, he needs to know what's been going on. My stomach churns with nerves, but I have to tell him. I take Dan's hand and give it a squeeze.

"Dan, I need to tell you something."

His worried eyes travel up to mine. "She hasn't left me has she?" His voice is small and trembling. My heart breaks for him, he looks so hurt and despondent.

I shake my head and grip his hand a little tighter. "No, sweetie, no. She wouldn't do that. She loves you."

His sad eyes travel down to our hands. "Then where is she?"

I wish I knew. "Look, Dan. I need to tell you something. It's not about Lucy, but it could have something to do with her disappearance." Tears start to fill my eyes, I try to control them but it's no use, Dan's sad eyes have done me in. He stares at me with a questioning frown waiting for me to continue. I clear my tightening throat and take a deep breath. "Dan, the night I was attacked…it was Monica." He blinks rapidly with a deepening frown and goes to speak, but I raise my hand to stop him. I need to get this all out before I crumble with guilt and regret that I hadn't told anyone sooner.

"Monica faked her death and came to the penthouse that night to kill me. She's a crazy, fucked-up, dangerous woman, and she's still in love with Max. She threatened to kill him if I didn't leave him. That's why I pretended to lose my memory, I was trying to protect him."

Dan stares at me incredulously then he looks away, his brow creasing as he tries to understand. "I knew something was going on, but..." He shakes his head at the weight of information. Suddenly his searching eyes fly up to mine, then they dart all over the place. I can tell by his expression that he's fitting the pieces together in his mind. "But… Max is still in love with you… And last night you two were together… It's Monica, isn't it? She's taken my Lucy hasn't she?" It's not really a question. He stands quickly and paces the rug dragging his hands through his hair. "For fuck's sake, Viv! You should have warned me!" He stops and glares at me with anger and disbelief. "You should have fucking told me at the very start!… Did Lucy know?" I nod sheepishly. His eyes widen in disbelief. "Shit! And neither of you thought to go to the police? What is wrong with you two?" he yells in exasperation.

"She could be…She could be…" He can't say it, the words catch in his throat as he collapses down onto the sofa, tears of anger and sadness rolling down his cheeks.

"I'm so sorry, Dan. Lucy wanted me to go to the police but I was so scared that Monica would hurt Max, I—"

He quickly stands and pushes past me, marching toward the door.

"Where are you going?"

"I'm doing what you both should have done in the first place. I'm going to the police!" he yells, not looking back.

I quickly stand. "I'll come with you."

He stops abruptly and turns to face me. His angry eyes burn holes into me. "Don't bother! You've done enough!" Then he leaves, slamming the door behind him.

He's right. I've caused all this. It's all my fault. *What the fuck am I going to do?* Collapsing into the sofa, I sit with my head in my hands and cry. *Oh, Lucy. I'm so sorry.*

After a few moments of feeling sorry for myself, I decide to pull myself together and follow Dan to the police station. They need to know what I know. Dan doesn't even have a picture of Monica.

Feeling sick, I walk into the kitchen for a glass of water. Images of Lucy being subjected to the same things that Monica did to me suddenly invade my mind. My belly knots. Poor Lucy's been dragged into this mess because I was stupid enough to think I could handle it on my own. How did I ever think I could handle a psychotic murderer?

I feel sick to my stomach. Leaning my hands on the edge of the sink I lean over it as a wave of nausea makes me retch. As I drink some water from the tap, my eyes land on a small glinting object on the draining board. I stare at the tiny shard of glass for ages. *The window!*

My head whips up, and I stare out the window at the metal fire escape outside. It runs the vertical length of my building and after I'd found that broken glass the other day I was convinced that Monica was using the fire escape and my kitchen window to get into my flat.

My eyes travel to the ceiling. I always wondered how Monica knew when I wasn't home. As far as I know she only ever came here when I was out. She seemed to know about all my movements and visitors too! She knew we'd gone to France. She's been listening. She's been listening to every conversation.

My wide eyes eagerly scan every inch of my kitchen. I jump up onto the counter and search the tops of my cupboards, but I can't find what I'm looking for. I keep searching, and then suddenly, it's glaringly obvious. The extractor fan in the kitchen wall above the boiler, has dust on most of it, but there are clean parts where the dust has been disturbed. I reach up to get a closer look. I can't see anything at this angle so I jump down and grab my toolbox.

Once I've removed the screws, I pull the face off the fan and there it is! A small black lead with a tiny microphone on the end. The lead disappears out through the air duct in the wall. I jump down and quickly pull out the nails I'd hammered into the window frame and then I throw it open. I jump up onto the sink top and lean out to find the wires. They go upward to the flat above. *You clever bitch!*

Monica's recruited Sandra to spy on me. I thought it was odd that Sandra hadn't told me she was living upstairs. She hadn't told anyone. Why would she do that unless she was hiding something? She seemed edgy and nervous last night too. It all makes sense. Monica rents the flat upstairs and puts Sandra in it to watch my movements and report my every word.

Fuck! My brain cogs whir ferociously, kicking up a notch to a higher gear when I suddenly realise that Sandra must be communicating with her somehow. *I need to get that number.*

I quickly head to my bedroom, close the door, and call Vinnie, but it goes straight to answer-phone. I leave a message for him to call me back, and then I search for Mike's number in my contacts. My finger hovers hesitantly over his number. *Can I trust you?*

Vinnie told me not to trust anyone. But I know Mike, he could never be part of this. And he's the only one I know who might have the skills to be able to help me right now. All Monica's calls to me were made from a private number. If Mike's as good as I think he is, he should be able to find out what that number is.

"Hello?"

"Mike… It's me," I whisper. "I need your help."

"Viv? Why are you whispering, is everything okay?"

"Erm, I can't talk now, but… Can you trace a private number for me?"

"Er, yes… But I'd need the phone the call was made to, and the trace has to be done straight after the call was made… Why?"

Damn!

"Okay, if I give you a number can you find out which numbers it's been calling or receiving regularly?"

"You know hacking into someone's private records is illegal, don't you," he says, sarcastically.

"But is it something you can do?" I ask impatiently. There's a short uneasy pause. I anxiously chew my thumbnail waiting for him to respond.

"Yes, of course. But—"

"And can you trace the location of the phone?"

"Viv… You know I can but what's going on? Why do you need to trace this number?"

I let out a sigh of relief. "Lucy's gone missing. I think Max's ex-girlfriend has kidnapped her."

"But… I thought she'd died?"

"It's a long story. Look, can you do it or not," I ask impatiently. My whole body is now buzzing with adrenaline.

"Yeah… I'm driving, but I'm nearly home. Text me the number and I'll get back to you as soon as I can."

"Okay, thanks." I quickly end the call and text him Sandra's number.

I can't sit still. I haven't heard from Vinnie and I don't want to involve Max, not yet. If Mike can find out Monica's location then I can tell the police, and they can track her down and arrest the fucking bitch. I can only hope that she hasn't harmed Lucy yet. I hope and pray she's only taken her to punish me and hasn't done anything to her out of spite. A thought suddenly crosses my mind. Why hasn't Monica contacted me to gloat? My stomach knots and the nausea returns.

Thirty minutes tick by achingly slowly. I'm going nuts just pacing the room waiting for Vinnie or Mike to call me back. *Where is everybody?*

I can't sit here doing nothing so I make the decision to go up to Sandra's flat and make her tell me where Monica is. I put the taser Vinnie gave me in my back pocket, the pepper spray in my jacket pocket, and I pick up my trusty old baseball bat. I don't want to have to use any of them on her, but if Sandra doesn't tell me where she is, I'll have something to threaten her with.

I stand outside Sandra's door hiding the baseball bat behind my back then I knock loudly.

"Sandra? It's me, Viv," I say, in a friendly voice. No response. I knock again, still nothing, so I put my ear to the door. I can't hear anything. *Maybe she's gone out?*

I dial Sandra's number and press my ear against the door. I can hear it ringing from inside. "Sandra! Open up!" Still no response. *Shit!*

Then I get an idea. I know Lucy used to have a set of George's keys. His daughter wanted one of us to keep them in case of emergency, so I quickly run down to her flat to try and find them. I look everywhere. Lucy isn't the tidiest of people. Every drawer is crammed with crap but I finally find them and run back upstairs.

I listen at the door before I try the keys, but I still can't hear anything so I unlock the door. I'm surprised to see the chain is on. Someone must be inside.

"Sandra?" I call out, but she doesn't answer me. "Sandra,

it's Viv. I need to speak to you." My heart pounds in my chest and adrenaline courses through my veins. The flat is pitch black and there's a weird chemical smell in the air. *Acid? Oh no.*

I wedge the baseball bat into the gap and force the door chain. It takes all my strength to break it and the door bursts open, banging back against the wall. The light from behind me doesn't travel far into the flat, and all I can see is a couple of feet in front of me. I try the light switch just inside the door but it doesn't work so I take my phone out with shaking hands to find the torch setting.

Shit! You idiot. The battery is almost dead. I shine the torch around the small hallway, my eyes are wide and straining to see in the dark beyond the dim torch light. My cautious brain is telling me to leave, to go and get help, but I feel compelled to stay. Something is very wrong here, and I need to find out what it is.

The layout should be the same as my flat so I head forward toward the living room on shaking legs. It's so dark. The windows must be boarded up because there's not a hint of light coming from anywhere. My ears strain to listen for any sound, but all I can hear is my own nervous, shallow breathing.

I hold the torch in one hand and raise my baseball bat in the other. If anything touches me, I'm going to swing at it. And probably die from fright.

Just as I enter the living room, the battery warning beeps twice and then the torchlight suddenly goes off, plunging me into darkness. *No! No, no, no. Not now!* My phone dies.

I put my arms out as far as I can and I make my way to what should be the window, I need to get some light in here. My leg bangs into something hard and immovable, making me stumble forward. Reaching out to feel the object, it feels like a metal cage of some kind. *What the fuck is that?*

I nervously feel my way past it and I head to the window to try and find some light. My fingers find the windowsill and slide up what feels like a hard, plastic sheet. I try to pierce it with my fingers, but it's too tough. I dig at it with my nails and manage to tear a small hole, stretching it as much as I can, but it doesn't want to give. A small shaft of light from outside beams in through the tiny hole. As my eyes adjust, I look back at the living room then I gasp in horror as my incredulous eyes land on the object I'd bumped into. It's a black metal dog cage bolted to the wooden floor. Lucy's unconscious body lies inside it.

"Lucy! Oh, my God, Lucy!" I run to her, drop my bat on the floor, and pull at the heavy padlocked chain wrapped around the cage door. I try to put my hand through the bars, but they're too narrow. "Lucy! Can you hear me?"

I can't see if she's breathing or not. Her face is partially covered with her hair. All I can see is a cut on her lip and blood on her hands, legs, and bare feet. She's wearing the dress she had on last night, but it's torn and bloodied. She doesn't move. I'm terrified that I'm too late.

"Lucy!… Lucy!…" I yell at her with tears flowing down my cheeks, but she doesn't move. She doesn't answer me. "I'm going to get help!"

A sudden movement in my peripheral vision makes me jump. I quickly stand up when I hear a soft, sniffling, moaning sound on my left. All my senses are on full alert. My heart is beating wildly in my chest, and I'm absolutely terrified.

I can't see anything, but I hear the sound again. As my eyes adjust to the dim light, I realise it's coming from a small bundle in the corner of the room. "Sandra? …Is that you?" I whisper, shakily. She moans again. I rush over and crouch down in front of her. She's curled up in a tight ball shivering with fear, and trying to back away from me. "Oh, my God!" I take my jacket off and lay it over her scantily clad body, she's clearly in shock. "It's okay, I'm not going to hurt you." She lifts her battered and bruised face to look up at me, she looks petrified, and she's shaking like a leaf. "Where's the key for the cage?"

She shakes her head, her bottom lip quivering. "She has it," she says, in a muffled, croaky voice.

"Who, Monica?"

She nods quickly, she looks so frightened. "I'm so sorry, Vivienne. I'm so sorry," she mumbles, sniffling. It's difficult to make out her words. "She said she'd kill my mum and dad..." Sandra bows her head and sobs uncontrollably into my jacket.

"I know…" My heart goes out to her. I know exactly how frightening and persuasive Monica can be. "Where is she, Sandra?" I ask, rubbing her shoulder. She raises her head, her left eye is almost swollen shut, and she has some deep cuts on her cheeks. As she looks up at me, her right eye widens and her face contorts into a mask of fear. She's looking past me, above my head. I quickly turn around as Monica swings my baseball bat and cracks me on the side of the head with it. A searing pain shoots through my skull, and all I can hear is the loud crack of breaking bone and Sandra's screams as I fall to the floor in a crashing heap.

Blackness envelops me like a dark, velvet blanket. The pain ebbs away and I feel like I'm floating. I feel lifeless and cold, and I can taste the blood in my mouth.

I'm being dragged across the floor by my feet, but I can't feel anything. My eyes intermittently focus on the ceiling above, until Monica's deranged, smiling face comes into my blurred vision. She stands above me holding my baseball bat in both hands.

"Oh, how I've longed for this moment!" she sneers, leering down at me with hate filled eyes.

I don't move. I can't move. I just stare up at her, waiting.

Rage emanates from every pore as she screams and raises the bat above her head.

I love you, Max. I close my eyes.

NINE DAYS OF HELL

The soft back and forth of something gently rubbing my hand pulls me from the comfort of my deep sleep. My eyelids are heavy and protest when I try to open them. Drawing in a long, deep breath, I slowly prize them open.

I can't focus straight away, but I'm aware there are several faces staring down at me. The rubbing on my hand has stopped, and the pressure has increased to a firm squeeze, almost crushing my knuckles.

As my focus eventually sharpens, I see Lucy and Dan with tears in their eyes sitting on my left. I close my eyes as a tear slips down my cheek. I'm so happy to see her alive and well. As my focus travels to the end of the bed, I see Vinnie and Jan, Sylvie and William, and John, smiling down at me. No one has spoken. They all look very emotional and choked up.

My eyes finally find the face I've been looking for. Sitting on my right, with my hand clasped between his, his beautiful blue, tear-filled eyes search mine. His brow is creased with worry, his unruly hair is all over the place, he has major stubble, and his handsome face looks utterly exhausted. I need to tell him. He's been here before and I need to put him out of his misery.

"Max…you owe me an apology for that stunt you pulled in the helicopter… but I still love you." My mouth is dry and the words come out soft and croaky.

His teary eyes close. A lonely tear trickles down his cheek

as he pulls my hand up to his lips and kisses my fingers. "Thank God," he smiles, weeping.

Everyone starts to talk at once. Max stands and bends down to kiss me tenderly on the lips. "I thought I'd lost you," he says, in a choked voice. "You don't know how long I've waited to hear you say that."

His familiar scent invades my nose. I breathe it in as I reach up and cup his face in my hand as he brushes the tears from my cheek. Kissing me again he looks up at everybody with a big smile on his handsome face.

Vinnie catches my eye with his cheeky grin and arched brow. He holds a yellow builder's hard hat in his hand and he puts it on the end of my bed. "I bought you a prezzie!" he chuckles. Then his smile dissolves and his eyes glisten. "Don't you ever scare me like that again," he chides, smirking.

"I'm sorry," I murmur. Max hands me a drink of water. I'm parched and I drink all of it. "Where's Sandra, is she okay?"

Max scowls at me for a moment. I know he's probably mad at her for letting herself get involved with Monica in the first place, but it wasn't really her fault. His expression softens as he sits and takes my hand again, rubbing the back of it with his thumb. "She's fine… She actually saved your life." I frown at him. I don't know what happened after Monica had clubbed me with the baseball bat. The last thing I remember was her standing over me, raising the bat above her head, preparing to bring it crashing down on my skull.

"You'd placed your jacket over Sandra, and she found your pepper spray in the pocket so she lunged at Monica before she could lower the bat and she sprayed her with it."

Wow! I never knew Sandra had it in her? "So, did they arrest Monica?" Max eyes me warily. I look up at the others, they all have the same expression. "Well?" I ask nervously.

Max clenches his jaw and his eyes become dark. "She got

away."

Oh no.

"Don't worry, baby. Vinnie gave the police all the details of her new identity, it shouldn't take them long to track her down." The look on his face tells me he's not going to hold his breath any more than I am. I try to push her out of my mind. I don't want to spend the rest of my life being haunted by that crazy woman.

I look over at Lucy. "I'm so sorry, Luce. I should never have put you in danger like that." Her teary eyes gaze down at me as her bottom lip quivers. "If it wasn't for your bravery and Mike's know-how, I probably wouldn't be here," she smiles, sadly.

Mike… I forgot about him. I look over at Max. "What happened, how did you find us?"

"Vinnie called me. He said he'd received an urgent message from you but he couldn't reach you on the phone so I came over to your apartment. When I couldn't find you there, I called Mike." He looks down, sheepishly. "I… I thought you might be with him." I squeeze his hand and smile up at him, shaking my head. He just shrugs it off. "Anyway, Mike told me everything. He said you'd asked him to trace a phone number and that you thought Lucy had been kidnapped by Monica. He'd already traced the phone to your building so I just hammered on every door until I found you." His sad eyes, glistening with tears, search my face. "I thought you were dead." He closes his eyes, while he struggles to contain his emotion.

Sylvie dabs the tears from her eyes. "Vivienne, I want to thank you for protecting my son. You have remarkable courage. I'll always be indebted to you for that."

The whole room falls silent at her words, and a lump jumps into my throat.

"You're a good little actress," William says, smirking at me. "You had me!" he adds, smiling down at me and lightening the atmosphere in the room.

"I'm so sorry, to all of you," I sigh. "I should have—"

"Yes! You should," Max scowls. "And if you think I'm ever going to let you out of my sight in future, you'd better think again," he huffs, his frown deepening. "No more secrets, Vivienne. Ever."

My belly churns and I look away. I have a secret. A secret that I've never told to a living soul, not even Lucy. To say it out loud might make it real, and I couldn't bear it to be real.

I wake to a quiet room. The soft light coming from the bedside table and the dark windows, tell me it must be evening. I look down at my side to see Max sleeping with his head resting on the side of my bed.

"Max." He doesn't wake. I run my fingers through his hair until his sleepy eyes flicker open and find mine.

"Hey, baby. How do you feel?"

I feel like I did that first time I'd been in hospital, after drinking myself into oblivion and falling over in the gent's toilets. My headache is pounding against my skull, and my neck is stiff and sore. But the sight of Max hurts me even more, he's exhausted. "Max, you should go home and rest, you need to sleep," I mumble sleepily.

"I don't want to leave you." He says it like a little boy not wanting to be sent to bed after supper.

I smile and pat the bed. "I've missed you, come and give me a cuddle." I gingerly move over to make some space. He smiles and kicks his shoes off then he gently lowers himself onto the bed beside me.

"You don't know how badly I've wanted to feel you in my arms," he sighs. Very carefully, he wraps me in his arms and kisses me gently on the top of my head. I close my eyes and stroke his hand, then weave our fingers together. "Vivienne…" he whispers, pausing for a moment. "Why didn't you tell me what she did to you? Why did you make me think you didn't love me anymore? Don't you know how painful that was for me?"

I open my eyes and try to look up at him, but my head

hurts too much. "I'm sorry. I wanted to tell you, but I just couldn't take the chance that she'd hurt you. I couldn't bear to lose you."

He sighs deeply and squeezes my hand. "You must have been so scared. I can't even imagine… I've thought that I'd lost you four times in as many weeks. I don't think I could survive any more losses."

Four times? He's exaggerating. An awful thought enters my mind. I pull the sleeve of his shirt back to check his arm for fresh wounds. I'm so relieved to see that there are none.

"Baby, I made you a promise. I haven't broken my promise, but… I have been drunk many times since you told me I meant nothing to you." He pauses to take a deep breath, his arms tightening around me. "I can't tell you how close I came to cutting myself again, especially when I thought you were still in love with Mike. I was so jealous I wanted to go and beat the fuck out of him."

I manage to turn my head without too much pain. "How do you think I felt when I'd sacrificed my happiness only to see you dating again so quickly? I thought that woman you were with was your new girlfriend."

He smiles down at me, with that bone-melting smile. If I wasn't tied to this bloody machine, and feeling so weak and exhausted, I would demand to have sex with him right now. I've missed those eyes, that smile. Just the way he makes me feel. His eyes become serious, as they search mine. "Vivienne, there'll never be anyone else for me…only you." He leans down and kisses me tenderly on the lips. His kiss evokes my butterflies as his words fill my heart with joy. He pulls back and stares down at me with a strange look in his eyes. "I haven't forgotten. And I *will* ask you that question," he looks around the room, "when the time is right," he smirks, then he lowers his eyes and a worried frown enters his brow. "But…if you've changed your mind, you'd better say it right now. I don't think I could—"

I raise my hand and rest my fingers across his lips to silence him. "I haven't changed my mind. If anything, these last few weeks have made me realise how much you mean to me. I need you, Max. I love you so much. Being apart isn't good for either of us."

His gorgeous smile returns as he takes my hand and kisses my palm.

"Does my mum know what happened?" I ask, tracing my fingers along his arm.

"I went to see her, to tell her you were in the hospital. She was high on God knows what. But she came in to see you a few days ago, and she looked like she'd made the effort to arrive sober."

"Really?" I'm surprised, I can't remember the last time I saw my mother sober. "Did she ask you for money?" His expression tells me she did.

"She won't accept my offer of rehab," he huffs. "I told her I'd pay for it, but she still isn't interested."

I'd always hoped Mum would sort her life out one day before the guilt, drugs, and alcohol finally kill her. But she's in too deep, and when my father left her it just got worse and worse.

"When can I come home?" I ask, resting my head back on the pillow.

"That depends. How do you feel?"

"Weak, tired, my head hurts, but other than that I feel okay."

"Doctor Alexander wants to carry out a few more tests. He wants to keep you here for a few more days, and I agree. You've been through so much, Vivienne. You need to rest."

"How long have I been here?"

"Nine days… For me? Nine days of hell."

My eyes ping open. "Nine days?"

"Vivienne, you've been in a coma since we brought you here. They had to resuscitate you in the operating theatre, and it was touch and go for the first forty eight hours."

I can hear the emotion in his voice. I had no idea. "I'm sorry." I squeeze his hand to reassure him, but I'm shocked to hear it.

"Vivienne, I thought I'd lost you. I never want to experience that kind of pain ever again." His voice is tight with emotion. "And if you think that hard hat is only a joke? Think again! You're going to be wearing that hat for the rest of your life."

I smile and close my eyes as he tightens his arms around me.

GOING HOME

"Good morning, beautiful."

I peel my eyes open to see a pair of smiling blue eyes gazing down at me. Max has got a white rose between his teeth and a big grin on his handsome face. I take the rose out of his mouth and smell the petals.

"Thank you. My two favourite things to wake up to." I feel so much better this morning, apart from the dull headache that just won't quit. It's been a week since I woke up from the coma. Ironically all I've wanted to do since I woke up, is to sleep.

Doctor Alexander has carried out a bazillion tests and he is very pleased with my progress. I've had my stitches out, and physio to help build my muscles, but I still feel incredibly weak. He said it would take time to fully recover but if my scan this morning doesn't throw up any nasty surprises, there's a good chance I'll go home today, I can't wait.

Max looks so gorgeous and handsome in his suit, and he smells amazing, he's turning me on. Since I've been feeling better it's been difficult for me not to drag him into bed with me every time he visits, he just makes me feel so horny.

While I was in the coma, Max had brought another bed in so he could stay with me, but when I woke up from the coma I talked him out of staying here. He's so busy at work, catching up with everything he'd postponed while I was sleeping that I wanted him to go home and rest properly. Besides, he turns me on so much that it's just too tempting to have him here. He's been staying with me every night until I fall asleep, and he always comes back early in the morning to visit me before he goes to work.

"Hmm, you look good enough to eat. How about a quickie before you leave?" I smirk, pulling him closer.

His eyebrows shoot up and a silly grin spreads across his lips. "Well, I'm game, but I think we might make my mom blush."

I turn to face Sylvie with wide eyes and crimson cheeks. "Oh! I'm sorry, Sylvie, I didn't realise you were here."

She stifles a laugh. "Don't be sorry, dear," she chuckles. "You're obviously feeling better."

"Yes, much better, and I'm starving." I start to push myself up into a sitting position but I'm struggling, my muscles are still weak so Max helps me and sorts out my pillows.

"You certainly look much better today. I'll get you something to eat." He kisses me on the lips then he puts the rose in a small vase on the bedside table. "They're going to do another scan this morning and then maybe you can come home."

I catch his eye and waggle my eyebrows. "Oh, I hope so."

Max leaves the room and I reach down to take Sylvie's hand. "I noticed William was out of his pyjamas the last time I saw him, does that mean he's left the hospital?"

"Yes, and he's doing very well. It's so nice to have him home again." She looks so relieved and happy.

I squeeze her hand. "These last few weeks must have been awful for you."

"You can say that again," she smirks, then her opaque eyes become serious. "I was so worried about you, Vivienne. We all were. And that awful woman is still out there somewhere. I swear, if I ever get my hands on her I'll—"

"They'll find her, Sylvie. They will. She can't run forever." She nods and offers me a weak smile, but I can tell she's worried that Monica hasn't finished with us yet. My stomach churns. We're none of us truly safe until she's found. But even Monica with her warped perspective must realise she can never come back.

"What about Cole?" I suddenly realise that no one has mentioned him.

She huffs out a sarcastic laugh. "He's not forgiven her for Charlie's death, none of us will ever be able to do that."

"No, you're right, that was unforgivable. I still can't understand why she would do that to her own child." A shiver runs down my spine. "If…when she's found, she's obviously going to need some kind of psychiatric care. There's got to be a reason why she'd do all those terrible things."

Sylvie straightens her back and frowns angrily. "You don't feel sorry for her, do you?"

"Me? No," I huff. "After what she's put me through? The sooner she's behind bars or six feet under, the better."

Max comes back with a tray of scrambled egg, toast, and orange juice. He makes me comfortable and then he hands me my breakfast. "I have to go." He kisses me on the forehead.

"Will you be gone long?" I mumble around my mouthful of food.

"I've got a meeting, but I'll be back in a couple of hours. Lucy's coming in to see you soon. I love you, baby." He kisses me on the top of the head. "Eat it all," he says, on an arched brow. "I want you strong and healthy before you come home," he adds, with a knowing look. I know exactly what he means.

Can't wait.

Sylvie talks to me while I eat my breakfast. It's so nice to have solid food again. She's very excited about William being home, and she tells me all about her plans for organising a celebratory dinner when I get out of the hospital.

When Lucy arrives they have a quick chat like old friends, then Sylvie leaves.

"Ooh, look at you all wide awake!" Lucy giggles.

"Yeah, I feel good." I really do feel good, especially after that yummy breakfast. I push the table away and run my eyes over Lucy's face. Her cuts and bruises have almost gone, and she looks happy too. We haven't had a proper talk yet, every time she's popped in for a visit, I've been asleep.

"Have either of you forgiven me for putting you through all that hell yet?" I ask warily.

She raises an eyebrow. "Viv, don't beat yourself up about it. We're all okay, that's all that matters."

I cringe and reach for her hand. "Dan was furious with me when I told him about Monica."

"Yeah, I know, but he's over it now. He's more upset that you'd stopped him from using Max's yacht," she chuckles.

"I'll make it up to him," I smile, patting her hand. "So, tell me. What actually happened that night at the club? How the hell did you end up in that cage?"

Her expression changes, it can't be easy going over her ordeal again.

"Me and Dan had another fight, and I told him the wedding was off," she says, rolling her eyes. I raise an accusatory eyebrow and shake my head at her. "Anyway, Sandra came over to talk to me, and I was rattling on about Dan, you know me, I like a good whinge," she says, shrugging. "Then she handed me a glass of wine and asked me to go out with her to the terrace so she could have a smoke, so I did… The next thing I knew I was squashed inside a metal cage in a dark room and I couldn't get out. Every time I woke up, Monica kept injecting me with something that made me sleep so I don't remember much at all. But I do remember hearing them arguing. Sandra had tried to open the cage and let me out, but Monica caught her. She really laid into her and gave her such a beating. She broke her wrist and fractured her jaw."

My belly rolls remembering how beaten and bruised Sandra had looked that night. "I haven't seen Sandra, what happened to her? Did Max press charges against her?" I ask nervously. I know Sandra would never have done any of it if she hadn't been threatened, like I was.

"No, he didn't. She stopped Monica from killing you with the bat, and she probably saved all our lives. She attacked Monica with the pepper spray she'd found in your jacket pocket."

Clever girl.

"Sandra knocked her to the ground and managed to take the bat away from her, but she got away. More's the fucking pity," she huffs, folding her arms across her chest.

"Luce, I'm so sorry. You must have been so stressed out with all my problems and lies. It's obvious you were taking it out on Dan, and that's my fault," I cringe. If I'd just said something in the first place, none of this would have happened.

"Well, a near death experience does help to put everything into perspective," she smirks.

"Hey, what about George? Does he know what happened in his flat?"

"Yeah, his daughter brought him over to have a look. Monica had boarded up all the windows and pretty much trashed the place. I think he's going to sell it now, though."

"Hmm, sounds sensible. How bad is it?" I ask, pointing up at my head. I still haven't seen what the damage is yet, but if it's anything like the last time I'd better brace myself.

She tilts her head and runs her eyes over my face. "Well…you look like you've been hit over the head with a baseball bat," she smirks.

"Great. Very helpful. Have you got a mirror?"

"What? And let you crack it with your ugly mug?" she chuckles. She reaches into her bag and hands me the mirror. I'm scared to look, my poor head has been through so much lately, I don't know what to expect. I gingerly lift the mirror.

My cheek has a fading bruise across the cheek bone, and I've got a short red scar on the side of my head just in front of my ear. Other than that I look pretty good apart from a small cut on my forehead and a bloodshot eye. I check my teeth. All present and correct. I roll my head around, my neck isn't stiff anymore either, but my hair is a bloody mess. It's obviously been washed but it looks dull and lifeless, a bit like how I feel.

"Eeuuww, I'm going to need your hairdressing skills to sort this out," I huff, handing the mirror back. "Anyway, how about you? How do you feel, Luce?"

"Yeah, I'm okay," she smiles. "You were very brave coming to save me like that. Or very stupid!" Her eyes glisten, then she looks down at her hands. "You could have got yourself killed."

I reach across and squeeze her hand. "We looked out for each other, that's what friends do."

"I'm so glad you and Max are back together," she says, with tears building in her eyes. "If for no other reason than to even up my table numbers at the wedding," she smirks.

"So, have you finally set the date?"

She smiles a big, beaming, happy smile. "Yes, and Josh is going to be Dan's best man."

"Well, I hope you've given me time to get rid of all the bruises before the wedding photos?" I chuckle.

"Yes, I have. The wedding is set for August twenty-ninth, so you've got three months to heal."

"Good… Did you get the venue you wanted in France?"

"Er…no. We'd messed them about with the date and we couldn't really afford to fly everyone out there anyway. There's about fifty of us. Even with my parents help, it was too expensive so we've booked the church, and I'm going to have a look at a few venues here. I'm sure we'll find something suitable, and if she's well enough, we'll pay for Dan's grandmother to fly over."

What a shame. She'd set her heart on France. "I thought you wanted a winter wedding?"

"And have a big red nose in all the photos? Don't be daft!" she chuckles.

I feel sad, Lucy had such a clear idea of how her big day was going to go, but it sounds like she's compromising on everything.

Lucy says her goodbyes when the nurse pops in to tell me that I'm going for a scan. Once the scan is done, one of the nurses helps me take a shower and brush my teeth. I feel good but my leg muscles are still very weak. I've been lying flat on my back for two weeks, even with the physio it's little wonder that my muscles can't cope. The nurse leaves me sitting up in bed reading a magazine.

Max arrives an hour later looking breathtakingly handsome. His big smile crinkles his eyes as he strides into my room. "Hey, beautiful," he says, leaning down to kiss me on the lips. I'm glad I brushed my teeth. I wrap both arms around his neck and pull him closer so I can kiss him properly. I've got butterflies in my stomach and a throbbing in my groin. Just looking at him makes me want him. The kiss evolves into a long, passionate but gentle trade of tongues and lips. I've missed this.

He draws my bottom lip through his teeth as he moans and breaks the kiss leaving me breathless. "Baby, you've given me a woody," he sighs, leaning his forehead against mine. I can't open my eyes, his scent is completely intoxicating.

He pulls back and kisses me on the forehead. "Good news, baby. Your scan and test results were all fine, you can come home."

"What? Really? What, now?" I'm so excited.

"Yes, now," he laughs. Then I get the eyebrow. "But… You're to take things easy, do as you're told, and rest. Them's the rules."

"I will, I promise. Oh, I'll be so glad to get home." A

happy smile spreads across his face and then he gives me a sideways look as he moves to the wardrobe and starts to pack up my things.

"I've already moved everything out of your apartment. All your stuff is at home now."

I wouldn't want to go back there anyway. Too many bad memories. "Thanks, I'll put it on the market as soon as I'm back to normal."

"I already did," he says, without missing a beat.

Hmm, a discussion about it would have been nice.

Once all my stuff has been packed away, Max helps me dress. Doctor Alexander arrives to give me some tablets to take with me. "These painkillers are very strong and only to be taken if you feel that the paracetamol isn't effective enough. I want you to take it easy, Vivienne. Rest and relaxation are paramount for your recovery, but if you have any problems or are worried about anything at all, please call me," he says, smiling at me in that fatherly way of his. "And, in the nicest possible way, I hope I don't see you for a very long time!" he smirks.

I laugh and thank him for everything he and his team have done for me.

WHAT'S THE MATTER WITH ME?

Max helps me into the Range Rover, throws my bags in the back and slides in beside me. His hand sits firmly on my thigh as he negotiates the traffic home.

We arrive at the basement of the Foxx-Tech building. As we park up, Vinnie arrives in the Mercedes and parks alongside us. His beaming smile as he gets out of the car, lights up his rugged face. "Good to have you back, Miss." He grins, giving me a gentle kiss on the cheek. Vinnie takes the bags from the car as Max scoops me into his arms and heads to the lift.

"I can walk you know." He gives me the eyebrow so I rest my head against his shoulder and let him get on with it.

We arrive at F1 where Jan is waiting at the penthouse door with a great big smile on her face. "Oh, Vivienne, it's so good to see you," she beams.

"Thanks, Jan. Oh, and I'm so sorry to hear about your mum." She nods and a moment of sadness flickers across her face but then her smile takes over again.

"Thank you, Vivienne. Welcome home."

Max carries me into the penthouse and walks me through to the living room. He gently lowers me to the sofa and puts my feet up, then he props some cushions up behind me. He's going over the top and fussing over me far too much.

"Max, I'm not made of glass."

He stops and looks at me with a serious frown. "Baby, please, just humour me. I thought I'd lost you. I'm just so happy to have you back, I want to take care of you."

"I'm happy to be back," I smile, tracing my fingers over his hand. "But…"

His frown returns. "What? What is it?" he asks nervously.

I glance over my shoulder toward the kitchen, I can hear Jan and Vinnie talking and laughing. I reach up and grab the bottom of his tie, pulling him down to me. "I thought we'd, you know…" I gaze into his eyes and waggle my eyebrows at him.

His eyebrows raise for a moment as his confused eyes search mine, then his super-sexy smile appears and his eyes begin to heat up with desire. "Are you sure you're ready for that?"

I tug on his tie again, pulling him closer to me until we're almost touching. "I've missed you. I need you. I'm ready. Right now." He picks me up in a flash, I wrap my arms around his neck as he carries me upstairs, kicking the door closed behind us.

He slowly lowers me to my feet. I'd expected him to rip all my clothes off and ravage me, but he takes his time. As he removes his shirt, my greedy eyes trail all over him. I rest my palms on his chest and lean forward to kiss his M.F. tattoo. He stares down at me with scorching blue eyes then he kisses me gently on my scar, forehead, eyes, cheeks, nose, lips, chin, and neck. I start to swoon and sway on my feet. He has this incredible way of melting my bones. He strips me slowly, kissing every inch of bare flesh, then he lays me down on the bed and removes the rest of his clothes, never taking his eyes from mine. His gorgeous body revealed, I drag my eager eyes all over every perfect inch of him. *I've missed you.*

He crawls his way up my body and rests on his forearms either side of my head. The weight of his body pushes me down into the mattress. His cock twitches against my sex.

We lie there staring at each other, silently appreciating the other's beauty. I smooth my hands up his biceps and over his shoulders. I notice that he doesn't flinch anymore when I trace the scars on his back. As he circles his hips into mine, I push up to increase the contact. His eyes drop to my mouth, then bounce back to my eyes. I'm lost in his beautiful blue eyes as they scorch me to my core with longing and hunger.

Reaching up, I weave my fingers into his silky hair and pull him down to me. Our lips softly meet then he pulls back, he grazes his lips against mine, then he pulls back again. It's so soft and gentle but so erotic and arousing. My sex throbs with anticipation, I can't hold back any longer. I wrap my legs around his hips and lift my head from the mattress. He meets me halfway and we devour each other in a passionate, urgent kiss that triggers all my nerve endings. I've waited too long for this moment. He's like a drug, and I'm the junkie needing my fix. I moan into his mouth as he deepens the kiss. Wrapping his arms underneath me he crushes my body into his, then he rolls us over so I'm on top of him. I break the kiss and stare down at him. He's so handsome, and he's all mine.

I kiss his eyes, his cheeks, his lips, his neck, then I trail my lips and tongue over his throat and chest. His intoxicating scent invades my nose, and his skin tastes so good. He gently runs his hands through my hair avoiding the scar as I kiss my way along each of his scarred forearms, then each of his palms. His hooded eyes are fixed on mine, neither of us speaks.

I move down his body kissing, nipping, and lapping my way down to his hips. Kneeling between his legs, I run my hands along his thighs. He lets out a soft groan when I lower myself and run my tongue along the full length of his twitching cock, from balls to tip. I feel his body flex when I take him in my mouth and lick the head of his pulsing shaft before plunging him deep into my mouth, sucking and licking.

"Baby, you'd better stop, you're going to make me come if you keep doing that," he says in a raspy voice. The thing is, if I keep doing this I'm going to come too. I can feel the heat in my sex, the throbbing pressure is building and pretty soon I'm not going to be able to stop it. He's the most sensual, sexy man I've ever met. I love everything about him. But most of all, I love the way he makes me feel.

He sits up and pulls me into his arms. "I need to be inside you." His throaty voice and the look on his face sends a pulse through my sex. He kisses me hard. I wrap my arms around his neck and my legs around his body. He lifts me onto his cock making me moan with pleasure as his hot, hard shaft penetrates me deep. I know it won't take me long, I can feel the pressure building. I break the kiss, panting into his mouth.

"I've missed you."

"I've missed you more, baby. Open your eyes." I do, but the look on his handsome face as he tries to control himself, and the delicious sensation of his cock inside me, triggers my orgasm with such intensity that I cry out, throw my head back, and shudder with wave after wave of erotic pleasure. Max joins me as he tightens his arms around me, buries his face in my neck and comes with a primal growl, shuddering as the last drops leave his body.

We hold each other for a moment panting, sweaty, and breathless, then he pulls my head back and kisses me tenderly. "I've missed you," he whispers, against my lips.

"Me too." I lean my forehead against his as we catch our breath.

He rolls me onto my back with his twitching cock still inside me. Brushing the hair from my face he searches my eyes with two beautiful pools of emotion. "You fascinate me, woman," he whispers, gazing into my eyes. "I'm a lucky guy."

I gaze up at him with a certain amount of scepticism. He's wrong. I'm the lucky one. How I ever managed to win this man's heart is a mystery. He could have anyone he chooses, and he chose me. Maybe I'm still in a coma and this is all just a crazy dream? *Please don't let this be a dream.*

A frown slips into his brow. "Okay, where do you go when you do that?" he smirks.

"Am I dreaming?" I ask, in all seriousness, reaching up to stroke his face. "Am I going to wake up and find that none of this is real?"

His frown disappears, and his scorching eyes pour out with love. "No, baby. It's not a dream." He lowers his lips to mine and kisses me softly. His cock twitching and growing inside me so I tighten my legs around his hips and push up to increase the pressure. The soft kisses soon turn into all-consuming passionate ones, I can't get enough of him. Our tongues glide and flick in each other mouths, and our hands roam eagerly over each other's bodies. He pulls out and re-enters me on a low growl, the depth and intensity makes me moan with pleasure as he fills and stretches me. Without missing a beat, he throws my leg over and skilfully manoeuvres me onto my side. Spooning me, he takes me from behind, his hot, minty breath heats my neck as he strokes my clit with his fingers while pumping me hard.

I cry out a long moan as the pressure builds in my core and I feel close to another mind blowing orgasm. He softly bites my shoulder as his powerful thrusts tip me over the edge. I hold my breath, my legs stiffen and I cry out his name as the intense rolling orgasm permeates throughout my body, right down to my toes. He growls in a low throaty voice, pumping faster as he reaches his own release, blowing hot panting breaths into my neck.

My returning headache thuds against my skull but I feel too blissfully happy to pay it much attention. I've never had such amazing sex. The man is incredible. I feel well and truly Foxx'd!

As we float down from our heady cloud, I reach up and run my hand through his hair as he tightens his arms around me, dropping soft kisses on my shoulder.

"You, are an amazing woman," he whispers into my ear, nibbling my lobe. He runs his hand along my hip and down my thigh, caressing and squeezing, the tingling sensation makes me shudder. "I've missed you so much."

I turn myself around to face him, he pushes my hair behind my shoulder and gazes lovingly into my eyes, then he rolls onto his back and pulls me onto his chest. A long, deep, contented sigh emanates from his lips as he closes his eyes. I absently trace the letters on his chest with my fingers as I gaze at his handsome face.

"How do you feel?" he asks, still with his eyes closed.

"Happy," I sigh, contented and sated.

He raises his head from the pillow and opens his eyes, smiling that amazing smile. A mild frown soon appears. "I'm glad to hear it, but you've just got out of the hospital, and that was pretty intense, do you have any pain?" His worried eyes search my face.

I smile up at him and shake my head. "No." If I tell him I have a banging headache, he'll probably think it's his fault for flinging me all over the place. But I'd rather suffer the headache than miss out on the incredible sex we've just had.

"Are you sure?"

"Max, stop fussing. I'm fine, really."

He leans forward and kisses me on the head. "I'll go and run a bath, then you need to eat. You've lost too much weight," he says, on an arched brow. I watch his glorious arse disappear into the bathroom and then I pull his pillow into my chest inhaling his scent. I feel so happy right now.

"Vivienne?... Baby? Hey, sleepy head wake up, the bath is ready."

I open my eyes to see Max's crystal blue eyes smiling down at me. *I must have drifted off.* He scoops me into his arms and carries me into the bathroom. I catch sight of myself in the mirror. I look pale, thin, and my hair is a mess.

He lowers us into the tub, taking his usual position behind me, and then he pulls me back into his chest. I relax my head against his shoulder as he drags a soapy sponge all over my shoulders, neck, and arms, then he makes me sit forward so he can wash my back.

I'm loving the attention and when he's finished, I lie back so he can run the sponge over my breasts and stomach. I flinch and giggle when he hits my tickle spot just above my hip.

"I love the way you laugh," he says, folding his arms around my shoulders. I lay there enjoying the nibbles and nips as he kisses my neck. The tingling sensation reverberates in my groin. I feel so horny right now. I've just had two of the most amazing orgasms, but I'm ready for more. If that's what a bang on the head does to you? Bring it on.

I run my hands along his thighs, either side of me.

"I've missed our baths," he whispers, nibbling my ear. I tilt my head to accommodate him as his lips softly trail down my neck and along my shoulder. A sudden buzzing noise disturbs the moment. I'm so turned on right now that the interruption is actually quite annoying. Max reaches up and presses a button on the intercom.

"Yeah."

Jan's soft voice comes through the speaker. "I'm so sorry to disturb you, Sir. But I've made a late lunch and I wondered whether you will be down or—"

"Or did you want a survival kit sent up?" Vinnie interrupts, chuckling in the background. I blush.

"Vincent, really." Jan chides, telling him off. I can imagine she's blushing right now too.

"We'll be right down," Max smirks.

I don't want to go anywhere, I'm perfectly happy right where I am. I turn myself around to face him and sit across his hips, straddling him. His cock twitches beneath me as I circle my hips. I place my hands on his shoulders and lean in to kiss him.

It starts as a gentle kiss, but it triggers an aching need deep inside me so I wrap my arms around his neck and deepen the kiss. I want him. I need him. He's mine, and I can't get enough of him. He breaks the kiss panting short breaths across my lips, then he smirks.

"Miss Banks, are you trying to take advantage of me?"

Without hesitation, I answer, "Yes."

His eyes smoulder with hunger then he kisses me deep and hard. I drag his bottom lip through my teeth and reach down into the water wrapping my hand around his pulsing shaft. Rising up slightly, I lower myself onto him, groaning out a long moan of pleasure as my muscles contract around him. He leans his head back against the tub and watches me with hooded, smouldering eyes. Short, sharp breaths escape his lips as I rise and lower myself slowly at first then faster and faster, grinding against him. I keep my eyes open so I can enjoy the pleasure on his face as the pressure builds. The friction is perfect, the sensation almost overwhelming. Gripping his shoulders I writhe up and down, causing the water to spill over the edge of the tub. He holds onto my hips, never taking his blazing eyes from mine.

"I'm close." I whisper as the sensations build to an intense peak. His parted lips twitch into a circle, his eyes conveying his pleasure. He pounds into me with urgency as my shattering climax triggers and consumes me. Throwing my head back I cry out his name as we come together.

My headache comes back into focus pounding against my skull as the built up pressure from my orgasm slowly ebbs away and my breathing slows down.

Max sits forward and kisses me on the nose, then he leans his forehead against mine. "Jesus, Vivienne. You're going to kill me." He breathes, against my skin. "But what a way to die!" he smirks.

Max lifts me from the tub and puts me on my feet. I stare out at the amazing view of London as he wraps me in a big towel.

"Oh, that's okay. I need to wash my hair," I say, throwing it off and walking through to the shower. I watch him walking past me out of the bathroom, until the hot jets steam up the glass, then I wash and condition my hair.

"Vivienne!... Jesus! Are you okay? What happened?"

I open my eyes. I'm lying on the shower floor, and Max is crouching down beside me. He's fully dressed and soaking wet. *What the hell happened to me?* I look up at his panic-stricken face. "I'm fine. I... I just slipped on the soap," I murmur trying to stand up, my muscles are so weak. He helps me up and turns the water off.

"You're not fine. You passed out."

"No I didn't, I slipped." *Did I pass out?*

"Don't move!" he commands, then he goes to get a towel. Wrapping it around me he carries me through to the bedroom. He sits me on the edge of the bed, then he starts to dry me off.

"I'm not a child, Max," I smirk, as he rubs me dry through the towel. I stand up, unwrap the towel and use it to dry my hair. He eyes me with disapproval, frowning big time.

"Did you bang your head?"

Did I? I don't think so?

"Vivienne, did you bang your head?" His tone is harsh, he's clearly worried but I don't want him to stress out and go all Mr. Protective on me again.

I stop drying my hair and look up at his concerned face. "No. I didn't. Look, I told you, I just slipped on the soap. I'm fine. Honest."

He eyes me sceptically, the big worry frown hasn't left his brow. He drags his hands through his hair, a tell-tale sign that all is not well in Max's world. "What was I thinking? You've just got out of the goddamn hospital."

"Max, I'm fine," I smile, reaching up to cup his cheek in my hand. I rake my eyes over his handsome face and rise up on my toes to kiss him. His eyes soften for a moment but then his determined expression returns.

"No, you're not fine. You should be resting. Christ! We've just had an intense sex-a-thon. It's too soon, you should be taking things easy."

"Max—"

"Ah, ah, no," he says, pulling away from me. "I'm not taking any chances, Vivienne. I've only just got you back. Stay! Right there." He turns and walks to the wardrobe to change out of his wet clothes. I walk through to the bathroom to take something for my headache and to brush my teeth.

"Vivienne? Goddammit!" He barges into the bathroom and stares at me through the mirror.

"What?… I'm brushing my teeth," I grin.

After giving me the eyebrow, he stands beside me and brushes his teeth, slipping me the occasional sideways glare, then he wanders through to the bedroom and waits for me to get ready.

Max is sitting on the bed as I walk to the wardrobe. I feel him watching me, I know he's worried that I've overdone it, and maybe I have. I don't know what happened, but I'm sure it was just the heat of the bathwater and then the hot shower that caused me to pass out. At least I hope that's all it was.

I was going to wear my jeans, but I change my mind and dig through some of my boxes to find my sexy underwear. Something silver glints in the bottom of one of the boxes. *Oh my goodness, where did these come from?…Lucy.* I giggle when I see the pair of silver handcuffs lying in the bottom of my underwear box. They're not mine, but I'm sure I can make good use of them at some point.

I make a show of putting my stockings on, I can feel his eyes travelling up my legs as I slowly pull them up, then I step into the navy dress I know he likes me in and I put my heels on too. When Max and I were apart, I'd never wanted to dress up, but now we're back together it makes me feel good, and I know how much he loves the stockings. I walk toward him and stand between his legs resting my hands on his shoulders. His appreciative eyes travel all the way up my body finally landing on my mine. Reaching up he runs his hands over my behind and down my thighs.

"Stockings… Hmm," he murmurs, shaking his head. "You're killing me," he smirks, flashing that crooked smile of his. "Come on, Jan's made us some lunch, and you need to eat." He stands and curls his arm around me then we head down to the kitchen.

Jan and Vinnie stop their conversation as we enter the kitchen. "Oh, Vivienne, it's so good to have you home," Jan says, beaming a big smile. "I've made your favourite." She gets up and moves to the oven.

"Yeah, nice to see a bit of colour back in your cheeks, Miss," Vinnie grins, waggling his eyebrows. I blush, they must know what's kept us upstairs for so long.

Max pulls my stool closer to him and rests his hand on my thigh, giving it a gentle squeeze as Jan dishes up my absolute favourite. Mac n' Cheese. I'm starving so I tuck in.

Max and Vinnie talk about guy stuff, so I take the opportunity to ask Jan about her mother. I feel bad that I wasn't there for her when her mother died. Apparently, she'd been ill for some time, but I can see in her face, it's not been easy for her.

When he's finished eating, Max wanders off to make some calls in his study while I take a second helping of Mac n' Cheese. Max had pulled a face when Jan offered me a glass of wine, so I finish my water and put my dishes into the dishwasher.

When Jan finishes tidying the kitchen she removes her apron. Vinnie's going to take her home so I give her a hug before she leaves. "I've prepared something for dinner and I've left it in the fridge," she says, kissing me on the cheek. Once they've gone, I wander through to the study to find Max.

I can hear him talking on the phone as I enter the study. A strange feeling comes over me, and I suddenly feel lightheaded. Max is sitting behind his desk, his eyes flip up to mine as I walk in and stop abruptly, my body shuddering involuntarily. This room holds so many terrifying memories for me, and suddenly they all come rushing back. My hands shake, my breathing becomes fast and shallow, my stomach churns, and I can't help but cast my eyes to the wall behind the door. There's nothing there but a freshly painted wall, but I can still see the blood in my mind. I've had many nightmares about that night but I thought I'd managed to get over it.

I feel hot and cold at the same time and it feels like all the air has been sucked out of the room.

A soft hand strokes my cheek. When I open my eyes, I'm looking up at the living room ceiling, until Max's face comes into view. His worried eyes search mine.

Not another blackout? "What happened?" I ask nervously. My head is resting in his lap. He stares down at me with a worried frown, clearly distressed.

"Baby, you passed out again. I'm going to take you to the hospital. This isn't right," he says, nervously.

Again? What's the matter with me? "Max, it's just…I haven't been in that room since that night. It was a bit of a shock that's all. I thought I was over it but the memories of Monica just came flooding back." I sit myself up then he pulls me into his lap and folds his arms around me.

"I'm sorry, baby. I should have realised."

I raise my hand to smooth his worried brow. "It's not your fault. Besides, I'm not going to let that woman ruin the rest of my life."

"Do you want to talk about what happened?" he asks

softly.

We haven't really spoken about it yet. Vinnie must have told him what he knew, but I know Max is waiting for me to tell him everything. The trouble is, I don't really want him to have the gory details swimming around in his head, I know how it will affect him. He'd just obsess over it, and that wouldn't help either of us. Max has conquered a lot recently but I sense he's close to the edge, and I don't want to be the one to push him over it.

"I know you're worried about me, Max, but I'm fine, really! I'm a tough cookie," I smirk. He smiles, but it doesn't quite reach his eyes.

FRAGILE

We kick our shoes off and lay on the sofa watching an old movie until Lucy and Dan arrive for a visit. Max had invited them over to cheer me up. He thought I'd still be in bed convalescing, but I've been in the hospital for two weeks, and I've been away from Max for too long to want to hide myself away in the bedroom. Not unless he's in the bed with me.

Lucy's brought a bottle of wine so Max goes into the kitchen to get some glasses.

"Do you really think you should be drinking after passing out earlier?" he asks, when I point out that he hasn't poured me a glass.

Lucy and Dan turn to look at me. "You passed out?" Lucy asks, with a concerned frown.

I throw Max an arched brow. "Well, that was your fault. You shouldn't have taken advantage of me three times in a row."

Max actually blushes. "I…No… I."

Lucy giggles as he stutters his way through a denial. "Hmm, I'd heard you were good," she grins, waggling her eyebrows. Max just shakes his head and begrudgingly pours me a small glass of wine.

"Cheers," I say, raising my glass. "To surviving."

We all clink our glasses together. "Amen to that," Dan smiles.

Lucy starts to tell me all about the bridesmaid dress she

has chosen for the wedding, but she refuses to discuss her own dress in front of Dan so Max takes him out to the terrace. Dan is under strict orders not to eavesdrop so they close the door behind them. Lucy's dress sounds amazing. It sounds like a dress that a fairy-tale princess would wear and I can't wait to see it.

"We've got three months until the wedding but I'll need you to have a fitting done soon, maybe next week?" she asks, sneakily topping up our glasses while Max isn't looking.

"Yes, of course. I'm hoping to go back to work next week, but if you tell me when, I'll take a day off."

"You're going back to work?" Her eyebrows shoot up in surprise. "Are you sure that's not a bit too soon?"

"Oh, don't you start! I think Max is going to be difficult about me going back, but I'm fine, and I can't sit around all day doing nothing. It's just not me."

"But Max said you passed out."

I sigh and twiddle my hair in my fingers. "What can I say? He takes my breath away." Lucy laughs and rolls her eyes.

"So what about your venue? Have you found anywhere yet?" I ask eagerly. Her expression changes. It's obviously not going as planned for her. I feel bad, she had such high expectations for her wedding.

"We're looking at the hotel where Mum and Dad had their anniversary party. They do a very reasonable package for weddings."

I'm not surprised it's a dump. I try not to flinch. No wonder they're doing a reasonable price, they'll be needing the custom. They've only just reopened a couple of months ago since the environmental agency closed them down. I suddenly have a great idea, but I need to speak to Max first. "How many guests will you have at the wedding reception?"

"Well, the last count was fifty-three, if Dan's grandmother can make it."

Hmm.

The door to the terrace opens and Dan pokes his head through. "Is it safe to come in yet, I'm freezing out here," he smirks, shivering.

"My hero," Lucy giggles.

Max comes and sits beside me, laying his hand on my thigh. I can feel him searching out the top of my stocking through my dress. When he finds it, he squeezes my thigh and leaves his hand there. The heat sends a tingle through my skin and brings a smile to my face.

We laugh and talk for ages. It's been nice to relax with my friends and so good to catch up on everything that's happened while I've been off the radar. I've really enjoyed myself. Max wouldn't let me have another glass of wine, insisting that I had to take things easy until I'm fully recovered. The building headache thudding in my skull put me off having another drink anyway so I didn't bother to argue the point.

As the evening wears on my eyelids begin to droop. My first day home has been quite energetic to say the least so I do as I'm told when Max tells me I need to go to bed. Lucy and Dan give me a big hug then they say goodnight. Once they're gone, Max picks up my shoes and carries me up to bed.

After brushing our teeth, Max leaves the bathroom while I clean my face and brush my hair. As I pad into the bedroom, he strides toward me gloriously naked. My tired eyes feast on his magnificent physique. As he unzips my dress and lets it fall, pooling at my feet, I can feel his appreciative eyes scanning over my semi-naked body. I know how much he loves the stockings and sexy lace underwear so I just crawl into bed with it on and wait for him to join me. I'm feeling horny.

He lies beside me on his side, propped up on his elbow. His hooded eyes trail up and down my body as his hand traces a soft path down my stomach, hip, and thigh. His fingers graze the tops of my stockings and he lets out a long, happy sigh. "You, in these saucy little things, drive me crazy, you know that?"

I watch his eyes greedily enjoying the lace. Rising up from the mattress I push him onto his back and lie on top of him. "No…*You* drive *me* crazy." I kiss him softly on the lips and then I feel his arms curl around me as he deepens the kiss. His cock begins to twitch, and my sex begins to throb.

He rolls me onto my back and hovers above me, staring down with scorching blue eyes. "You need to rest. You've had a very long day," he murmurs, kissing me chastely on my forehead.

Wait, what? No!

Before I can argue, he rolls onto his back, closes his eyes and sighs deeply. I'm all turned on and frustrated. I don't want to go to sleep. I snuggle into his side resting my head on his chest with my leg over his hips. He squeezes me in his arm and runs his other hand up my thigh, stopping at my stocking top. After a few moments, I realise he really is going to just go to sleep, even though I can feel his cock twitching and pulsing beneath my thigh. I lift my head and kiss his chest, his eyes remain closed so I kiss his shoulder then his neck. His eyes are still closed! I start to wonder if I'm just not turning him on, but I can feel his cock moving under my thigh. I crawl over him again and lie on top of his body, he still doesn't open his eyes.

"Go to sleep, Vivienne," he rasps, with a crooked smile.

You stubborn… I hover over his face then I kiss him lightly on his left eyebrow, then his right eyebrow, then his cheek and throat. His eyes remain closed, but his breathing has become more rapid and his cock is now really hard. I circle my hips into his and very softly graze my lips over his mouth then I suck on his bottom lip and drag it through my teeth. Staring down at him, a big beaming smile spreads across my face. "It's only a matter of time, baby." His eyes open and stare at me in that sexy way he has. The next thing I know, his hands are in my hair pulling me down to his lips, and he kisses me hard. *Finally!*

Breaking the kiss, he stares at me for a moment then he rolls me onto my back and kisses his way down my body. He frees my breasts from the cups of my bra and rolls his hot tongue over each aching nipple, dragging them through his teeth and sucking them before trailing his lips down my stomach and over my knickers.

He kneels between my thighs and lifts my legs up in front of him. I hold them there as he begins to drag my knickers off throwing them aside, then he removes my stockings one at a time, kissing my legs as he does it. He parts my legs and rests them on his shoulders, stroking them with his eager hands. He kisses me softly on each thigh, then lowers himself down and kisses me at the apex of my groin, nipping and lapping. I close my eyes and arch my back as his tongue invades my sex, flicking, licking and sucking my vulnerable bud.

I weave my fingers through his hair as the pressure builds in my core. I feel myself begin to quicken and the sensation has me writhing and moaning with pleasure. He has the most amazing tongue, and as much as I try to draw it out for longer, the glorious assault triggers a shattering orgasm making me shudder as it passes through me like electricity.

I open my eyes and watch him crawl up my body with my calves still resting on his shoulders. He enters me slowly, watching my face the whole time. He pulls out and re-enters me, closing his eyes briefly as the sensation takes him over. His powerful thrusts become more and more urgent as the pressure builds. Suddenly he slows, I can tell he's close to his release by the look on his face, but he slows, pulls back, and rests back on his heels.

He moves my legs from his shoulders and pulls me upright. I fling my arms around his neck and my legs around his waist as he lifts and lowers me onto him. Holding my waist in his big strong hands, he starts slowly then builds to a faster pace. The friction sends a delicious tingle through my sex, and I know I'm going to come again in this position. I bury my face in his neck and bite him lightly on the shoulder before my head rolls back as a wave of ecstatic pleasure consumes me all over again.

"Good girl," he says, in a raspy voice. Rising up on his knees, he buries his face in my neck as he reaches his climax. His hips bucking wildly until he pumps out the last drops and growls a low moan of pleasure into my neck.

I'm exhausted, sated and thoroughly content. Now, I can sleep.

REMEMBERING CHARLIE

"Good morning, beautiful."

I open my sleepy eyes to Max's handsome face smiling down at me. He's deliciously naked from the waist up, his hair is damp from his run, and he has very sexy morning stubble. "I've got to go to work for a bit, will you be okay?" he asks, stroking my cheek. "Jan's downstairs, so you're not on your own."

I'm a little disappointed that he has to go, but the poor man has a company to run, and I know it's selfish of me to want him to spend every moment with me. I reach over to Max's pillow to take the white rose and smell it. It's become somewhat of a ritual now, and it's so romantic.

"Will you be gone long?" I ask, twirling the rose in my fingers.

"Just a couple of hours. Greg Taylor is a new client, but he's an old friend of Parker's so I want to meet with him personally as a favour to Parker."

Greg Taylor...Why is that name familiar?

He kisses me on the lips then he walks to the bathroom. I watch him go, I could watch his predatory walk and fine ass all day.

I'd had another nightmare last night. It had woken me with a jolt in the early hours, so I'd sneaked out of bed to go and dry the sweat from my face in the bathroom. Luckily, I didn't wake Max, I don't want him to worry about it and I hate that I'm still besieged with these constant reminders.

A sharp pain in my head makes me wince when I sit myself up. *Urgh! When will you ever stop.* I've got some painkillers in my handbag so I haul myself out of bed to go and find it. I quickly take the strong painkillers that Doctor Alexander had given me before Max comes out of the shower, he'll only worry if he knows I'm still getting headaches.

I wander into the bathroom and brush my teeth. Catching sight of Max in the shower through the mirror, I can't help but stare as he lathers the soap all over his body. *Lucky soap!* Max seems to have brought out an animalistic quality in me that I never knew I had. I've never felt this horny and turned on my whole life. Maybe it's because he's so easy on the eye, but I think it actually goes deeper than that. He's woken up all my senses at once, and I feel totally alive when I'm with him. He'd said that about me when we first met, and now I realise what he meant.

Max waits for me to have a quick shower before he leaves for the office. He's worried I'll pass out again, but I feel fine apart from the headache. Once I'm out and dry, he gives me a chaste kiss then he turns to leave. Turning back, he grabs the towel and pulls it off my body, dropping it to the floor. He stands there staring down at me with hooded eyes trailing up and down the length of me. "I just wanted something to take with me." Then he hits me with that smile of his, the one that makes my heart flutter and awakens all the butterflies.

Once I'm dressed, I head down to the kitchen to get some breakfast. Jan greets me with a smile and hands me a bacon sandwich and some orange juice. While I munch through my sandwich, she tells me all about her mum. They had a really close relationship by the sound of it, which saddens me about my own mother. We've never had that kind of closeness. Mum was always too drunk or too high to notice I was even there most of the time.

Jan gets a call which puts a frown on her face.

"Everything okay?"

"Oh, it's another urgent document I need to sign at the solicitors for my mother's probate. Why they couldn't ask me to sign it when I was there two days ago, I just don't know," she huffs, checking her watch.

"You don't have to babysit me, you know. Why don't you go and get it sorted, I'll be fine on my own. Besides, Max will be back in a couple of hours."

She thinks about it for a moment. "Well, it would help if I could leave early, are you sure you'll be okay?"

"Jan, I insist. Just go. I'm fine, really," I smile. "And don't worry about the kitchen, I'll tidy up, it'll give me something to do."

Jan hesitates for a moment. "Well, if you're sure." I roll my eyes and give her the eyebrow.

After Jan leaves and I've stuffed my face with another bacon sandwich, I wash the dishes and clean the worktops. As I have time to kill, I decide to go and find my phone and my laptop so I can organise my recent photographs and check my emails.

My phone is in my handbag upstairs but I can't find the laptop, so I head back downstairs. After checking the living room, the only place I can think it would be is the study. That awful feeling comes over me again as I walk toward the study door. I hate how this is affecting me, it's ridiculous! It's not like Monica is going to be standing in the room pointing a gun at my head again. *That couldn't happen twice could it? Oh, for heaven's sake, Viv. Get a grip.* I push the door open and march into the study, then I let out the breath I was anxiously holding once I'm inside and no crazy people are jumping out at me. *See?*

I laugh at my own stupidity and search the room for my laptop. When I find it, I realise I'll have to plug it in as the battery is completely dead, so I sit in Max's chair and wait for it to power up.

While I'm waiting, I glance around the walls. Max's family pictures are all neatly hung together in one space.

The photograph of Charlie and Max that I'd taken just before Charlie's death, brings a smile to my face and a tear to my eye. He was such a cute little boy. I loved how he called me Auntie Viniven in his squeaky high voice. I miss him dearly, and I'm sure Max does too. My heart twists. Max was so good with him, he was born to be a father.

The wall that he referred to as 'our wall', still remains empty. He told me that he wanted it to be filled with photographs of us, our children, and family pets. Coincidentally, it was the wall my blood was smeared all over the night Monica tried to kill me. *How ironic.* I stare at the blank wall. My stomach rolls, bile rises in my throat and I feel like I'm going to be sick. I grab my laptop, leave the room, and run upstairs to the bathroom.

Leaning over the toilet bowl holding my hair back I heave, but nothing comes up, so I wait a few moments for the nausea to pass. Once it does, I walk over to the basin and splash my face with cool water.

"Well, that'll teach you for stuffing your face, you greedy moo!" I say, to my scowling reflection. I'd been on liquid food during my coma, and then light meals once I'd woken up in hospital, but since I've been home I've done nothing but eat. And double helpings at that.

I stand sideways on in the mirror. My stomach is lovely and flat, but if I keep eating double helpings it's not going to stay that way, and I haven't done any exercise for weeks.

I brush my teeth to get rid of the awful taste in my mouth and then I walk through to the bedroom. Plugging my laptop in, I lie on the bed and wait for it to power up. My phone buzzes with a text message from Max;

```
Hey, beautiful.
I hope you're taking
things easy!!
I'll be home soon.
I love you.
X;-)
```

I text him back;

```
I'm being a very good girl.
I'm conserving all my energy
```

```
so I can be a very bad girl
when you get home!
Xx:-)
```

I wait for his reply with a smile on my face.

```
Can't wait!
X;-)
```

Once I've stopped grinning, I check my emails and clear out all the spam. It's very nice of these people to contact me so regularly, but I really don't need a penis enlargement, Russian girls, or a free spin in an on-line casino. Lucy has sent me some pictures of the bridesmaid dress she's chosen for the wedding, and she asks if I can make it to the fitting on Friday morning? I send her a reply and make a note of it in my calendar.

All the gang at work have sent me emails wishing me a speedy recovery and then I notice an email from Sandra.

```
Dear Vivienne,
I can't tell you how sorry I am to have
played a part in Monica's vile and hateful
mission to hurt you and Lucy. I'm ashamed of
what I've done.
I stupidly fell for her lies, and I thought
she really cared for me, but I realise now
she was just manipulating me.
She knew I was gullible and weak, and she
threatened to kill my parents if I didn't
follow her instruction. I'm so sorry, I know
I can never make up for what I've done but it
was never my intention to hurt you, and I
hope that one day you will find it in your
heart to forgive me.
I've left the magazine, the press have made
my life unbearable so I'm going back to my
parents for a while. I sincerely hope you
recover from this terrible ordeal and I wish
you all the very best.
Sandra.
```

I know Sandra isn't to blame, and I don't hold any bad feeling toward her, but I just can't bring myself to reply. I will, but I'm not ready to deal with it just yet.

To keep my mind from trawling over all the horrific events I've had to endure recently, I busy myself with organising my photographs. I suddenly realise the only photographs of Max and I together are the paparazzi shots of us taken at Brands Hatch. I have lots of Max and Charlie together, but I delete anything with Monica in it. I refuse to have to look at her face ever again. I see it enough in my dreams, I'll be damned if I'm going to see her on my laptop too.

The sound of footsteps running up the stairs makes me stiffen.

"Vivienne?" Max's voice calms my racing heart. He strides into the bedroom with a frown on his handsome face. "Vivienne, where's Jan?" he asks, walking toward the bed.

"She had to go out," I say, jumping up onto my knees and pulling him down to me for a kiss. I wrap my arms around his neck to pull him closer, but he's resisting me.

"I told her to stay with you until I got back," he says, angrily.

I pull him down, but he's still resisting me. "She had an important call from the solicitor about her mother, I told her to go. I've been fine." I pull him down to me again, this time, his eyes soften and he lowers down to kiss me on the lips.

Breaking the kiss he puts me at arm's length. "How do you feel? Any headaches? Blackouts? Tell me the truth."

"Nope," I lie. I haven't blacked out but the headache I've had since this morning, just won't quit. His eyes and smile do their worst and pretty soon I feel my bones melting. I push his jacket from his shoulders and let him finish taking it off as I loosen his tie and start to open his buttons. He watches me as I finish unbuttoning his shirt and I gaze in awe at his gorgeous body. His hard muscles bunch and ripple under his honey coloured skin. I lean forward and kiss the M.F. tattoo over his heart.

"Baby, why do you do that?" he asks, in a soft, raspy voice.

I blush and look up at him. I'm surprised by his question.

I think I've always done it since I found out that its significance had everything to do with his parents and nothing at all to do with Monica. "Because it's a symbol of love…if it means a lot to you, then it means a lot to me too."

He stares down at me with wonder in his eyes. "They would have loved you." He pulls me into his arms and kisses me deeply, reverently.

Max takes his time to undress me, kissing me randomly all over my body. Then he gently pushes me back onto the bed. He lies beside me, softly stroking his fingers up and down my stomach and over my hip bone, then he drags them up and over my breasts tantalising my skin with every stroke.

I lie there staring up at his eyes as they follow the movement of his fingers. He's got something on his mind. I watch him, waiting for him to spit it out, but he says nothing. Although what he's doing feels very nice, I can tell that he's zoned out. I do it a lot myself. Whatever he's thinking about has taken over, and I feel like I'm going to have to prompt him to tell me what's bothering him.

"Max?…Where do you go?" I ask, smiling up at him. His fingers stop moving, and his eyes lower before slipping me a sideways glance. "Sorry… I was just thinking."

I wait patiently for him to finish his sentence, but he doesn't. "About what?" I ask, reaching up to stroke his cheek.

His eyes travel over to my laptop on the end of the bed. A photograph of Charlie's cheeky smiling face fills the screen. My heart clenches. Charlie's death is still very hard for Max. I sometimes wonder if he'll ever truly come to terms with it. He wraps his arms around me and rests his head against my chest. I stroke my fingers through his hair and kiss him on the top of his head. Laying in each other's arms, we remember Charlie in our own individual ways.

I wake with a jolt and pull my hand up to my throat. Monica's bony fingers crushing my windpipe are no longer there as I wake from my nightmare. I'm lying on my side. Max is spooning me with one arm beneath me, one arm draped over my side, and his leg is resting over my hip. It's pitch black and deathly quiet and when I glance at the clock I see that it's just after four in the morning. I have a terrible headache and I need to get some painkillers. I don't think I can wait until morning. I gently lift his heavy leg off of me and slither out from his arms. He moans and frowns but thankfully, he remains asleep.

I quietly pad into the bathroom and close the door before hitting the light switch. The bright light hurts my eyes and I feel lightheaded and dizzy. Neither of us ate last night. We ended up talking about Charlie and just fell asleep in each other's arms.

I find the pills and take them quickly. They're the ones Doctor Alexander gave me, he said they were strong but they don't seem to be very effective. Rinsing a flannel under the cold water tap, I rest it against my forehead to try and ease the thumping in my skull. *When will you ever stop?*

After a few moments, I turn off the light and wait until my eyes have adjusted to the darkness, then I open the door and make my way to Max's side of the bed. I check to see he's still asleep then I grab his shirt from the floor. As I stand up again, I sway with dizziness. Maybe it's low blood sugar? *Maybe I should eat something?*

Once I'm steady on my feet I put his shirt on and go downstairs. I can't sleep now, I'm wide awake. I pad downstairs and wander into the kitchen, but I really don't think I can eat until this awful headache subsides, it's making me feel sick. I wander back into the living room and sit in the big swivel chair overlooking the magnificent view of London. Curling my feet underneath me, I gaze out at the bright city lights of the bustling metropolis as the haze of dawn begins to pale the sky.

My mind trawls over our conversation earlier. Max talked quite a lot about Charlie. Monica had cruelly made him believe that Charlie was his son. Even though that turned out to be another one of her twisted lies, Max was genuinely devastated when he found out the truth. He'd have made a wonderful father to Charlie. I've often thought that had he taken Monica back, Charlie may still be alive. Although Max hasn't said it out loud, I know becoming a father and having a family of his own sits very highly on his agenda. And that worries me because—

"Baby? Are you okay?"

I look up to see Max standing on the bottom step of the staircase rubbing his tired eyes. He's completely naked and his hair is all over the place. He looks so adorable.

"Yeah, I was hungry so I came down for something to eat," I lie. I've been doing that a lot lately. I try to convince myself that it's only a white lie as I did come down for something to eat, I just couldn't face it with my swirling stomach. He doesn't need to know, and he also doesn't need to know that I'm still having nightmares, he'll only worry.

I stand and walk toward him when I realise he's not going back to bed without me. He curls his arm around me and kisses me on the top of my head, then we walk back upstairs. Once his head hits the pillow he's out like a light, while I stare up at the ceiling.

WHO IS FIONA?

I peel my eyes open and focus them on Max's smiling face hovering over me. I can smell the fragrant petals of the white rose lying on his pillow.

"Thank you." I sigh, lifting the rose and smelling the petals. It means a lot to me that I wake every morning to a beautiful white rose. He doesn't know it, but I've saved them all and before they dry out, I've pressed them all in a special book. It's silly, but I just couldn't bear to throw them away.

His bare chest, damp hair, and morning stubble, means he's been for a run and hasn't begun to get ready for work yet. "Shower or tub?" he asks, with a cheeky grin. I take a deep inhale and have a long, satisfying stretch to iron out all the kinks.

"Sex," I sigh, seductively.

His eyebrows raise and he hits me with his knee-trembling smile. "I hoped you'd say that," he grins, "but I need to take a shower first, I'm all sweaty." He starts to walk away so I reach up and grab the waistband of his shorts and pull him back.

"Oh, no you don't!" I giggle. "That's part of your rugged manly charm." I kneel up on the bed and push his shorts down his legs. His rigid cock springs free and bounces up and down as he kicks his shorts off. I take him in my hand as it pulses in my firm grip. I run my other hand up his chest and around the back of his neck to pull him down to me for a kiss. He obliges without hesitation and fists his hands in my hair. I flinch slightly when he grazes my scar, but it only hurts for a second so I ignore it. The pounding headache is harder to ignore, but I refuse to let it interfere with my amazing sex life.

Max moans softly into my mouth then he pulls me up to my feet. Breaking the kiss he buries his face in my breasts and softly bites my erect nipples, dragging them through his teeth. I hold his head in my hands and thread my fingers through his damp hair.

He lifts me from the bed. I wrap my legs around him and throw my arms around his neck, kissing him as he walks me to the wall then he props my back up against it. On a low growl he enters me, cupping my behind in his hands. The deep penetrating thrust has me gasping for breath. I dig my fingernails into his back as he pulls out and thrusts in over and over again, building the pressure and increasing the friction. I bury my face in his neck and bite his shoulder as the delicious feeling overwhelms me. The sweat drips from his hair, and I feel my hands slipping on the hard flexing muscles in his shoulders. His scent is intoxicating and totally arousing. The intense feeling of his cock rubbing inside me brings me to the point of no return.

"Max!" I gasp, urgently.

"Look at me, baby. I need your eyes on me." His voice is ragged and raspy. I know when I open my eyes and see the carnal desire in his, I'll be done. I open my eyes, and sure enough, the ecstasy on his face detonates my release as wave after wave of shuddering sparks resonate throughout my body. He grunts a succession of low growls when his final thrust pins me to the wall as he finds his own release.

We're both unable to speak until we catch our breath, then he hugs me tightly to his chest and walks us through to the bath.

Stepping into the empty bath with me still wrapped around him, he then turns the taps on. Leaning his back against the tub and resting his head back against the edge, I stretch my legs out behind me and lay on his warm hard body, resting my head against his shoulder. We silently wait for the tub to fill and for our breathing to even out.

"That was amazing," I sigh, relaxed and contented. I know my experience with sex is limited, but I've never known sex like this. "Is it always this good?" I ask, before engaging brain to mouth. I suddenly worry what his answer will be. He's had so many more sexual partners than I have. That thought suddenly evokes a pang of jealousy, knotting my stomach.

I feel him raise his head so I look up at him, nervous of his reply. The look in his eyes floors me. "When you love someone, it's always this good," he says, in a raspy voice.

I lean in and kiss him softly on the lips. "I love that you love me."

We lay in the warm water for ages. Max keeps adding hot water to keep the temperature up. He strokes my back for a while then he rests his hand on my behind. I raise my head to look at him. "Aren't you going to be late for work?" We've been in the bath for the best part of an hour.

"I'm not going in today," he sighs, his eyes still closed. He looks so relaxed.

I kiss him on the chin. "Good. I'll have you all to myself."

He chuckles. "Well, you've proved that you're definitely getting your strength back," he says, opening an eye and raising a cheeky eyebrow, "so I thought I'd take you shopping. There's a fundraiser coming up next week and I thought we could go shopping for a gown." He kisses me chastely on the tip of my nose then he closes his eyes again.

"I can borrow one of Lucy's."

"The red one?" he smiles.

"Yes. Why, what's wrong with it?"

"Absolutely nothing. You looked beautiful in it, and I

like you in red, but there are going to be lots of events coming up so you'll be needing more than one dress."

A thought suddenly enters my mind and makes me feel uneasy. "But won't the press be there?" I ask on a nervous frown.

"Of course."

"But—"

"But what?" he asks, raising his head and looking at me with confused eyes. "Don't you want to go?"

"Yes, but…the press will want to take pictures and ask questions."

"And?" he shrugs.

"But you don't tell them anything. You've been notoriously private. You never talk to the press. What should I say if they ask me about you…or us?"

He smiles his knee-trembling smile, the one that almost stops my heart. "You tell them that you're my fiancé, that you're madly in love with me, and you can't wait to marry me."

I smile and roll my eyes. "That's easy. But what if they ask me about Monica, or about what happened?"

"Just say 'no comment'," he shrugs. "Besides, I'll be with you, you won't have to deal with them alone. Come on, let's get out of here before we prune," he chuckles, squeezing my behind.

While Max gets dressed, I quickly take another couple of painkillers. The headache from hell is ever present and starting to piss me off. I put on my satin underwear and lace top stockings. If I'm trying on evening wear I'll need a pair of heels with me too so I put on my grey pencil skirt, black top, and killer heels. I style my hair into soft waves and apply some mascara and lip gloss. Apart from the fact that I've lost weight, I'm amazed at how good I look, considering the trauma I've been through lately.

Max walks up behind me as I stand in front of the full-length mirror, running his hands over my hips and down my thighs. "You know I really like these," he smirks, feeling the lace tops of my stockings through my skirt.

"Really? I don't think you've got the legs for them, personally," I smirk. He digs his fingers into my tickle spot and makes me cry out. "Okay, okay!" I giggle. "I'll buy some more."

His sexy smile creeps across his lips as he rests his chin on my shoulder and wraps his arms around my waist. "I love your laugh, and I love whatever it is you're doing to me."

The look on his face floors me. "Ditto, Mr. Foxx." I haven't been outside for ages. If I wasn't so keen to get back to a normal routine, I think I'd drag him back to bed and smother him in kisses. That smile gets me every time.

Jan has prepared a light breakfast and I manage to eat some toast and drink some coffee. My stomach doesn't feel as queasy this morning, but I do feel very tired. We say goodbye to Jan and head for the lift.

"So, where are we going? I know a great little shop near my office building."

He squeezes my waist and smiles down at me. "I was thinking Knightsbridge." He shrugs.

"Pff, I couldn't afford a dress from there," I blurt, giggling. That's like, super rich territory.

"You're not buying it, I am."

"No. No, I'm sorry Max, but I can't let you buy my clothes. And that reminds me, we need to sort out some arrangement of housekeeping. I can't live with you for free, it's not right. I'll be back at work next week so we need to discuss my contribution."

Max stares at me with a heavy crease in his brow and an open mouth. "Are you talking English? Because none of what you just said made any sense," he scowls.

Now it's my turn to stare at him in utter confusion. "Max, I—"

"Vivienne," he interrupts, "please understand, that as much as I appreciate your concern, I am a little insulted that you would even think that I would ask you to contribute financially toward our home. I make more money than we could ever spend in a dozen lifetimes."

I blush. My small pittance of a wage against his colossal earnings is ridiculously unbalanced, but it's not my way to take without giving back. I wouldn't feel comfortable.

"Max, if we're to be a partnership, a real partnership, I need to bring something to the table."

He reaches down to take my hands in both of his. The look on his face floors me. "Vivienne, you've brought everything I could ever want or need to this relationship. I couldn't buy what you bring to the table, and I'm rich," he smirks. "Money's just money," he shrugs, "and if I want to spend it on you? I'm afraid you have no choice."

"But—"

"And another thing," he interrupts, arching his brow. "You're not going back to work next week. It's not like you need to work."

"Max, I want to go back to work. I like my job. I'm good at it, and I'm not going to just sit around waiting for you to come home every night, that's just not me." I can see the irritation on his face, but I'm not backing down on this one. I run my hands up his chest waiting for his mood to soften, but I can see he's not going to give in anytime soon. "Max, photography isn't just my job, it's my passion."

His eyes soften, and I know even though he's not happy about it, he understands. "You could have your own studio, you don't have to work for a crummy magazine anymore. I know people who could—" I reach up to silence him, softly placing my fingers across his lips.

"I know you want to help, but my dad always said, if you want something in this life you have to work hard for it. You have to earn it. You of all people must understand that."

He sighs, then he smiles, giving me a look that I can't quite determine.

The lift arrives at the basement, and as he doesn't

comment any further on the topic I feel like I may have won that round.

Max takes me to a very expensive clothes shop. As we enter, a flamboyant, well-dressed man minces toward us and greets Max with affection. He obviously knows him very well.

"Mr. Foxx, how divine of you to honour us with your presence today. And may I say you get more and more handsome with each passing day. But enough about you, let's talk about me!" he says, in a very camp, very crisp, English accent. He's like a character from Downton Abbey. If it were a comedy.

"Davis, this is—"

"Ah, yes, you must be Fiona. Charmed, I'm sure," he interrupts, eagerly.

Fiona?…Who the hell is Fiona? I frown and turn to Max. His face is tight, and he's positively glaring at Davis.

"Awkward!" Davis sings, realising his faux pas. His cheeks turn pure crimson and his crisp English accent suddenly slides into more of an East-End twang as he mutters an apology. "Bugger. Note to self…never guess a name," he laughs nervously. "I'm so sorry. Let's start again shall we?"

Max, who seems to have forgiven him, introduces me as his fiancé. Davis kisses the back of my hand making me blush, and he returns to his camp, crisp, English accent.

"Vivienne dah'ling. I'm cock-a-hoop to meet the woman who's finally going to take him off the market and up the aisle, so to speak." He grins at his innuendo. "Many have tried and failed miserably. I was beginning to wonder if he might be one of us," he whispers conspiratorially, swiping a sideways glance at Max, who's rolling his eyes. They obviously enjoy their badinage. Davis lifts my left hand and holds it up. "Oh, dear. I hope the lack of an engagement ring is merely an oversight dah'ling?" he asks, frowning at Max.

"Oh, he's not officially proposed yet," I stutter awkwardly.

"Why ever not?" Davis asks incredulously. "Oh, of course. I heard about your recent tribulations with Monica," he adds, with a sympathetic smile. "Terrible business. Wretched girl. I never cared for her very much."

I suddenly realise Davis must have known her too. And then my mind starts to wander. *How many women has Max brought to this shop? Tons I'll bet.* A pang of jealousy knots my stomach. I know it's ridiculous to feel jealous, he's been honest about his past and as far as I know, all the women he'd dated were just casual affairs, nothing serious, except… Who is Fiona?

Knowing I could be one of many to have been brought here takes the dairy off a little bit.

"So, what can I do for you today, Mr. Foxx?" Davis asks enthusiastically.

"We need a few evening gowns and lots of lingerie," Max answers, smirking.

"Oh, don't we all dah'ling." Davis hooks his arm through mine and starts to walk. "I've got some fabulous couture that will look amazing on you, Vivienne." He walks us down a few steps to a lounge area with two massive ornamental mirrors, cream sofas, and a low glass table. A woman arrives with a silver tray and two glasses of Champagne, she sets it down on the table and asks to take my coat, then she disappears. Max sits on the sofa while Davis shows me to a changing room which has wall to wall mirrors and a small chaise long.

A few moments later, the woman reappears with a clothes rail full of gowns. Davis looks me up and down for a moment. "Oh, you're tiny," he says, then he hums and haws for a moment before pulling three gowns from the rail and then he brings them into my changing room. "Just call me if you need any assistance, Vivienne. I'll be right outside." Then he closes the door.

I undress, and check the gown for a price tag but I can't

find one anywhere. I step into it and pull it up. It's a stunning piece of art. The fabric is a patterned velvet and satin mixture in a rich, purple colour. It goes well with my colouring. It's beautifully made and extremely comfortable to wear. I'm not sure about the one shoulder thing, but it looks very nice. I step out and walk to the lounge to show Max. His appreciative eyes run up and down my whole body.

"That's gorgeous," he says, still trawling his eyes over it.

Hmm, I think it makes me look older than I am.

As I'm stepping out of the gown, Davis barges into my room with an armful of new gowns. "Oh!" I yelp, surprised that he's just waltzed in without knocking.

"Oh, dah'ling, don't worry about me," he smirks. "I'm so gay you couldn't straighten me out with a steam roller. I'm much more likely to shove you in the cupboard and run off with your dreamboat of a boyfriend," he sighs wistfully.

I stare at him a little gob-smacked.

He arches a glossy brow. "That was a joke, dear. I'd never do that to one of my esteemed customers…well, maybe just this once," he giggles.

I chuckle at him as he helps me into another gorgeous dress, which is even lovelier than the first one. It's a strapless shimmering tube of blue crystals with a back slit. *I quite like this one.* It doesn't have a price tag either.

"If you don't mind me saying so, Vivienne, you were made to wear fabulous gowns."

"Thanks," I blush.

"Well, you should see some of the women I have to shoe-horn into these things," he mutters, rolling his eyes. "It's a testament to the quality of the stitching that they survive the strain."

When I show Max, he says he really likes it, but I haven't seen that look in his eye yet. The one that tells me he really, really likes it. I try on dozens of dresses until I'm starting to feel like I couldn't face another one. They're all very nice and some of them are very glamorous, but none of them have registered that special look in Max's eye that I was hoping for.

Davis walks in to help me out of the dress. I've got used to him being in the room while I'm standing there in my underwear and he's been very helpful. He's brought what I hope to be the last dress. My headache is growing worse, and I've already finished the pack of painkillers I'd brought out with me.

"Vivienne, I'll be honest, I thought these were a little old for you, but these ones here were gorgeous on you," he says, pointing at the ones I liked.

"But this one," he says, holding it up, "this is the one for you, and I know Mr. Foxx will adore it," he smiles, waggling his eyebrows.

I look at it on the hanger. It certainly looks very nice and I love the colour, but as soon as I put it on, I know it's going to blow Max's mind. This is definitely the one.

Davis gazes at me in awe. "Well, dah'ling. In that dress, you could even turn *me* butch."

I look at it from every angle. It's very fitted and hugs me in all the right places. It has long sleeves, a thigh high split and a plunging deep V-shape at the back. The satin fabric is a rich shade of red with an intricate sparkling lace overlay, and it has a very small train at the back. I look like a movie star going to the Oscars.

"How much is this Davis?" I ask nervously.

He gasps in mock-shock. "Dah'ling girl, when a man offers to buy you couture, one must never ask the price," he chides.

"But—"

"No, no. Please desist. I shall never divulge that information. Even if you tortured me with the hideous screechings of an x-factor finalist. Or made me wear nylon. Or forced me to eat double egg and chips at a greasy spoon," he shudders. "My lips are sealed, dah'ling," he says, dramatically like he's delivering a line from

Shakespeare.

"Well, is it under or over five hundred pounds?"

He laughs. "Oh, dear girl. How you jest." I just stare at him waiting for him to spill the beans. "Dah'ling. If I tell you how much it costs, I'll have to kill you, and I've just had my manicure." He gives me a smile then wafts out of the room and holds the door open for me.

As I walk out to the lounge, Max has his head down talking on the phone. He looks up at me and immediately stops talking, his eyes tell me that this is the one. They drag up and down the dress getting darker as they travel all the way back up to my eyes.

"Stunning," he whispers, then his super-sexy smile spreads across his handsome face. I turn to show him the back view. "Oh, my God. You're killing me," he rasps, rising to his feet. He picks up both glasses of Champagne and walks his predatory walk toward me. Handing me a glass, he leans in to kiss me softly on the lips as he runs his hand down the exposed skin on my back. It sends a sensual shiver up my spine.

"We'll take it, and whatever else Vivienne liked," he says, to Davis never taking his smoldering eyes from mine. "You look beautiful," he whispers, before clinking our glasses together and taking a sip of his Champagne.

"Max, it's very exp—"

"Ah, ah. No. Please don't," he says, arching a brow. "You're worth every penny. And I want to buy you nice things." His eyes become hooded and dark and I can feel myself being drawn in as a dull throb pulses in my groin. As I stare into his scorching eyes, I feel myself begin to sway. I place my hand on his shoulder and push onto my toes to kiss him. "Thank you," I whisper against his lips.

He inhales deeply then releases a long sigh. "I'd better call Grace back. I kind of left her hanging," he smirks.

As I change back into my own clothes, I suddenly feel very hot and dizzy. I sit on the chaise long and wait for the moment to pass. *I should have eaten more at breakfast.* Just the thought of food churns my stomach.

"Are you alright, Vivienne?" I look up and see Davis's worried face staring down at me. "You look pale, shall I get Mr. Foxx?"

"Oh, no. I'm fine. It's just very warm in here." He regards me for a moment longer. *Please don't mention it to Max.*

"Why don't you sit in the lounge, it's much cooler out there. I'll bring you some water."

I take a few deep breaths before I stand up. He's right, the lounge is much cooler, and I feel better out here. Davis brings me a selection of lingerie in exactly my size. He's very observant. I pick out the red set to go with my new dress and some stockings.

"We'll take them all," Max says, without batting an eye. Then he throws me his sexy smile.

Max gets a phone call as Davis shows me some lovely red shoes to match my gown and a cute little clutch bag, but I decline. I think Max has spent quite enough on me already.

"Thanks, Davis, you've been so helpful." I reach out to shake his hand, he kisses the back of it instead.

"Vivienne, it was entirely my pleasure, and I hope to see you again soon."

Max shakes his hand and asks Davis to have the items delivered so we leave the shop empty handed.

"Can I buy you a coffee?" It's the least I can do after being treated to all those lovely things.

"Sure." He takes my hand, lacing our fingers together, and walks me down to a little café. The waitress takes our order batting her lashes at Max, who seems oblivious to her attempts to catch his eye. It makes me smile. I love the fact that he seems not to notice.

"What?" he asks, on a frown.

"Nothing," I smirk.

"Max. Hi, what are you doing here?" We both look up

and Max smiles when he sees her.

"Fiona. I thought you were still in New Zealand?"

A tall, gorgeous, willowy blonde walks over to our table. He stands and greets her affectionately, kissing her on both cheeks. Max introduces me without mentioning the word fiancé or girlfriend which jars me a little, and now I know who Fiona is. Maybe he doesn't want her to know I'm his fiancé? But then I'm not his fiancé yet, he hasn't proposed.

She only gives me a quick cursory glance before directing her eyes back to Max, still resting her hand on his arm. "Max, I'm so sorry I wasn't here for you. I heard about poor Charlie, it was shocking. That must have been awful for you," she says, stroking his arm. He just shrugs and nods. "Did they find Monica yet?"

His face tightens. "No. Not yet."

"You poor darling, you should have called me, I'd have flown straight home," she says, cupping his cheek in her hand.

Hmmf.

Two other women call to her from the doorway. "Oh, I'd better go, my friends are waiting. It's lovely to see you again, Max. I've missed you. I'll see you next week at the ball." She smiles, leaning forward to hug him and then she kisses him on the lips.

Really?

"Oh and here's my new number." She reaches into her bag and hands him a card. "Call me!" She kisses him again then glances down at me before turning to leave. Max watches her walk all the way to the door before sitting down again.

The unreasonable jealousy knotting my stomach sours my mood. I don't want to feel like this, and he's given me no reason not to trust him, but I still feel like a visitor in Max's world. Of all people, I know how awful it is to live with a jealous partner. Mike's jealousy made life very difficult for me sometimes. I don't want to be like that, but

I just can't help the way I feel.

"Who is she?" I ask, trying to mask my irritation.

"Fiona?…Just an old friend," he shrugs.

"An old girlfriend?" I didn't mean to say it out loud, but it just came out.

"Yeah," he nods, stirring his coffee without so much as a hint of awareness that I might be a bit put out by that.

I try not to show it on my face but my possessive streak has kicked in and robbed me of my confidence. Fiona is stunning, in fact, all the other women he's been out with are stunning. I don't know what the hell he sees in me?

Something tells me that my feelings are plastered all over my face when he reaches over and takes my hand in his. "Vivienne, she's just a friend. I've stayed friends with a lot of women I've dated, but it doesn't mean anything."

Maybe not to you. I pull my hand out of his. I hate how jealous I feel. It's not like me at all. I quickly change the subject. "I've got a fitting with Lucy tomorrow for my bridesmaid dress."

"Okay, I'll get John to drive you there."

"No, it's okay, I'll go on my bike." I don't look up at him. I know he's going to protest, but I'm still miffed at the prospect of bumping into all his ex-girlfriends every time we go out.

"Vivienne, I don't want you riding that bike. It's dangerous," he frowns.

"Pff, dangerous? I've faced death twice just staying at home. How bad can it be?" I immediately regret saying it. He flinches and lowers his eyes. I know he still feels guilty that he wasn't there to protect me from Monica the first time she tried to kill me. The second time she tried, it really hit him hard. I feel bad for bringing it up, but my pride stops me from apologising, and his guilt stops him from pushing the point any further.

We walk back to the car. Max curls his arm around my waist and we walk in silence. My niggling brain is doing overtime.

As we leave the car park, he lays his hand on my thigh. "Are you mad at me, baby?"

Yes!...No!...Urgh, I'm mad at myself. If I'm honest with myself, I'm acting like a jealous idiot because I know it's only a matter of time before he realises I'm all wrong for him. I'm wrong for him in ways he doesn't even know yet. *I'm going to have to tell him...*

"Baby?"

His concerned expression melts my heart. He's done nothing to make me think that his feelings for me aren't real, but I can't for the life of me understand why he's chosen me.

You'll change your mind when you know the truth. "No, Max. I'm not mad at you." I sigh. "I've got a headache, and I'm just tired that's all." I rest my head back against the seat and close my eyes. I'm not ready to tell him yet.

We arrive back at the penthouse without speaking two words to each other. I've felt Max staring at me trying to figure out my mood. He can see something's bothering me, but I'm sure he thinks it's something he's said or done. The reality is, everything he's said and done just makes it harder for me to tell him what I need to.

Maybe he'll come to his senses and I won't need to tell him anyway... "I'm going to go and lie down for a while," I say, heading toward the stairs. I can feel his eyes on me, but I feel too emotional to talk to him, and I really need to be by myself for a while.

"Can I get you anything? You haven't eaten all day."

I don't turn around. "No, I'm fine. I just need some sleep." The tears prick my eyes so I keep on walking.

The room is dark when I feel Max's arms pulling me into his chest. He lies behind me, spooning me, kissing me softly on the shoulder, and then he lets out a long sigh. I hadn't intended to, but I must have slept for hours, and now I'm wide awake.

"Max?..."

"What is it, baby?" he asks snuggling into me.

"Why didn't you tell that girl I was your girlfriend?" I feel his breathing pause. I regret asking him now but it's been on my mind ever since I saw Fiona and realised I had so much competition out there. If he's still friends with all his ex's, surely he's going to realise he's picked the wrong girl sooner or later.

He props himself up on one elbow and waits for me to look up at him.

"Who Fiona?" he asks, a little surprised. I don't answer, and I'm thoroughly embarrassed by my insecurity. "I didn't realise I hadn't." He takes in a deep breath and lets out a long sigh. "Vivienne, I understand. I do," he says, searching my eyes. "If Mike were to show up when we were out together I'd feel the same way. Believe me, I see how men look at you, and I don't like it." His frown deepens. "You're mine, and you have nothing to worry about. I love you and I never want you to doubt that." The sincerity in his eyes floors me, and I hate myself for being so insecure and needy, it's not a trait I recognise.

He kisses me softly on the lips then he lies back and pulls me onto his chest. "Please don't take the bike tomorrow," he whispers. "I'm just worried that you might have another blackout or something. Davis told me you felt dizzy this afternoon. I just want you to be safe."

Oh. I kiss his tattoo and snuggle into him. "Okay."

ALL WRONG FOR YOU

I wake to the shrill, irritating sound of my alarm clock. I throw my arm out of the covers and whack the snooze button as the piercing noise stabs into my skull like a sharp knife. *Hell-fire I'm going to have to change that sodding alarm.*

Max left for work very early this morning for an important business meeting. He woke me with a kiss and told me John will drive me to the fitting. I didn't bother to argue because he's right! I have had a few blackouts since I got out of the hospital. The blackouts are frightening, and I thought I was going to pass out yesterday while I was trying on the dresses, but I think it was just low blood sugar because I hadn't eaten much at breakfast. I'm sure it's nothing to worry about but better safe than sorry.

When Max left, I was all set to get up and make a start sorting through all my boxes from the flat, but I was still feeling so exhausted and I couldn't be bothered to move.

Just five more minutes…

"Vivienne?…Vivienne. May I come in?"

Huh? I open my eyes to see Jan's head poking around the bedroom door. I blink and squint at the bright sunlight pouring in through the curtains.

"Vivienne, I've brought you a cup of coffee."

I drag myself up and rest my head against the headboard. I'm disoriented, and when I look down, I find my white rose is squashed and stuck to my arm. "What time is it?" I croak.

"It's eleven o'clock. I didn't want to disturb you but I'll be leaving in a minute. I have an appointment at the solicitors."

"What? It can't be?" I look at my alarm clock. *Shit!* "I'm late." I throw the covers back and race into the bathroom. "Sorry Jan," I yell. "Thanks for the coffee."

I quickly shower and throw on some clothes then I call John.

I meet him down in the basement and he drives me to the shop for my fitting. Lucy's left me tons of messages asking me where I am. I'm forty minutes late.

"I'm so sorry, Luce," I say, running toward the shop. She's standing at the door waiting for me with a face on.

"Where the hell have you been? I've been calling you," she says, hugging me. "You look terrible," she adds, holding me at arm's length.

"I know. I'm sorry. I overslept."

"You should tell him to give you a break, you look exhausted," she smirks.

"Sorry. Will they still be able to do our fitting?"

"Yeah, come on."

Lucy and I change into our respective dresses. I almost cry when I see Lucy's wedding dress, it's really beautiful. It's ivory with a structured bodice, a full skirt and off the shoulder sleeves. My dress is in the same style at the top but has a much narrower skirt and is a lovely shade of burgundy. Both our dresses have to be altered, mine especially. I've lost so much weight recently that although it's my usual size, it just hangs off me.

The dressmaker makes me stand on a raised platform while she pins the dress. I ask her to leave me some wiggle room just in case I put weight on now that I'm getting back to normal.

"Is it hot in here?" I can feel perspiration on my upper lip, and I'm starting to feel a bit lightheaded too.

"Viv! Viv! Can you hear me?" I open my eyes to Lucy's worried face peering down at me. It takes me a moment to realise I'm lying down.

"What happened?" I ask, trying to sit up. Lucy pushes me back down. "Just lie still for a minute. You fainted."

Someone hands Lucy a glass of water. "Shall I call an ambulance?" the person asks.

"No! No, I'm fine. I just felt a bit queasy that's all," I say, pushing myself up. Lucy helps me stand up and walks me to a chair.

"Here, drink this," she says, handing me the water. I take a sip then I finish the whole glass. I didn't realise I was so thirsty.

"Viv, I think you need to go to the doctor, or back to the hospital. Maybe you should have another scan or something," Lucy says, kneeling in front of me. "You're so pale and look at you, you're shaking like a leaf and skinny as a rake." My hands are shaking, and I feel sick. "Have you passed out before? Since you came home from the hospital, I mean?" I look away sheepishly. "Oh, Viv," she scolds. "Does Max know?"

I shake my head. "He'll only worry, and I'm sure it's just because I haven't eaten. I just need to build my strength back up that's all."

Lucy eyes me sceptically. "Viv, I've never known you not to eat. You're a human dustbin for chrissake. I'll get you something from the café next door," she says, starting to rise.

"I'm not hungry. I can't eat with this headache, it makes me feel sick."

She shakes her head with a worried frown. "If you've lost your appetite then there's definitely something wrong." Suddenly her eyes widen and she searches my face with a funny look on hers. She grabs me by the shoulders and gasps, "Oh, my God… You're pregnant."

My headache pounds even more, when I hear the joy in her voice. "No, I'm not," I murmur.

Her smiling eyes search my face. "Well of course you are. Dizzy spells, sickness. It makes sense. You've got morning sickness, you're pregnant." Lucy's smile slowly disintegrates, and a worried frown takes over. "What's the matter?" she asks, as tears pool in my eyes. I can't speak past the lump in my throat. "Oh, Viv, don't cry. Come on, let's get out of these dresses and then we'll go and find somewhere to talk."

As we leave the shop, John is waiting for me in the Range Rover.

"Wait here," Lucy says, then she walks over to speak to him. "We're just going for some lunch and then I'll bring her home," she tells him. He nods and waves at me then pulls away from the kerb.

My phone vibrates in my pocket. It's a text from Max;

```
Hey, beautiful.
I'll be home in a couple
of hours. Your gowns have
been delivered.
I look forward to the
lingerie fashion show!
I love you
X;-)
```

My heart twists.

```
Can't wait!
Xx:-)
```

I turn my phone off and put it back in my pocket. We walk to the wine bar on the corner and sit at a table in the window. Lucy waits for the waitress to take our order before asking me any questions. I can see the concern in her eyes when I order a large white wine.

"Are you sure you should be drinking alcohol?" she asks, arching her brow. I just huff out a sarcastic response.

I need a drink .

Lucy eyes me warily, trying to gauge me. I haven't spoken since the dress shop because the lump in my throat is still there, along with the threat of tears as soon as I tell her what's swirling around in my brain.

When the drinks arrive, I take a couple of mouthfuls.

Lucy does the same, still eyeing me with caution until she gets a phone call.

"It's Max," she frowns, handing me her phone. I immediately cancel the call and hand it back to her. She looks surprised for a moment and then I get the eyebrow. "Viv, what's going on?" I just stare out the window, watching the people go by. "If you're not pregnant then you need to see a doctor to find out why you're fainting and feeling sick. And if you are pregnant… why are you so unhappy?"

Her phone rings again. "It's him again."

"Don't answer it," I mumble, still staring out the window. She reluctantly turns her phone off and places it on the table shaking her head. I stare down at my glass and spin the stem in my fingers.

"Viv, talk to me, please… If you're worried about what Max will think, then don't. That man loves you so much, and quite frankly, I think he'd be over the moon if you were pregnant."

Oh, God. My heart twists and my eyes fill with tears. I've tried, but I can't hold them off any longer.

Lucy reaches across the table and squeezes my hand. "Viv, please talk to me." She hands me a napkin to dry my tears and patiently waits for me to speak.

"I'm not pregnant… I can never be pregnant."

Lucy's shocked, sad eyes trail over my face. Then she asks the inevitable question. "Why not?" I briefly close my eyes and take a deep, calming breath then a large gulp of wine as my mind searches through the painful memories I've tried so hard to bury.

"Dad was away filming in India. He'd been away for months and months and my mum couldn't cope, so she drank more and more. She'd started to take drugs now too. I was about ten years old but I knew what she was doing, and I hated it." I flick my eyes up to Lucy. I have her full attention. Reluctantly, I continue. "The house was always full of strangers, especially at night. I think some of them were her boyfriends… anyway, I would often wake up in the middle of the night and find three or four people passed out in the living room. The whole place stunk, and it was littered with beer cans, food, empty bottles, weird shaped spoons, and what I now know, was cocaine." I glance up at Lucy again, she just waits patiently for me to continue. That familiar feeling of dread coils in my stomach as the vivid memories unfold in my mind.

"If Mum was still conscious when I woke up, she'd make me go to the kitchen and get her some food. She called it 'the munchies,'" I huff. "Some of the people were regular visitors, some of them were new, but there were always people in the house at night.

One night, a man came into my room and just stood over me, watching me. He didn't look like all the other men, he was smart and dressed in nice clothes. He came in and sat on the edge of my bed and stroked my face. He reminded me a bit of my dad. He had a nice smile and kind eyes. He said, 'You're so pretty, like a little doll.' …He just stared at me for ages and then he stood up and left." The memory of him speaking those words is crystal clear and makes a shudder run down my spine.

"I fell asleep and woke up again a bit later. The same man was sitting on my bed. I felt cold. I looked down and I saw that he'd pulled the covers back, and he'd pulled my nightie up to my chin. He was… touching me, and he had a horrible look on his face. I cried, I was so scared, but he put his hand over my mouth."

I hear Lucy gasp but I can't bring myself to look at her. I just keep staring at my glass of wine, spinning the stem in my fingers.

"I could hear my mum laughing in the next room, but she didn't come for me. The man was… touching himself, and then when he'd finished he looked so angry, and he told me not to say anything or I'd get into trouble, and then he left… I was so scared. I hid in my wardrobe." I take another mouthful of wine then I place it down on the table and stare into the glass.

I can feel Lucy's eyes on me, but I can't face her reaction just yet, and she hasn't spoken a word. I, on the other hand, can't seem to shut up.

"I stole a rounder's bat from school, and I kept it beside my bed in case the man came back… And he did. Two weeks later he crept into my room one night and closed the door behind him. I screamed and screamed but my mum didn't come for me. I swung the bat as hard as I could but I couldn't stop him. He held me down and…" I shudder, closing my teary eyes.

"He raped you didn't he?" Lucy whispers.

I screw my eyes tight. The tears stream down my face as the horrific sights, sounds, and smells of that terrifying night come flooding back.

"Oh, Vivienne. I'm so sorry. I'm so, so sorry. Why didn't you tell me?"

"I've never told anyone, not even the police. I was too afraid of him." His face flashes into my mind and makes me feel sick. I'll never forget his face.

"What happened after that, I mean surely your mum—" I interrupt her with a sarcastic laugh then I take another mouthful of wine.

"My teacher noticed the bruises on my wrists and shoulders, she called social services. When I was taken into care, they examined me and found that I'd been raped but I never said a word, I never told a sole. I just wouldn't talk about it. Not even to my dad." I look up at Lucy's sad face. "That's why they divorced, because of what happened to me that night." I take another drink, my hands are shaking.

"They told me I'd never be able to have children… I was ten. I didn't understand it then…But now…"

Lucy weeps as she holds my hand and squeezes it tightly. "Jesus, Viv… I…I don't know what to say?" There's nothing anyone can say.

I catch the waitress's eye and order another large wine

for both of us. Lucy waits for the girl to take our order and leave.

"Does Max know?" she asks hesitantly.

I laugh. I don't know why but I do, and I can't stop laughing. "There's no point. He won't want to marry me now." The laughter turns into sobs of self-pity. I can feel people staring at me, but I don't give a shit. I need to let all the pain and anguish out. I've buried it and carried it around with me for far too long.

"Of course he wants to marry you. The guy's besotted with you. He loves you so much," Lucy says, drying my tears.

I shake my head. She's wrong. "You saw what he was like with Charlie. He's aching to be a father. He's dedicated a whole wall to our family photo's for fuck's sake."

"Has he told you that? Have you talked about it?"

"How can I talk about it? It's not something I can give him."

"You can adopt or—"

"No!… No…I can't marry him. It's too selfish of me to even think about taking that away from him."

"Viv, you're not thinking straight. That's the wine talking. Maybe—"

"No, Luce. I am thinking straight. For once my mind has never been clearer. I can't marry him. I love him too much to deny him his chance to become a father. I've just been kidding myself."

"Viv, you need to talk to him."

"And say what? Hey, Max. I love you so much that I want you to forfeit your own happiness to make me happy… Pff!"

"Viv, you're being ridiculous. The man deserves to make his own mind up about it. You need to tell him, you need to talk about it. And you need to do it now."

I finish my glass and order another. I feel like drowning my sorrows, and the last thing I want to do is to go home and face the music.

Lucy calls Dan to tell him where we are and that we're going to get a cab home later. Lucy's advice is to come clean and talk to Max about it, and she's right, but that would only seal my fate and I'm not ready for that yet. I'm too much of a coward. Too selfish.

I love Max, more than I've ever loved anyone. I don't want to lose him. But I don't want to see the pain in his eyes when I tell him that I can never give him children. I've selfishly kept that to myself. But who am I to deny him his future, his right. And why would he still want me when he finds out?

The drinks keep on coming and as I haven't eaten at all today, I'm completely legless by my fourth glass.

The end of day work crowd has started to arrive, and the music is turned up a couple of notches. Lucy comes back from the ladies room looking decidedly shifty.

"Viv, we should go, you're pissed as a fart," she shouts above the music, arching a brow.

"Ah, don't be a moo-bag Loosh, less-have-a-dance," I slur, then giggle and hiccup simultaneously. "Come on." I grab her arm and slither off my stool. I drag her over to the tiny dance floor and start bouncing to the music. Lucy stands on the edge of the dance floor scowling at me. She tries to drag me away but I resist, pulling back.

"Viv, come on, we need to go. Max is on his way."

"You called him?" I ask, glaring at her. She just nods sheepishly. The thought of admitting to him that I can never give him a family, churns my stomach. I'm not ready to face him yet.

"No! I don't wanna go." I pull out of her arm and stagger backwards, bumping into a group of guys and spilling their drinks. "Oops, sorry," I slur, giggling and trying to focus on their faces. The room is spinning. *Man, I'm pissed.*

I start to wobble on my heels, and one of the men puts his arm around me to steady me. "Are you alright, love?"

Suddenly I don't feel so good. *Oh, no!* He asks me again. I just bend at the waist and throw up all over his shoes. Everyone scatters and yelps as I evacuate the wine from my stomach.

It finally stops, and someone on my left holds out a white handkerchief so I grab it and clamp it over my mouth. I'm still heaving, but nothing else comes up.

"Here, get yourself some new shoes." I straighten and my unfocused eyes land on Max's angry face as he hands the poor man some cash.

I fling my arms in the air. "My shite in nighning armour," I giggle, then I burst into laughter at my drunken mistake. He doesn't find me funny at all, and just continues to glare at me while I sway on my heels. "Grumpy-drawers," I grumble, staggering on my feet.

"You're drunk," he grates, frowning angrily.

I burst out laughing again, everything seems so funny. "I am…Just a teeny, weeny, teeny bit," I giggle, trying to show him a teeny-weeny amount with my uncoordinated fingers. "That's because I've been drinking," I smirk.

He continues to glare at me shaking his head, which just makes me laugh even more.

"Dance with me," I mumble, pulling his arm, but he stands rock solid and gives me the death stare. I'm finding it hard to focus on him as the room continues to spin. My knees buckle and Max quickly catches me before I fall, scooping me into his arms. I wrap my arms around his neck. "Do you love me, Max?" I ask, trying to focus on his face. I know he does, I just need to hear him say it. He just looks straight ahead, clenching his jaw. When I realise he's not going to even bother to humour me with a reply, I suddenly feel very melancholy. "You won't," I mumble. "Not when you know." I rest my head against his shoulder. My blurry eyes land on Lucy, who's scowling at me.

"For fuck's sake, Viv," she sighs angrily, then she marches off in front of us.

When I hit the fresh air, I feel worse. My drunken headache is hammering against my skull and I feel sick again. Max buckles me into the front seat, opens my window and gives me a plastic bag. "Use this if you're going to throw up," he scowls, then he rests my head back against the headrest and moves my hair out of my eyes.

"I'm sorry," I murmur sheepishly. He scowls at me, clenching his jaw then he slams the door shut. He's obviously very angry with me when he pulls away from the kerb with a screech of tyres.

"What the fuck was she doing getting so drunk? She's only been out of the god-damned hospital for three days. I've been worried sick. I've been calling all afternoon, and neither of you answered."

"I'm sorry, Max, she's just…it's… She passed out at the fitting and she's been a bit depressed so I took her out for a drink to try and cheer her up."

Oh, no. I'm going to be sick! I heave another glass of wine into the plastic bag. I feel so hollow, I didn't think there was anything left.

Max drops Lucy off at her house, he walks her to her door and they stand and talk for a while, then he drives us home without a word.

He carries me up to the bedroom and sits me on the edge of the bed. Holding onto me with one hand he takes all my clothes off. I keep flopping over, I just can't keep myself upright. The room is spinning too much and my head is pounding.

"I'm sorry," I murmur, but he doesn't say a word, he just shoots me an angry glare. When I'm naked, he sits on the bed beside me.

"What did you mean when you said I wouldn't love you anymore when I knew? Knew what?"

I rest my spinning head against his shoulder and close my tired eyes. "I'm ahhronforyou."

"What?"

"I'm all wrong for you."

MAYBE I WAS WRONG

I wake to the sound of the shower running in the bathroom. I'm lying on my side, naked, and clutching an empty plastic bowl to my chest. *What the?….. Oh, yeah…. Oh, no.*

I have an awful taste in my mouth, a thumping headache, and my stomach rolls as I slowly recall what happened last night. *Oh, God!*

There's a faint whiff of vomit in my hair, churning my stomach even more. Dragging myself out of bed, I quickly run to the bathroom and barge through the door. Standing over the toilet with my hands resting on the seat, I heave several times and then kneel down and wait until the nausea passes.

"Vivienne!" Max appears at my side and pulls me up, then he sits me on the toilet seat. He kneels down in front of me, naked and dripping wet from his shower, searching my face with worried eyes. "You look awful," he scowls.

Thanks.

"I've made an appointment with Doctor Alexander for twelve o'clock."

"No, I'm fine," I mumble. "It's my own stupid fault for drinking on an empty stomach."

He huffs an agreement. "When was your last period?" I'm shocked at his direct question. Even he thinks I'm pregnant.

If only. I shake my head and lower my eyes. "No… It's

not that." His eyes narrow on me. "I'm on the pill," I lie.

"Lucy said you passed out at the fitting yesterday, and you've been having headaches and sickness since you left the hospital. You should have told me, Vivienne."

"I didn't want you to worry."

"Jesus!" He drags his hand through his hair. "I am worried. I should have made you go to the hospital that first day you collapsed in the shower. How the hell can I take care of you if I don't know what's going on?" he asks incredulously. "I don't want you taking chances with your health. For chrissake, Vivienne, you've just got out of the hospital, you have to tell me these things." His eyes lower for a moment, and then they return to mine with renewed concern. "Lucy said you were depressed. Why didn't you tell me?"

Thanks, Luce. Big mouth. "I'm not. Stop fussing." I go to stand up but he stops me and gently pushes me back down.

"Is it me? Is it something I've said or done to hurt you?" The look on his face melts my heart. I briefly close my eyes to avoid its effect. I don't want to cry.

"No. It's not you." I smooth his cheek with my palm. "The headaches have been getting me down, that's all." I try to smile at him but I'm struggling to hold on to my resolve. I don't want to cry, I might never stop.

He searches my face for ages, trying to read me. "Are you worried about something?" he asks softly.

Petrified… You're going to hate me when you know. I shake my head and force a smile. "No." I can't say any more than that, the lump in my throat is choking me. I can see in his eyes that he knows there's more but thankfully, he doesn't push for it.

"I need to brush my teeth." I stand up and move past him to the basin. I watch him through the mirror as he dries himself off. I can see by the worry line in his brow that he's confused and concerned. When he leaves the bathroom I take some more painkillers to relieve my thudding headache, and then I take a quick shower. My mind is all over the place and my belly knots with anxiety. *Maybe he doesn't need to know?* Lots of women can't have children. Some of them go through their whole life never knowing why? *Can I really live with that lie hanging over my head?*

It's no use. I can't lie to him, or myself. I need to tell him the truth. I can't put it off any longer, it just isn't fair. I've been burying my head in the sand for way too long. We'd said no secrets. And mine isn't one you can brush under the carpet, or bury out of sight. My secret affects us both.

We've survived so much together during our brief relationship, and Max has overcome so many emotional obstacles to be where he is right now. But if I don't tell him the truth, how will he ever trust me again? He's offering himself to me, and giving so much, more than I ever could have wished for, but I can only offer him a limited version of myself in return. One that I know will never be enough for a man like him. I owe him the truth. He deserves the truth.

When I'm dressed, I find Max sitting in the kitchen. My eyes drink in his handsomeness and my heart clenches knowing that if I tell him, that could be the end of us.

He looks up and drags his eyes over my body. I'm going to miss those eyes. The way he looks at me like I'm a treasured possession that he could never live without. I crave his eyes on me.

"What's the matter?" he asks frowning. I suddenly realise I'm just standing there staring at him.

"Nothing." I force a smile and take a seat at the island. Max drags my stool closer to him and lays his hand on my thigh. His touch plays havoc with my butterflies, as usual.

"Good morning, Vivienne. Bacon sandwich?" Jan asks, pouring me some orange juice. My stomach rolls. I feel empty, but I really couldn't eat.

"Just toast, please." I notice Jan and Max exchanging a look before she turns to make my breakfast.

Max reaches into his pocket and throws four empty blister packs onto the counter. I instantly recognise them as the strong painkillers I've been taking to try and get rid of this constant headache.

"You should have told me about the headaches," he says, searching my face with a hurt expression. I look down and fidget, wringing my hands in my lap, but he places his hand over mine to still them.

"There you are, Vivienne." Jan puts a plate of toast in front of me. Max sighs in frustration and finishes his coffee.

"I've got to make a call, please eat your toast." He stands and mutters something under his breath, then he walks out of the kitchen.

I nibble at the toast but I really don't want it.

"Vivienne, you look troubled, is there anything I can do to help?" Jan asks, taking a seat opposite. I push the toast and orange juice away. "You really should eat something. The sickness will pass," she adds, with a knowing smile.

Oh, not you too. "Can I have some milk?"

Jan jumps up and gets me a glass of cold milk. I drink it, then I notice that the toast has disappeared from my plate. Jan just smiles at me and gives me a little wink.

When Max returns, I notice him eyeing my empty plate. He takes my hand, and then we head off to the hospital for my appointment.

I sense that he's still mad at me for my drunken behaviour last night when he doesn't speak during our ride to the hospital. The car journey is less uncomfortable when he receives several phone calls breaking the awkward silence.

My pounding headache has got much worse on the way here, and I'm so glad I didn't eat anything. I'd be so embarrassed if I threw up all over the DB9.

As we approach Doctor Alexander's office, my nerves kick up a notch. The headaches have been pretty constant since I left the hospital, there's got to be a valid reason for them. My mind starts to conjure up all kinds of unwanted explanations. *What if he tells me that I've got a clot, or a brain tumour. Or worse! Shit! What if he's got my medical records and he tells Max before I do?*

Doctor Alexander asks me how I've been since I left the hospital, but Max answers for me.

"She's not been herself, and she's been way too active. She hasn't rested at all." he says throwing his hands in the air. "She's blacked out several times. She's not eating. She's been drinking alcohol, *and* she's gone through all these since she left the hospital!" He throws the empty painkiller packs onto his desk.

Doctor Alexander picks up one of the empty packs and raises his eyebrows. Then he offers me a reassuring smile. "Vivienne, on a scale of one to ten, how would you describe the pain in your head?"

I look up at Max, who's still frowning, even though his eyes convey his concern. "Sometimes it's a five, sometimes it's a ten," I answer honestly.

"And you've lost your appetite?"

"Yes, if I eat I feel sick."

"And how are your sleeping patterns."

"I sleep okay, but I've had a few nightmares since… erm…" I suddenly stop when I realise that I haven't told Max about the frequency of my nightmares, or the content.

Max stares at me incredulously. "Why didn't you tell me?" he asks, with a hurt expression and sad eyes. I don't answer, I just stare down at my knotted fingers in my lap.

Doctor Alexander stands, drawing our attention. "I'd like to do an ECG, and we'll do a blood test, a urine test, and another CT scan."

"Okay," I mumble, embarrassed that my urine sample will no doubt be pure alcohol. *Pee-no Grigio.* My stomach rolls at the thought.

"Mr. Foxx, I'd like to do these tests now, you can wait in

the visitors room if you like. I'll call you when all the tests have been completed." Max looks irritated at being dismissed. He rises reluctantly and kisses me on the top of my head before he leaves the room muttering under his breath.

Once he's gone, Doctor Alexander takes me through to his examination room for the blood test. He also checks my temperature and blood pressure, then he looks in my eyes and ears. Apparently, my blood pressure is a bit low and according to the doctor, I'm very dehydrated.

After all that, he takes me downstairs for the ECG and CT scan. Once the scans have been done, he asks me to produce some urine so I head off to the toilet with my little plastic pot.

I hand the sample over and then I wait for Doctor Alexander in his office. He returns thirty minutes later with the results.

"Well, Vivienne, I'm happy to tell you that it's all good news," he smiles. "Your scan and ECG were absolutely fine. Your headaches and nausea seem to be the result of low blood pressure, iron deficiency, dehydration, and good old fashioned stress."

He takes off his glasses and places them on his desk, then he smiles at me sympathetically. "Your physical injuries speak for themselves, and I have to say, you've been remarkably lucky to have recovered so well, but you've also had to deal with a lot of anxiety over the last few weeks. I can see the tension in your body now." He's right, my shoulders are up, and my hands are clenching and releasing all the time. "Tension can build up in the muscles causing prolonged headaches and of course, the attacks you suffered were particularly brutal. Anxiety can deeply affect your well-being. I can refer you to a—"

"No! Really, I'm fine," I interrupt, forcing a smile. *I'm not going back into therapy. No way.*

He looks surprised for a moment, but he doesn't push it. Putting his glasses back on, he clasps his hands on the desk in front of him.

"You're a healthy young woman, Vivienne, but the body really does need time to repair itself, and I can't tell you how important it is to rest after the injuries you've sustained. Furthermore," he says, raising an eyebrow, "misuse of pain medication isn't advisable. Apart from the obvious dangers, it can cause irritation in the stomach lining, which in turn, can create nausea and vomiting. I'm going to give you a new prescription with an enteric coating, but you must follow the dosage exactly." He waits for me to respond. I nod sheepishly. I know he's right. I've been taking the painkillers almost hourly. "I would also suggest that you eat a healthy, balanced diet. Lots of green vegetables, lots of water and above all, rest."

"Thank you, Doctor."

"Not at all," he smiles. "I'm afraid there's nothing I can prescribe for the nightmares other than maybe talking about them with Max. It's often better to share the things that frighten us, rather than storing them up and letting them become more powerful than they really are."

He's right again. But the thing that frightens me the most, isn't something I want Max to know.

Doctor Alexander walks me down to the visitor's room. A wave of nausea hits me when I see Max through the window, anxiously pacing the room.

"I'm just going to the loo," I say, letting the doctor walk ahead of me.

Just as I open the door to the ladies room, I hear Max's worried voice. "Is she pregnant?" My stomach rolls and I quickly hide behind the door leaving it open just a crack so I can see the two of them. Doctor Alexander looks surprised by his outburst.

"Er, no, Mr. Foxx. Vivienne isn't pregnant. But she's absolutely fine, all her test results were very good. She just needs to rest, rehydrate, and try to avoid anything that may cause anxiety. She's experienced a considerable amount of trauma recently. She just needs to heal."

"Thank God!" Max sighs, dragging his hands through his hair.

Wait, what? Thank God?…Thank God I'm okay? Or thank God I'm not pregnant? Which is it?

"Where is she?" he asks, looking past the doctor. I quickly close the door and run to the cubicle to throw up.

Once I've sorted myself out and drunk some water from the tap, I suck on a tic-tac and pat my face dry. Then I try to organise my expression into a less traumatised one before I leave the toilets.

"There you are." Max strides toward me and wraps me in a tight hug, then he kisses me on the lips. He's obviously very relieved, but I'm not sure why? I thought he wanted children. I could have sworn that he harboured the desire to become a father someday.

Maybe I was wrong?

YOU DON'T KNOW ME AT ALL

As we walk to the car, Max is beaming like an idiot, which just puts me more on edge. As soon as we get in the car he receives a call from Grace, and they have a lengthy discussion about an upcoming meeting with the Japanese. It gives me time to think on the way home.

If he really doesn't want children, maybe I won't have to worry about telling him? I'm confused, I'd always thought he wanted to be a father. You could see how happy he was every time he and Charlie were together.

When we enter the lift on our way up to F1, he curls his arms around me and kisses me tenderly on the lips. I rise up to deepen the kiss. It's just something my body does. It's automatic.

"Baby, I'm so glad you're okay. I was so worried about you. You've been acting so strange lately, I thought… I thought maybe you were having second thoughts about marrying me," he says, lowering his head. The worry line is firmly back in his brow. I reach up and smooth his cheek. I need to ask the question that's been burrowing a hole in my brain all the way home.

"Max…You seemed relieved when you found out that I wasn't pregnant. Don't you want children?" Nerves suddenly make my voice waver.

His cautious eyes search mine and then he shakes his head. "No. I don't," he says, with almost a guilty expression.

No?… Relief washes over me and I finally release the breath I was anxiously holding. He takes my face in his hands and scorches me with his loving eyes. "Vivienne, I've only just got you back. I'm not ready to share you yet. It feels like we haven't spent any time together and I want you all to myself… at least until our wedding."

Oh… My heart sinks to the pit of my stomach.

His eyes sparkle as he gazes lovingly into mine. "I'd like to take you on a romantic honeymoon, just the two of us. We'll have plenty of time to make our beautiful babies after we're married." I swallow and try to remember to breathe as his scorching eyes blaze with love. He takes me in his arms and kisses me with a passion that breaks my heart. Tears threaten my eyes but I try to hold them off and fight them back.

I have no choice…I have to tell him….But how?

He walks me into the living room and takes my coat, then he tells me to sit down and rest. "Are you hungry?" he asks, pulling my shoes off and lifting my legs onto the sofa. In a daze, I just shake my head. I couldn't eat anything right now, my stomach is churning.

Crouching down beside me, he takes my hand in his as his concerned eyes trail over my face. I'm on the verge of tears, and I know he can see it, but I'm scared. I don't want to tell him. I can't.

"Baby, is there something wrong?"

Oh, Max, please don't make me say it.

"Baby, you've been through so much recently, it's no wonder that you've been getting stressed out and depressed. Who wouldn't? As the doctor said, it's going to take time for you to heal." His eyes drift down to our hands. "I should have realised that you were suffering from nightmares about Monica. Christ! I think we've all had those." His sad eyes return to mine, full of guilt about him not being here to protect me. "Baby, I can't imagine how terrified you must have been."

My throat tightens and a sudden flashback to Monica's

brutal attack plays in my mind. "It's not your fault," I whisper, squeezing his hand. My eyes drift over to the study door. I can still see Monica's snarling face while she was choking me. The smell of blood still lingers in my nostrils, and the occasional sharp stabbing pains in my scars, serve as constant reminders of her horrific attacks. I don't need to be asleep to see those images in my mind, they come and go at will. But they're not the things that'll be keeping me awake anymore. They're not responsible for the overwhelming anxiety I feel right now.

Reaching up, he strokes my cheek. "Baby?" He follows my eyes to the study door. I look down, but he lifts my chin with his finger. I stare into his crystal blue eyes willing myself to come clean.

I need to tell you, Max. I need to tell you, but I don't know how?

"What is it, baby? Is it the house?…We don't have to live here if there are too many bad memories for you?"

I shake my head and force a smile. "No, it's not the house."

His smile crinkles his eyes and lights up his face. "Once we're married and start a family, we'll move out of here anyway," he shrugs. "I want our kids to have a big garden with swings, a tree-house, a pool, and lots of room to run around."

My heart twists. Closing my eyes, I rub my forehead. *This is so hard.*

He lifts my chin with his finger forcing my line of sight to rise. His smile fades as his cautious eyes search mine, trying desperately hard to read me. "Do you have a headache?" I nod in response. "I'll get you some painkillers. You need to rest, baby. And you need to eat," he frowns. "I'll go and make us some lunch." He stands up, and as he turns to walk away, my whole body turns rigid.

No! I need to tell you. It's now or never. "Max!" He turns back, waiting for me to continue but I can't. The words are trapped behind the lump in my throat. Instead, I force out a smile. "…I love you."

His face lights up with that heart-stopping smile, holding my gaze for a moment longer. "Love you more, baby." Then he walks away to the kitchen.

Once he's left the room, I swing my legs off the sofa and sit nervously on the edge. *What am I going to do?* Tears stream down my face. *Why can't you just tell him… Just fucking tell him!* As I look up, my blurry eyes land on the photograph of Max and Charlie. *Oh, God. I can't.*

I run upstairs to the bedroom and fling the wardrobe doors open. Grabbing my suitcase from the top shelf, I throw it on the bed and start to chuck all my clothes into it. My stunning new red gown hangs in amongst all my clothes. I stare at its beauty for a moment and then I sweep it aside and pull all my dresses and jackets from their hangers, throwing them in the case.

I run into the bathroom and scoop up my toiletries, then I run back out to the bedroom. My feet shudder to a stumbling halt when I see Max standing beside the bed looking at my open suitcase. The pain and disbelief etched on his face, crushes me. His fearful, questioning eyes land on mine.

"What are you doing?" His voice breaks and it's barely a whisper.

"I…I'm sorry, Max," I mumble, choking on my tightening throat.

He starts to walk toward me and I immediately back up, which stops him in his tracks. "You're leaving me?… But I just got you back." His incredulous voice tugs at my heart, and the look on his face takes me back to that night in France.

On shaky legs, I quickly move to the bed and throw my stuff in the suitcase. Tears blur my vision as I hastily try to close the lid. I can't speak, and I can't look at him.

"But why?" I don't answer. I can't answer. My trembling fingers fumble with the catches but I can't get them to close. "Why?" he yells, making me jump.

Suddenly he grabs me by the shoulders and spins me around to face him, but I can't look at him. I'm so ashamed that I've deceived him for so long. "Why are you doing this?" he asks, shaking me. "Vivienne, answer me."

I look up into his teary, fearful eyes. "I'm so sorry."

He searches my face with such pain in his eyes that I can't look at him anymore. "Vivienne, I don't understand. Please, baby. Please tell me what I've done to make you want to leave me?"

My heart twists and I bury my face in my hands, sobbing my heart out. Max grabs my wrists and pulls my hands away. "Vivienne, please. Talk to me."

"I'm sorry," I murmur feebly.

"Sorry about what?… Answer me!" he yells, exasperated.

I whip my head up. "I can't marry you!" I yell, sobbing. I instantly feel his hands release my wrists and he staggers backward, collapsing down on the edge of the bed. His wide, fearful eyes stare up at me, scanning my face for answers.

"But I thought…" His voice breaks with emotion. My heart shatters into a million pieces as I look down at the saddest eyes I've ever seen. "You said you loved me… You said you wanted to marry me… What changed?" The pain and disbelief in his voice makes my heart ache. My knees buckle and I collapse onto the floor with my head in my hands, sobbing.

"Is it Mike?" he asks, in a harsh tone.

I whip my head up to face him. "No!"

"Are you still in love with him, is that it?" he asks, clenching his jaw.

"No!… It's… I can't…" The words choke me.

His confused, watery eyes search mine, pleading with me to release him from this pain. "Please, Vivienne. Please tell me what the fuck is going on!" he yells, angrily.

I can't look at him anymore but he has every right to be angry. Burying my face in my hands, I cry my heart out.

Suddenly I feel his tight grip around my wrists, pulling

my hands away from my face. He's too strong for me to stop him. "No! Don't look at me."

Kneeling down in front of me, he releases my wrists and gently holds my face in his hands, then he softly wipes the tears from my cheeks. "What is it, Vivienne? Please, baby. I don't understand. Please tell me why you're doing this." He patiently waits for me to respond, but now he's right in front of me, gazing at me with all that love and fear in his eyes, it's even harder for me to form the words. I lower my eyes and dig deep for the words I know I need to find. He deserves the truth.

He tilts my head to raise my line of sight and suddenly his expression changes. "Look, baby. Forget what I said. If you want to have kids straight away I'm okay with that. I just wanted you to myself for a little longer," he smiles. "I was just being selfish," he adds softly.

My heart breaks and my guilt comes crashing to the surface. "No!... *I'm* selfish!" I yell in frustration, pushing him away from me with all my strength. His stunned expression kills me. "Yes! Me!" I yell, almost screaming. "*I'm* the one who's selfish! It's all a lie, Max. I should have told you the truth about me, but I didn't! I've been deceiving you this whole time... I can't have children...There! I said it!... I can't marry you because I can't have your children! I kept it from you because I couldn't bear the thought of losing you, but it's all a lie! A selfish fucking lie! And now you're going to hate me for it. You happy now?"

As my last word rings out, a deathly silence ensues. The pain and sadness in his eyes is exactly what I had expected to see, but it still breaks my heart. I turn away from him, scrambling to my feet, then I walk to the bed to try and close my suitcase. The quicker I get out of here, the better.

Max suddenly appears beside me, pulls the suitcase from the bed and throws it against the wall, the contents scatter all over the floor. I yelp as he grabs my arm and swings me around to face him. My heart is pounding in my chest and

I gasp as he pushes me back against the wall, planting his hands on the wall either side of my head. His furious expression scares me for a moment as his wild, stormy eyes search mine. I'm stunned and speechless.

After a long moment and a deep breath, he releases a weary sigh, then he closes his eyes and leans his forehead against mine.

"You don't know me at all," he whispers with emotion quivering his voice. He pulls back and looks deep into my eyes with two burning pools of love. "Whether we have kids or not, that's not why I love you. And I do love you, Vivienne. With all my heart." His sincerity takes my breath away as burning tears fill my eyes.

"I'm all wrong for you," I murmur. "I know how much you loved Charlie. It hurts me to know that I can never give you a child of your own. You'd make such a wonderful father."

He sighs and kisses me on the forehead, then he pulls me into his chest and wraps me tightly in his arms. "And you'll make a wonderful mother to the children we adopt, if that's what we choose to do… I don't know what's around the corner, baby, but as long as I have you, it doesn't matter."

I'd worried about this moment for so long, building it up in my mind to a painful peak of loss and regret. But once again he's totally blown me away. I don't know what I've done to deserve his love, but I know with all certainty that I wouldn't want to live without it.

We hold each other until my tears finally stop. I sigh into his chest. "I'm sorry, Max. I should have told you."

"Yes. You should. We don't keep secrets from each other. Them's the rules, remember?" He kisses the top of my head then he lifts my chin with his finger. Our eyes meet as he wipes the tears from my cheek and gazes down at me with love pouring from his eyes. Love for me.

"Why me?… Of all the women you could have chosen, why me?"

His eyes scorch me to the core. “Because with you I’m alive. Everything makes sense. Everything feels right…” A small questioning frown slips into his brow. “Do you ever get butterflies in the pit of your stomach?”

I nod and smile. “Every time I look at you. Every time I think of you. Every time I’m with you.”

“Yeah,” he smiles, “me too. We belong together, baby.” He kisses me. Rising up on my toes I deepen the kiss.

BLUSHING HANDCUFFS

Lying naked on the bed, sprawled over Max's chest, I watch him sleep. His handsomeness is only surpassed by his amazing capacity to love, and I feel truly blessed that he's chosen to give his heart to me. I trail my fingers over his M.F. tattoo, kiss it gently, then I rise from the bed.

Slipping into one of Max's shirts, I leave him to sleep as I head down to the kitchen. We've not eaten since this morning, and after all the drama of today and the incredible sex that followed, I actually feel really hungry. I suddenly realise my headache is hardly noticeable too.

Jan has left us some meals in the fridge so I heat up some chilli and I cook some new potatoes and green beans. As I'm just about to dish up the food, a warm pair of arms circle my waist from behind and Max rests his chin on my shoulder.

"You scared me. I woke up and you were gone," he says, kissing my neck. I put the pot down and turn around to face him. His unruly bed hair is all over the place, and his sleepy face looks so adorable.

"Max, I'm so sorry about—"

He kisses me to shut me up. "There's no need to apologise," he whispers against my lips. Pulling back, he hits me with those amazing eyes. "And I don't want it to be an issue between us. We have each other, that's all I care about."

I fling my arms around his neck and rise up to kiss him

back. His hands squeeze my behind as he grinds his erection into me. "Max, sexy as you are, and irresistible as you may be, dinner's ready and I'm starving."

He pulls back and gives me that knee trembling smile. "I'm impressed. No black smoke and no need to call the fire brigade," he smirks. "Your cooking skills are improving, Miss Banks."

I pretend to look offended until he kisses me again and I begin to melt in his arms. Breaking the kiss he releases me and walks to the fridge to get the wine. My eyes drink in his semi-naked handsomeness, he looks so sexy in just his board shorts sitting low on his hips. I sway, then I drag my eyes away when my stomach grumbles and I realise I'm supposed to be dishing up the dinner.

As we tuck into our meal, Max asks me how I'm feeling. I have to think about it for a moment, but I actually do feel okay. My stomach isn't knotted into a tight, anxious ball anymore, and my headache is a much less aggressive version of what it has been lately. I'm also acutely aware that now I've been able to tell Max the truth, an enormous pressure has been lifted from my shoulders.

My niggling brain does, however, still wonder if Max will resent me at some point in the future, but I can't foresee the future so I can only hope that I'll be enough for him as I am. I'm going to cling on to that hope with both hands.

"How did your bridesmaid fitting go?" he asks, out of the blue. I cringe, I'd almost forgotten about that. That was the day I got shit-faced and threw up all over that poor man's shoes!

"Fine. I'll have to go back for another fitting in a couple of months." I stare down at my plate. Poor Lucy still hasn't found her ideal venue and I feel sorry that she's had to compromise on so much. She can't have her reception in that dismal, dive of a hotel. The last time I was there, the function room smelled of old beer, and the food was disgusting.

"Baby? Where do you go?" Max asks, with a chuckle.

"What? Oh, sorry. I was just thinking… Do you have any friends in the hotel business?"

He raises his eyebrows and reaches for his wine glass. "Sure. Why?"

"Well, originally Lucy and Dan wanted to get married in the South of France, but they can't afford the venue and to fly everyone out there. So, now she's thinking about getting married over here. But they still want to have their honeymoon in France, and because their budget is limited, she's looking at this really nasty, cheap hotel which even the homeless wouldn't look at twice."

"How many people are they inviting?"

"Fifty-ish."

He shrugs. "I'll make some calls."

"Thanks, I'd appreciate that. She's been such a good friend to me, I'd like to help her if I can."

He leans on his elbow with his wine in his hand and then he looks at me thoughtfully. "What would your dream wedding be?" he asks in a soft, raspy voice. I blush and spin the stem of my wine glass, watching the liquid swirl around inside.

"I've never really thought about it," I shrug.

"Never?" he asks sceptically. "I thought every little girl dreamed of their wedding day. You start planning your lives from the age of ten," he smirks.

I stop spinning the glass. At ten years old, any dreams I'd had were destroyed the night that man came into my room. After that, the only plans I made were what I would do to him if I ever saw him again. I didn't even go out on dates like all my other friends until I was almost twenty. I dated Mike for a whole year before I'd even let him touch me. So deep were the scars, it took me a long time to trust anyone.

"Baby? Are you okay? You look pale."

"Sorry, what?"

Max puts his glass down and drags my stool closer to his, then he pulls me into his lap so I'm straddling his legs and facing him. He wraps his arms around me and kisses me softly on the lips. "Do you trust me?" he asks, pulling back to search my eyes. I nod. "Good," he smiles.

I wait for him to elaborate but instead, he kisses me again, igniting all my senses and then he stands and walks upstairs with me still wrapped around him.

"Now, how about that fashion show?" A million butterflies invade my belly.

Max lies with his back against the headboard as I walk out of the wardrobe wearing one of his suit jackets, a bow tie, and my killer heels. He wants me to model the new underwear he bought me, and although it looks great on, I feel very self-conscious. I'm not sure I really know how to do 'sexy.'

My heart is racing, and I'm so nervous, especially when I see the look on his face. His eyes light up and trace all over me, but he pays special attention to the lace tops of my stockings.

"You really have the most gorgeous legs," he says, in a low throaty voice.

The jacket is slightly open revealing my sexy new underwear, so I tease him a little by opening the jacket a little wider as I slowly walk toward him. His greedy eyes take it all in, and I can see his chest rising and falling with heavier breaths.

I feel something in his pocket so I pull it out, it's one of his ties. His eyes land on it and then flick up to mine. "What are you going to do with that, tie me up?" he smirks, salaciously. I smile wickedly and shake my head. Pulling my hand out of the other pocket I jangle the silver handcuffs in the air. "No. That's what these are for." His eyes widen, and if I'm not mistaken I've just surprised the hell out of him. That makes two of us, I haven't got a clue what I'm doing.

I kneel onto the bed and straddle his hips. His erection twitches under the sheet. He grins at me and holds his hands out in front of him. I rather awkwardly snap one of the cuffs onto his wrist and then I push his arm up above his head. By the look on his face, he wasn't expecting me to do that, and if I'm honest, neither was I. I'm just making this up as I go along.

"But how am I going to touch you?" he asks, in all seriousness.

"You will… But not yet," I smirk.

He slowly raises his other arm above his head, his eyes never leaving mine, and with shaking hands, I thread the cuff through the wrought iron headboard and snap it closed on his other wrist.

"There!" I say, with a satisfied smile. I have no idea what I'm doing, but so far, so good.

I quickly scoot off the bed and pull the sheet all the way down revealing Max's pulsing erection and phenomenal physique. The sight of him sends a throbbing pulse to my core. His breathing has become deeper, and his eyes greedily trace over every inch of me as I walk to the end of the bed and slowly open the jacket, letting it fall to the floor. His eyes feast on the red lace.

Okay…now what?

He glances at the tie in my right hand with a questioning frown, then he flicks his narrowed eyes back to mine when I improvise and tie it around my right thigh, then I slowly crawl onto the bed. I watch his eyes as they darken with desire, empowering me all the more.

I run my hands over his feet and up his calves, knees, and thighs, pushing his legs wider apart so I can kneel between them. He writhes at my touch, and his breathing deepens. I kiss his thighs and hips, making sure not to touch his twitching shaft. Even as he rolls his hips to make contact, I deny him the pleasure. His rock hard abs bunch and ripple as I kiss them, then I let my hands skim over his soft, warm skin. He watches me eagerly as I crawl up and straddle his stomach, laying my hands on his chest.

"You shock me, Miss Banks," he growls in a low, throaty

rasp with a salacious grin on his face.

That makes two of us. I smile and lean forward to kiss the underside of his scarred forearm. He tries to lean his head forward to touch me, but I pull back. "Ah, ah, ah. Not yet." I whisper seductively. I feel so powerful right now.

Sex with Mike was always in the missionary position, and not very imaginative. It was probably my fault because I was a late starter and I had no point of reference. But Lucy would often enlighten me on her and Dan's bedroom antics which always sounded like so much fun. That's where the handcuffs came from, she must have left them at my flat.

Looking at Max cuffed to the bedpost, I realise my inner sex goddess has been awoken. I think I could really get into all this kinky stuff. I just wish I knew what I was doing.

I sit on his stomach and untie his red tie from around my thigh. Pulling it through my fingers, I lay it over his eyes and tie it around his head. "No peeking now."

"Woman! You fascinate me," he growls, with a big smile on his face.

Once it's secure, I kneel up and get off the bed. Then I watch him as he tries to figure out what I'm going to do next. *Good luck with that.* It's like the blindfolded leading the bewildered.

I kick off my shoes and take off my bra and knickers, but I leave the lace top stockings on. I suddenly realise I should have done that before I'd blindfolded him but it's too late now. Then I stand at the side of the bed. His mouth is open and his breathing is quick and shallow. He's totally aroused and his cock pulses with anticipation. He's so sexy, even more so now that he's so vulnerable.

I lean over him without touching him, or the mattress, and I lick my tongue across his lower lip. He groans with pleasure and pushes himself up to try and kiss me, but I pull away.

Watching him for a moment, I feel the pulse in my sex

throbbing with excitement as he swallows then opens his mouth and licks his lips in anticipation of my next move. He has such gorgeous, kissable lips.

I quietly move further down the bed and lean over to run my finger up the sole of his foot. His head lifts up, and all his neatly packed abdominals tighten under his golden skin. I move back to the top of the bed and trail soft fingers over his chest and arms, then along his throat, and then I run my fingers softly over his lips. He wriggles and writhes, moaning a soft groan each time I touch him.

I quietly move to the bottom of the bed again. Crawling up his body, I lick my tongue up his inner thigh and then blow on the wet trail. He moans and lifts his head, pulling on his cuffs. I plant soft kisses over his happy trail on his lower belly, then I kiss his hips and all around his cock without touching it. Then, very slowly, I drag my tongue from the base of his twitching shaft right up the length of him and lick away the bead of his arousal at the tip.

He pulls against his restraints. "Baby, I need to touch you," he moans, throwing his head back.

I take him in my mouth and begin a slow rhythmic movement, sucking and licking. I hear him gasp and then his breathing quickens and his hips rise and roll as I begin to speed up. As I slowly increase the pressure and speed, he pants out short, sharp breaths, moaning his approval. I feel the head of his cock expand as I bring him close to his release, but I stop just in time to prolong it. I'm not ready to let him come yet, I'm enjoying myself way too much.

I kiss my way up his torso and across his magnificent chest, then I continue up his throat, along his jaw, nibbling his earlobe, and then finally, I kiss him deep and hard on the lips. He groans with pleasure as our tongues collide in each other's mouths. His kiss is hot, hungry, and full of want. Dragging his bottom lip through my teeth, I pull back to look at him. He looks insanely sexy, and I feel like I have him in the palm of my hand. In reality, I'm just the moth drawn to his bright and intoxicating flame.

His breathing is ragged, and his chest moves quickly. "I need to see you," he groans. I lick my tongue across his lips and slowly kiss my way back down his body, then I lift his hard twitching cock and slide myself onto him. He hisses out a loud moan, pulling on his handcuffs as he fills and stretches me making me moan with pleasure. Lifting and rolling his hips, I rise and lower myself faster and faster creating the perfect friction.

"I need my hands on you," he groans, between panting breaths. His lips twitch and the vein in his neck pulses as his impending orgasm builds to its peak. But I can't release him from his cuffs, the sensation is too good to stop now. He's close, and I'm nearly there. I grind and rise as his hips pump into me like a piston.

"Oh!" I cry out repeatedly, as the raw and powerful vibrations of possibly the best orgasm I've ever experienced, ripple out from my core. Max holds his breath and then he yells out a long, deep growl of gratification as his body ejaculates with shuddering thrusts.

Riding him until the very last moment of ecstasy, I fold, and lay on his chest. Exhausted and utterly satisfied.

Neither of us speaks. Our breathing is almost at the same fast rate and the sweat is dripping off us. After a few moments, I hear Max rattling his cuffs.

"Baby, that was incredible. You blow my mind," he sighs. "Can I get out of these now? I need to touch you," he says, rattling his cuffs again. I lift my head and reach up to remove his blindfold. He blinks and smiles down at me with a questioning frown. "Have you done that before?"

I blush and shake my head. "Never," I answer shyly. "That's a first for me." I feel quite chuffed with myself until he raises an accusatory eyebrow. I sit up, feeling indignant that he doesn't believe me. "Seriously. I promise you, I've never done anything like that before. They're not even my handcuffs. I found them in one of my boxes."

He looks at me in awe then he shakes his head. "Well, I hope you've got the key."

I blink at him for a moment. "Key? Don't they just pull apart?" I ask innocently.

Max's brow wrinkles with confusion then he looks up at the cuffs and gives them another shake. "No, baby, you need a key. You do have the key don't you?" he asks nervously.

"Ahh…I'll have a look." I blush and quickly scoot off the bed to find the box that the cuffs were in. I search through all the boxes, but I can't find a key anywhere. *Oh, shit.* I pad back out to the bedroom. "Erm…I'll have to call Lucy," I cringe. "Maybe she's got the key."

"Wait. What?" he says in a panic. He looks up at the cuffs and shakes them again, but even I can see they're not going to budge.

"I'm sorry, I didn't know," I say, trying not to laugh. I feel stupid for being so naive, but it is kind of funny.

He looks at me incredulously. "You're kidding me, right?" I shake my head and burst out laughing. "Vivienne! It's not funny!" he grumbles.

"Okay, okay. I'll call Lucy," I giggle. I grab my phone and dial her number.

"Hey, Viv. How are you? Did you tell him yet?" she asks nervously.

"What? Oh, yes. It's alright, everything's fine."

"Thank fuck for that. I told you it would be."

"Erm, Luce…changing the subject, do you have a pair of handcuffs?" I ask tentatively.

"Yeah, but I don't know where they are. Why?"

"Well, I found them, but I can't find the key."

"Oh, yeah, I lost it."

"What?" The line goes quiet and then Lucy suddenly gasps and begins to giggle.

"You didn't?" She asks in an accusatory tone. "Viv! You saucy mare. I didn't think you had it in you?"

I blush. "Neither did I."

I look over at Max. "Well?" he asks, exasperated.

"Look, Luce, I've got to go, I'll call you later." Lucy's

raucous laughter continues as I end the call and gingerly turn to face Max. "Where do you keep your toolbox?" I ask, suppressing a smile. He gives me one of those withering looks. The trouble is it just makes me laugh even more. I take a quick photo of him with my phone then I grab his shirt from the floor.

"I'll go and have a look for it… Erm, you just wait here," I giggle. I pull the sheet over him and leave him muttering and shaking his head in disbelief.

I run downstairs giggling to myself, and I finally find the toolbox in a cupboard in the kitchen.

"Oh, hello, Vivienne, how did your appointment go?" Jan asks from behind me.

Shit! I straighten and clutch the heavy toolbox to my chest. Her smiling eyes trail over my stockings and Max's shirt, then they land on the toolbox.

"Is everything alright?" she frowns.

I blush instantly. "Erm…yeah. Erm… Back in a minute," I mumble, moving forward. My eyes widen and I stop dead in my tracks when I see Vinnie walking into the kitchen with bags of shopping. He stops and looks at me, and then at the toolbox.

"Problem, Miss?" he asks warily.

"No… I just need to…erm…I, ah…"

Vinnie puts the bags down and reaches forward to take the toolbox. "Here, let me help you with that."

"No! It's fine," I blurt. "I've got it." I put my head down and scuttle out of the kitchen running back upstairs.

Max's eyes land on mine as I enter the bedroom. He looks quite comfortable and almost resigned to the fact that he's chained to the bed. I put the toolbox on the floor and rummage around in it, looking for something that might cut the chain between the cuffs.

"That one," he says, when I pick up the heavy, red handled cutters. I kneel either side of his chest and I try to get a hold of the chain in between the blades, but it just slips about all over the place. I look down at Max, who's smiling up at me shaking his head. "You really haven't done this before, have you?" he grins. I blush and cringe, I'm so embarrassed. I try to get a grip on the chain, but I haven't got the strength to cut it.

A light knocking on the bedroom door has both of us looking at each other, and then at the door.

"Guv', do you need any help?"

I cringe and look down at Max. He gives me that withering look again and raises an eyebrow. "Yes, Parker. I'm afraid we do," he says rolling his eyes and sighing deeply. "Come in. We might as well make this as embarrassing as possible," he smirks, shaking his head.

I scramble off his chest and make sure I'm fully covered before Vinnie enters the room. He walks in and falters ever so slightly when he sees Max cuffed to the bed, but he hardly breaks his stride, and he doesn't say a word. Without missing a beat, he takes the cutters from my hand and kneels on the edge of the bed. A couple of seconds later, they're off, and Max lowers his arms, rubbing his wrists back to life.

"Thanks," Max sighs, avoiding eye contact with Vinnie.

"No worries Guv'," he says, pinching his lips together to suppress a smirk. He pulls out a leather pouch from his inside pocket and takes a fine metal stick from inside it, then he picks the locks and releases Max from the cuffs. "Do you want me to fix these?" Vinnie asks, holding the cuffs up and trying not to laugh. I can't look at him, I'm too embarrassed.

"No. Just get rid of them," Max says, rubbing his wrists and leaning his head back against the headboard.

"Right-oh, Guv'. You might want to try cable ties next time, they're a lot easier to cut off." I can see Vinnie's shoulders bouncing as he silently chuckles his way out of the bedroom.

I cringe. "Oh, my God, that was so embarrassing."

"You think?" Max grins, shaking his head and rolling his eyes. Suddenly he jumps forward and grabs me, throwing me down on the bed. I yelp as he pins my arms above my head and hovers over me. "You amaze me," he smiles, searching my eyes.

"Amaze, or amuse?" I cringe. "I'm sorry, I was trying to be all sexy, and I made a right balls-up."

His super-sexy smile spreads across his handsome face. "Baby, you are sexy. Look what you do to me." He grinds his erection against my thigh and pretty soon my shirt is ripped open and his hands are all over me.

DOUBT

The sun creeps in through the curtains and stirs me from my sleep. I open my eyes and feel Max's arm tighten around me as he exhales a long, sleepy sigh. I lay sprawled across his chest, thoroughly comfortable and content. I don't feel sick or lightheaded, and I don't even have a headache. Things are looking up.

If anyone had ever told me that I'd fall in love with an insanely rich, devastatingly handsome man, who was head over heels in love with me, I'd have laughed in their face. But here I am, in the arms of my gorgeous paramour who loves me just as I am, with all my flaws, foibles and naivety.

I'd worried myself to the point of illness about telling him that I couldn't have his children, and yet he took it all in his stride, and if anything, I feel much closer to him now. I could never match him financially, that's a given. But of all the cruel twists of fate, I'd like to have been able to give him sons and daughters. What woman wouldn't for the man she loves.

Max's phone rings. I lift my head and rest my chin on his chest. He reaches out to the phone and slides it off the bedside table. I notice the caller ID says 'Fiona'.

Fiona?…From the café?

"Yeah," he says, resting his head back on the pillow. I lay my head back down on his chest and listen. I can hear a woman's voice but I can't distinguish the words.

"Uh-huh…Yeah… I'll try…Yeah, thanks, you too." He ends the call and slides his phone back onto the table.

"Who was that?" I ask, circling his tattoo with my fingers. His chest stops rising for a moment.

"Oh, just work. I forgot I have a meeting with a client across town this morning, that's all," he says, rubbing his eyes to look at his watch.

I didn't know Fiona was a client? "What, now? But it's Sunday."

He leans forward to kiss me on the top of my head. "I know. I won't be long. I'm going to take a shower."

He gets out of bed and walks into the bathroom. I wait until I hear the shower running before I check his phone. Sure enough, it was Fiona calling him, and when I check the call log, he's made seven calls to her since Thursday.

Hmm. My green eyed monster begins to hurl a ton of questions at me. He's never mentioned her since we saw her at the café, why does he have to meet her today? And why did he refer to her as a client? She wasn't a client three days ago, she was an ex-girlfriend.

I quickly replace the phone and lie back when I hear him coming. He hasn't shaved his morning stubble, which he normally does for work. When he emerges from the wardrobe, he's wearing black jeans, converse, and a dark grey t-shirt with a matching suede Harrington jacket. He looks gorgeous, but he normally wears a suit for meetings with his clients. He shoves something into his inside pocket, walks over to the bed and bends down to kiss me. His minty breath and intoxicating scent wafts into my face.

"Go back to sleep, you need to rest, remember? I'll be back soon." His eyes linger on mine for a moment, then he smiles, picks up his phone, and leaves.

I reach for his pillow and curl into a ball around it. My niggling suspicious brain kicks into gear and I feel the gnawing pangs of doubt creep into my mind, sapping every ounce of confidence out of me. *What if he's changed his mind about me?*

I lay there for a while, torturing myself with thoughts of him with Fiona in some cosy little flat somewhere. *He had the perfect out yesterday, why didn't he take it?*

My brain cogs whir into motion, churning my stomach and filling my head with all sorts of unwanted explanations. She's probably asking him what the hell he's doing with someone like me. And he's probably telling her that he'd moved me in because he felt guilty about Monica beating me to a pulp, and now he doesn't know how to get rid of me. They're probably laughing about my cock up with the handcuffs too. *Jesus! I'm so bloody naive.*

My cautious brain flips between doubt and absolute certainty that he's had time to think about everything and has now changed his mind about me. My crushing insecurity takes hold, winding me up and pissing me off.

I throw the covers back and haul myself out of bed. If I'm going to stew over him cheating on me, I'm going to need to speak to Lucy, she always knows what to do. We arrange to meet at Java's.

I shower and dress, then I head downstairs.

"Ah, Vivienne. Just in time," Jan says, catching me before I get to the front door. She's got a breakfast tray in her hands which she was apparently just about to bring upstairs. I'm actually quite hungry, so I decide not to argue and I march over to the island to tuck in.

"I'm so happy to hear that you've been given the all clear," she smiles. "It must have been very worrying for you," she adds, handing me a glass of water.

It was, but not for the reasons she's thinking.

"Jan, do you know who Fiona is?" I ask, munching through my bacon sandwich. Her expression changes ever so slightly, but she just shakes her head. For some reason, and I don't know why exactly, I just don't believe her.

"Were you going out?" she asks, changing the subject.

"Yes, I'm going to see Lucy."

"How will you get there? I'm afraid all the boys are busy. Does Max know you're going out?"

Her questioning, and the fact that I have to explain my movements, irks me. It's not her fault, I was already in a mood. I stop chewing and stare at her. "Last time I looked, I was a free woman. And I've survived this long without a chauffeur, I'm sure I can manage," I snap, regretting it immediately.

"Oh, yes, of course," she says, a little taken aback by my outburst. "I'm sorry, Vivienne. It's just that I'm under strict instructions to make sure that you're eating and taking care of yourself."

I know it's not Jan's fault, but I'm irritated by Max's control over me when he clearly doesn't have any control over himself. I drink the rest of my water and pick up the other half of my bacon sandwich. "You can tell Max that I've eaten, I've drunk all my water, I've even washed behind my ears and tied my own shoelaces. And now I'm going to spend the day with my friend." With that, I turn on my heel and head for the door.

I feel awful talking to Jan like that, she's not to blame for how I feel so I turn back and poke my head into the kitchen. Jan is sitting at the island looking a bit upset.

"I'm sorry, Jan," I mumble sheepishly. "I'm a little grouchy this morning, I'll see you later." She doesn't say anything, she just looks up at me and smiles. Now I've made my peace, I leave.

Lucy is already waiting for me when I arrive at Java's. I'd decided to walk so I could clear my head, but it took me a lot longer than I thought.

"Hey, Viv, I was beginning to think you'd forgotten all about me," she smiles.

I order us a couple of lattes and two chocolate muffins. When I join her at the table she's almost bouncing in her seat.

"Well? Tell me all about it then," she grins, but when I don't smile back and answer her straight away she gives me a wary look. "Don't tell me he's still handcuffed to the bed?" she smirks.

"What?…Oh, no. Vinnie cut them off," I say, preoccupied with more important woes.

Lucy laughs and shakes her head. "Oh, my God, he'll never live that down." Her smile fades and morphs into a more concerned expression. "So, why the long face? What's the matter? I thought you said he was okay about the kids thing?"

"He is… He was… Oh, I don't know."

"Viv?"

"He says he loves me, and he said that it didn't matter to him that I couldn't have children, but…"

"But what? What's the matter?" Lucy patiently waits for me to find the words.

"I think he's seeing someone else, one of his old girlfriends."

"Don't be stupid," she scoffs. "Why would you think that?"

"Because he got a call from her this morning and then he made some excuse about having to meet with a client. But I know he's gone to meet her, I saw her number on his phone, and they've been talking a lot lately too."

"Well, maybe she is a client." I give Lucy the eyebrow. "Oh, come on, Viv," she chides. "He poured his heart out to me when he thought he'd lost you, the man's ridiculously in love with you anyone can see that. And why would you think any of that has changed?"

"Guilt." I look down and pick the chocolate pieces out of my muffin. I've lost my appetite for it now.

"Guilt about what?"

I've never told Lucy about the whips, and why Max self-harms. I didn't want to betray him by blurting his secrets to the world. Not that Lucy would do that, but people always talk, and if the press ever found out about his secrets, they'd slaughter him.

I thought he'd conquered that part of his life. I thought he no longer carried the burden of his guilt. He promised me that he'd stopped self-harming, and I've seen no evidence to the contrary, but people don't just change overnight. It's obvious, he's just found a new way to deal with things.

"Luce, Max has guilt issues. He's had them ever since his parents died when he was a little boy. He blames himself for their deaths. He was with them when they died and he tries to save people because it helps him feel better about not being able to save his mum. He did it with Monica, and now he's doing it with me."

Lucy blinks at me with confused eyes. "But what does that have to do with anything?" she asks, shaking her head.

"He saved Monica from her abusive father, then she dumped all over him breaking his heart, and then I turned up. I saved him from his broken heart, and more importantly, from being killed by Monica, so now he's in my debt."

Lucy stares at me open mouthed. "Fuck me. Cautious Viv is back in the house." she scowls, shaking her head.

I sit back and exhale a long, unhappy sigh. It seems pretty straightforward to me.

Lucy leans forward with a big frown on her face, pushing her coffee aside. "I've never heard such a load of old bollocks," she chides. "Mike was a dick. He loved you, but he was an idiot to himself because he was jealous and stupid, and that's just what you're doing. You're bailing out before you even know the facts. Just like when you thought Max would dump you because you couldn't have kids." I huff out a sarcastic response. "Maybe this woman is a client. Maybe you're over thinking everything like you always do, and creating a problem that just isn't there. Caution is good when you're crossing the road, Viv. But unless you know for sure that he's cheating on you, you're just going to drive yourself nuts, and quite possibly, drive a wedge between the pair of you." Lucy takes a deep inhale after her lecture and then she sits back in her seat, frowning at me and shaking her head. I can see that she's disappointed in me. I'm disappointed in me. I've never been a jealous person, and I hate that I've become so possessive and needy. But I've never felt this way before. I've never loved this way before.

"Lucy, how can someone like me ever be enough for someone like him?" I ask in all seriousness.

She sits forward and takes my hand, giving it a gentle squeeze. "Beats me. You could curdle milk with that face." I flinch, then I offer her a half smile. I know she's only joking but I'm not really in the mood for humour. "Look, Viv, it's very simple," she sighs. "He's just a man. He has feelings, desires, and insecurities, the same as the rest of us. He's probably thinking the same thing about you."

"Pff, I doubt that."

"Well, that's your problem, isn't it? You doubt everything. You're too cautious for your own good," she smirks, shaking her head.

She's right. I am cautious, but life has taught me to be that way.

"So, did you tell him why you couldn't have kids?" she asks tentatively. I just shake my head. "Why not?" I suddenly feel really uncomfortable and I begin to fidget in my seat. "What are you afraid of?" she asks softly.

"I can't tell him why, it'll just make me more of a victim and—"

"And what? You're worried that he'll want to save you?… Viv, I think you should give the man more credit. He loves you, and if you can't see that, then you're a fool."

We sit in silence for a while as I absorb Lucy's words. I've always been so guarded, it's difficult for me to let down the barriers and open myself up. But she's right. I need to have more faith in myself, more confidence. Until this morning, Max has never really given me cause to doubt his love, but it happened so fast for us, how can we really know for sure that we're right for each other?

"Viv… Oi! I'm talking to you."

Huh? Lucy glares at me across the table. "Oh, sorry…

What did you say?"

"I was asking you how you were feeling. The last time I saw you, you were throwing up and passing out."

"Oh, yeah, I'm okay. I think I'd just worked myself up about telling Max. The doctor said I was fine and since I told Max, I actually haven't felt so bad."

"See!" she scowls. "I told you all your problems were self-inflicted. What about work? Are you going back to the magazine?"

"Yes, I hope so. Maybe next week if Frank will take me back." I cringe. Poor Frank must be fed up with me by now. I've had so much time off lately.

"Well, that's good. Your life has been so crazy, it'll do you good to get some normality back."

"Crazy, is the operative word," I smirk.

"Do you think they'll ever catch that psycho-bitch?" Lucy asks with an arched brow.

"I hope so." An involuntary shudder shimmies up my spine. "I never want to see that woman again. Ever."

THE TRUTH?

Lucy and I say our goodbyes and I take a slow stroll through the park on my way home. She's right about me, I am too cautious, and I need to stop analysing everything. Harder to do than say when you've spent your whole life asking 'what if?'

When I finally get home, I realise I hadn't taken my key-card with me so I have to ring the doorbell. Nobody answers.

Great! Stupid key! Why don't we have a number code or something? I can't call anyone because I stupidly left my phone on charge in the bedroom. *Great. Just great.*

I pace the foyer for a moment, muttering to myself about what an idiot I am, then I decide to go down to the Foxx-Tech office to see if anyone can help me. Max said he was visiting a client across town, and I don't even know if the office is open on a Sunday?

I walk to the lift and head down to have a look. As the doors glide open, I see a young woman sitting behind the reception desk so I walk over.

"Hi, I'm Vivienne, from F1."

"Oh, yes, good afternoon, Miss Banks. How can I help you?"

"I foolishly forgot my door key and I wondered if Mr. Foxx kept any spares here?"

She smiles and looks down at her screen. "I'll call Mr. Foxx for you," she says, reaching for the phone.

"He's here?" I ask, a little surprised. I thought his meeting was across town.

"Yes, he's in his office."

"Oh, good. I'll just go and see him then." I walk away from the desk.

"But, Miss Banks—" I ignore her and head to his office.

As I walk toward his huge frosted glass doors, I can see that Grace isn't in today and I make the hasty decision to just barge in. If he's up to something, I'm not going to give him any warning. I push against the doors and barge straight in.

Max is sitting behind his desk and two other men are sitting opposite him. They're having a heated discussion but everything stops when Max looks up in surprise as I enter. The thing that strikes me immediately is that Max isn't wearing the same clothes he went out in this morning. He's wearing a suit and tie.

"Oh. I'm so sorry," I mumble, shuddering to a standstill. I blush and quickly back out of the office. *Shit!*

Max suddenly appears. "Vivienne, where have you been? I've been trying to call you," he says with a worried frown.

"Erm, sorry, I went to see Lucy. I didn't know you were busy. I'm sorry, I forgot my key," I mumble pathetically.

"Vivienne, how many times have I asked you not to go out on your own, especially not without your phone." His irritation is obvious.

"I'm sorry." I feel like a child being told off, but he's right. I should have taken my phone with me. And my door key. Max hands me his key and looks back at his office, I sense that I'm holding him up from something important.

"I'm sorry, I'll go." I turn to walk away but he pulls on my arm to stop me.

"Is everything okay?" he asks, searching my face.

"Yeah." I force a smile and then trail my eyes up and down his suit.

He leans in to kiss me on the lips. "I've got to get back

to the meeting but I'll be home in an hour, okay?"

I notice he looks a bit edgy. I nod toward his office. "Everything alright in there?"

He drags his hand through his hair and exhales a big sigh. "Yeah, nothing for you to worry about. I'll see you soon." He waits for me to walk away before disappearing back into his office. I'm tempted to walk back and listen at the doors, but I know there are new cameras everywhere now so I just head back to reception. I sidle up to the desk and wait for the young lady to look up at me.

"Hi. Erm, I was just wondering, when did Max, I mean, Mr. Foxx arrive this morning?" I ask trying not to blush.

Her eyebrows shoot up in surprise, but she answers me almost immediately. "About an hour ago."

I just nod, smile, and walk away. *So where has he been until an hour ago?*

In the lift, I mull everything over in my head which just winds me up even more. I've always been a thinker, sometimes it's a good thing, sometimes it just makes things worse. Today it's the latter.

I let myself in and I run upstairs to the bedroom. The jacket he had on this morning isn't in his wardrobe. I hate myself for doing it but while he's not here, I take a peek into all his drawers and cupboards. I'm not sure what I'm looking for, but I hope I don't find it, whatever it is.

After I've searched through the bedroom, I head to the study. I get that awful sinking feeling every time I come in here. I try to ignore it as I take a seat in Max's big leather chair. His top desk drawer is locked so I go hunting for the key. I remember him hiding my bike keys in one of the filing cabinet drawers, so I look there, and sure enough, I find it.

Unlocking the desk drawer, I find his diary nestled in amongst some papers and folders. A sudden wave of guilt that I'm prying into his personal things makes me hesitate, but the overwhelming curiosity takes over so I quickly remove the diary from the drawer and flick through the pages.

As I begin to read some of the entries, I realise they're all about me. I flick the pages back to the first page with any writing on it. It was the day I was working at Great Ormond Street Hospital. I remember when he'd taken me to Italy for our first date, he'd told me that day was the first time he'd ever seen me. I hadn't seen him, I was busy working, but I remember the day very well, and I remember Charlie.

WED 28th January:

11:00hrs Charlie, G.O.S.H, Directors meeting:

Charlie led me to the most beautiful girl I've ever seen.

She has a boyfriend!

Vivienne Banks - Photographer/Star-Biz Magazine

Who are you???

THUR 29th January:

Can't stop thinking about that girl...

Call Frank, need information and contact number.

He knows Frank? The next few pages are blank so I keep flicking through until I find some more entries.

FRI 27th February:

Foxx-Glove Gala Charity Ball - Royal Albert Hall

Order flowers for Mrs. Savchenko

Pick up Jade at 4:45pm

Saw Vivienne again, she has the most beautiful eyes!

So it was you who text me that night. I continue to read, only to find that he's poured his heart out in every page.

SAT 28th February:

8:45hrs Meeting - Mr. Goldsbrough - Savoy

Saw Vivienne outside Java's

Still has boyfriend! (Mike)

This woman is driving me crazy.

21:00hrs - Jamie - Launch - Gallery

Take Tickets for Chymeira & Cheque (Jamie's Prize)

Vivienne was there. Couldn't resist any longer, spoke to her for the first time.

Beautiful, intriguing, funny!

Great news - No more Boyfriend.
Slight problem with direction, balance, & alcohol. Took her to the Hospital.
Falling for this girl, big time! She fascinates me.

SUN 29th February:
22:45hrs - Flight to Paris

Went to visit Vivienne in Hospital before the flight.
I didn't want to leave her. Can't wait to see her again.
Need to know if all finished with Mike. (Hope so.)

MON 2nd March:
07:30hrs Meeting - Phillipe at Four Seasons George V - Paris
12:15hrs Flight Home
15:00hrs Flight to NY - Meetings & Charlie (Disney world)

Cole visiting Mom & Dad.
Call Vivienne - UK time.
Not sure if Vivienne is still in love with Mike, hope not. He sounds like an asshole!
Sent Parker to keep her safe and find out more about Mike!

THUR 12th March:
Vivienne - Check up at Limberton

No show!!
Rang Vivienne, got a mouthful. (Cole being a dick as usual.)
Explained the sitch. Rescheduled appointment for 1pm
So pleased to finally get Vivienne on her own. She makes me nervous.
Took her to dinner - Rome - Mike is definitely off the scene.
Broke every rule, but couldn't help myself.
She's beautiful, funny and…Perfect.
Had butterflies all night, what's that all about???
When we got back from Italy, I didn't want to let her go.
Monica showed up. Another suicide attempt - Hospital
What's wrong with me??

I've completely fucked up any chance with Vivienne.
I'm an asshole!!!

FRI 13th March:
08:30hrs - Meeting - Heads of Dept.

Big fight with Monica about Vivienne when we got home from the hospital.
She wants us to get back together - Never going to happen!
Fight escalated, then she dropped the bomb. Charlie's my son.
How could she do that to me? Why now, when it's too late?
If today couldn't get any worse, Vivienne left a message, she never wants to see or hear from me ever again. I've lost her. I've fucked it all up. She deserves so much better.
Found a blade, but it wasn't enough. Went to the room...

Tears threaten my eyes. *Friday the thirteenth certainly wasn't a lucky day for you, was it?* Or me, for that matter. It pains me that his only mechanism at the time for dealing with this kind of heightened emotion, was to harm himself. It must have been so isolating not to be able to talk to someone about how he felt inside.

My heart breaks. I remember the look in his eyes when he'd talked about finding out that Charlie was his son, or so he thought. Friday the thirteen was indeed a shitty day all round. That was the morning that I'd gone to the penthouse to retrieve my phone, and to hopefully see Max again. But that morning Monica had answered the door to me and she revelled in her shameless attempts to ward me off and have him to herself.

The next five pages are blank. He'd obviously chosen not to commit whatever he was feeling to his diary, almost as if those days had never existed.

WED 18th March:
07:45hrs - Flight to NY - Taking Monica home & meetings NY office.

Spent time with Charlie. Took him to the Knicks game. He loved it.

The next nine days are empty so I eagerly flick ahead.

FRI 27th March:

14:00hrs - Red Ball Fundraiser - Emirates

Finally, something good happened! Vivienne was working at the event!

One look at her and I was lost in her beautiful brown eyes. I've missed those eyes.

I tried to talk to her, but she shut me out. I can't stop thinking about her.

20:00hrs - Dinner with Fiona

Cancelled dinner. Need to find Vivienne, can't get her out of my mind.

Traced her to Chymeira. Couldn't take my eyes off her, she fascinates me.

Took her for dinner at Ravi's - Think I might have told her everything! Hope not! Don't remember getting home.

It makes me feel better knowing he'd cancelled his plans with Fiona to come and find me, but it still troubles me that he's talking to her again but hasn't made any mention of her at all.

SAT 28th March:

Woke up at 7am with a terrible hangover! Never drinking Jack Daniels again! Parker told me off about getting drunk.

Found Vivienne sleeping in the guest room, she looked so beautiful. I'm in love with this woman. I know she feels something for me, I can see it in her eyes, but she ran away and wouldn't answer any of my calls. What the fuck did I tell her last night???

HAVE TO GET HER BACK.

Traced her phone to the 'Jelly Bean' - Motorbike. (That's got to go!)

Mike gone for good - Finally!

Told Vivienne that I'm in love with her, it felt awesome.

Vivienne's apartment was trashed - (Mike.- deal with him later) Perfect excuse to bring Vivienne home.

Visited Dad in Hospital, no change.

Found out Monica is in UK with Charlie. - Need to see him

ASAP.
Vivienne's fighting against her feelings for me, not sure why? She's curious about my locked room, my tattoo, and my scars. Can't tell her about me yet. She'll run. She's had enough truth for now. I can't lose her again.

SUN 29th March:

08:30hrs - Brands Hatch

Amazing!! Vivienne just blows me away.
Her bike's got to go. Ordered new car for her.

Lunch with Anne & Paul

Perfect afternoon.
Vivienne finally told me she loves me. It felt fucking awesome!!
She's the one. She makes me so happy.

16:00hrs Charlie & Monica visiting.

Charlie breaks my heart. Need to find more options for his treatment.
Dad had another stroke. He's stable at the moment. Really worried about him.

MON 30th March:

09:00hrs - Meeting at Bank

11:30hrs - Taking Charlie Flying.

Woke up with Vivienne in my arms. I couldn't be happier. Everything about her is perfect.
She insists on going to work. Need to change that.
I told Monica I'm going to marry Vivienne, she seemed very happy for me.
Vivienne still won't say yes! Why is she hesitating????
Took Charlie Flying - We had a wonderful morning together, he loves flying.
Had to rescue Vivienne from her apartment. (Need more security)
Charlie very sick - called the doctor out. - Monica says it's the medication???
Visited Dad - no change.
Paid Mike a visit.
Had to tell Vivienne about my parents. She seemed to

already know I was self harming, but I didn't tell her everything about me. It's too soon She'll run!

TUE 31st March:

11:45hrs Flight to Germany - Meeting at Embassy – Kurt Becker

Vivienne took Charlie to the zoo.

Meeting dragged! - Deal eventually signed off.

Vivienne found out I'd visited Mike. SHIT!!!

She ran. - Refused to take my calls.

Why does everything good in my life always fall apart.

WED 1st April:

Got home around 3:30am Penthouse door wide open! Jan and Monica gone! Charlie unconscious in bed! Rushed him to hospital. - Coma...

Test results are Unbelievable! Monica has been poisoning Charlie!

She fucked off with money & my gun. Trencher looking for her. No trace yet.

Vivienne came back. I need her. Can't do this without her.

THUR 2nd April:

R.I.P Little buddy x

I may not have been your father, but I've loved you like a Son and will always hold you in my heart. Forever.

Fly with the angels my little one.

X

Vivienne found out about my room. She shocked the shit out of me when I got home. But in spite of all my fears, instead of running, she overwhelmed me.

Today, I felt the full force of her love for me, and although I don't yet deserve her, I feel truly honoured and blessed to have her heart.

I quickly flick forward through the pages, but Charlie's death is where it all ends. I wipe the tears from my cheeks and return the diary to the drawer, carefully placing it back where it was. Then I lock the drawer and hang my head in shame.

For a man to commit his feelings to paper like that is

unusual to say the least, but if I ever needed attestation of his love for me, it's right there in black and white.

In spite of that, it doesn't take long for my niggling suspicious brain to fire out more questions about why he lied to me about Fiona this morning. Why didn't he just say that she had called? Why did he have to tell me it was a client calling? And why did he change his clothes?

I wander through to the living room and sit at the piano. My mind isn't really focused on the notes as it should be, but playing usually helps to clear my mind.

As I butcher my way through the intro of Claire De Lune, I'm interrupted by Max as he suddenly appears out of nowhere and leans on the top of the piano.

"What are you playing?" he asks, smiling down at me. I stop and close the lid, embarrassed by my ham-fisted attempt at Debussy's classic. I suddenly realise he's not wearing his suit anymore and he's back in the clothes he left the house in this morning.

"Why have you changed?" I ask abruptly, wishing I hadn't said anything at all.

"Changed? I haven't. I'm still madly in love with you no matter how badly you play."

Huh? Oh, there you go, changing the subject. My cheeks heat up. I hate my jealous streak. It's probably uncalled for but I can't control it. All this jealousy and possessiveness is a totally new experience for me. And if I'm honest, it's not something I handle with any finesse.

I stand and walk over to the window, leaving him leaning on the piano.

"What's the matter, baby? Do you have a headache?" Before I have the chance to answer, he's standing behind me wrapping his arms around my waist and leaning his chin on my shoulder. His soft lips kiss me lightly on my neck, sending tingles down my spine and a dull thud deep inside. I close my eyes and tilt my head to accommodate him. It's a natural, instinctive reaction to his feather-light kisses, until I realise that I've succumbed to his innate charm and so I force myself to snap out of it.

I turn my head to face him and breathe in, but there's only his scent pervading my nostrils. There's no foreign perfume lingering on his collar. I turn back to the window.

"Baby? Is everything okay?"

"How was your meeting with your client this morning?" I ask, staring out at nothing in particular. He continues his tantalising path along my neck and throat.

"Fine. It got a little heated, but we resolved the situation in the end," he sighs, breathing a hot breath across my neck.

"You mean, the men I saw in your office?" I ask, leading him exactly where I want him.

"Yeah," he chuckles, "you barged in right in the middle of it."

He doesn't know that I'd already asked his receptionist what time he'd arrived at the office, and now he's just confirmed that he's not told me the whole story about this morning.

"And what about the meeting you had with Fiona, how did that go?" I feel him pause momentarily, then his arms tighten around my waist and he begins to nibble on my earlobe.

"Very well," he says, in between nibbles.

Is that it?…Very well. So, what do I do now? He hasn't denied it, and if I keep on badgering him I'm going to sound like the nagging wife.

"You didn't tell me she was a client," I say, trying not to be side-tracked by the attention he's paying my earlobe. I have to admit, it's turning me on.

"She isn't," he says, without missing a beat.

What? But…

He spins me around in his arms and gazes down at me with his scorching blue eyes and sexy smile. My heart flutters and I feel my bones melting under his gaze.

"Her father is, or was. He's an old friend of the family."

Oh… So I guess I'm going to be bumping into her quite a lot then.

Great!

After distracting me with his super-sexy smile and a succession of feather-light kisses, he informs me that we should hurry up and change. Sylvie has invited us for Sunday lunch so I park the million more questions I have for him, and I store them up for later.

RIVER OF NEED AND WANTING

In the car on the way over to his mother and father's house, he squeezes my thigh and looks over at me with an edgy expression. "Baby, my sister will be there today."

Wait. What? "You have a sister?" My wide eyes stare at him waiting for an explanation. I'm physically stunned. No one's ever mentioned a sister before. Not Sylvie or Jan. No one.

"You never told me you had a sister."

His eyes slide back to the road ahead. "She's not really my sister. We didn't grow up together," he shrugs, "she was never officially adopted, but Mom and Dad have always treated her like a daughter. She's twelve years older than me, and I don't see her very often since she and her husband moved to South Africa."

I continue to stare at him realising there is so much I still don't know about this family.

"What's her name?"

"Olivia." His eyes dart back over to mine. "She's very nice, you'll like her." He smiles, but I sense an undertone of something that he's not comfortable with. I just don't know what it is.

After negotiating the speed bumps in a tree lined, private road, we pull up to a huge pair of wrought iron gates which swing open almost immediately.

The long gravel driveway leads us toward a huge ivy-covered house, no....Mansion. There are several cars parked around the ornate fountain in the middle of the driveway, and as we come to a stop, a suited man walks toward the car and opens Max's door. Then he walks around to do the same for me. I can't quite get used to the pomp and ceremony. *Surely even rich people know how to open a car door for chrissake.*

I struggle to walk with any dignity on the gravel in my killer heels, but I do my best before taking Max's outstretched hand to steady myself.

As we enter the beautiful, spacious hallway, I can't help but look up at the incredible artwork on the ceiling and walls. The vintage Italian decor is simply stunning, and the imposing central staircase sweeps up to a galleried landing where the decoration continues. The glistening droplets of crystals on the impressive chandelier, sparkle and glint in the sunlight from the overhead stained glass dome right at the top of the house. I've never seen anything like it.

"They're all in the family room, Sir," the man in the suit says.

"Thanks, Jimmy."

Max pulls me into his side and walks me toward a large sitting room. I can hear the chatter as we approach the open doors. As we enter, the chatter stops and all eyes are on me. I shrink at the attention until I hear a familiar voice.

"Ah, Vivienne. You look beautiful." William struggles to his feet and walks toward us with a stick to steady himself. He greets me with a beaming smile and reaches down to take my hand in his.

"I thought this was supposed to be a casual lunch, just the six of us?" Max grumbles. William just smiles and arches an eyebrow. "You know your mother's been dying to tell everyone," he chuckles. "Just humour her."

I feel Max release a deep sigh before unravelling his arm from around my waist to shake his father's hand. Then he hugs his mother, who's just bounded over like an excited gazelle. I suddenly feel exposed and nervous.

"Darling, I'm so glad you came," she says, as Max kisses her on both cheeks. Her smiling face swings over to mine as she reaches out a hand toward me. "And Vivienne, I'm so happy you're here," she says, pulling me into an affectionate hug.

Sylvie quickly positions herself in between Max and I, then she links her arms through ours with a big beaming smile on her face. "Everyone? This is Vivienne, Max's fiancé."

"Mom," Max chides looking very uncomfortable. He throws me a small cringe over the top of his mother's head, and I'm sure my expression is priceless. I blush instantly as everyone stands and walks toward us. I feel like an exhibit.

One by one, Sylvie and William introduce me to the family and friends attending this not so casual lunch. All the women's eyes glide down to my left hand, looking for the engagement ring that isn't there, and I have to keep explaining that Max hasn't officially proposed to me yet.

"We never thought we'd see the day, did we, Sylvie?" chuckles the lady introduced to me as Mary, Sylvie's cousin. "I always thought he'd marry Fiona." I recoil slightly at her words. They must have been very close for Mary to think that. "I've heard great things about you, Vivienne. Least of all your incredible bravery. That was a terrible business with Monica. I heard you suffered at her hands more than once. And poor Charlie, that was awful," she says, without stopping to take a breath.

"Now, now, Mary. There'll be no talk of that evil witch in my house," Sylvie says, scornfully. "And stop badgering poor Vivienne. I'm sure she'd like to forget all about it. She doesn't need you giving her the third degree." Sylvie takes Mary by the arm and manoeuvres her away from me.

William takes me by the elbow and walks me over to the fireplace. He's a little unbalanced on his feet and so he rests his hand on the mantelpiece to steady himself.

"Vivienne, I just wanted to talk to you while I have the

chance," he says, with an apologetic smile. "Sylvie and I have a great fondness for you, I hope you know that we both care about you very much, and we couldn't wish for a better daughter in law." I blush and look down, his words have moved me. "I know I'm no substitute for your father, but I just wanted to let you know that I'd be honoured and so proud to walk you down the aisle when you and Max get married." I look up with glistening eyes. "If that's what you would want?" he adds, nervously.

I'm choked up, and I have to swallow the lump in my throat before I can speak. His kind eyes search my face as I blink the tears away and nod my approval with a smile. "I would like that, very much."

"Good. That's settled then," he says, smiling broadly. He squeezes my hand then he leaves me to find Sylvie.

William's kindness has left me feeling very loved, and lucky to be a part of such a loving family. I didn't realise how much I missed my own parents.

Blinking my tears away, I look for Max. We'd become separated during the meet and greet. When I find him, he's standing in front of a woman I recognise.

Fiona!…The old family friend…Hmmf…The ex-girlfriend…The girl Mary thought he'd marry. Great. My green-eyed monster has hitched a ride and joined the party.

Until last Thursday, Max had never mentioned her, ever. And I distinctly remember when I first met him, he'd said that he didn't do relationships.

They look very comfortable together and they burst into laughter at the same time. She reaches up to stroke his cheek but he doesn't flinch or move, he just accepts it willingly. My hackles rise immediately.

"Hi, I'm Olivia."

I begrudgingly turn away from Max and Fiona to face the woman standing beside me. She's a lovely looking woman with soft brown eyes, and pale blonde hair. She has a warm smile, and in her arms, she's carrying a newborn wrapped in pale blue blankets and wearing a tiny little knitted cap. Now I understand the uncomfortable look in Max's eyes when he told me I would meet Olivia today.

"You're Max's sister," I blurt.

"Yes, it's so nice to meet you, Vivienne." She smiles at me warmly. "And this is Mason," she adds proudly, looking down at her gorgeous baby. My eyes dance over his perfect little features as he yawns out a big sigh and uncurls his tiny hands, still blissfully asleep.

"He's beautiful," I sigh, reaching up to touch his tiny little fingers.

"Yeah. He is." Olivia coos. "It'll be your turn next, Vivienne." She smiles, totally unaware that her comment has just torn my heart from my chest.

There are never any warnings for moments like these. You can't introduce yourself with, 'Hi, I'm Vivienne, I was raped as a kid and I can never have children.' It's just not the done thing.

I've never been one of those women who dreamt of nothing else but being married and having children. The traumatic events of my childhood certainly put paid to any thoughts of a fairy-tale future. God knows it took me a long time to learn to trust anyone enough to even begin a relationship, and knowing I could never have children, marriage seemed like a pointless pursuit. Instead, I'd built up my barriers brick by brick, and I'd carved out a modest living focusing all my energy on my photography. Poor Mike, he never really stood a chance with me.

Up until recently, 'the love of my life' was just a thing other people had. Other happy people, like Lucy. How could I know the love of my life was waiting for me around the next corner. Max was a big surprise. And now that I've found my prince, no one could be more shocked than I am, to find that I really do want the fairy-tale ending…

"Vivienne?… Would you mind?" My eyes dart up to Olivia's confused face. I suddenly realise I'd zoned out again. I don't even know what the question was. I'm still holding onto Mason's tiny little fingers and gazing into his gorgeous little face which is now wide awake and staring up at me in wonder.

"Sorry… Miles away… Your baby's beautiful," I say, smiling up at Olivia.

"Would you mind holding him for me while I fetch his bottle?" she repeats, chuckling at me.

Oh, no. "Yes, of course. I'd love to." My heart pounds in my chest as Olivia hands over her prize possession. He stirs and pulls a face as I cradle him in my arms. He feels so small and fragile. All the maternal instincts I never knew I had, suddenly flow through me like a river of need and wanting. I can't take my eyes off him.

A warm hand rests on the small of my back, and I feel Max's hot minty breath against my cheek as he peers over my shoulder at Mason. I look up at him and take a deep inhale. "He's beautiful isn't he?" I sigh.

Max gives me a look that almost brings me to tears. I know he wants this for us, he just doesn't have the courage to admit it.

Olivia returns with a bottle. "Would you like to do the honours?" she asks.

"Actually, I think Vivienne may need a drink," Max says, raising an eyebrow. "Mom's kind of sprung all this on her without any warning."

"Oh, yeah," Olivia giggles. "Mom can be a little overpowering. But you settling down is a big event for her," she says, with a cheeky grin. "And the prospect of more grandchildren sends her positively giddy," she adds, taking Mason out of my arms. I stiffen. That's what they all expect from our union, more children. What a disappointment I'm going to be when they find out. My mood plummets, and suddenly I'm feeling hot and breathless. "Why don't you show Vivienne the lake? It's beautiful at this time of year," Olivia says, offering the bottle to Mason.

Max curls his arm around my waist and begins to lead me

away. Remembering my manners I turn back. "Lovely to meet you, Olivia." My eyes drift back to Mason and a strange sense of loss builds in my heart.

"You too," she smiles. "I'll catch up with you later, I've got tons of stories about Max," she giggles, waggling her eyebrows.

We walk through to the massive kitchen. A couple of the waiting staff nod hello to us both and then leave the room with trays of wine and canapés.

Max pours me a large glass of wine, assessing me warily as he hands it to me. I paste on a fake smile. I don't want him to see how emotional I'm feeling.

"Wow. You do this every Sunday lunch?" I smirk.

Max just shoots me a look. "Hardly. Mom's just a little excited about me finally settling down. She was beginning to think the rumours about me being gay were true," he smirks, rolling his eyes.

I gape at him in mock-shock. "Wait. You're *not* gay? Oh, well, I only date gay men. I'm sorry, but you'll have to go." He smiles that bone-melting smile, and then he leans me up against the counter crowding my space. His lips are achingly close to mine, and his eyes blaze with intent. He tilts my head up with his finger and gazes into my eyes for the longest time.

Searching my eyes, his expression slowly morphs into apprehension. "Baby, I'm sorry. I wasn't sure how you'd handle it. I saw your face when you were holding Mason, you looked so sad." I stiffen and try to lower my head but Max pulls my gaze back up to his. "You don't have to pretend with me, Vivienne," he says, softly.

"…I am sad. Not for me. I'm sad for you. You should be with someone who can give you a family, someone who can—"

"Don't," he says, searching my eyes and clenching his jaw. "Don't feel sad for me. I'm the happiest guy on the planet. I have you. You're all I want."

"But—"

The staff interrupts our moment bringing the empty glasses back into the kitchen. Max reaches down to take my hand. "Come, let's go for a walk."

He leads me out to the rear gardens. There are acres of land in every direction, and big, majestic, ancient trees dot the landscape. As we silently walk hand in hand, my mind is all over the place and I feel an ache deep inside. *What if he's wrong?* What if in five, ten, or fifteen years, when everyone around us is bathing in the glory of their children, what if he resents me? It's not like he doesn't have other options. There are plenty of women, Fiona for one, who would love to be in my position and who could give him the family I know he truly wants.

When the path finally ends, Max scoops me into his arms to save my heels in the grass and then he walks us further along to a beautiful lake set in amongst the woods. Setting me down on my feet, he drapes his arm around my shoulders and we gaze out at the idyllic scene.

"I have to apologise for my mom," he smirks. "I had no idea she was going to invite so many people."

"No, don't apologise. She's just happy for you." I look down and fidget when I realise telling Sylvie I can't have children may be just as hard as it was telling Max. "Did Sylvie have any children of her own?" I ask hesitantly.

He takes a moment to answer, still staring straight ahead. "Yeah," he sighs. "She had two sons. Daniel died at four months, his heart hadn't developed properly during the pregnancy. And Joseph was stillborn."

My heart drops. I don't know which is worse, not being able to conceive, or having them only to lose them so cruelly. I look up at Max, he's clearly moved. His expression is tight and the sadness is obvious. Even the loss of two souls he'd never met seems to have affected him deeply. Or is it something else? Is it me who saddens him?

In his diary, he'd said I was perfect, but I'm far from that, I'm imperfect. Maybe now he's starting to realise he's made a big mistake.

Max uncurls his arm from around my shoulders and walks down to the water's edge. He's deep in thought as he picks up a couple of stones and throws them across the lake, skimming and bouncing across the surface until they plop into the water and disappear.

Standing with his back to me, he bends to pick up a couple more stones, feeling their weight and smoothness in his hand. He draws his arm back to throw the next stone.

"You never told me how you really felt." My question makes him pause, then he throws the stone with much more force than the last.

"About what?" he asks, still with his back to me.

"About me not being able to give you any children. I know you want them."

He throws the next stone and then he shoves his hands in his pockets, staring out at the ripples on the lake. After a deep sigh, he speaks in a low, raspy voice. "I can't lie to you, Vivienne… I was devastated."

And there it is. His confirmation of something I'd known all along. Even though I knew it deep inside, it hit me like a freight train and there was nothing I could do about it.

"It's funny," he shrugs, "I never thought I'd ever want to settle down and have a family, not after what Monica did..." Max takes his hands out of his pockets and drags one through his hair. "But when Charlie was born, something inside me changed. I knew I wanted to be a father someday." He turns to face me, but I nervously look down as he starts to walk toward me. Stopping in front of me, he lifts my chin with his finger raising my line of sight to his sad eyes, making my heart twist and sink in my chest.

"When I saw you with those kids in the hospital, you were so natural with them and yes, of course, I thought about us having a family of our own one day. But it doesn't change how I feel about you."

My eyes begin to water and the lump in my throat tightens.

"Come on you two lovebirds. Dinner's ready." Mary's chirpy voice startles me. I quickly blink the tears away and paste on a happy face before turning toward her. She's standing at the edge of the pathway, far enough away not to notice my tears or to have overheard our conversation. I'm grateful for that.

Max lifts me into his arms and carries me over the grassy bit, then he puts me on my feet once we're back on the path. Taking my hand, he smiles down at me, although it doesn't quite reach his eyes.

Mary walks ahead, talking for England all the way back to the house. I couldn't tell you what she'd said, I was replaying Max's words over and over in my head which gave me little room to notice anything else.

My stomach was churning and I wanted to leave. The thought of spending the afternoon fending off questions about our future, scared the hell out of me. But what excuse could I give? Sylvie and William had gone to so much trouble, and even if I did leave, my troubles would only come with me.

Before we enter the house, Max pulls me back letting Mary go on ahead.

"Baby, I meant what I said. I love you." His eyes search mine. "I can see it in your eyes that you doubt me, but you shouldn't."

"Come on you two." Mary chides.

Max gives me a reassuring squeeze as we follow her into the house.

The dining room is huge with an enormous, glossy wooden table in the centre. William is sat at the head of the table with Sylvie at his right hand side. Max and I sit beside each other opposite Sylvie. Olivia and her husband are beside me. There must be twenty four people chatting and laughing as we take our seats. I glance up at Max, he looks so calm and poised. He hides his emotions very well.

"Vivienne, how nice to see you again." I look up to see Fiona taking her seat opposite me. "I'm Fiona," she smiles, "we met at the coffee shop last week."

I smile politely. "Yes, I remember." *How could I forget.*

"I love your dress, you have such a great figure for it too," she says, unravelling her napkin and laying it across her lap.

"…Thanks." I'm a little taken aback, she hardly even glanced at me when we met last week, but now she seems very interested in me.

I watch her for a moment as she scoops her long blonde hair over one shoulder. She has an elegance about her, not to mention her stunning good looks, and she literally radiates with confidence.

"I feel terrible for not introducing myself properly last week. I'm afraid I was in a bit of a rush that day. I'd just returned from New Zealand and my girlfriends and I were on a mad shopping spree," she laughs.

"Oh, that's okay."

Max begins to ask Fiona about New Zealand as Olivia draws my attention by placing her hand on my arm. "Did Max show you the lake?"

"Oh, yes. It's really beautiful." I notice Olivia's baby isn't with her. "Where's Mason?"

"He's up in the nursery, sleeping hopefully," she smirks. "I love him dearly, but I miss my sleep," she says, pulling a face. "Make the most of it, Vivienne. While you can still have a lie in. Once you start a family, you can kiss goodbye to a straight eight hours." Thankfully, Olivia's husband draws her attention away from me so I don't have to continue the conversation.

Max and Fiona are still talking and laughing loudly about people and places they both have in common. I feel his hand settle on my thigh as he feels for the lace tops of my stockings giving me a reassuring squeeze, but his attention is still focused on Fiona as he absently pours me a glass of wine.

"I hear congratulations are in order," Fiona says, lifting her empty wine glass toward Max. He stands and leans across to pour her some wine even though the waiting staff are busily doing just that. She bats her lashes at him, then she slides her eyes over to me and raises her glass in salute. "He's a very lucky man." She smiles, disingenuously.

The clinking of crystal as William taps his glass with his fork, cuts through the chatter.

"Everybody, please." He waits for the room to fall silent. "Please raise your glasses to baby Mason, the youngest member of our family. Cute as a button and no doubt Sylvie and I will spoil him rotten." We all raise our glasses at once. "To Mason."

"I'd like to also welcome another new member to our family. One in which Sylvie and I are truly indebted." William takes Sylvie's hand and gives it a loving squeeze.

Oh, no! Please don't. I feel everybody's eyes on me as I shrink in my seat.

"Her courage and love for our son, kept him from the wrath of She-who-will-not-be-named," he says, arching a brow. "And we couldn't be happier to welcome her into our family…To Vivienne."

Max's left hand squeezes my thigh as he raises his glass along with everyone else. I'm so embarrassed as I look up at William and Sylvie with roasting cheeks and a shy smile. Once the toast is over, the chatter resumes.

Max leans over to me, I see Fiona's eyes following him, studying him, then she looks away as he whispers in my ear. "Welcome to my crazy family. You'll get used to the embarrassing moments of which, if my mother has anything to do with it, there will be many," he smirks, then he kisses me tenderly on the cheek before continuing his conversation with Fiona.

The dinner was delicious, even though my churning stomach didn't make it as satisfying as it should have been. Fiona commandeered most of the conversation at our end of the table, talking about her experiences in New Zealand and reminiscing with Max about earlier times. I could see that they got on very well and had slipped into an easy rapport with each other. I would have felt more of an outsider if it wasn't for the gracious attempts of Olivia and Sylvie to include me in their conversations.

Max never took his hand from my thigh throughout, choosing to negotiate his food with only his fork. I could tell Fiona had noticed this, and I'd hoped that in some way it may have irritated her as she was starting to irritate me.

The woman was just too perfect. Beautiful, interesting, funny. A worthy adversary. She hadn't said or done anything specifically, and I know it's just my irrational jealousy rearing its ugly head, but there was something about her that irked me. I think it was her smile.

Every now and then, as she was talking to Max, she seemed to check me out. Every time I caught her doing it, she'd smile. I'd seen that cat-like smile before from Monica, the one dripping with insincerity. Maybe I was just being paranoid. But as far as I'm concerned, one Monica in a lifetime is quite enough.

While the coffee is being served, some people disappear out to the gardens to have a cigarette. Mary suddenly appears at my shoulder in between me and Max, leaning on the back of our chairs.

"Well, Vivienne. You've survived the first of many family gatherings. I hope we haven't scared you off," she chuckles.

I smile up at her and shake my head. Her gaze lifts away from my eyes, above my head, and follows something into the room. "Oh, isn't he adorable," she sighs, watching Olivia walk into the dining room with Mason in her arms. "I expect you'll be wanting to start a family of your own pretty soon. We Foxx's love our cubs," she says, her smiling eyes now fully focused on me.

I blush, and quickly excuse myself from the table.

"Where are you going?" Max asks nervously.

"I just need to use the bathroom," I stutter.

"I'll show you where it is," Fiona says, rising from her seat. I don't look at Max although I can feel his eyes on me, but I do notice the lingering, knowing look Fiona gives him.

She links her arm with mine and walks me up the sweeping staircase to the first floor. "Whatever you do, don't tell Mary any of your secrets. She's the biggest gossip this side of Nagasaki," she smirks. "I really do love your dress," she adds, squeezing my elbow.

Fiona's going out of her way to be nice to me, but something doesn't quite sit right. I can't put my finger on it yet.

She shows me to a beautiful, dark marble bathroom. "Here we are." She gives me a strange look and sweeps her eyes all over my face as if sizing me up. "I'll leave you to it," she smiles, pulling the door closed.

I lock it and move to the basin to check out my face in the mirror. I choose not to have a full blown conversation with my reflection in case Fiona's still waiting outside. I still feel uncomfortable about Mary's comment. And I wanted to ask Fiona about her and Max's relationship, but if I'm honest, I don't think I could handle the information.

Once I've taken care of business, I wash my hands and check myself out in the mirror before leaving the bathroom. I walk along the lush, carpeted gallery toward the staircase and stop to admire some of the incredible paintings.

Giggling from down below draws my attention. As I peer over the banister, I see Max and Fiona walking across the hallway into a room opposite the dining room. He has his arm wrapped around her waist, and she's leaning into him with her arm around his waist. Something she's whispering into his ear has him laughing out loud. All my nerve endings jangle at once.

"Are you alright, Vivienne?" Mary asks, walking toward me up the stairs.

"Oh. Yes. I was just admiring the beautiful paintings," I stutter. She smiles and carries on walking to the bathroom.

I hesitate at the top of the stairs then I slowly make my way down toward the room Max and Fiona had gone into. As I enter what appears to be a library, I feel immediately uncomfortable. They're both sitting with their backs to me on a small couch opposite the fireplace. Fiona's hand is stroking the back of his neck, curling the hair at the nape of his neck through her fingers, and he's just letting her do it. Her soothing words hit me like an anvil. "Oh, Max. I'm so sorry. I know how much you want a family. Maybe…maybe you should just cut your losses and move on. You're the catch of the century. Any woman would be proud to stand by your side and give you the family you want."

You told her? It felt like a slap in the face. "Why would you do that?" My voice breaks as tears begin to fill my eyes. Max and Fiona turn to face me at the same time. "Why would you tell her?"

Max's face is shocked and even from here, I can see the tears in his eyes. He's confided in her. Baring his soul to her. But it's me he should be talking to. Not her.

"She was just trying to help." He stands, dislodging Fiona's hand and then he starts toward me.

"Don't!" I yell, holding both my hands up. It stops him in his tracks. My eyes ping-pong between them. Fiona's face has a hint of a smile, Max just looks sad and confused.

I turn and bolt for the front door, flinging it open. The cold blast of air hits me as I run blindly out and down the steps toward the long driveway.

"Vivienne!" Max calls my name but I keep on running, my heels twisting in the gravel. Suddenly, he catches me around the waist bringing me to a shuddering stop, lifting me from my feet. I kick out as I try to wriggle free. He tightens his hold, and I feel his chest heaving in and out against my back. "What the fuck are you doing?" he asks, with ragged breath.

"Put me down!" I yell, trying to wriggle out of his arms.

"Why are you running?"

"Put. Me. Down!"

He does, then he spins me around to face him, now holding me by the tops of my arms.

"What the fuck are you doing?" he repeats angrily as his dark eyes search my face for an answer.

"What am *I* doing?" I yell. "What are *you* doing telling *her*? You told her about me, didn't you?"

"Who, Fiona?" he asks incredulously.

"Yes! Fucking Fiona!" I yell, exasperated. "The ex. The woman that Mary seems to think you were going to fucking marry!"

His stormy eyes glare at me. "Is that what this is all about? You're jealous of Fiona?" He's almost laughing at me when he says it which hurts me even more.

"You told her that I can't have children. We've barely spoken about it ourselves, and yet you found it so easy to confide in a woman who clearly wants you for herself."

He shakes his head and looks at me like I'm a raving loony. "She's just a friend."

"Like fuck!" I yell. "I know you've been talking to her behind my back." He gives me a look that tells me I'm right, and suddenly his expression softens and he tries to pull me into his chest but I resist him and stand my ground.

Exasperated at me, he clenches his jaw and exhales a long frustrated sigh, dragging his hand through his hair. "Vivienne, I don't know how many times I have to tell you that it doesn't matter to me. I love you, and I—"

"Of course it fucking matters to you. You're talking to your ex-girlfriend about it. I'll bet she could give you what you want. I'll bet little Miss Perfect is just dying for you to come to your senses and dump me for her!"

We glare at each other like two boxers on fight night.

"You're being ridiculous."

"Am I?" I goad, gritting my teeth. "I don't think so. I'm damaged goods. You're only with me because you feel guilty about this!" I raise my hand to point at the scar on the side of my head, his eyes follow.

I suddenly notice a crowd gathering at the steps watching us, but I don't care. I'm fucking angry.

Max drags his hands through his hair in exasperation. "Look, Vivienne," he says, trying to calm down. "I've had a really shitty day. The last thing I need is to have a shouting match with you on my mother's front lawn. Why don't we just go inside and talk about this calmly?"

"*You've* had a bad day?… Really?" I grate sarcastically.

His eyes flare, and suddenly his anger is back. "Yes! As a matter of fact a really fucking shitty day! The meeting that you so rudely barged into this morning was with a company trying to sue me and ruin my reputation, all because one of my treacherous, two-faced lawyers has been dealing behind my back! And to top it all, our servers have been hacked! I'd say that constitutes a pretty fucking shitty day, wouldn't you?" The look in his eyes would normally make me back down, but I'm way past the point of being able to control my mouth. Anger seethes inside me and so far, he's said little to assuage it.

"Yeah, I would! But where were you for the rest of the morning? With Fiona?" I spit it out and leave it hanging, but when his eyes confirm it, I feel sick to my stomach.

"It's not what you think," he says softly, shaking his head and clenching his jaw.

"Really? Try me!" I snap, staring him out.

He drags both hands through his hair and his angry frown deepens but his voice remains soft. "Her sister, Sarah, couldn't have any kids. They'd tried for years and then they tried I.V.F., and now she's pregnant. I just needed to talk to Fiona about it, that's all. I just thought that maybe—"

"What?" I interrupt, throwing my hands in the air. "That I.V.F. would fix me?" I see Fiona walking toward us over Max's shoulder. "Oh, great!" I huff, turning away. Max reaches for my arm to stop me from walking off again. His expression and angry tone of voice startles me.

"What do you want me to fucking say, Vivienne? Am I disappointed that we can't have kids? Yeah! Of course I am! It fucking kills me! I'd give my right arm to have a child like Charlie, but there's nothing I can do about it! Not one goddamn thing!"

I stare up at his hard, dark eyes. Suddenly everything feels so hopeless. I know he loves me, but how long will that last when one of us just feels wholly inadequate. Steeling myself, I lower my voice. "No… That's right… There is nothing you can do about it… Not with me, anyway. Goodbye, Max." I turn and start walking. I hear a low hum from the spectators gathered on the steps behind me and then Fiona's voice cuts through.

"Max, just let her go. She needs to cool off, and so do you."

As I trudge down the long driveway, the ache in my heart makes me almost immune to the biting cold air around me. I just feel completely numb.

I hear a car pulling up alongside me. I expected to see the DB9, but it's Olivia's husband Rick. He gestures for me to get in.

"Olivia wanted me to make sure you got home alright," he says, softly, swiping a nervous sideways glance in my direction. I don't speak. I just stare straight ahead with tears in my eyes and a hole in my heart. "Whatever it is…I'm sure it'll work itself out," he offers, kindly.

Will it?

KEEP CALM AND CARRY ON

Rick had given me a lift home, and I'd paced the floors reliving every word from Max's lips before finally going to bed, where I'd cried myself to sleep at God knows what-o'clock.

It's just after six in the morning. Today is the first day since I met Max that I haven't woken up to a beautiful white rose nestled on my pillow. My heart sinks as I sprawl out across the empty bed. He didn't come to bed last night. For all I know, he didn't come home either.

Home… This isn't my home, not anymore. Max's confession of his disappointment didn't come as a surprise, nonetheless, it can't be ignored no matter how much I want it to be different.

Our relationship seems to have lurched from one catastrophe to another. Surviving most of them is a testament to our love for each other, but this time it's different. I'm the one inflicting pain this time, and I love him too much to drag it out any longer.

I puff out a sad, weary sigh and bury my face in his pillow drawing in his scent. The swirling sickness in my stomach prompts me to get up and head to the bathroom. I haven't felt like this since I'd seen Doctor Alexander for a check-up a few days ago, but the tension from yesterday seems to have brought it all back.

I hang over the toilet bowl and heave the contents of my stomach. Once the nausea dissipates, I take a shower and try to do something with my hair.

As I sift through all my clothes and underwear, I'm careful not to take anything that I didn't buy myself. When I've packed the last of my boxes, I stack them in a neat pile against the wall and then I grab my rucksack and crash helmet.

Today, I'm going to go grovelling back to Frank in the hope that he'll still have a job for me, and after that, I'll move back to my flat. A quick clean exit, I owe him that much.

Jan hasn't arrived yet, so I leave her a note and I put it under my key-card on the hall table, then I take one last look around and leave with a heavy heart.

I park my bike in my usual parking slot and I'm relieved to find that my building pass still works. It's still early so hardly anyone is in the office when I arrive. I head to my desk and make myself comfortable waiting for Frank to show up.

Oh, no.

"Sweetie!" Clive's squealing voice interrupts the peace and quiet of the empty office. "O.M.G!" he announces dramatically. "Girlfriend, I didn't expect to see you here today," he says, bounding over like a lamb in springtime. I stand and let him give me a hug, then I prepare myself for the million rapid fire questions I'm about to receive. "Frank didn't say you were coming back today, why didn't you tell me?" he scowls.

"He doesn't know yet," I cringe. "Do you think he'll be alright? I've had so much time off lately."

Clive cocks his head. "For good reason," he huffs arching a brow, or trying to at least. "So, anyway. Tell me. How's things? How are you?" His eyes search my head. He's looking for the scar but it's hardly noticeable anymore.

I haven't got the strength to tell him about my latest depressing revelation, and I don't really want to hear it said out loud either, that would make it final so I just nod and shrug. "I'm good."

Frank arrives just in time to avert Clive's rebuttal. He's carrying a small cushion and walking like he's just got off a very wide horse, wincing with each stride.

"Oh, ah, Frank? Have I still got a job?" I ask on a cringe. He does a double take, then he gives me a poor attempt at a smile then a small grunt as he slowly passes my desk. "Is that a yes?" I whisper to Clive as I watch Frank shuffling to his office, grumbling under his breath.

"I think so," Clive giggles, smoothing his brow.

"What's the matter with him? He's walking like his shorts have been over starched."

Clive leans in toward me and giggles. "Vasectomy," he whispers.

"Oh," I cringe. "Poor bugger."

"Yeah, he's been a bit of a cantankerous old grouch since his wife made him go for the chop," he giggles. "It's been a bit chaotic while you've been away too. Oh. and Sandra left all of a sudden after…well, you know. But I'm sure Frank would have told me if you had been fired," he adds, rising from the corner of my desk. "You grab the coffees, and I'll go and see what's on today's agenda." He minces off to Frank's office and disappears inside.

I'd forgotten about Sandra, I still haven't sent her a reply. While I wait for Clive to return, I take a couple of the tablets Doctor Alexander gave me for the headache that's slowly getting worse. Then I walk over to the coffee machine and check my phone for probably the millionth time, but there are still no calls or messages from Max. If he was trying to hurt my feelings more than he already has, he's done it with knobs on.

I bristle as my mind explores the idea that maybe he went home with Fiona last night. I'm sure she knows exactly how to comfort him. Suddenly my stomach rolls and a wave of nausea washes over me. Running to the ladies toilets, I barge through the door and lean over the toilet bowl. Nothing comes up, but I haven't eaten anything yet. Once the feeling passes I head back to my desk.

Clive comes striding back from Frank's office with a smile. "So. You're all good on the job front," he says, reaching for his coffee and taking a seat on the corner of my desk. "You may have an assignment later on today, he's just waiting for confirmation. He asked that you catch up with all your emails and organise Ed's data from last night's red carpet at Leicester Square. Gus will need all the data by noon today."

I nod and take a sip of my latte. I'm feeling much more relaxed now that I know I still have a job.

Clive eyes me suspiciously over the rim of his mug. "Are you okay, you look a little green around the gills?"

"Yeah, I'm fine," I lie. I'm not ready to talk about last night yet, especially not with Clive.

"I didn't think you'd come back."

I avoid his eyes for a moment, trying to organise an answer that won't provoke any more questions. "Why not? I like working." I shrug nonchalantly. I can see Clive's brain cogs whirring so I cut in with another question that will hopefully push the conversation away from me. "So, have you and Luke set a date yet?"

Clive gives me his, I'm-so-in-love, look and fans his face. "I'm going to be a June bride," he announces, coyly.

"This June?" I ask, realising that it's only a few days away.

"No. Next year, silly. It's going to take a lot of preparation. We're going for the whole shebang. Marquee, swans, live band, fireworks, everything. Don't tell Luke I said that," he whispers, "he's trying to keep to a budget, but I want it all, and I want it covered in sequins." he sighs.

"I don't doubt that for one minute," I smirk. "Have you booked a photographer yet?"

"No, not yet."

"Well, don't. Call it my wedding gift."

His eyebrows leap upward in delight. Clearly a sign that his Botox is due for renewal sometime soon. "Really? You'd do that for me?" he asks, clapping his hand over his heart.

"Of course. I'd be happy to." Clive gives me a huge hug, almost knocking me out of my chair, and as he pulls away, I distinctly notice his eyes glistening with tears.

"Okay, I'd better get some work done or Frank will definitely fire me."

"But, what about you? How are things with your drop-dead gorgeous boyfriend?" he asks excitedly.

"Oh, yeah, great. Erm…I'll tell you all about it later, I really should get started." I cross my fingers and pray that he'll take the hint. Surprisingly, he does and almost skips away from my desk.

After a couple of hours of sifting through the photos Ed took at last night's premier, I organise them into great, good, okay, and what were you thinking? Then I put them all on a stick and take it to Gus.

When I return to my floor, I see my phone ringing on my desk so I run to catch it before it rings off. I hesitate when I see Lucy's number on the screen. I had hoped that it would be Max, even though I don't really know what to say to him.

"Hey, Luce."

"Hi, Viv. Where are you, you sound out of breath? Oh, shit. You and Max aren't—"

"I'm at work," I interrupt quickly.

"Already? Are you sure that's wise?" she asks hesitantly.

I let out a deep sigh. "It's more a necessity right now, Luce."

There's a slight pause before Lucy speaks. "What now?" she asks flatly, sounding resigned to the fact that something drastic has happened. I glance around the office, checking that no ears are on me.

"I'm moving back to my flat tonight, I'll tell you all about it later."

"What? Oh, no. Friggin' hell, Viv. I thought you'd got through all that?...Look, I know you can't talk right now, I'll meet you after work, okay? And Viv...keep your chin up."

I've been at work for three hours, I've finished all my jobs, and it's still only ten o'clock so I decide to go for an early lunch. I manage to sneak out of the office before Clive can grab me. I'd like to avoid him completely but I know that's going to take some doing.

I wander in the opposite direction from the bars and cafés we usually frequent at lunchtime and I find a quiet spot in a small café on one of the back streets. It's more like a greasy spoon, but I know Clive would never think to come looking for me here so I have half an hour's peace to contemplate the rest of my life.

I have a sudden urge to call my mum, just to see how she's doing. I haven't seen or spoken to her for so long, and even though our relationship is fractured to say the least, I always feel drawn to her when I'm feeling at my lowest. It's probably just an instinctual feeling and I don't act on it, there's no point.

Walking back to the office, I take one last look at my phone but there are still no calls or messages from Max. He's obviously had enough and who could blame him. A man like him doesn't need to settle for second best. He's surrounded himself with luxuries and perfection, it's laughable that he could ever have loved me at all. I miss him.

My headache pounds as I walk toward my desk. I hadn't eaten anything for fear that the nausea would return so I grab another coffee to fill the void in my groaning, empty stomach.

With nothing much to do, I take out my camera and give it a thorough clean. Once I've put it all back together again I hear Frank's strained voice calling to me from his office doorway. I turn to see him gesticulating for me to go over so I bag up my camera and head to his office.

"Frank?" I push the door open and stifle a smirk as I watch him gingerly trying to sit in his seat, groaning with every movement. Once he's settled, he lets out a sigh of relief and scowls up at me. "Are you alright, Frank?" I ask, pinching my lips together so I don't giggle.

"No." he barks, sarcastically. "Women! Mrs. Rosenthall has a lot to answer for!" he grumbles.

"Yes, well, I'm sure giving birth to your six children would have been nothing compared to what you're going through right now, Frank." I say it with as straight a face as I can manage.

He gives me an indignant scowl. "Clive's got a big mouth." I shrug and nod. I'd have to agree with him there. He winces as he reaches for a folder on his desk. "This just came in. The clients name is Madame S," he says, raising an eyebrow, "she's an eccentric wealthy Russian, and she's got an exhibition of her artwork at a club called the…ah," he pulls his glasses down from the top of his head, "the Stock X-Change Club."

"The Stock Exchange?"

"No, no, it's a club, a bondage club," he says avoiding all eye contact. I raise both eyebrows and stare at him, a little bemused. It doesn't sound like the kind of venue or material I'm used to photographing.

"I know what you're thinking," he says, shrugging, "sounds a bit weird, but it's just an exhibition of her art. The club doesn't open for its regular business until the evenings. All you have to do is take a few shots of the artwork and you're done."

"And who's coming with me?" I ask, hoping it will be Ed. He winces as he leans forward to hand me the folder and then he rests back in his chair. His face is starting to sweat.

"Ed's out on a shoot, and Jason decided to hand in his notice at the worst possible time. As if I haven't got enough to deal with already!" he grumbles. "You'll have to go alone, you can handle it."

Oh. Really?

Frank huffs out a painful sigh and then he levels his eyes on mine. "You don't have to go, Vivienne. I can sub it out if you're not comfortable with it? No pun intended," he smirks.

"No, that's okay."

"Good. I'll have a cab waiting for you out front."

STOCK X-CHANGE

The cab drops me at the entrance to the Stock X-Change Club. It looks like a theatre entrance but there are no windows. I stare up at the big, black, shiny double doors. It looks closed, and the overhead sign isn't illuminated. I start to wonder if Frank's made a mistake. It's then that I spot an intercom at the side of the doors. I press the buzzer and wait.

"Yes," the sharp voice asks.

"Erm, hi! I'm Vivienne from Star-Biz magazine. I'm here to photograph the artwork." I say, trying to sound as professional as possible.

"One moment, please."

After a few moments, one of the double doors opens enough to let me slip inside and then it's quickly closed and locked again. A good looking man wearing just a pair of leather trousers and a leather collar, introduces himself as Sebastian. He lazily trails his eyes all over me before leading the way down a flight of stairs.

It's dark inside, save for a low, red light set into the bare brick walls. My eyes take a moment to adjust. As I follow him down the stairs, I find myself trailing my eyes all over him. His long hair, strong physique, and striking features remind me a little of Max.

At the bottom of the stairs, he leads me along a short corridor which then opens out to a large dark room. A steep metal staircase leads up to the balcony, which wraps all around the entire upper floor. There are old fashioned wooden stocks at set intervals all around the upper balcony.

The DJ booth sits at one end of the room, and a long, fully stocked bar at the other. The ceiling has a gantry of lighting and several items hanging high above the dance floor. I see two trapeze bars, some kind of rack with loops hanging off it, and three thick coloured ribbons tied up out of the way.

As I walk onto the dance floor area I notice it's covered in sexually explicit images. I stare at one trying to work it out, there are more than two bodies mixed up in the image but I can't quite figure it out. Suddenly my eyes pop open wider as I finally realise what I'm looking at.

Wow!

"Ah, you must be Vivienne." The lady's soft Russian voice startles me, and I feel myself blushing as I drag my eyes away from the floor. A tall woman of an indeterminable age slinks toward me in a tight fitting, knee length, black dress, which hugs her voluptuous figure everywhere it should. Her makeup is impeccable, and her white blonde hair is glossy and coiffed in a sleek, heavy bun at the nape of her neck.

"I'm Nova. Nice to meet you," she smiles, with a voice like melted chocolate.

"Hi." I smile nervously, trying not to show my surprise. I was expecting something a bit more leather and chains. Instead, she looks like a powerful business woman.

"Have you ever been to a club like this before, Vivienne?"

I blush. "Wha…er…no. I can't say I have." I feel her eyes gliding slowly up and down my body then they land on mine. I find it impossible to look away.

"You're very beautiful," she says, in a matter of fact way. "You'd make a good model here," she adds, tilting her head.

Before I have the chance to protest, she turns and walks

toward the stairs. I look around for the man who had brought me in here, but he's disappeared so I follow Nova up the metal staircase.

We walk a short distance along the balcony.

"This is the Purple Room," she says, standing at the entrance to a room entirely decorated in hues of purple. It has a long, low stage at the centre with three shiny, silver poles fixed to the stage and the ceiling. Either side are plush velvet, button backed sofas lining the walls. The decoration is very stylish and, dare I say it, classy.

I turn to Nova to comment on the room but she's already walking out the door. I quickly catch up and follow her along the balcony to another room.

"This is the Red Room." She stands at the door while I walk through to take a look. My eyes are drawn to a huge four poster bed set in the middle of the room. It has no canopy, and each of the dark wooden posts have silver rings attached at varying heights. A wooden rack on the far wall has varying lengths of whips, canes, and floggers, hanging in uniform rows. My eyes linger on the whips as a flashback to Max's room of guilt suddenly hits me. I shake my head to clear the image from my brain and I cast my eyes over to the bed. It has red satin sheets and all around the bed are red velvet chairs and small tables, obviously for the spectators.

Wow! "You must go through a lot of sheets," I mumble to myself.

"Yes. It's an expensive hobby but very rewarding."

Shit! She heard me. I blush again and avoid looking at her as she beckons me to follow her to another room.

"This is the Creche." I stare into the room and fight the urge to speak my mind. How could anyone even think about bringing children to a place like this. I feel Nova staring at me as my eyes blink rapidly. It's a fairly innocuous room, apart from the black, over-sized crib, a high chair, and various dolls and teddy bears. *This is just sick.*

"Some of my guests have an adult baby fetish. Paraphilic infantilism," she says, calmly, as if she knew she had to explain it.

Oh?... Oh!

"I cater for most needs," she adds, walking on. She shows me the 'Wet Room', which has a massive Jacuzzi in it. 'The Rubber Room' which is self-explanatory, and finally she stops at the top of the stairs, having come full circle.

There is one more door but she doesn't offer to show it to me, and I don't ask. Each room I've seen has been carefully decorated and facilitated with all the paraphernalia required for each type of fetish. I've heard about these places, but this is the first time I've ever seen inside one, it's certainly an eye opener.

"Do you have a preference?" Her eyes slide over to mine and lock on to me with inquisitive intensity.

I swallow and blush. "Erm, it's not really my thing," I mumble shyly.

She smiles and reaches her hand up to my cheek. "And what is your thing?"

"What? No! I..." I try to speak, but I have no idea what to say so I close my mouth again and fidget.

"Oh, come on, Vivienne. Don't be bashful," she purrs. "Everybody has sex, everybody has fantasies. Release your inner goddess, you might enjoy it." She grazes her fingers down my cheek and turns to walk down the stairs.

My stomach tightens, my mouth has gone dry, and I realise I'm still standing like a statue on the top step while Nova is almost at the bottom, so I quickly run down to catch her up.

"Nova, the brief said you had some artwork to photograph?" I ask hesitantly.

"Yes, that's right. Come, I'll show you."

I follow her across the dance floor to a pair of black doors with crystal doorknobs. Before she opens them, she turns to face me. Her hooded, violet eyes search mine as she speaks. "This is the White Room, Vivienne. Open your mind, let the art speak to you. This is what I want you to photograph. My living statues."

Huh? Living what?

Nova slowly opens the doors. My eyes have to adjust to the stark contrast of the bright, white interior. The only colour in this room is the black, leather clad, semi-naked bodies of six figures bound, chained, or hanging from metal frames in varying forms. Each one stands on a low white pedestal, each with its own spotlight.

Oh, I got it. They're waxworks. Like a kinky Madame Tussaud's.

"I'll leave you to it." Nova says, backing out of the room and closing the doors. I stand there gazing around the stark space. The white walls are totally bare. I'm guessing the photographs will eventually be hung all around this room.

I take my camera out, remove my jacket and begin to check the lighting, while I figure out which angles I'd like to use. A smile seeps across my face. This is the weirdest assignment I've ever had, but I find it strangely fascinating. The lighting in the room is excellent for some really stunning monochromatic shots.

The first statue I pick, is a naked woman kneeling down with her hands bound at the wrists behind her back. She has a tiny waist and her perfectly toned, pear shaped bottom is resting on her heels. Her arms are tied together by leather straps at evenly spaced intervals right up to the top. She has a black velvet collar around her neck, and her long brown hair is braided down her back.

I take a few shots from behind, then from the side, and then I move around to see the front. The workmanship is remarkable, she's so lifelike. Her eyes are lowered to the floor and her full red lips are a stark contrast to her pale, white skin. She is completely naked apart from her collar, and I notice she has been sculpted to look very natural with one boob slightly bigger than the other.

I take a few more shots from the front. *Fuck!* I suddenly jump and fall backwards as the eyes flick up and land on mine. "Oh, my God. You're real." Her eyes immediately return to the floor as I stare at her in shock. A little unnerved, I stand up and walk over to her. Reaching out a trembling hand, I touch her pale skin. It's warm. "I'm sorry, I didn't know you were real. I mean. I didn't… I thought you were… Oh, shit."

The girl's eyes flick back up to mine. She even rolls them at me with a small smile curling her lips. "It's okay," she whispers.

"What? But…I mean, don't you mind being like this?" I ask, looking around at all the others who don't seem to have moved a muscle.

"No. We don't," she whispers. "But we mustn't talk," she adds, lowering her eyes.

"Oh, sorry…I… Sorry."

I watch her revert to her statuesque pose. They're all so good at it. The room is deathly quiet and totally still. Gathering myself together, I move on to the next one.

I found it fascinating. The human body truly is a work of art although, I'm not sure I could handle being bound and displayed like they were. Some of the contraptions looked way too uncomfortable to me. My feeble attempt at kinky sex with Lucy's handcuffs certainly pales into insignificance with what I've seen today. And somehow, although I don't suppose I will ever step foot in a place like this again, it's been an experience that I'll never forget.

As I'd moved around the room some of them gave me eye contact, one of them even winked at me, and when I'd bashfully lowered my eyes, I wished that I hadn't when they landed on the man's erect penis held firm by the cock ring at the base of his eye-wateringly large manhood. Embarrassment aside, I continued until all of them had been photographed from every conceivable angle.

"Thanks, everyone," I say, as I bag up my camera and walk to the doors. None of them reply.

As I leave the White Room my eyes have to adjust to the dim light in the main room, where Sebastian is waiting for me. My eyes trail over his impressive chest and tight, neatly packed abdominals. "Madame S asked that you meet with her tomorrow for dinner, to discuss the photographs," he says, walking me to the front door.

"Where, here?" I ask nervously. I'm not sure Frank will be happy about that. Then again…

"No, at her home, this is the address." He hands me a black business card with her details engraved in silver filigree.

"Oh, okay." I follow him back up the stairs, popping the card into my pocket to give to Frank when I get back to the office. "Do they have to stay in that room for long?" I ask, thinking how uncomfortable it must be.

"Until the Mistress dismisses them," he says, in a matter of fact nonchalance, holding the door open for me.

"Thanks." I step out into the bright sunlight, squinting at the harshness of it. Looking back, I see the large, black, shiny door closing and then I hear the lock click into place. *Wow. It's another world.*

The cab is waiting for me so I dump my bags in the boot and jump in the backseat. As we pull away from the kerb, I watch the busy people in suits and ties and designer clothes walking past the entrance of the club, and I wonder to myself how many of them would ever visit a place like that. From what I've read about these clubs they're inhabited by all walks of life. It makes me smile when I realise I've just spent the last two hours wandering around one myself. And then I begin to wonder about the people I've just photographed. They all have parents, siblings, colleagues and friends. I wonder if they know what they get up to in their private lives.

When I return to the office, I bump into Clive on my way to Frank's office.

"Hey, sweetie, where have you been?"

"Frank sent me out on a shoot." I blush, recalling some of the sights I've seen today. Should I tell him where I've been? Oh, what difference does it make. "It was a fetish club. The Stock X-Change." Clive's expression stiffens and his eyes flare. *Oh, my God.* "You know it?" I ask, wishing I had dialled down the shock in my voice.

"No! Erm, yeah. Erm, maybe?" he cringes.

I smile and shake my head. "Whatever floats your boat," I chuckle. He seems to relax when he realises I'm not going to reprimand him for his choice of entertainment. I start to walk on to Frank's office, then I turn back. "Hey, which room?" I ask, narrowing my eyes. He looks all around him before answering, just to check the coast is clear.

"All of 'em!" he shrugs. I raise my eyebrows. I'm not sure if I'm shocked or just in awe. "Except for the creche, that just ain't my thing," he adds, frowning. I feel surprisingly relieved. "Hey, did you meet Sebastian?" he asks, waggling his eyebrows.

I nod, with a cheeky smile. "Oh yes."

I carry on to Frank's office checking my phone yet again before knocking on his door. Still no calls or messages from Max. All I can think is that he's chosen to cut all communication with me. Jan has probably found my note and told him that I've packed up all my stuff. He's probably glad he won't have to see me again. He's probably even had all my stuff couriered over to my flat by now. I sag, feeling hurt and lost without him.

"Yeah!" Frank barks as I knock on his door. I push the door open and see Frank's sweaty, pained expression as he sits behind his desk. He looks awful.

"Job's done. I'll put the photographs on a drive for you. This is the woman's address," I hand him Nova's card, "she wants you to meet at her house for dinner tomorrow night to discuss the photos." I turn on my heel and start to leave.

"Vivienne, I can't go. Look at me. I can't even lift my

coffee mug without breaking a sweat," he grumbles.

"Shouldn't you go back to the hospital?" I offer, wincing at his obvious pain.

"No way. The surgeon was a sadistic female. She's not getting her hands on Angus and the twins ever again."

I smirk at the name he's given his manhood, then realise I shouldn't be laughing at his misfortune. "Talking of sadistic females, what about Nova?"

"Who?"

"Nova. Madame S," I say, pointing at her card.

"Can't you go? She's paid well over the top for these photographs, I'll make it worth your while and I'll even give you a bonus," he says, pleading with his eyes.

"But—"

"Please?"

"It better be a big bonus."

NO ME WITHOUT YOU

I head back to my desk and copy all the photographs onto my spare drive and my laptop. As I flick through the images, I can't help but feel proud of my work. These photos are stunning, regardless of the content. Who would have ever thought I'd be good at photographing submissives in a fetish club? I can just see it now… 'Ah, Vivienne, thank you for coming to the interview. May I see your portfolio? Good heavens, is that a cock ring and an anal plug?' I laugh out loud at the scenario in my head.

"What's so funny?"

I gasp as Max's voice startles me. I stare up at him standing in front of my desk. His eyes are dark and stormy, and his frown is deep. He looks sexy as hell, evoking the butterflies in my stomach and making my heart skip a beat. I quickly flip the lid of my laptop down and push my seat back.

"Wha… What are you doing here?"

"I could ask you the same thing." he says, without a flicker of humour. He stares me out for a few moments, then his eyes slide from my face and he marches off toward Frank's office. I watch him with bewildered eyes and an open mouth. Max doesn't knock, he just barges into Frank's office and closes the door behind him.

Clive comes bounding over. "What's going on?" he asks excitedly.

I shake my head and close my mouth. "I wish I knew."

A few minutes later Max comes out of Frank's office. My eyes trawl over his sexy frame as he strides that predatory walk of his back to my desk. His dark eyes are on me the whole time. Reaching for my hand, he barely stops walking and tugs me to my feet. "Wait, where are we going?" He doesn't answer me, so I pull back. "My camera." He stops and lets me pick it up from my desk then begins to stride off again. "Wait. I need my drive." Again he stops and lets me pick it up, then begins to stride off again. "Oh, wait! My laptop." This time, he stops and takes my camera bag from my hands and throws it over his shoulder, then he scoops the drive and my laptop into one hand and bends to grab me around my thighs. I yelp as he throws me over his shoulder in a fireman's lift.

"Wait! My crash helmet."

"Fuck your bike," he grumbles, marching through my office as everyone stops what they're doing and stares at us. I raise my head to see Clive with his hand raised to his lips. Then he smiles and waves at me.

"Er…goodbye, sweetie."

I have no idea what Max is up to, and if he doesn't put me down soon, I'm likely to throw up all down his back. He doesn't even put me down when he takes the lift down to the lobby, and he hasn't bothered to explain himself either.

"Max! What are you doing?" I ask, trying to wriggle free. I get nothing. It's like talking to a brick wall. "Max, please. What the fuck is going on?"

I feel a sharp sting as he smacks my behind. "Watch your mouth," he growls.

The look I get from our new receptionist is priceless as Max carts me out of the lift and through the lobby. I raise my hand and give her a wry smile and a wave, as he barges out through the door and marches toward the street. He places me on my feet, wincing as he does it. I must be too heavy or something. He opens the car door then he glares at me until I get in. Walking around to his side, he throws my stuff on the backseat and then slides in beside me.

"Buckle up," he growls, then we screech away from the kerb.

Other than his obvious anger, I can't read him. He hasn't looked at me and I can see his jaw clenching the whole time. I must have really pissed him off when I caused a scene at his parents' house yesterday, but he has to take some of the blame for that. He hurt me when he told Fiona that I couldn't have children. How could he have been so thoughtless? I don't know what to say, or do, so I just nervously wait for him to explain himself.

In silence, he drives to the Foxx-Tech building. He just abandons the car at the kerb, takes me by the elbow and drags me along beside him into the building.

"Max I—"

"No talking," he interrupts, sternly.

I huff out a sigh of exasperation, this brooding male thing is becoming very annoying. Why doesn't he just tell me off and have done with it?

His personal lift is waiting with doors open. Even as we ascend, he still doesn't bother to say anything. He's cold and distant. I'm starting to wonder if I might have packed something that didn't belong to me in one of my boxes. Or maybe he's found out that I'd read his diary. *Oh, shit.*

The lift stops on the twelfth floor. The doors open to a bright, white, brushed steel and blue glass reception area which is clean and spacious looking. A smiling, well-dressed man sits behind the main reception desk.

"Good afternoon, Miss Banks. I'm Casper." I feel uneasy for a moment wondering how he knows my name. Casper doesn't address Max other than with a small nod.

Max marches me down the corridor to the left of the main reception, to a huge office also in white, brushed steel and blue glass. The walls are covered in massive photographs, the furniture consists of a large steel and glass desk in front of a panoramic window, which looks out over the park. Royal blue leather sofas, a couple of chairs, and a low glass coffee table take up the rest of the space. Max walks ahead of me and dumps my stuff on the desk.

"Where are we?" I ask, looking around the office. At least our argument will be in private. Max doesn't answer, he just leans back against the desk folding his arms over his chest and crossing his feet at the ankles. His face is stern and hard, and he hasn't stopped clenching his jaw. His eyes follow me as I walk to the wall to study the pictures. My pictures. The aerial photos I took of the Foxx-Tech building. *Hmm… They're good.*

I remember taking these photographs from Max's helicopter. I'll never forget that day. He was trying to frighten me with his daredevil antics. He was angry with me because he thought I was still in love with Mike. I shake my head at the irony. At the time, I thought he was dating Grace's daughter. It turns out my best work seems to be achieved when I'm under pressure.

"You hurt me, Vivienne."

I turn to face him as a flutter of butterflies invade my belly. "*I* hurt *you*?" I huff, irritated that he still doesn't seem to appreciate what he did was totally out of order.

"Yes. You did," he scowls.

"Pff. I don't understand. How—"

"No! That was quite obvious when you stormed off yesterday. And even more obvious when I got home and found all your belongings packed away in boxes." He bites out the last word, clenching his jaw.

I lower my eyes for a moment, but why should I feel bad, he's the one who decided to cosy up with his ex-girlfriend and tell her about our private problems. The memory of her gloating smile after she'd been stroking his neck and saying 'maybe you should just cut your losses and move on' really starts to piss me off.

I fold my arms over my chest and stare him out. "Max. You'd better just spit it out because I'm at a loss to understand how any of this is my fault."

His eyes darken as he takes a deep breath, puffing out an aggravated sigh, his angry glare still in force. "You ran. You left me."

"Can you blame me?"

His eyes soften, all the hurt and sadness coming to the surface. "Vivienne, I get that you thought I'd betrayed you by talking to Fiona, it was stupid and thoughtless, and I'm sorry… But you accused me of being with you out of guilt," he huffs, clenching his jaw. "How could you even…That really hurt me."

I lower my eyes and shuffle on my feet. When I look back at him, the anger has returned to his eyes. "And how could you even *think* that I'd ever cheat on you. That's not how I roll. You should know that by now."

I unfold my arms and shove my hands in my back pockets. His accusing glare is making me feel uncomfortable, I can't look at him.

"You've proved to me more than once that you don't trust me, Vivienne. That hurts, and it makes me so angry."

I lift my eyes to his in defiance. He's not the only one who's hurting.

"Is that why you didn't come home last night? Because you wanted to punish me?" I ask angrily. He puffs out a small, sarcastic laugh as if I've just said something funny, then he pushes himself away from the desk, dragging his hands through his hair.

"I needed some space to clear my head. I needed to…" he trails off and looks away.

"To what? Be with Fiona?" I couldn't help it, I just blurted it out.

His hurt eyes narrow on me, then he starts to walk toward me but I turn away and walk to the window, staring blankly out at the London skyline. Unwanted images of her stroking his neck swim around in my head.

"Vivienne, nobody's perfect, least of all me. I know you have doubts, and yes, I'll admit it… so did I." My heart sinks and tears threaten my eyes. I hear him releasing a long, tired sigh and in it, I hear his pain. "Until I realised… Baby, there is no me without you. Without you, there's no point." I close my eyes as tears prick them, my heart leaps in my chest and the breath I was holding comes sighing from within. I feel his warm hands on my waist and his hot breath across my cheek as he stands behind me. "I've done all my thinking, Vivienne. I know what I want. You're my once in a lifetime love and I want you, exactly as you are… What do you want?"

I spin around. His nervous eyes search my face as I reach up and smooth my fingers down his cheek. "You… I want you."

His watery eyes close briefly then he kisses my palm before wrapping his arms tightly around me. "Don't ever do that to me again," he whispers, his voice laced with emotion.

Gazing into his loving eyes, I whisper, "I love you."

"I love you too, baby… Apparently, more than you realise," he adds shaking his head, then he leans down and crushes his lips to mine. I rise up on my toes meeting him half way.

UPPING THE ANTE

As we lay in each other's arms, naked and breathless, I lift my head from his chest and kiss his tattoo. "What if someone walks in on us?" I whisper, spotting my bra and knickers hanging off one of the chairs, and my jeans in a crumpled heap on the floor.

"Like who?" he murmurs, tightening his hold.

"Like whoever runs this office. What if—"

"They won't," he says, opening his eyes. "Nobody's coming in here."

"How can you be so sure? Or did you tell Casper to warn you when his boss returns?"

"His boss is already here," he says, leaning forward to kiss me on the top of my head.

"Yeah, I know *you're* the boss, but who runs this office?" I ask, wondering how much coverage the back of the sofa will give me from the angle of the doorway should someone burst in.

"You do."

I whip my head up to face him. "What!?"

His gorgeous blue eyes smile back at me, but I'm too bewildered to succumb to their usual effect. "These are your new offices. The studio is through that door over there," he nods toward it, "Casper will take care of all your administration, and the interviews for your new assistant are scheduled for tomorrow."

"Max, no! I can't—"

"Of course you can," he smiles and closes his eyes resting his head back down on the cushion.

I stare at him incredulously. "No. I'm sorry, but I can't let you do this. It's too much."

"I didn't really do anything," he sighs. "Besides, your work speaks for itself. You've got three new clients already. I showed your aerial photographs to some of my friends, and they want you to do the same thing for their companies. Casper has already scheduled their appointments for next week."

I sit up and look around at the incredible office with wide eyes and an open mouth.

"But Max, I can't afford a place like this. And I can't let you spend your money on me. I told you, I don't feel comfortable being in anyone's debt."

He opens his eyes and levels them on me. "Firstly, I'm not *anyone!*" he frowns. "And secondly, it hasn't cost me a thing…much." He smiles, then reaches up to tweak my nipple. I smack his hand away which makes him smile even more. "I mean it," he chuckles. "I got you a great deal. The fella who owns this building is a very nice man and very, very smart. He knows a good investment when he sees it." His eyes sparkle and his roguish grin lights up his face.

"But Max, how can you even think I'm ready for something like this? I mean…" My brain's gone to mush and my heart is racing in my chest, it's a ridiculous idea. The thought of branching out on my own scares me to death.

His big blue eyes gaze lovingly up at me, and he reaches up to stroke his fingers down my cheek. "Vivienne, you once told me that photography wasn't just your job, it's your passion. We should always strive to do the things we feel passionate about."

Me and my big mouth. "But Max, you're asking me to jump in at the deep end. I haven't earned this position yet."

He smirks and pulls me back down to his chest, stroking

my hair. "Baby, the deep end is the best end. It's where all the big fish are."

I lift my head and rest my chin on his chest. "And what if I get eaten by sharks? What if I drown?"

He chuckles softly to himself. "You won't. Besides, you'll have me as a lifeline."

Something inside my belly stirs, and this time it has nothing to do with Max, or sex. I know…shocker. This time, it's excitement about the possibilities that lay ahead. Maybe I could actually achieve something worthwhile, make a name for myself in the job I love. My father would be so proud. I'd be stupid to turn this incredible opportunity down, but how could I pay him back?

"What about Frank?"

"What about him? Vivienne, it's just a shitty magazine. You're way better than that."

I go to speak, but I'm actually gob-smacked for a moment. "But… I still couldn't afford this."

"Vivienne, you can, and you have. You've paid your rent for the next three months, and you've bought all your own equipment. Plus, your staff salaries are covered for a few months too, all from the sale of your apartment."

I sit bolt upright. "You sold my flat? But…how?… What if we'd split up?"

He gives me a shifty look and arches a brow. "Then I'd own your old apartment and an empty office," he shrugs.

"*You* bought my flat?" I ask in a high, squeaky voice as I blink at him in disbelief.

He lowers his eyes sheepishly. "Well, I didn't want you to be homeless if the worst happened," he mutters.

I stare at him utterly gob-smacked, shaking my head. "Max… I don't know what to say… I…" I'm actually speechless.

He strokes his hand down my cheek, his eyes searching mine. "Look, baby, you can do this. Just look at those photographs." His eyes slide over to my incredible work hanging on the wall. I must admit, I'm really quite proud of them. "They're amazing. I can point you in the right direction, but the rest is up to you."

Tears hover on my lower lashes then spill down my cheeks. He's overwhelmed me with his kindness. "…Thank you."

He sits forward and holds my face in his hands, his eyes now blazing with intent. "You're welcome. Now shut up and kiss me."

A light tapping on the door intrudes on our moment. Max bites my lower lip and drags it through his teeth before resting his forehead against mine. "We'd better get dressed." He whispers, before kissing me chastely and pulling away.

"Yeah," he says, as we both hustle to get dressed.

"Sir, Grace has just called down, your meeting with Peter Melling is scheduled in thirty-five minutes."

"Okay, thank you, Casper. Please tell her I'm on my way."

"Yes, Sir."

Max leans forward to grab his phone from the floor. Grace had been trying to call him, but he'd put it on silent. I suddenly notice the long red welts on his back. They run between his shoulder blades and continue down to the middle of his spine. They look painful, and raw, and very new. Feeling sick to my stomach, I stand motionless just staring at them.

"Oh, Max…" He turns to face me and instantly reacts when he sees my face. His eyes lower, he knows I've seen them. "Why?" He doesn't bring his eyes back up to mine, he just stands up and begins to put his shirt on. I watch him, waiting for an explanation.

"I thought I'd lost you," he murmurs in barely a whispered voice, cagily glancing up at me.

"And if you had lost me? What then?" Fear curdles my stomach. I can't bear the thought of him going back to that way of life. I wait for him to look at me but he doesn't so I walk over and put myself in his line of sight, lifting his chin with my finger. “I thought we’d got past all that?” I whisper, searching his eyes. My heart clenches for this beautiful man standing before me. He’s so strong and powerful in so many ways, and yet his heart makes him so vulnerable. In the darkest moments of his life, he’s turned to pain for comfort, for solace. Like an addict he’s stumbled backwards because I wasn’t there to protect him. Or rather, I was the cause.

With a heavy heart I offer him a reassuring smile and smooth my fingers over his cheek. Walking over to the window, I stare out at nothing in particular. I can’t get the image of Max beating himself out of my head. I’d hoped his propensity to self-harm had been overcome. Clearly, it only lies dormant. But what was the trigger? Me leaving him? Or him mourning the loss of the children we would never have? Either way, it all comes back down to me.

“Baby, we’ve got to go,” he says, softly. I blink the tears from my eyes and then I look for my boots. Max had flung them every which way in his eagerness to get me naked.

“I’m meeting with Peter from the Dorchester about our charity ball on Saturday, why don’t you come with me,” he says, doing up his tie. “You can have a look to see if it’s a suitable venue for Lucy and Dan’s wedding.”

I hop on one foot trying to get my boot on. I never think to sit down, it would make life so much easier. “Oh, I don’t think their budget would stretch to something that grand,” I say, finally getting my boot on. Max steadies me as I attempt to put the other one on.

“Then it’s just as well you’re sleeping with the man who can get it for a very good rate,” he smirks.

“You’re kidding.”

“I kid you not,” he smiles, then he winks. “I’m more than just a pretty face and a smokin’ hot body you know.”

I throw my arms around his neck and pull him down to me. “Max…You are the kindest, most generous person I’ve ever known. The way you love me, and the wonderful things you do for me… One day I hope I can do something just as amazing for you," I whisper in between kisses. "You may be an old man by then, but you'll be my old man."

He chuckles and nuzzles my nose then he rests his forehead against mine. "Baby, just having you back is enough. Please, don't ever leave me again."

"I won't. I promise."

Peter greets me with enthusiasm and shows me around the function suites. Max hangs back a little while I absorb all the information Peter's giving me about the different wedding packages they provide. He's not mentioned any costs yet, and he still has to check that the date is available. While he wanders to his office to check his diary, I turn to see Max smiling at me.

"What?" I ask, smiling back.

"I love to see you happy," he grins, with a glint in his eye.

I walk up to him and slide my palms up his chest and around his neck. "You make me happy," I whisper, as a dull thud hits my groin from his oh-so-sexy smile. All I want to do is snog his face off, but I feel it would be inappropriate considering where we are, and especially now that Peter's on his way back to us.

"I'm afraid we have a slight problem with the date, Vivienne. I'm afraid it's already booked out."

"Oh," I sigh. "Oh, well, never mind. Thanks anyway." I feel totally deflated. I leave the men to discuss their business and I take a wander around the lobby. It would have been a lovely venue for Lucy, and I would have felt so proud to see her laughing and dancing in such beautiful surroundings on her special day.

After a while, Max comes striding toward me. His predatory walk and sexy smile alerts my butterflies and brings a smile to my face.

"France," he says, before he actually reaches me.

"I'm sorry?"

"Lucy and Dan wanted to get married in France, right?" I nod, but I'm still not sure where he's coming from. "My yacht's in the South of France. It has plenty of room, and they can even get married on board if they want to. Lucy and Dan can stay on it for their honeymoon, while you and I spend some time at the chateau. It's perfect."

I know I've glazed over by now, and as I close my mouth to swallow, I'm guessing it was gaping open while I tried to take in what he's just said. "What do you mean? You'd let them use your yacht? In the South of France?"

His super-sexy smile spreads across his face. "Yeah… Well?… What do you think?"

"I…they'd…they'd love it. But, how much would it cost?"

Max wraps his arms around me and leans in to kiss me on the nose. "I can get them very special rates at the hotel you stayed in before and on the flights, the rest will be our wedding present."

I shake my head, dumbfounded. "Max, that's too much. I can't let you do that."

He leans back to look at me with serious eyes. "Vivienne, when you were in the hospital, I got to know Lucy a little better. She's an important part of your life, and she's been a good friend to you."

"Yes but—"

"Call her. Tell her the good news." I gaze up into Max's smiling eyes. He's serious, and all of a sudden I feel totally overwhelmed. A small frown slips into his brow. "What's the matter?" he asks softly.

"You keep upping the ante. How am I ever going to repay your generosity?" I ask in all seriousness.

His eyes become hooded and dark, as his arms tighten around me. "I can think of a million ways, and they all involve you being naked." He smiles. His knee-trembling, heart-stopping, mega-watt smile hits me right in the groin as I melt in his arms. "Call her."

"Hey, Viv. I've been trying to call you for the last half

hour. I'll have to work late tonight so I won't get to your flat until seven-ish. Will you be alright until then?" she asks, sympathetically.

Oh, I forgot. She still thinks we've split up. "Luce, forget what I said earlier—"

"Fuck me, Viv. Your relationship is up and down like a whore's drawers."

"Yeah, I know. Sorry. Anyway, I've got some amazing news to tell you. Please tell me you haven't booked that dump of a hotel yet?"

"What? Oh, no. I haven't been able to bring myself to do it yet," she groans, obviously feeling as unenthusiastic about it as I was.

"Well don't. Max has—" Suddenly my phone is wrenched from my hand.

"Hi, Lucy, it's Max. …Yeah, good thanks. Listen, what's your final count on the wedding guests? …Fifty three? Okay good. I just wanted to let you know that Vivienne and I would like to give you your wedding gift early. ….Well, we've just organised your whole wedding. I'll get Vivienne to email you all the details for your invitations. …What? …My yacht in the South of France. …I'm totally serious." Max quickly pulls the phone away from his ear and looks at me with a big smirk on his face. "She's screaming," he shrugs. "Lucy, I'll pass you back." Max hands me the phone, I can hear Lucy screaming and yelling as I bring it to my ear.

"Luce, calm down."

"Oh, my God. I can't believe it. Is he serious?"

"Yes. Totally." I pull the phone away as Lucy squeals again, and I imagine she's jumping up and down a lot too.

"Viv, I don't know what to say. How can we ever thank him? It's incredible."

"I'll email you the details later," I say, trying to get a word in above Lucy's constant squealing.

I still can't quite believe Max would do that for Lucy and Dan. But in my heart, I know he's really doing it for me, and it makes me feel very humble.

As Max drives us home, I think about how lucky I am to have found such an amazing man to share my life with. My niggling brain still harbours doubts about my inadequacies, but I have to cling on to the hope that he means what he says, and that he won't resent me further down the line. After those thoughts leave my head, a new batch of questions pop into my brain. What company name should I use? I wonder if Ed would be interested in being my assistant? Frank would kill me if I poached him.

"Does Frank know I'm leaving the magazine?" I blurt, realising I just suddenly disappeared from the office this afternoon without telling him where I was going. Not that I had any choice in the matter.

"Yeah, I told him when I went to see him this afternoon."

I shake my head at him and narrow my eyes. "That was a bit self-assured of you wasn't it?"

Max cocks his head and swings his cheeky smile over to me. "I could say the same about you, Miss Banks. Frank said something about you promising him an exclusive on our wedding photos?"

I blush and turn away as he smirks at me big time. "I had my fingers crossed at the time. Besides, I'd barged into his office and demanded to use the tech and printing departments. It was just for leverage, that's all." I can feel him grinning at me, but I don't look at him. I never seem to be able to do anything sneaky without him finding out about it.

ALMOST EVERYTHING

When we arrive at F1, Jan greets me with a hug before she leaves for the day. She looks very smart.

"Going anywhere nice?" I ask.

"Yes, Vincent's taking me to the theatre and then dinner for my birthday."

"Oh, no," I gasp. "I didn't know it was your birthday. I'm so sorry, Jan, I would have bought you a gift." I feel awful. I know Max's birthday is the fourteenth of February, but I had no clue about Jan's or anyone else's for that matter.

"You did," she smiles. "I received a beautiful bouquet of flowers, a bottle of my favourite perfume, and a rather nice bottle of Chateauneuf Du Pape."

I glance up at Max. "You could have told me," I whisper as Jan leaves the penthouse.

Max hands me my equipment and I head upstairs to unpack my boxes as he heads to the study to make some calls.

When I walk into the bedroom, all my boxes have vanished. On further inspection, I find all my stuff has been neatly assigned to the wardrobes and cupboards.

I want to send Lucy an email about the address of the marina for her wedding, so I head down to Max's study to get all the details. I don't bother to knock as I can't hear him talking to anyone so I just wander in. Max is sitting in his big leather chair reading a large piece of yellow paper.

The look on his face puts me on edge. He's just staring down at it, he hasn't even noticed I've entered the room.

"Max?" He suddenly looks up with a deep worry frown set in his brow and he immediately crumples the paper in his hands. "What's that?" I ask, walking toward him.

"Oh, nothing." Once he's crumpled it into a tight, hard ball, he tosses it in the bin. Judging by his expression, whatever it was has put him in a bad mood.

"I just wanted the details for Lucy," I ask, but he doesn't seem to have heard me. "Max? Is everything okay?"

"Yeah…everything's fine." I hear the words coming out of his mouth, but his body language tells a different story. "Sorry, what did you want?" he asks, avoiding my eyes.

"I just wanted the details of the marina to send to Lucy."

He seems distracted. He takes a minute to write down the information, then he hands me the piece of paper. "Get her to send me a list of her guests so I can make the reservations at the hotel and organise the flights," he says, as if he's talking to his p.a. I study him for a bit longer but his mind is elsewhere, so I leave him and head back upstairs.

Once I've emailed Lucy, I head down to the kitchen to make dinner, or rather, to heat up whatever Jan has left us in the fridge. *I really should learn how to cook.*

Jan has made a chicken casserole so I pop it in the oven to heat through. As I'm boiling some vegetables to go with it, I hear Max talking to me from the doorway.

"I've got to go down to the office, I'll be back in a few minutes." He seems edgy and he doesn't wait for me to respond, he just leaves.

I stare at the empty doorway for a moment, then I quickly run to the front door and look through the spy-hole. I see Max in the lift as the doors close. I quickly run to his study and start rummaging in the small bin beside his desk, where he threw that yellow piece of paper. *That's strange.* It's not here. I unravel all the balled up papers that I can find, but nothing seems out of the ordinary with any of them. I sit back in his chair wondering where the hell it could be, I'm sure I saw him chuck it in the bin. I try his top desk drawer, but it's locked. Opening the filing cabinet, I look for the key in the same place I'd found it the last time, but it's not here either. What was on that piece of paper, and where is it now?

The faint whiff of burning vegetables hits my nose. *Oh, crap!* I run to the kitchen, open a window, and waft the tea towel around, trying to get rid of the awful smell before the smoke alarm kicks in. The green beans are now completely charred to the bottom of the pot.

"Need some help?" Max asks, leaning up against the doorway with a big smirk on his face. I hadn't heard him return.

"Sorry, I can't even boil bloody vegetables." I huff, trying to scrape them into the bin but they just won't come off the bottom of the pot.

"It's a good thing I'm not marrying you for your culinary skills," he chuckles, walking up behind me. He takes the pot out of my hand, looks at the charred remains inside it, then he throws the whole thing in the bin.

"I'm really rubbish at this aren't I?" I sigh, cringing at my ineptitude.

He pulls me into his arms and buries his face in my neck. "Yes. You are," he chuckles, nipping my neck and shoulder. The sensation of his lips on my bare flesh evokes my normal reaction and I rise up on my toes, throw my arms around his neck, and pull him closer to me. My hands weave through his silky hair as he trails his lips up my throat, along my jaw, and finally over to my eager lips as he devours me in a passionate kiss.

Breaking the kiss, he pulls back and gazes down at me with scorching blue eyes. He's turned my bones to mush with his kiss. I drop back down to my heels, trailing my eyes over his handsome face. His nose wrinkles slightly. "Are you burning something else?"

I blink up at him for a moment. "Shit! The casserole." I

hear him laughing at me as I run to the oven and yank the door down. Another two minutes and it would have been crunchy.

We sit at the island and pick at the edible parts of the casserole.

"So, what do you think my company name should be?" I ask, suddenly feeling nervous.

"I already asked Casper to organise the stationery so you'd be up and running for tomorrow," he says, nonchalantly.

"Really? So what is it?"

"Vivienne Foxx Photography." I shake my head and smile. "What?" he smirks. "My name isn't good enough for you?"

"Oh, no, it'll do nicely. Although, I can't imagine what the press will have to say about it."

"Fuck the press." He lays his cutlery down and takes a sip of wine. "We've sorted out Lucy and Dan's wedding, but where do you want to get married?" he asks, searching my eyes with his seductive gaze. A flash of excitement surges through me at the thought of becoming Mrs. Foxx. He's the hottest guy on the planet, and he's all mine.

After a moment's thought, I push my plate away and finish chewing my mouthful.

"I don't mind," I shrug. Max narrows his eyes on me and I realise that sounded a bit uncaring. "It's just that, well, I don't have any family except for my mum, and I only have a handful of friends, so a big lavish wedding seems a little pointless. Besides, you haven't asked me yet," I point out with a smirk and an arched brow.

His lips tip up in a crooked smile. "Fair comment, Miss Banks." Suddenly his expression becomes serious. "I can't wait to marry you, the sooner the better." He drags my stool over and pulls me into his lap, wrapping his arms around me, still gazing into my eyes.

"We can't get married before Lucy. I'd hate to steal her thunder, especially after what I've put her through recently," I say, rolling my eyes.

"Hmm, I guess you're right. But I'm not waiting for long, Vivienne. You're mine. Forever. And I want to make it official." He leans in to kiss me tenderly on the lips, just as my phone rings in my pocket. I ignore it and kiss him back, wrapping my arms around his neck.

My phone rings again a few moments later. Max pulls it from my pocket and we both look at the screen. It's not a number I recognise but Max's expression suddenly changes, it would appear that he does. I take the phone out of his hand and answer the call, staring at him the whole time. He looks edgy.

"Vivienne Banks."

"Hello, Vivienne. It's Nova."

My mind has gone blank. "Who? …Oh, Nova. Yes of course, sorry."

"I spoke with Frank, he said you've left the magazine, is that right?"

"Ah, yes. That's right."

"That was quick," she laughs.

I cringe. "Well, it was kind of a spur of the moment thing."

"Do you still have the photographs? Frank wasn't sure where they were."

"Yes, I've still got them but—"

"Good. I'd much rather deal with you, Vivienne. I don't think Frank understands my art quite as well as you seemed to. But don't worry, I've already paid him for your services so we can deal directly from now on. The only thing is, I'm afraid I can't make our appointment for tomorrow evening."

"Oh, I see. Well, you're very welcome to come to my new office, it's on the twelfth floor of the Foxx-Tech building." *That doesn't sound weird at all.*

"Oh, how wonderful, would Wednesday be okay, say, ten o'clock?"

"Yes, Wednesday will be fine, I look forward to it."

"Excellent, I'll see you then… Ah, would it be possible to speak to Max?"

I'm startled by her request, and she asked for him by his Christian name, they must know each other. "Erm, yes. One moment." I hand the phone to Max. "She wants to speak to you."

Max frowns at the phone then he flicks his eyes up to mine as he takes the call. "Nova… Yes, she is… Ah, yeah, thanks… She did what?" His eyes widen on me, then they lower to the floor. "You didn't…okay, thanks… I will… You too. Bye."

Max slides my phone onto the counter. I can sense that he's not going to tell me what their conversation was about and I can feel him tensing up.

"You didn't tell me you'd met Nova," he says, still not looking at me. The penny drops and my stomach knots into an anxious ball.

"Are you a member?" I ask, as nonchalantly as possible, watching his eyes as they avoid mine. "The Stock X-Change Club… Are you one of Nova's customers?"

He shakes his head. "No," he says, softly.

"But you went there recently, didn't you? That's where you got the new marks on your back, isn't it?" I can see that he's ashamed and he doesn't want to tell me, but I need to know why he went there. I've seen what goes on in that club and his reticence irritates me. I hate it when he tries to hide things from me. I lift my chin, my voice now much more direct. "Which room did you use? I've seen them all." He throws me an angry glare. I know he doesn't like the idea that I've been there, even though it was just for work and not during opening hours.

"I didn't go to the club," he says, clenching his jaw.

"Where then?"

He brings his eyes up to mine and to his credit, he doesn't look away. "I went to her house… After you ran away, I needed to…" he trails off, leaving his sentence unfinished. But I already know why he went there. He needed to inflict pain on himself, and she was the one to do it.

It sickens me to ask, but I need to know. "Did you sleep with her?"

"No! Of course not," he snaps, defensively.

"Have you ever slept with her?" I hate asking, but I have to. "I just need to know before I strike up a business relationship with this woman." I don't think I could handle it if I knew he'd slept with her.

"No. Never. …It's not like that. She understands why I need to… Besides, Nova's tastes are much more feminine."

She's gay?

He takes a deep breath and releases a long sigh. "It's not what you think. You of all people know I've never been able to cope with loss… Fiona had been asking me questions about Charlie, which brought all the pain of his death back to the surface, and when you and I had that fight… I really thought I'd lost you this time. If I'm honest, the pressure has been building ever since I found you that night in a pool of blood. I just got to the point where I couldn't handle it anymore. You had disposed of all my whips, so I went to see Nova."

"But you did handle it…before… both times I was in the hospital, you didn't do it then. Why this time?"

His sad eyes burn into mine. "Because this time, you'd *chosen* to leave me. It's very different." He lowers his eyes and my heart sinks. I can't chastise him for feeling. The poor man's known more pain and loss in his short life than anyone should. I place my hands on his cheeks and lift his bowed head.

"I know you miss Charlie, and I know how hard it was for you to find out that we'd never have children of our own. But you can't punish yourself for things you can't control. It hurts me to know that you would do that to yourself because of me. I'm not worth it, Max. Please, don't do it again." I lean in to kiss him tenderly on the lips.

As I pull back, he opens his mouth to speak, but I interrupt him. "What were you reading earlier in your study? The yellow letter, you seemed to be affected by it. What was it?"

I can see the walls going up over his eyes, brick by brick. "Nothing for you to worry about." He smiles, but the smile misses his eyes completely.

I don't know whether it's a weakness or a strength that I decide not to push him on it, and my phone ringing again interrupts the moment. It's another unknown number, but I'm glad of the distraction. "Hello."

"Miss Banks, it's Casper. I'm sorry to call you so late, but I just wanted to let you know that I'll be syncing your work schedule to your phone. You'll find it in your V.F.P app. And if you could email me a link to your portfolio, I'll set it up on your new database. I'll see you in the morning, Miss Banks."

"Ah, yes. Thanks, Casper. See you then." The nerves about tomorrow set in and make my hands shake. I quickly store his contact in my phone and look for the app.

"And so it begins," I smirk, sliding my phone onto the counter. "Hey, does that mean I'm C.E.O. of my own company now?" I ask, trying to lighten the mood.

Max smiles, leaning in for a kiss. "You are. And I'm very proud of you. I think your father would be too."

NEW VENTURE

Max wakes me with soft kisses all along my shoulders, neck, and throat. "Good morning, beautiful," he whispers, before continuing his sensual path across my skin. I can't open my eyes yet they're still too sleepy, but I won't pass up the opportunity to be romanced by the hottest guy on the planet. Nope. Uh-uh. Never going to happen. No matter how tired I am.

I peel my eyes open to see his devastatingly handsome face hovering above me. I'll never get used to how handsome he is.

"Morning sleepy head," he smiles. Wrapping his strong arms underneath me, he pulls me onto his chest. I lay sprawled out on top of his body as he circles my back with his fingers.

Kissing his tattoo, I then proceed to yawn in his face. "Oh, sorry," I murmur, blinking the sleep away.

He laughs at me then opens his eyes. "Are you excited?" he asks, softly brushing my hair out of my face. My eyes widen when I suddenly realise today is my new company's first day of trading.

"Oh, shit." I feel the panic rising as nerves get the better of me and I start to feel nauseous. "I'm going to balls it all up, aren't I?"

Max laughs and rolls his eyes. "You'll be fine… It's not like you have to cook anything," he smirks, but then his expression becomes more concerned. "I don't want you going anywhere alone anymore. I've assigned John as your personal bodyguard. Whether it's shopping or visiting a client, you must take him with you. There's no negotiation on this, Vivienne." His face is deadly serious. I know this has something to do with that yellow letter he received yesterday, and I'm dying to ask what it said, but I know him well enough to know that he's not going to tell me.

"Okay," I shrug, begrudgingly. "What time is it?" I ask, laying my head back down on his chest. I feel him lifting his arm to look at his watch then suddenly, I'm on my back and he's hovering above me.

"It's time for me to show you how much you turn me on," he grins. I can feel his solid erection against my thigh as a throbbing pulse hits my sex. Reaching up to hold his face in my palms, I pull him down to me for a kiss. Now, I'm wide awake and horny as hell.

I stand under the hot water unwilling to move. Max gave me a thorough workout this morning, he's an amazing lover, and although I enjoyed every delicious moment of it, it's left my muscles weak. As I rinse the soap out of my hair, I start to feel a bit queasy and my head feels hot and fuzzy. I turn the water off and lean against the glass until it passes. Suddenly, another wave of nausea hits me and I run to the toilet.

"Baby? Are you okay?"

I feel Max's hand on my back. I don't want him to see me like this but I know I haven't finished yet so I stay put. My body shakes, and the bile hurts my throat as the final heave takes all my energy and I collapse down onto my knees. Max goes to the basin and returns with a cool, wet flannel, then he crouches down in front of me. He's dressed and ready for work looking gorgeous, as usual. I take the flannel and wipe my face. "I'm sorry."

He gently rubs my shoulders. "What are you apologising for? I thought you were starting to feel better?" Concern softens his voice.

"I am. I think it's just nerves. You know, big day and all."

He smiles and kisses me on the top of my head. "Baby, you're going to be fine, I promise. Come on, let's get you up off the floor." Max helps me to my feet, then I have to literally push him out of the bathroom so I can finish getting ready. He's worried. I can see it in his face. But I'm sure it's just nerves unsettling my stomach.

Once I'm dressed and ready, I grab my phone and head down to the kitchen. Max looks up as I walk in, his eyes lazily drag all over my tight, figure hugging dress showing his appreciation with a sexy smile. It's a mutual appreciation, Max looks good in everything, but there's something sexy about a good looking guy in a well-made suit, that really stirs my hormones.

"You look beautiful," he purrs.

"Good morning, Vivienne. What would you like for breakfast?" Jan asks.

I can smell the bacon but for some reason, it's churning my stomach. "Erm, if you have any, I'd really like sardines on toast," I say, popping myself up on the stool next to Max. He drags it closer to him, resting his warm hand on my thigh seeking out the lace tops of my stockings. I hear him sighing to himself, he really likes me in stockings.

"I'm sorry, Vivienne, did you say sardines? Only, I thought you were allergic to fish." Jan says, with a questioning frown.

"Oh, yeah. That's right, I forgot." I really fancied them too. "I'll just have a bagel with ham, cheese, peanut butter, tomato, and pickle." Jan gives me a wide-eyed sideways look before walking over to the fridge. It's not my normal breakfast request I know, but now my stomach's empty, I'm hungry.

At ten minutes to eight, Max and I head off to work. It feels strange and exciting. The lift stops at his floor. "Have a great day at work, baby," he says, before kissing me softly and walking off. He turns to throw me a sexy smile and a cheeky wink before the doors close and I descend to the twelfth floor. My floor.

My knees are shaking when the doors open, and I immediately see Casper's smiling face behind the desk in reception. He's a good looking man, probably in his early thirties, and he dresses impeccably. He reminds me a lot of Idris Elba, only Casper's eyes are a pale hazel colour, very striking against his caramel skin.

He smiles, rising to his feet. "Good morning, Miss Banks."

"Casper, please just call me Viv or Vivienne. I'd feel much better if you did," I smile, trying not to blush. He's older than me, it just feels weird.

"Two of your interviewees have already arrived," he whispers, pointing behind me. I hadn't even noticed them sitting there. My stomach churns with nerves.

"Okay, could you give me ten minutes and then send the first one in."

I open the door to my new office. The clean smell of new furniture is the first thing I notice as I walk in, but then the delicate fragrance coming from the bouquet of white roses sitting on the coffee table takes over. I pick up the small white card nestled in amongst them.

Good luck on your first day!

M

X ;-)

I smile, but then the realisation that I've got to make this work brings on a bout of nerves. My stomach knots so I walk to my desk and take a seat while my heart beats a million miles an hour in my chest. *What am I doing?*

I quickly send a text to Ed, asking him to call me. I'd feel much better if he was here. A polite knock at my door has my body turning rigid. "Yeah? I mean, Yes?"

Casper pokes his smiling face around the door, then he walks in. "It's a latte, extra shot, no sugar, right?" he says, putting a steaming hot coffee on my desk.

"Yeah, thanks. How did you know?"

He smiles and places some files next to my laptop. "It's my job to know," he smirks. "You've got four people interviewing for the job today. Their resumes are great, but it's Mr. Foxx's policy that all employees within the Foxx-Tech umbrella must sign a formal contract and a non-disclosure agreement before they can begin. If any of the applicants seem agreeable to you, just let me know, I'll do a background check and take care of all the formalities, okay?" I nod, bewildered. "This is your leather bound portfolio," he says, sliding a big heavy folder onto my desk. "I had it made up last night from the photographs you sent me, and they've all been uploaded to your database as well."

Casper's efficiency stuns me. "When do you sleep?" I ask, wondering how he got all this done in such a short amount of time. He just shrugs like it's nothing.

"Are you ready?"

I stare at him with a fearful cringe. "I don't know, am I?"

He smiles and starts walking to the door. "Drink your coffee before it gets cold," he smirks, then he leaves closing the door quietly behind him.

In spite of my nerves, the interviews go surprisingly well. Although the applicants have experience, they actually make me realise that I'm better at my job than I'd ever given myself credit. Their photographs are very good, but I can instantly see the errors they're making. The fact that they can't see them is worrying.

Ed knows how I work, and his technical skills and eye for detail are a quality lacking in the people I've met this morning. I check my phone, but he hasn't got back to me yet so I decide to start organising Nova's photographs for our meeting tomorrow. The photographs I had taken at Nova's club are exceptional and very artistic. I'm proud of them, and I was right about the black and white, it gives them sophistication and creates a very striking mood. I'm especially proud of the images I'd taken of the first girl, the one I'd thought was a waxwork. She looks stunning. I'm going to have to ask Casper to show me how to upload all these into the database, but I think I'd blush my arse off if he saw them.

My phone rings.

"Hi, Viv. It's me."

"Ed. Thanks for calling me back. Listen, I don't know if you've heard, but I've left the magazine."

"Yeah," he laughs. "Clive's told everyone. He said you were manhandled off the property by your boyfriend. Frank's been pulling his hair out. He's only got me left now."

Not for long. "Actually… I was wondering if you'd like to come and work for me?" I ask hesitantly.

"For you?… Don't tell me you've started a rival magazine. I think Frank would commit hara-kiri if he found out," he chuckles.

"No, we're not a magazine, just freelance photography. Max has some very wealthy friends and clients who need publicity and marketing material. I can't promise anything yet, but I think between the two of us, we could really achieve something… What do you think?" The pause makes me nervous. "Ed?"

"When can I start?" I can hear the grin in his voice.

"When can you get here?"

We agree to meet for lunch to talk about it. Just as I finish the call with Ed, my door opens and Max strolls in with a big grin on his face. His cool, arrogant swagger has my eyes grazing up and down the length of him.

"Well? …How did it go this morning?" he asks, perching on the corner of my desk with a smug smile on his face.

"Great. And I've just spoken to Ed. I asked him if he wanted to be my assistant and he said yes. He's perfect for the job." I lean back in my chair trying not to think about the incoming I'm going to get from Frank when he finds out.

I notice Max's eyes slide down to my open laptop. The screen displays the image of Nova's female submissive bound in leather. I watch his eyes as they trail very slowly across the image. "Stunning," he whispers, to himself.

The girl?

"You have an amazing talent, Vivienne. You should be very proud of your work," he says, still looking at the image.

"I am, but I'm still nervous about my ability to make this work. I hope you don't expect too much," I cringe.

He stands and pulls me to my feet, wrapping his arms around my waist. His smiling eyes search mine as he leans down for a kiss. "Baby, I expect you to be amazing, because that's what you are." His passionate kiss unfurls all my inner longing. He has a way of hypnotising me with his eyes until all I want to do is rip his clothes off and make mad, passionate love to him. "Your body drives me crazy," he whispers, running his hands all down my back, cupping my behind as he drops feather-light kisses all along my throat and neck. His touch fires up my need for him as I become putty in his hands. "Crazy-good," he adds, nuzzling my neck. I feel his hard erection pressing against me.

"Lock the door," I whisper, reaching up to loosen his tie.

"Oh, baby, believe me," he says, in a raspy voice, "I want nothing more than to take you right here, right now, but I'm afraid I can't. I have to meet Fiona in town, and then I have a meeting with my lawyers."

I pull back and let my expression tell him how I feel about that. *Why her?*

"I'm sorry, baby. I'll make it up to you, I promise," he says, kissing me on the forehead.

I hate myself for asking but I can't stop myself. "Why are you meeting Fiona?"

"Oh, she's just helping me with something, that's all," he says, turning to walk away. "Have a good day, I'll see you at home." He winks, smiles that toe-curling smile, and then he leaves.

I feel like a whirlwind has just entered my office, stirred my emotions into an erotic bundle of need, and then left me wanting. He has such a powerful effect on me. Even his touch leaves me feeling like I've just had the best sex ever.

In spite of my non post-coital euphoria, I'm annoyed that he's still seeing Fiona. How could he not realise that I wouldn't be comfortable with that? Especially not after what happened on Sunday. Men! Why have you always got to spell it out for them.

As I sit at my desk, stewing over Max's insensitivity, my eyes wander over to my laptop. I'm going to have to bite the bullet and get Casper to show me how to upload these to the database, but I should be on my way to meet Ed, so I leave the laptop open and ask Casper to take care of it while I'm out at lunch. I don't bother to call John. It's not like I'm going very far, and I'm still a bit miffed about Max seeing Fiona. Sometimes he just makes me feel like being a rebel.

HOW MANY WARNINGS DO YOU NEED?

I arrive at the wine bar a little early and take a seat in the window. As I watch the world go by I suddenly spot Mike walking past, he looks terrible. I tap on the window but he doesn't look up, so I tap louder. This time, he looks up and sees me. I know he recognises me, but he walks on. I quickly run to the door and yell his name. He stops and reluctantly turns to face me. His eyes stay on the ground, and he shoves his hands deeper into his pockets.

"Mike, what's the matter?" He looks in a bad way like he's carrying the weight of the world on his shoulders. "Mike?"

"Nothing." He goes to walk on again.

"Mike. Wait! Why won't you talk to me?" He stops, warily raises his eyes, and then he slowly makes his way over to me. "Come on, I'll buy you a drink."

I order him a beer and we sit on opposite sides of the table. He stares down at his pint, only occasionally flipping his eyes up to mine.

"You look good," he says, eventually.

"I wish I could say the same for you," I blurt, instantly regretting it. "What's happened? You look awful." He shrugs and takes a sip of his pint. Placing the glass back down on the table, he stares into it, running his fingers up and down the sides of the glass until all the condensation is gone. "Mike, tell me. What's happened?"

He shrugs and leans back in his seat. "I lost my job, and I lost… Oh, fuck it. What does it matter?" he sighs angrily.

"How did you lose your job?"

His lips turn up in a snarl. "Someone called my boss and reported me for illegally obtaining private information. No guessing who that was." His words are dripping in sarcasm.

Max?…No. …Why would he? I know I asked Mike to help me trace Monica's phone, but surely he didn't get into trouble over that? "Is there anything I can do?" I ask hesitantly.

His eyes flick up to mine and stay there. His expression is hard, almost hostile. After a long pause, his expression becomes sad and he finally speaks. "You could leave him and come back to me, where you belong." His eyes stay fixed on mine, forcing me to look away.

Not this again. "Mike, I thought… What about Michelle? What about—"

"I don't love Michelle." Suddenly he reaches across the table and takes my hand, his sad eyes searching mine. "Viv. I've missed you. I know I did a stupid thing, and I know I hurt you, but I need you, Viv. I still love you." His words hit me like a sledgehammer. He holds my hand in a tight grip and his eyes are full of hope and longing.

"Mike, I…" I don't know what to say that won't hurt his feelings.

His hopeful expression disappears and his eyes darken. "Max is no good for you, Viv. I know you think you're in love with him, but he's put you in the hospital twice. He's going to get you killed."

I stare at him with wide eyes as my heart pounds in my chest. He's being totally unreasonable. "Mike, that wasn't his fault, it was—"

"His fucked-up ex? Yeah, I know," he snarls. "But she's still out there somewhere, and you know as well as I do that she's going to come back. For you."

"But—"

"Christ! How many fucking warnings do you need?" I blanch at his comment, and the look in his eyes frightens me.

"Viv? Everything alright?" I look up to see Ed standing at the side of our table.

Mike suddenly releases my hand, pushes his beer aside and stands quickly, his eyes still burning into mine. "Don't say I didn't warn you," he mutters before leaving.

Ed sits down eyeing me with concern. "What was all that about?"

I watch Mike march out of sight. "Oh, just Mike being Mike," I say, forcing a smile.

"Well, here I am, boss," Ed grins.

We spend the next hour or so discussing our new venture over lunch. Mike had managed to thoroughly ruin my appetite so I asked the waitress to put mine in a doggy bag for later.

Ed and I head back to the Foxx-Tech building and I introduce him to Casper, then I show him around the office.

"Fancy," Ed smirks as he wanders around the studio, and what will be his workstation. He takes a look at all the new equipment and seems impressed by the quality. "I think I'm going to like working for you, Viv." He wanders back into my office and looks at the aerial photographs I'd taken of the Foxx-Tech building. "These are incredible. Will we be doing more of these?" he asks, with a big grin on his face. I nod and smile back. His face lights up with a big smile. "Cool."

Ed and I spend some time sorting through Nova's photographs on the database. He sighs and gives me a hurt look. "I got a boring award ceremony, and you got beautiful naked women in a bondage club. Why am I never that lucky?"

I waggle my eyebrows. "Stick with me, kid. We'll be meeting this client tomorrow. If you play your cards right, who knows?"

While we're sorting through all of Nova's images and making our notes, I pick at my food from lunch to appease my growling stomach, then I leave Ed in Casper's capable hands to sign all the contracts. I check my phone for the millionth time, but Max hasn't contacted me yet. My mind starts to wonder whether he's still with Fiona, but it irritates me when I think of her so I try to push her out of my mind. Mike's words begin to float around my brain instead. I'm sure Max wouldn't have reported him, Mike was one of the people who had helped me the day Monica kidnapped Lucy. Something Mike had said, '*how many warnings do you need?,*' makes me think about that yellow letter Max had in his study. Whatever he'd seen had rattled him. Was it a warning? From Monica?

Once I've prepared a layout for tomorrow's meeting, I finish the rest of my lunch, pop some freshly printed business cards into my purse, and head upstairs to the penthouse.

Jan is busy preparing a meal in the kitchen. She gives me a strange look then she heads to the fridge to pour some wine.

I take a seat at the island. "How was your evening last night?"

"Oh, it was lovely. We saw La Boheme by Puccini, which was beautiful. And then we had a meal at Langan's Brasserie. It was a marvellous evening," she beams.

"Wow. Vinnie certainly knows how to wine and dine you doesn't he?"

"Yes. And…he gave me these," she smiles, pointing at her delicate gold earrings.

"Oh, Jan, they're lovely."

"Now, enough about me, how was your first day at your new job?" she asks, clinking our glasses together.

"It was good. It went much better than I thought it would, but I'm absolutely pooped."

"Why don't you go and take a nice long bath, dinner will be ready in an hour or so," she says, kindly.

"Yeah, good idea. Do you know when Max will be home?" I ask, trying not to sound too bothered.

"Anytime now I should imagine, he hasn't left any messages to the contrary."

I head upstairs with my wine and run the bath. My bones ache from all the tension of my first day, and a long soak is just what I need. I take another sip of wine but my stomach isn't feeling too good so I leave it on the side and undress.

During our lunch, I'd had the fancies for some prawns. I've always been allergic to fish, but lately I've really fancied it so I took a chance, and up until now I was feeling okay.

I lean back in the tub, resting my head against the edge and I close my eyes.

"Hey, beautiful." His voice makes me smile. I open my eyes and turn to look up at him.

"Whoa! Did you have something done?" Max asks, eyeing me with a strange look on his face.

Huh? His wide eyes are on my lips, and his expression is definitely worried. "What? …What's the matter?" My lips feel numb and tingly, and my voice sounds funny.

"Baby, what have you done to your lips?"

I sit up in a panic and even from this distance, I can see my reflection in the mirror looks odd. I pull my hands up to my face and feel my lips, they're very swollen. *The bloody prawns!*

Max immediately calls out Doctor Alexander who arrives to give me a shot. He assures me that the swelling will go down soon enough. He asked me if I had any allergies so I felt like a complete numpty when I told him that I was allergic to fish and that I'd eaten prawns. His face was a picture. I apologised to him for having to come out and treat me. Considering it was a self-inflicted act, I couldn't apologise enough.

"Why did you eat the fish if you knew you were allergic to it?" Max asks after the doctor leaves. It's a perfectly valid question. I just wish I knew the answer.

"I don't know," I mumble. "I just had a taste for them." Max gives me the eyebrow, enough said.

"So, how was your meeting with the lawyers?" I ask, changing the subject.

"Boring." He moves behind me and kisses my neck. He undoes the belt on my robe and lets it fall and pool at my feet. His hands skim my hips, stomach, and up to my breasts as my head falls back against his shoulder. His teeth gently nip my shoulder as his fingers roll my nipples, gently pinching them into erect buds. I reach up to weave my fingers into his hair, and I tilt my head to pull him down for a kiss. It feels strange, my lips are still numb in places.

"Doesn't that hurt?" he asks softly. It does a bit, but not enough to stop. I turn around and wrap my arms around his neck, rising up onto my toes to deepen the kiss. My body has some unfinished business with him. Lifting me off my feet, I wrap my legs around his waist, and groan into his mouth. He walks us over to the bed and sits on the edge with me still wrapped around him. I break the kiss and stare down into his handsome face.

"How was your meeting with Fiona?" I'm angry with myself for asking. I shouldn't let that woman bother me, but she does.

"Fine," he answers, before burying his face in my neck.

'Fine' is not enough, and as much as I want to appear aloof, I fail miserably with my next question. "What did you have to see her about? It must have been important to cancel having sex with me?"

I feel him pause for a beat, then he softly bites my neck and in a heartbeat, I'm lying on my back with him hovering above me. His hooded eyes scorch me with dark carnal desire.

"I said I'd make it up to you." He smiles that sexy, full

on, mega-watt smile.

As soon as he begins his leisurely trail of feather-light kisses along my throat, neck, and shoulders, I close my eyes and everything else just fades away. His tongue circling my nipple, and teasing it with his teeth, sparks a heat deep inside. He softly kisses his way down my stomach and across to my hip. My hands weave into his hair as he continues down to my sex, nipping and lapping.

"You're so beautiful," he whispers against my skin. I can't speak. My body is tingling and writhing beneath him as his tongue invades my sex and begins its gloriously tantalising assault. It doesn't take me long, and as his hands dig underneath me to cup my behind, I roll my hips to the intoxicating rhythm of his expert tongue.

As the first wave of pleasure hits me, causing me to cry out his name, he doesn't stop or slow down, and although the intensity of his tongue against my throbbing sex is almost too much, I come again as a second more powerful orgasm shudders through me and rolls out all over my body.

As the remnants of the most amazing orgasms leave me weak and sated, he crawls up and kisses me softly on the lips. "See? I told you I'd make it up to you." I can sense his smile, but I can't open my eyes. I'm still floating on the euphoria of Max, and his incredible tongue. "Was that good?" he asks, in a raspy voice.

I eventually peel my eyes open and stare up at his smiling, sexy face. "Crazy-good," I whisper, smiling back. I wrap my arms around his neck and pull him down for a kiss. I can feel his solid erection pulsing against my thigh, and I can taste my arousal on his tongue. I wrap my legs around him, tilting my hips to accommodate him. Leaning on his elbows, he holds my face in his hands, burning me with his scorching blue eyes, then with a shudder he enters me with a deep, pleasurable growl. I close my eyes and cry out as his powerful thrusts fill and stretch me as my muscles contract around him.

"Open your eyes. You know I need to see them," he whispers, in a ragged voice. The sight of him gazing at me with all that love in his eyes, fills me with a hunger so deep. I pull myself up to kiss him hard. He's mine, and I need to possess him. He pounds into me with urgency, his pleasure showing on his face and in the soft moans emanating from him.

Max pulls me with him as he rolls onto his back, still inside me. I break the kiss and rise up placing my hands on his chest as I rise and fall onto his thick shaft. Throwing my head back, my body absorbs all the delicious friction of his thrusts, and as my impending orgasm builds to the point of no return, I cry out his name. I feel his chest muscles tighten as his thrusts become more aggressive. With a deep, throaty growl, he joins me, shuddering with each burst of his hot seed.

Collapsing down onto his chest, he wraps his arms around me and kisses me on the top of my head. "I love you, baby," he whispers, softly. My heart skips a beat. I love those words coming out of his mouth.

"Me too," I whisper on a long, contented and exhausted sigh.

We didn't make dinner. We didn't leave the bedroom. When you're in love with a man who looks like he does, it's hard to think of anything else and the sex is amazing. Who needs food when you've got a Max in the bedroom.

JUST BECAUSE YOU CAN...

I arrive at my office in a panic because I'm very late.

I'd like to blame Max for making me late, but in truth it was my own fault. You'd think after last night's sex-a-thon I would have been exhausted, but I woke up feeling very horny this morning. I just can't get enough of him.

Even after our shower together, which was hot and steamy in more ways than one, we stood in the bedroom getting dressed, but as soon as I'd pulled on my stockings, his hands were all over me again and of course, I couldn't resist him.

So now I'm very late, very flustered, and my headache from hell has returned with a vengeance. Today of all days. Nova is going to be here in less than an hour, and I'd wanted to be relaxed and prepared before she arrived. Fat chance. Plus, it's Ed's first day and I'm showing him a very bad example.

"Good morning, Vivienne." Casper says, with a cheery smile. "Ed called, he said to tell you that he will be here as soon as he's spoken to Frank and collected his equipment from Star-Biz." He walks with me to my office. "I'll get you a fresh coffee, and I've added another appointment to your schedule. It's another company requesting aerial shots for publicity material. Looks like you might have hit on a niche market for this type of work."

"Oh, good. Is it in London?" I ask, throwing my bag on the desk and walking to my personal en-suite bathroom. I got ready in such a rush this morning that I still haven't finished my makeup, and when Nova arrives, I'd rather look like a confident woman who's totally in control, than the nervous wreck I feel at the moment.

"No. It's an equestrian centre in Gloucestershire. They have a cross country course and they want a set of aerial shots to advertise their three-day event."

"Really? How did they know to call us?"

Casper just shrugs and smiles.

Max! How does he know all these people?

A sudden wave of nausea churns my stomach, and I feel hot and fuzzy. I stand over the toilet bowl and sure enough, even though my stomach is empty, I'm sick.

Casper comes running into the bathroom. "Vivienne, are you okay?" I hold my hand up to stop him coming in any further. This is too embarrassing to have an audience.

"I'm fine."

"You don't look fine," he says, filling a glass with water and handing me a damp flannel.

"It's just nerves," I mumble. "This is all a bit overwhelming, that's all." I thought I'd gotten over it, but everything has happened so quickly, and I don't even know if I can live up to Max's high expectations. He succeeds at everything he does. *What if I'm a total failure? …What if…*

"Vivienne? …Vivienne! Can you hear me?" I open my eyes and see Casper's pale hazel eyes staring down at me. "Are you alright?" I blink up at him confused, and then I sit up, trying to figure out how I ended up lying on the sofa.

"What happened?" I ask nervously.

"You passed out. I caught you before you went down, but you've been out for a few minutes. Should I call a doctor or Mr. Foxx?"

"No! …I'm okay, really." I swing my feet off the sofa and just sit for a minute. *Not this again.*

"Have you eaten this morning?" Casper asks, concern

softening his voice.

"Erm, no. Not yet," I mumble.

He shakes his head at me. "Well that won't do. You can't function without fuel," he chides. "I'll get you some breakfast. Just sit there for a minute." Casper leaves and I feel so silly.

I don't understand what's wrong with me. I've followed all the doctor's orders, well, most of them. But then I realise I've not eaten since I had those prawns yesterday. Max and I could be in the Guinness Book of World Records for the amount of sex we've had in the last twelve hours. It doesn't take a genius to work out why I'm feeling so flaky, my blood sugar must be very low.

By the time Casper returns with some orange juice, coffee, and a bagel, I'm sitting at my desk. I feel a lot better now. "You've got twenty minutes before your first appointment," he says, handing me the orange juice.

"First appointment?" I ask, a little confused. "There's more than one?"

He tilts his head at me like a dog. "Yes, it's in the schedule. I synced it to your phone, remember?"

I cringe. I'd forgotten to check it this morning. "I'm sorry, Casper. I haven't quite got the hang of it all yet," I blush. He must think I'm a complete moron.

"You have a lunch appointment with Mr. Foxx at twelve-thirty, and after that John will be waiting for you to take you to your two o'clock appointment with Mr. Adams at the George Ralph Institute across town."

My nerves jangle. That will be my first proper business meeting with a complete stranger, and I really don't know if I'm going to be able to pull it off. My appetite vanishes at the thought so I just drink the juice and coffee until my nerves have calmed down a bit.

Ed arrives ten minutes before Nova is due, and makes me feel a whole lot calmer. He'd called Frank yesterday to tell him he was leaving, but he went in to talk to him face to face this morning, and to pick up his equipment. Poor

Frank, he must be feeling like he's got a mutiny on his hands. Clive apparently asked Ed to enquire about a job for him too. As much as I love Clive, I don't have anything for him to do here. And I couldn't steal anyone else from Frank, that just wouldn't be right.

Casper announces Nova's arrival. She glides into my office looking like a Hollywood movie star. She obviously takes a great deal of pride in her appearance, but it's her natural elegance and poise that really sets her apart. Casper dutifully asks her if she would like anything to drink.

"Do you have Vodka?" she asks in all seriousness. It's ten in the morning.

Casper doesn't even flinch. "Straight up, or on the rocks?" he asks, helping her off with her coat.

"On the rocks, please," she smiles.

Casper leaves the room, and then my nerves really kick in.

"Good morning, Nova. Thank you for coming," I say, walking around my desk to shake her hand. "This is Ed, my assistant." Ed walks toward her and takes her hand, kissing the back of it with a silly smile on his face.

"Very nice to meet you," he says, in his smoothest voice. I chuckle to myself, he doesn't know she's a dominatrix, or that she's not interest in young men. He'll be so disappointed.

As Ed and I show her the images I'd taken at her club, she seems very pleased, although, every word she's uttered has been in Russian, which makes me nervous. She could be saying these photos are terrible. Ed talks her through the options regarding colour and size, and eventually she sits back and holds her empty glass up. Ed quickly takes the hint and pours her another Vodka. Casper had cleverly brought a bottle and a bucket of ice. This will be her third, but I'm not judging.

"Lapochka, I am very pleased with your work. I think we may have a very interesting future ahead of us," she smiles. Her eyes travel over to Ed and linger on his for a moment.

If I didn't know any better, I could swear she was interested in him. The poor dear, I think she'd eat him for breakfast. "Okay, now I must go," she says, rising to her feet.

"Oh, but you haven't told me which photographs you want yet," I splutter, rising to see her to the door.

She picks up her handbag, resting it in the crook of her elbow, drapes her fur coat over her arm, and then she walks toward me, reaching up to cup my face in her hand. "All of them. I want all of them," she smiles. "And don't forget, you and Max must come to my club. I make special night for you. Do Svidaniya," she says, kissing me on both cheeks.

"Let me walk you to your car," Ed says, offering his elbow. She smiles and takes his arm.

"Why don't we go for some lunch, I'm starving," she purrs, smiling up at him. Ed looks over at me for approval, so I shrug and smile. Before she leaves, Nova throws me a wink over her shoulder. The woman is a little bit bonkers, but completely fascinating, and something tells me she plays for both teams.

I may never see Ed again. I chuckle to myself and take a seat at my desk. I feel drained from the pressure of closing my first ever deal as an independent, but thrilled and excited to have at least one happy client on my books, and one happy assistant too.

My stomach growls with hunger. I check the time and slip into the bathroom to check myself out in the mirror. It's only ten past twelve so I decide to meet Max at his office instead of waiting for him to come down. I'm so excited about my first sale, and I want to tell him straight away.

"Casper, I'm off to lunch with Mr. Foxx, why don't you slip off for a while, I'll be back after my meeting with Mr. Adams." My belly churns. I hope that meeting goes as well as this one did. "Oh, and best not to mention what happened earlier." I wait for Casper to acknowledge me. I don't want him telling Max that I passed out again.

"Certainly," he smiles.

When the lift arrives at Foxx-Tech, I walk straight to Max's office. Grace isn't at her desk so I knock on Max's frosted glass door. There's no answer, so I knock again and wait, but there's still no answer. Pushing the door open, I poke my head in, but he's not here. His phone is lying on his desk. I assume he's just popped to another office so I stroll in to wait.

Standing at the enormous window, I take in the amazing view of London's bustling financial district. After a few moments, I pull his chair out and take a seat, swivelling it around from side to side. Something catches my eye in his bin. It's a scrunched up piece of yellow paper. The same colour as the one he was reading in his study. The one that vanished into thin air. I stop swivelling and reach down to take it out.

"Baby, I didn't know you were here." Max strides toward me without taking his eyes off mine, until he's beside me, then they slide down to the bin. His voice had startled me so I'd already dropped the yellow ball of paper back into the bin. He takes my face in his hands and leans down for a kiss. "How did it go?"

"Very well. V.F.P. has made its very first sale," I grin, shamelessly.

His eyes smoulder as he melts me with his knee-trembling smile. "I'm so proud of you, baby. How about we celebrate in style?"

"Okay," I grin. "But I've got another meeting at two."

His eyes gaze at me in wonder. "You're amazing. So calm and confident."

Ha! If only. I'm glad he thinks so, but in reality, every time I think about my next meeting, my knees quake and my belly rolls.

"Come on, I've got a surprise for you." He takes my hand and grabs his phone, then he leads me to the lift.

Once inside it, he takes me in his arms and kisses me, curling my toes. I almost tell him to take us home, but I can't be late for my next appointment. *Oh, there goes my stomach again.*

When we exit the building and walk to the car, Vinnie gets out and opens our door. I squeal with delight when I see Lucy and Dan sitting inside. "Oh! This is perfect," I giggle, trying not to cry.

Vinnie drives us to Carrigan's in Mayfair.

"Max we would have been quite happy with the Pizza Pit. You didn't have to go to all this extravagance," I say, stroking his cheek.

He smiles, that blistering, heart stopping smile. "Only the best for you, baby. Besides, you're paying."

"Huh?" I blink up at him, internally working out how much credit I have left on my card.

Lucy and Dan haven't stopped thanking Max for his generosity. He tries to play it down but I know how much this means to Lucy, and it's right that they show their gratitude.

During lunch, Lucy and I chat about my new job and her wedding, while Max and Dan talk about sports cars, yachts, and all the usual guy stuff. When the coffees arrive I check my watch, my belly churns as the meeting draws nearer.

"Hey, did you know Mike has lost his job?" Lucy asks, out of the blue.

"Yeah, I saw him yesterday, he looked awful."

"You didn't tell me you'd seen Mike." I look up to see Max frowning at me. I hadn't told him, not because I was hiding it from him, it just never came up.

"Erm, yeah, I saw him while I was at lunch with Ed yesterday." Everyone is looking at Max. His tone of voice and angry frown has completely changed the atmosphere.

Dan suddenly chips in. "He got the sack for breaking company policy and the law. It's his own fault. Cyber hacking is as bad as breaking and entering, or burglary. I told him he'd get into trouble sooner or later," he huffs, shaking his head.

"But he was only trying to help me trace Monica's phone." I feel like I have to defend him. He was only doing what I'd asked him to do.

Dan gives me an arched brow and a condescending look. "Viv, Mike's been hacking into stuff for months. Just because you can, doesn't mean you should."

I never knew that. Mike's computer skills were always way above my understanding.

"We should go. You're going to be late for your appointment," Max says, rising from the table, still frowning and clearly put out that I hadn't mentioned my conversation with Mike. Well, he hasn't bothered to elaborate on his meeting with Fiona, so I guess we're quits.

Max had already paid the bill before I got the chance to, which in a strange way dented my self-esteem, but it probably saved me from the embarrassment of having my card rejected.

John is waiting for me outside. Lucy, Dan, and I, hug it out before they get into the limo and Max gives me a chaste kiss. "Have a good meeting," he says, but I can see he's still angry with me.

GENEVA

"Hi, John," I mumble, getting into the range rover.

"Ma'am," he nods.

Once we're on our way, I look into the rear-view mirror to watch his expression.

"John, has Mr. Foxx been receiving any hate mail?"

His brow twitches and his eyes briefly swing up to mine then they look away. "Hate mail?"

"Yeah, you know, like threatening letters or something."

"Not that I'm aware of," he says, but I'm not convinced. "Why? Have you?" he asks hesitantly. I just shake my head and continue to watch him in the mirror until he looks away. Neither of us speaks for the rest of the journey, but I sense John's eyes repeatedly returning to the mirror.

For all my nerves and apprehension the meeting couldn't have gone better. Mr. Adams was younger than I had expected, and we got along really well. He was very down to earth and made me laugh, putting me at ease straight away. He showed me around each department of the institute. He wants internal, external, and aerial photographs for their new brochure. The building is very modern with the very latest architectural designs, and I'm really looking forward to the project. We shook on the deal, and he said he would send the contracts through later this afternoon, so now I have two clients on the books making me a very happy woman.

When John drops me off at Foxx-Tech, I head back to my office. Ed has left a message that he's still at lunch with Nova. Knowing Ed as I do, I should imagine he's using all his manly charms on her, although, I'd love to be a fly on the wall. I think he may have met his match with Nova.

Casper and I discuss the new clients, and then we organise my schedule for next week. I want to get started on the institute as soon as possible.

"You've got another meeting with a fashion brand tomorrow, it's a relatively small business, but very well respected within the industry. If we clinch the deal, it could be very lucrative. We'll also have to liaise with Mr. Foxx's secretary to book the helicopter for your aerial work. Would you like me to do that?" Casper asks.

"Oh, no it's okay. I'll call Grace. In fact, I'll go up and see her now." I want to speak to Grace, she may know something about the letters Max has been receiving. I get the feeling John knew more than he was letting on too, and it bothers me that Max won't talk about it. What is he hiding?

I head up to the Foxx-Tech office and find Grace at her desk.

"Vivienne, how lovely to see you, and congratulations on your new venture."

"Thanks, erm—"

"He's free at the moment, you can go in," she smiles.

"Actually, I wanted to ask you something, has Max—"

"Vivienne." I jump when he says my name. I turn to see Max standing in his doorway looking surprised to see me. "How did your meeting go?" he asks, walking toward me.

"Very well, thanks."

He wraps his arms around me then he kisses me in a possessive way that leaves me breathless and ready for sex. I hear Grace chuckling to herself.

"What are you doing here?" he asks, nipping my neck and earlobe. I blush and glance over to Grace, but she's occupying herself with some papers and pretending not to notice.

"Oh, I just wanted to book the helicopter for next week. I've got a job at the George Ralph Institute."

He smiles down at me and hugs me a little tighter. "That's great. But Casper can deal with that, right Grace?" he says, winking at her.

She smiles and picks up her phone. "I'll call him now."

Max pulls me into his office and closes the door. He walks us over to his desk and pulls me into his lap, kissing my neck and running his hand underneath my skirt. When he finds the lace tops of my stockings, his hand stays there stroking the material. While his face is buried in my hair, I take a quick peek at his bin, but the yellow ball of paper is now gone.

"Baby, I've got to fly to Switzerland this afternoon. I've got a meeting in Geneva, so I'll be gone until late Thursday evening. Come with me."

I sag, I'd love to go with him. I've never been to Geneva but I have responsibilities now. "Max, I'd love to come, but I have a meeting with a new client tomorrow, and I can't leave Ed on his own."

He sighs and nibbles my earlobe. "I've created a monster," he grumbles, tickling my neck with his lips.

I squirm and wriggle so he does it even more. "Stop!" I yell, giggling.

He pulls back and searches my face with a half-smile. "I'm so happy for you, baby. But you know I don't like being away from you, please come with me." His sad eyes make me hesitate, but I can't just abandon my business. I'll never get it off the ground if I don't get out there and hustle.

"Max, I can't. I'm sorry."

His frown says it all. "Baby, please tell me we're not going to have one of those relationships where my secretary has to book a slot with your secretary just so we can see each other?" he grumbles, stroking my thigh.

"No," I laugh, smoothing my hand across his cheek, "but

I did have you pencilled in for nudity and rampant sex at nineteen hundred hours. If you're going away, I guess we'll have to cancel."

He hits me with his sexy smile and crushes his lips against mine. Running his hand up to my bare flesh above my stocking, he squeezes my thigh and strokes a finger over my sex.

"Or, we could bring that forward?" he whispers against my lips.

Trying to be quiet while having sex on a desk, with Grace on the other side of the door, was tricky! I'm sure she knew what we were doing. The dead giveaway was when she knocked and had to wait for a couple of minutes for us to get dressed. We giggled and ran around picking up all our clothing from the floor.

I scoot into the bathroom to finish dressing, but I have to laugh when I hear Grace saying, "Sorry to disturb you, Sir, but I need your signature on these before you leave. Oh, and you may want to take care of that…you don't want to catch a chill." I peek out through the bathroom door. In his rush he'd forgotten to zip up his fly. Grace gives him a cheeky smirk before leaving the office.

"That wasn't embarrassing at all," he says, sarcastically when I emerge giggling from the bathroom.

"What time do you have to go?" I ask, putting my shoes on.

"In about an hour. Are you sure you won't come with me? I don't want to leave you." He pulls me into his arms.

"I don't want you to leave me either, but I can't. Promise you'll call me when you land." I rise up on my toes and kiss him softly on the lips.

"I will. And promise me you won't go out tonight. I want to know you're safe while I'm away. Parker's coming with me, but John will be in his quarters after he takes Jan home. I want you to activate the new alarm system as soon as she leaves," he says, firmly. I nod and smile, then I leave him to his work. Grace and I exchange a knowing smile, then I head back down to my office.

Ed has finally made it back from lunch. Apparently, Nova wanted to show him her club, and judging by his silly smile he's had a great afternoon.

"You must be good," I quip. "I'd heard she was gay."

He raises an eyebrow with a wry smile. "I don't let things like that stand in my way."

"As long as it doesn't hurt the business, I'm fine with that."

Casper has already organised the helicopter for next week and he talks me through my schedule for tomorrow, then we all call it a day and I head off home.

After Jan leaves for the evening, I set the alarm just as Max calls me to tell me he's arrived safely in Geneva. He's just about to leave for his meeting with his client.

"Jan's just left and I've set the alarm. Oh, and Lucy's coming round tonight to keep me company, I think she wants to go through the details of the wedding."

"Good. Any problems just call John, and I'll speak to you later, baby." A woman's voice calls his name in the background. My hackles rise when I realise I recognise the voice.

Fiona! What the fuck is she doing there? "Why is *she* there?" I blurt, wishing I'd given myself time to control my tone. There's a very slight pause before he answers which just fuels my suspicion.

"Actually, she's here with her father. I'm staying at his house tonight."

My blood starts to boil. "You never said." I try, but fail to control the anger in my voice.

"I didn't know. Not until I got here. Look, baby, I'm sorry but I've got to go, I'm having dinner with a client and I don't want to be late. Are you okay?"

No! Far from it. "Yes. Fine," I huff.

"Say hi to Lucy for me. I love you, baby."

"Enjoy your dinner," I mumble ungraciously. I wait for

the silence of him ending the call before I allow my anger to really kick in. "Bitch!"

REBEL

I take a bath then I throw my comfies on waiting for Lucy to arrive. Fiona being in Switzerland with Max has completely thrown me. But maybe it's like he said, maybe he didn't know she was going to be there. He did ask me to go with him after all.

While I wait for Lucy, I wander into the study. I know I shouldn't be snooping, but I can't help myself. I need to find the keys to Max's drawer, but when I try the drawer it opens. The diary and all the folders that were in it, have all gone.

Suddenly, I get a flash of inspiration. *The safe.* I remember Max telling me he hadn't changed the safe combination even after Monica had left him. She knew the combination, that's how she'd managed to steal all that money, twice. Any normal person would have immediately changed the code, but the reason he hadn't, was quite simply because he couldn't. The numbers he'd used were too significant to him. Too important. They're the day and month of the death of his parents. Three-zero-zero-three. The thirtieth of March. He uses the same code for the lift.

I try the code and sure enough the safe clicks open. A pang of guilt hits me for about two seconds, then I brush it aside and open the door. The safe is empty. *Where the hell are they?* If I had a diary and papers that I didn't want anyone to see, I'd try and hide them somewhere no one could find them. But other than his safe, where the hell else would he put them? Then it suddenly dawns on me that he must have a secure place in his office too. I'm going to have to get in there tomorrow while he's still away. If I'm lucky, he'll have used the same code there too.

While I'm mentally patting myself on the back for figuring out a plan of action, I feel awful for being so sneaky. It's wrong of me to be snooping around his private things, and I'm going to have to come up with a very good excuse to get into his office tomorrow. Since Monica broke into the penthouse, the whole place is under c.c.t.v. surveillance.

My phone jolts me out of my thoughts and I rush to the lounge to find it.

"Hey, Luce. Are you on your way?"

"Sorry, Viv. My mum's just called, she wants to pop round for a chat. Why don't you come here instead, she'll only be here for an hour, then we can go to the pub." I hesitate, remembering Max asking me not to go out while he was away. "Viv? You still there?"

"Yeah… Alright, I'll see you soon."

I change into my jeans, a smart top, and boots. If I take my bike I won't be able to have a drink, but I should be able to sneak out undetected and Max need never know. Besides, knowing Fiona's in Geneva has pissed me off. I'm feeling rebellious.

I park my bike and walk up to Lucy's flat. It feels weird being here again knowing that Max has bought my flat and it's now totally empty. I glance up the staircase that leads up to George's old flat. I still get shivers remembering that day.

"Hey, Viv." Lucy says, putting her coat on as she answers her door. "Come on, we might as well go straight to the pub. Mum's running late, she's going to meet us there."

"Oh, okay. But I can't drink, I've got the bike."

"I thought Max didn't like you riding that thing?"

"He doesn't know. He's away on business."

"Fair enough, but I'm not drinking on my own. You'll have to leave your bike here and get a cab home."

Knowing I have work in the morning, I decide to limit myself to just one drink. Because I'm still miffed with Max, I drank it really quickly while telling Lucy all about Fiona, then I hear myself ordering another before thinking about the consequences.

Lucy thinks I'm just being paranoid and tells me to forget about her. As far as she's concerned, Max can do no wrong. We haven't been on a night out for ages, so I take her advice and start to loosen up. By the time my fourth glass of wine is sitting in front of me, I couldn't give a shit about the consequences.

Lucy's mum Joan arrives. She's fun to be around, very flirtatious and always cracking jokes. She really loves a party. If I thought Lucy could sink the drink in record time, her mother is worse. We giggle and dance the night away until a familiar face scowling at me from across the bar, sobers my mood. He walks over to our table.

"You're going to get me fired," he says, frowning down at me.

"John, what are you doing here?" I'm irritated at his presence and too pissed to hide it.

"I've come to take you home, Ma'am," he says, arching a brow at me. "More importantly, what are you doing leaving the penthouse without telling me?"

I flick my semi-focused eyes up to Lucy. She and her mother have gone silent, just staring up at him in confusion. "John, I'm not a kid," I huff indignantly. "I'm quite capable of taking myself out for the evening."

"I know," he shrugs. "But if you'd told me, I could have brought you here and Mr. Foxx would have been none the wiser. Unfortunately, Mr. Foxx insisted that I install a tracker on your bike, which is how he found out that you had left the penthouse without me."

"You mean you would have covered for me?" I ask,

taken aback by his honesty.

"I've been assigned to you, that makes you my boss. I'd do whatever you ask, within reason," he smirks.

"Well in that case, pull up a chair while I finish my drink. The damage is done now anyway."

We didn't get off to a great start, but the more I get to know John, the more I like him. He sits with us laughing at Lucy's mum's jokes until I finish my drink. John's a good looking man and Joan couldn't take her eyes off him. Admittedly they were glazed by the amount of alcohol she'd been drinking, but John had certainly made an impact on her. Once I finish my drink and say my goodbyes, he drives me home.

On the way home, I ask John what he knows about Fiona, but he just shrugs and says he hasn't met her. I want to ask him about the letters again, but then my rolling stomach takes all my focus and I keep my mouth shut for fear that I will throw up in the car.

He sees me into the penthouse and I hear him on his phone talking to Max as I rush upstairs to the bathroom to be sick. I used to be able to handle my drink but lately the slightest thing upsets my stomach. Feeling rough, I don't even bother getting undressed, I just crawl into bed.

DON'T MAKE ME LIVE WITHOUT YOU

"Ooh, bad night?" Casper asks as I walk past his desk.

I glance up at him and grumble a hello as I carry on to my office. *No need to shout.* My head is banging, and although I've thrown up twice this morning, my rolling stomach tells me I haven't finished yet. *I'm never drinking again.*

I ignore my phone ringing in my handbag as I collapse into my chair and hold my head in my hands. I know it's Max calling, but I'm not in the mood for another fight. He'd called me earlier and told me off for going out last night. It annoyed me, but I felt too fragile to argue back so I just let him have his rant. This is just my own stupidity paying me back. *What was I thinking last night?*

Casper enters with a coffee and two paracetamol. The smell of the coffee churns my stomach. "Casper, would you mind getting me a tea instead. And could you answer my phone, he's only going to keep calling," I mumble, handing Casper my bag and pushing the coffee away.

"Sure." He takes the phone from my bag and answers the call on his way out. By the time he comes back with my tea, I'm in the bathroom throwing up for what I hope to be that last time. It seems to be a daily occurrence lately.

"Vivienne? Are you okay?" Casper asks, through the door. "I've brought you some tea, and Mr. Foxx said he'll call you later. He's leaving Geneva earlier than expected, so he should be home by six."

"Okay, thanks. I'll be out in a minute," I answer, splashing water on my face. I look awful. Hardly a good way to introduce yourself to a new client. I sort out my hair and makeup, then I drink my tea and take the painkillers. After a while, my stomach settles down and I feel more like myself.

John meets me in the lobby and delivers me to my appointment. He makes no mention of my drunken behaviour last night, which is a relief. All I want to concentrate on is my pitch to the client and controlling my nerves.

Thankfully Daisy Abbott-Taylor, the founder of her fashion brand, is very nice. Her clothing line is quirky but I love it. She's only young, very innovative, and has a great eye for shape and colour. She's met with several other companies, but seems very keen to book me after I explained how I would like to shoot her collection. I won't know for a couple of days as she needs to speak with her business partner, but I left feeling very hopeful about it.

Ed and I spend the rest of the afternoon tweaking our website and creating our online presence through social media and Youtube. Luckily Ed has a gift with anything technical. If it was left to me, I'd still be running around shoving paper flyers through letter boxes. I still have to pinch myself that I'm running my own business, but so far, things are going very well.

I've checked my phone a million times today, but apart from my telling off this morning, and a quick text to tell me he'd be home at six, Max hasn't called or text since. I have wondered if it's because he's spending time with Fiona and hasn't given me a second thought, but I suspect he's giving me the cold shoulder because I'd defied him yesterday. Part of me is irritated by his attitude, but part of me likes the fact that he worries about me. I miss him too, I hate not being able to see or speak to him.

When I leave my office, I think about going to Max's office to see if I can get in and have a snoop around, but I'm in trouble already for going out last night, I don't want to add breaking and entering to the list. I decide to bite the bullet and just ask him outright. Max was annoyed that I'd gone out on my own because, in his words, he thought it was dangerous. He's going to have to define that. He's clearly worried about something so if he wants me to conform to his rules, then he's going to have to be honest with me about those letters.

When I get home, Jan has left instructions on how to finish off the meal she's prepared for us, so as it's almost six already, I put the dish in the oven and I start to prepare the vegetables.

When the oven timer goes off, I put my book down and glance at my watch, it's already quarter past seven and he's still not home. He hasn't called or text, and when I call him, it goes straight to answer-phone. *Where the hell is he?*

I decide to call Jan.

"Hi, Jan, have you heard from Vinnie? Max said he would be home at six but he's still not here and I can't reach him on his phone."

"No, I haven't. I was starting to worry myself. I haven't been able to reach Vincent for a while now," she says, nervously.

Suddenly a loud pounding on the front door makes me jump. "Wait a minute, Jan, there's someone at the door."

I open the door and John barges in looking very agitated. "Have you heard from Mr. Foxx?" he asks, walking straight through to the living room.

"Er, no. And Jan hasn't heard from Vinnie either. Why? What's going on?"

John turns to face me, his expression frightens me. "You'd better sit down," he says, looking extremely nervous. It's not like him at all.

My stomach tightens. "Just tell me. What's happened?"

John stares at me for a moment longer, then he walks

toward me, his eyes searching mine. "Mr. Foxx's plane lost radio contact shortly after they left Geneva… There's been no contact with them since they took off."

"No. .. No!" My heart drops into my stomach, and my legs buckle underneath me. As I crumple to the floor, my phone flies out of my hand and I can hear Jan's high pitched voice calling my name. John picks up the phone and gingerly tells Jan the same thing. I feel sick to my stomach, and all of a sudden I feel like I'm suffocating.

"Breathe, Vivienne. Just breathe," John says, crouching down in front of me. I can't believe it. I don't want to believe it. I couldn't bear it if anything happened to Max or Vinnie.

"What happened? Did they… Did they crash? Why have they—"

"Ma'am, I don't know anything yet," he interrupts, squeezing my shoulders. "Trencher's in contact with the authorities in Geneva, he's going to call me as soon as he has any news."

My mind is racing with all sorts of scenarios, none of which I hope to be true. Suddenly the yellow letters come into my mind.

"Jan's coming over in a cab. She didn't want me to leave you on your own," he says, interrupting my thoughts. I quickly scramble up off the floor and grab the remote control to turn the telly on. My tears blur the screen so I swipe my sleeve across my eyes and scroll through the channels until I find the news channel. *Shit! Where is it?* They're talking about the fucking weather now. But the small yellow band of information running across the bottom of the screen, confirms everything John just told me.

'Breaking news: Private jet believed to be owned by billionaire Maxwell Foxx, missing shortly after take-off from Geneva. Radio contact lost. Search and rescue ongoing.'

I watch it over and over again, unable to think, or move,

or feel.

John wraps his arm around my shoulders and moves me to the sofa. "Sit down, I'll get you a drink." He starts to walk away, but I reach up and grab his sleeve.

"John! How am I going to tell Sylvie and William?" I ask in a panic. William is still so fragile, this could kill him. John's eyes lower as he shakes his head and clenches his jaw. I release his sleeve and sink back into the sofa as the tears stream down my cheeks. The pain in my heart grows deeper and more painful as the black cloud of realisation that I may never see Max again, slowly destroys me.

Jan arrives in tears and we hug each other sobbing as the lives of our loved ones hang in the balance. There's been no further information on the news, and several people have already called after seeing the report. I let John field all the calls, I'm in no state to talk to anyone right now.

I stand and pace. I can't sit still. I feel sick, and every time the phone rings my heart stops. "What am I going to say to Sylvie? I can't let her find out from the news," I say, trying to hold myself together.

"Would you like me to call them?" Jan offers.

"No. I should be the one to do it. I just don't know how I'm going to tell them."

"Ma'am, why don't I go and pick them up and bring them here, you should all be together," John says, handing me and Jan a drink. I don't want it, I just want to keep moving.

"Yes. Okay. I'll call them now and tell them you're on your way." With shaking hands I make the call to Max's parents.

Sylvie answers, and I'm barely able to get the words out that her son's plane has gone missing. Her tortured voice kills me as she asks the same questions we did. The same questions none of us know the answers to.

As Jan and I wait for John to return, my eyes land on the photograph of Max and Charlie. "We had a fight," I murmur staring at Max's beautiful face, "I'd been jealous and stupid, and… The last time I spoke to him, I didn't tell him that I love him." My voice quivers with emotion as I turn to face Jan.

"Don't torture yourself, Vivienne. Max loves you, and he knows how much you love him. We all do."

My phone rings. Without looking at the screen I quickly answer it. "Hello!"

"Vivienne. It's Mike. I've just been watching the news… I'm so sorry, are you okay?"

I dissolve into tears. "Oh, Mike…" I can't speak, and I collapse into the chair.

"Viv… I just wanted you to know that I'm here for you if you need me. If there's anything I can do… Anything. Just call me. I'm so sorry."

In floods of tears, I find it difficult to speak. After a few moments Mike hangs up and Jan puts her arms around me as my heart breaks into a million pieces. Everyone is thinking the same thing, that Max and Vinnie are dead.

When Sylvie and William arrive, I run to them and throw my arms around them both. We stand in a huddle crying. I don't want to let them go. "I'm so glad you're here."

John walks in and hovers beside us. "Ma'am, Trencher's sent a team to join in the search and rescue. They've picked up a faint signal from the aircraft's I-dent tracker and they've been able to track Mr. Foxx's cell phone. They're heading to the coordinates now."

"Thank God." William says, with tears in his eyes. "That's good news." He takes Sylvie's arm and they walk to the sofa, greeting Jan with hugs and kisses.

I stare up at John trying to read his face, he doesn't look as happy as William does. What is he not saying? I dry my tears and straighten my back.

"John?" His eyes meet mine, and I can tell he's anxious about something, but reluctant to say. He eventually nods for me to follow him to the kitchen. "What is it?" I ask, dreading the answer. My stomach is churning so badly and my hands are shaking.

"Ma'am, if Mr. Foxx's cell phone is still able to pick up GPS, why hasn't he used it to contact us? To call for help?" His worried frown transfers onto my face. Now my mind begins to reel with all the unthinkable possibilities.

"No! …No we can't give up hope, John. I want to know the minute anyone finds out anything."

"Yes, Ma'am. I'll be downstairs if you need me."

To keep myself busy I make some tea and coffee, and pour a large Scotch on the rocks for Sylvie. As I walk the tray of drinks into the living room, the doorbell chimes. I freeze and almost drop the tray.

"I'll go." Jan offers. We all stop and stare at the door and I'm relieved to see Lucy and Dan walking in.

"Any news?" she asks anxiously, walking toward me for a hug.

"No… Not yet."

For me, the next four hours and thirty-six minutes pass achingly slowly. Sylvie and William have kept us all strong. Their unwavering faith in the search and rescue mission, and their stories about Max, have kept me from falling apart. But even their determined faith that they will be found alive doesn't stop the fear from creeping into my mind. *What if he's been hurt? …What if he's dead.* I stand abruptly. I need to clear my head or I'm going to drive myself mad with worry.

"Are you okay?" Lucy asks.

"I just need some air." I walk out to the terrace and stare out across the night sky. The chilly evening air bites into my skin. My head is pounding, and although I haven't eaten or drunk anything, I feel sick. *Please be safe. Please, come back to me. I love you, Max. Don't make me live without you.*

A commotion coming from the living room has me anxiously turning around. John's arrived and he's standing with his back to me, busily telling the others something that has them enthralled with frowns on their faces. I take a step toward the patio doors, but then I hesitate. I can't read their expressions, they're all anxious, but I can't tell if it's good or bad news he's giving them. Sylvie and William suddenly embrace, holding on to each other for dear life, but I can't see their faces. Jan bows her head and sobs into her handkerchief. And I can't see Lucy and Dan from here. Suddenly John spins around and looks directly at me.

No…Please don't. My whole body stiffens.

As he walks toward me, sliding the patio door open, his anxious face relaxes into a smile. "He's okay, Ma'am. They're both okay. They're coming home."

Thank God! My knees buckle. John races forward to catch me and holds me upright as the floodgates open and tears of worry and joy intermingle down my cheeks.

Since the good news, everyone seems to have relaxed. I won't relax until he walks through that door and I can see him with my own two eyes. He hasn't called. I haven't heard his voice and until I do, I can't relax. Jan's organised some nibbles and drinks, and the room is full of chatter and the occasional bout of laughter. It's been a traumatic time for us all, but they're on their way home, and the relief in the room is palpable.

Three more hours pass at a snail's pace. As we wait for them to come home, my stomach knots and rolls. Trencher has called several times to update us on their progress but as yet, I still haven't spoken to Max. *It's been hours. Why hasn't he called me?*

Lucy and Dan have been great. Dan's kept everyone's glass or tea cup topped up, and Lucy's taken everyone's mind off the plane crash with the details of her wedding. My mind can't really focus on anything at the moment. John had said they'd both suffered cuts and bruises, but until I see him with my own eyes, until I can touch him and feel his lips against mine, none of it is real.

"Excuse me a moment," I mumble rising from the sofa.

"Viv? You okay?" Lucy asks.

"Yeah, just need the loo," I answer nonchalantly. The truth is my stomach is churning like a washing machine, and if I don't get to the bathroom soon, I'm going to throw up in front of everyone.

Once I'm sure I'm not going to be sick anymore, I wander over to the basin. My reflection makes me wince as I stare at my puffy, red-rimmed eyes and hollow cheeks. I look exactly how I feel. I splash my face with cold water and brush my teeth to get the taste out of my mouth. I'm exhausted and weak with worry.

Sitting on Max's side, I pull his pillow from the bed and hug it to my chest, breathing in his scent. Tears pool in my eyes as I rock back and forth clutching his pillow.

"Viv!" I look up to see Lucy's head poking around the door. "They're here. They've just landed on the roof." I bow my head into the pillow and sob loudly, unable to contain my emotion. The relief that he's home overwhelms me. As I gather my thoughts, I stand in a rush and throw the pillow on the bed. Wiping my eyes, I race to the door. Barging past Lucy, I head toward the stairs.

Everyone has congregated at the front door. Standing on the bottom step, I frantically search for Max over their heads as they welcome Vinnie home. He winces as they jostle and hug him. Jan wails with delight that her man is finally home safe.

My heart twists when I see Vinnie. He looks broken and bruised, his arm is in a sling and his jacket is torn and bloodied at the sleeve. Whatever happened to them must have been terrifying. Fear churns my stomach, I don't see Max.

Suddenly, I catch a glimpse of him. "Oh God!" I gasp when I see his cut and bruised face, he looks gaunt and exhausted. The front of his torn shirt is covered in blood. I want to run to him but I can't seem to move, I can't stop staring at him. His eyes search the eager faces waiting to greet him, and then they find mine. Tears flow down my cheeks and my heart aches when his tired, watery eyes focus on me with such relief.

He starts to walk toward me, never removing his eyes

from mine. He's trying to conceal it, but I can see he's in pain. Relief, adrenaline, fear, and joy surge through me. I'm so relieved to see him that even though I know I shouldn't, I run and launch myself at him. Burying my face in his neck, I sob my heart out. He hisses out a painful groan, but wraps his arms around me and squeezes me tightly to his chest.

"Vivienne," he whispers. His hot breath heats my skin as he buries his face in my hair and holds on to me for dear life.

Pulling back, I hold his face in my hands, searching his watery eyes. "Don't you ever do that to me again," I sniffle, as the lump in my throat strangles the words. I kiss him tenderly on each of his cuts and bruises.

He kisses me softly on the lips, then he closes his eyes and leans his forehead against mine. "I'm so glad to be home."

As he lowers me to my feet, I see him flinch badly. "Oh, Max, I'm sorry, you're in pain. Come and sit down." I help him remove his jacket, then I pull him over to the sofa. His shirt is drenched in blood so I help him remove that as well, but I can't tell where the blood has come from. He has a large dark bruise over his ribs on his left side, and a deep cut on his collar bone and shoulder, both of which have been sutured. "Where did all that blood come from?" I ask, gently running my fingers over his bruised ribs.

"Parker caught some shrapnel in his arm, I had to tourniquet it or he'd have bled to death."

"And what about you?" I ask, holding his face in my shaking hands.

He reaches up and takes one of my hands in his, then he softly kisses my palm. "Just a few cuts and a couple of cracked ribs, I'm fine," he smiles, playing it down.

"Here." Lucy hands Max a clean shirt and a glass of Jack Daniels. He throws it back in one go, then I help him on with his clean shirt and he rests back in the sofa, wincing at the pain in his ribs. Jan and I share a relieved smile.

Both our men are home safe, and I know exactly how she's feeling.

I have a million questions, but I hold back while Sylvie and William fuss over him as only concerned parents can. Max doesn't let go of my hand the whole time. When William asks him what happened, Max plays down the danger, but I can see in Vinnie's expression how terrifying it must have been for them both. We must all be eternally grateful for Max's experience that they managed to land safely at all.

As John waits to take everyone home, I reluctantly leave Max so I can see everyone off at the door. I give Jan a big hug, and I kiss Vinnie on the cheek. "I'm so glad you're okay. You gave us such a fright," I sniffle, blinking back the tears.

"You'd have to do better than that to kill me off," he smirks, "but I don't mind telling you, it was pretty scary," he chuckles. His eyes slide over to Max. "How you managed to land that tin can I'll never know, but I'm glad you did, Guv', you saved my life." His words begin to quiver at the end, and I can see them both exchanging a knowing look. The emotional experience they've both been through today has brought them closer, you can see it in their eyes. It makes me shudder to think they both could have been taken from us today.

"Come on, let's get you home for some much deserved pampering," Jan smiles, tearfully.

Lucy and Dan say their goodbyes hugging me tightly, and finally, we're alone.

"Can I get you anything?" I ask, walking back to him. He repositions himself on the sofa, wincing with every movement.

"Come here," he says in a throaty voice, patting his thigh. I carefully sit in his lap, resting my back against the armrest, trying not to touch him anywhere it hurts. His hand immediately runs up and down my thigh, his eyes following the movement until they slide up to mine.

"I thought we'd had it," he murmurs softly, shaking his head. "I thought I was never going to see you again."

I swallow the tightening lump in my throat as his eyes search mine with such sadness it breaks my heart. Reaching up, I run my fingers through his hair. "I'm so glad you're home. I was so scared, I thought I'd lost you." I'm choked by emotion.

He smiles and leans forward to kiss me, but his painful ribs abort that plan immediately. I gently push him back and lean forward, careful not to hurt him, then I softly kiss him on the lips, stroking my hand through his hair. I want to wrap myself around him and kiss him hard. I want to rip his clothes off and make mad, passionate, possessive love to him. I thought I might never see him again and I couldn't bear that. There is no me without him. But right now he needs tenderness and security. I lean my forehead against his and close my eyes.

"I love you, Max. Don't ever put me through that again."

BLOODY LETTERS!

Lying here staring at Max as he sleeps, has been pretty much all I've done since he made it home. He was going to go into work, but I put a stop to that, and Grace called to say that if he showed up at the office, she would have security remove him from the building. She'd already rescheduled all his meetings to next week and told him to relax, everything was under control.

Once I'd got him to bed, he'd slept for a while, but his dreams were disturbing. I wondered if he was reliving the crash. He muttered incoherently and his arm tightened around me, but he didn't wake up. He wouldn't let me go even in his sleep and so I was on tenterhooks until he finally slept peacefully.

As the sun rose and shone into the bedroom, it woke me up. Max was still sleeping so I just lay there staring at him, circling my fingers over his M.F. tattoo. I could gaze at his handsome face all day. To think I could have lost him, physically hurts. I couldn't bear to live without him. I crave him. I need him. *There is no me without you.*

"Didn't anyone ever tell you it's rude to stare?" he says, still with his eyes closed. He tightens his arm around me and takes in a deep breath, wincing at the pain, and then he releases a long painful but contented sigh.

"How did you know I was staring at you?" I ask, smirking.

His lips tip up at the corners and he opens a sleepy eye. "You were, weren't you?"

I shake my head and gently lean over to kiss him softly on the lips. "How do you feel?"

He opens both eyes and gazes up at me. The love pouring out of them stirs my butterflies. "Always better with you in my arms," he smiles, trying to raise his left arm, but the pain stops him.

"Max, you can't go tonight, you need to rest and recover."

"I'm fine. I promise. Besides, we can't let them down." He strokes my behind with his hand, and I can feel his erection growing under my thigh.

I shake my head at him and raise an eyebrow. "Breakfast first, Mr. Foxx. You haven't eaten for over twenty four hours. Then maybe we'll see about taking care of all your other requirements."

A cheeky grin spreads across his lips. "Yes, Ma'am."

Today is the Gala Charity Ball, which Max insists on attending in spite of all our protests to the contrary. His cuts and bruises to his hands and face are all fairly minor, but the broken ribs and the cut to his left shoulder are causing him a lot of pain. Every movement makes him wince. Even breathing deeply causes him pain.

While I rustle up some breakfast, I call Jan to find out how Vinnie is, then I call Doctor Alexander to ask him to visit, just to be sure.

Doctor Alexander arrives as Max finishes his breakfast. He gives him a thorough examination and prescribes rest, an ice pack to help reduce the swelling, and some painkillers. While the doctor visits, I scoot into the bathroom to take a shower. My stomach feels queasy again, but I guess it's all the stress of the last two days.

Once Doctor Alexander leaves, I prop Max up on some pillows, and then I sit next to him sipping my tea.

"I thought you only drank coffee in the mornings," he says, eyeing my cup.

"No, I've gone off coffee." Even the smell of it makes me feel ill. He tries to move his tray off the bed, but he struggles with the pain. "Here, let me do that. You shouldn't be lifting anything until your ribs heal." I get up and move the tray to the bedside table. He grabs the belt on my robe and pulls me toward him making me squeal. I almost fall on top of him. "Max, be careful."

"Baby, I've missed you," he sighs, untying my belt with one hand and opening my robe. His gaze trawls lazily up and down my bare flesh, caressing my skin with his eyes almost as if they were soft fingers. I can see his erection under the sheet. The plane crash certainly doesn't seem to have dented his libido. He runs his warm fingers over my stomach and down my hip, the tingling sensation fuels my need to touch him. I shrug out of the robe and let it fall to the floor as my eyes take in his gorgeous body. His eyes are trained on me, slowly making their way all over my nakedness. I want to pounce on him and kiss him everywhere, but I know I'm going to have to be gentle. I move away from him and watch his face as his expression alters.

"Where are you going?"

I walk to the end of the bed and kneel down between his feet. "To the parts that don't appear to be sore." I say, waggling my eyebrows. His face erupts into a big smile, and his cock pulses under the sheet.

"But I want to touch you." He reaches forward but his ribs put a stop to that and he sinks back into the pillows on a painful sigh.

"Just do as you're told and lie back. Let me take care of you," I whisper, crawling up the bed. I pull the sheet back and kneel on top of it, then I run my hands up his powerful thighs. I watch his face as I bend to kiss him on his hip, then his belly, and then over to his other hip. His eyes close as his head falls back to the pillow and he groans a soft noise of approval from deep in his chest. I can see his abdominals bunching. "Just relax." I whisper, trailing soft kisses all over them. His cock pulses and knocks against my breasts.

Very carefully, I crawl up and kiss his chest, his neck and throat, then as he opens his eyes, I kiss him on the lips. Our tongues meet and gently glide over each other, then I pull back and kiss him lightly on the cuts over his eyebrow, cheek, and nose. He tries to wrap his arm around me. "Ah, ah, ah. Just relax and let me take care of you," I whisper. He watches me with focused, hooded eyes as I make my tricky but careful path back down his body. I gently kiss the big black bruise over his ribs, and then I make my way back down to his thighs. Kneeling between them, I wrap my hand around his pulsing shaft and begin.

"I warn you baby, it won't take me long," he sighs, rolling his hips as I pump his cock with a tight grip. "You turn me on like crazy and I've been away from you for too long." He moans, absorbing the sensations. As I lower myself and take him in my mouth, I feel his thighs stiffen, and I hear his sexy groans of pleasure. "Oh, baby. That's so good," he moans softly.

I love the feel of him in my mouth. His taste is arousing, it's sexy and powerful and it turns me on. I feel the head of his cock expand and I know I won't have time to relieve my own pressure so I watch his face, drinking in his handsomeness and revelling in the powerful effect I have on him. I love to see him enjoying the moment when I tip him over the edge and he comes with loud, jerking movements as his hot spurts hit my tongue.

I swallow and kiss the tip of his still jerking cock, then I let it rest against his belly. His chest rises and falls in short shallow breaths, and the frown line in his brow indicates the pain he's feeling in his ribs.

"Baby, I'm sorry. I couldn't stop it, it felt so good," he says opening his eyes.

I smile and crawl up over his waist. "Don't be. That was sexy as hell. You're sexy. I love having control over you." I bend down to kiss his tattoo. He smiles up at me with that dazzling, seductive smile of his, and his eyes tell me everything.

Suddenly, my stomach rolls and I feel hot and nauseas. I can't stay here. I'm going to throw up any minute, but that could really put a downer on what just happened. I kiss him chastely on the chest and scoot off the bed.

"I'm just going to take another shower, I'll be back in a minute." I know my voice sounded convincing, but the speed I left the bedroom wasn't cool.

I shut the door and run the taps and the shower, to hide the sound of my imminent retching. *What the hell's wrong with me?* I've never reacted like that before.

Luckily having not eaten breakfast, nothing happens, and as the nausea passes I take a shower and wash my hair. Once I'm dressed, I help Max into some comfortable clothes and then I walk him down to the living room.

When he's comfortable on the sofa, I notice a pile of mail sitting on the hall table so I grab it and take it over to him. He opens every envelope except a large brown one, which he puts at the bottom of the pile.

That's it. That's the one. "Are you not going to open that one?" I ask, watching his face for his reaction. He doesn't give anything away.

"No, that's for Trencher," he says, nonchalantly.

"Really? But it's got your name on it." I wait for something to show on his face, a wary look, excessive blinking, anything. But his poker face is still firmly in play.

"Yeah, but it's for Trencher to handle. I'll send it down to Grace later."

"I can take it if you like? I'm going to Lucy's salon to get my hair done, I'll drop it in to Grace on my way."

Bingo! The small flicker of uncertainty in his eyes tells me I've hit the jackpot.

"...Okay," he says, hesitantly.

I put all his mail in the study, and I leave the brown envelope on the hall table to take with me. Obviously, I'm going to read it before I give it to Grace. I want to know what's going on, and if he's not going to tell me, then I'll find out for myself.

I notice Max is reading a report from the crash investigation team.

"So, what actually went wrong with the plane?" I ask, handing him some painkillers and snuggling in beside him on the sofa. He winces when he moves his good arm around my shoulders. Every movement seems to cause him pain.

"I don't know," he sighs. "The on board computer just died so we had to go to manual, but there was something wrong with the rudder. They're checking it out now," he says, resting his head back.

"Is that something that just happens, or could it have been tampered with?"

He lifts his head and looks at me like I've just asked the million dollar question. "I don't know. It shouldn't… But we'd better get it fixed before we start rolling them out next year."

"And what about your lawyer and the problems you've had at work?"

His eyebrow lifts into an irritated arch. "He got what he deserved. And as for the hackers? Luckily, they only got into the surface layer, they didn't get into the client database or deeper, but it was a wake up call."

I take a breath then I ask him, in a roundabout way, about the letter he's been hiding from me. "Is there anything else troubling you that you haven't told me?"

His brow lowers into a frown. "Like what?"

"Like the yellow letter you were reading in your study the other day? I know it worried you, I could see by your face."

He closes his eyes and rests his head back again. "Baby, that was just someone trying to piss me off. It happens in business all the time," he sighs. "It's nothing for you to worry about."

There it is again. The glib remark. The brush off. I can

tell he's not going to give me any further explanation. It's annoying that he won't tell me, but I'll find out one way or another.

I head upstairs to change and get ready to go to Lucy's salon for my hair appointment. I want to look glamorous for tonight's gala ball. I'm excited, but also really nervous. I've photographed plenty red carpet events but I've never actually walked down one myself.

"I'm off now." I bend down to kiss him goodbye. "I'll be back in an hour. Do you need anything before I go?"

He pulls me down for another kiss. "You. Hurry back." I gaze into his scorching eyes and hesitate. I find it hard to drag myself away from his mesmerising eyes, especially when he looks at me like that. "Go! You're turning me on," he smiles, puffing out a long sigh.

I walk to the door. "Max? Where's the letter for Grace?" It's no longer on the hall table.

"I got John to take it down for me," he says without looking up.

If I was suspicious about it before, I'm convinced about it now. He knew I'd read it. I leave the penthouse even more determined to get to the bottom of those bloody letters.

ONCE IN A LIFETIME LOVE

Lucy has done a fabulous job with my hair, and while Maggie is giving me rich, red lips and smoky eyes, Lucy paints my nails. I look amazing and I haven't even got my sexy new dress on yet.

When I get back to F1, Max is upstairs struggling to dry himself after his shower. I take the towel from him and dry him off, carefully avoiding his ribs and wounds. "Are you sure you're going to be okay tonight? I'm sure they'd understand if we cancel," I say, walking him over to the basin.

"I'm fine." He winces, gritting his teeth together as he reaches into the cupboard to pick up his shaving kit.

I drag the chaise long over to the sink. "Sit. I'll shave you. You'll end up cutting an ear off." He smiles, and slowly lowers himself uncomfortably to the chair.

As I lather up his chin, he stares up at me smirking. "You like bossing me around, don't you?"

"Pff, this might be the only chance I get for you to do as you're told," I smirk back. "Now sit still these are new blades, I don't want to cut you by accident." I tentatively start to shave him.

"You look gorgeous. I like your hair like that," he murmurs, skimming the back of my thigh with his hand. I try not to let him distract me, but it's difficult. He's sitting naked on the chaise, his scent is wafting into my nose, and I can feel his eyes burning into me. "I can't wait to marry you, Miss Banks." His velvety rasp makes me pause. I stop what I'm doing but I avoid looking into his eyes, staring into those hypnotic blues is fatal. His cheeks expand on a big grin and his hand moves up to my behind, caressing and squeezing.

"Mr. Foxx, if you don't hold still, I won't be responsible for the little bits of tissue paper you're going to have to wear on your chin tonight." He chuckles, then he takes a deep painful breath and closes his eyes. I try to ignore the butterflies and my desire to kiss him, and continue to shave him.

"I can't wait to see you in that dress," he whispers, opening an eye. I stop and give him the eyebrow, trying not to smirk. "Sorry," he smirks, "but you're very distracting," he murmurs. I give him the eyebrow again. "Okay, okay, I'll behave," he chuckles.

He lets me finish and wipe off the excess soap, and then I help him into the bedroom, sitting him on the edge of the bed. Once I've helped him into his tux and tied his bow tie, I start to get myself dressed. I can feel his eyes on me as I put on my new red lingerie and stockings.

"You do realise I'm going to be thinking about those all night," he says, in a velvety rasp. I smile and put on my pretty new shoes, the one's I'd said no to, but Davis had sent them anyway. Then I pull my new red gown from the hanger. As I step into it and pull it up, it feels so luxurious against my skin. Standing back to get the full effect in the long mirror, I almost gasp when I see myself. I look incredible. I feel so elegant and sexy.

"You look stunning," Max says, walking up behind me. He trails his fingers down my exposed skin, then he wraps his good arm around my waist and nibbles my neck and earlobe. "You make me so happy." I turn around to face him, he looks so handsome in his tux, and the look in his eyes melts my heart and stirs my butterflies. "Tell me," he whispers, searching my eyes. I reach up to smooth his cheek, then I rise onto my toes to kiss him tenderly.

"I love you," I whisper against his lips.

"I love you, more," he whispers back. His fingers trail down my exposed skin, right down to the V-shape at my lower back. It sends delicious tingles up my spine and a low thud in my sex. I breathe in his scent and lower back down to my heels.

"We'd better go, or we may never make it out of this bedroom," I sigh, reluctant to move.

He hits me with his bone-melting smile. "I'm good with that."

As we near the drop zone, I start to fidget. Max squeezes my hand until I look over at him. "Don't worry, baby. I won't let you go," he says, with a wink. "Just smile for the cameras and stay on my left, you can help protect me from any stray elbows," he smirks.

I tremble as we exit the car. The noise from the press is deafening. They're all shouting at Max to look their way. It feels weird being on this side of the barrier. They're shouting for information on what happened in the plane crash. I also hear some of them shouting out 'who's your new squeeze?'

Max holds my hand in a tight grip and keeps me close to his side, his bruised side. He stops right in front of the bank of photographers. "You look beautiful, just relax and enjoy it," he says, smiling down at me, then he bends to kiss me on the lips. It's a long, hot, lingering kiss and the press go wild. All my nerves evaporate, like he's just sucked them all out of me. He's just shown the world's press that I'm special to him, and it feels amazing.

After a few moments, we move along the line, stopping again to be photographed. Every journalist is trying to get Max to talk to them but he doesn't, he just smiles his mega-watt smile and gazes down at me every now and again to reassure me. Once we're in the main hall, Max introduces me to a few people. His left hand is firmly nestled on the exposed skin of my lower back as he walks me through the crowd.

"Max!"

A tall, pretty woman walks up to us, her eyes give me the once over before settling back on Max. "I didn't think you'd make it after your accident. How are you?" she asks, kissing him on both cheeks.

"I'm fine. Vivienne, this is Chloe, she's one of the organisers for tonight."

Another ex-girlfriend? I can see by her expression that I'm a bit of a surprise to her. She smiles, but it doesn't reach her eyes which are still surveying my dress. Before she has time to say anything else, Max excuses us and moves me on toward the bar. As we move through the room, I notice we're getting a lot of attention. Everyone is staring at us, then whispering to each other as we pass. Max nods hello to some of them, and stops to introduce me to others, until we finally end up at the bar. I feel like a fish out of water and the water's full of sharks.

Max hands me a glass of Champagne, but after one sip I decide to leave it on the bar and I order a glass of water instead. I just don't feel like drinking tonight. As Max is busy talking to an associate, I glance around the room, wondering how many of these beautiful women Max has dated in the past. I should imagine I'm public enemy number one right now.

"Vivienne. I didn't expect to see you here."

I'm sure you didn't. I paste on a fake smile. "Fiona. Hi. I can assure you, I was invited." I see her eyes slide down to Max's hand which is holding mine. She laughs and flicks her hair.

"No, I meant after Max's crash, I didn't expect either of you to attend. It sounded dreadful." Her eyes travel down my gown, then back up to my face. "You look stunning. That dress looks lovely on you."

If I didn't suspect her of having designs on my boyfriend, I could mistake that for a genuine remark. "Thanks. Are you here with anyone?" I ask, hoping for the best.

"No," she laughs, flicking her hair again. "I'm free and single."

Damn.

I find it hard to make small talk with her, she seems on edge around me which I find quite amusing, but her eyes keep swinging down to our interlocked hands, with any luck it's pissing her off. Max is still busy talking to his associate, so much to my delight Fiona makes her excuses and moves on.

"Man, that fella can talk," Max sighs, smiling down at me. "That's the trouble with these things, you have to talk to people you wouldn't normally spend time with."

Yeah, I know what you mean. It seems like every five minutes someone else interrupts us, but I love to watch Max, he's so confident and self-assured. Everyone likes him, and of course, all the women love him. He's never let go of my hand once, and he's introduced me to everyone. I've lost count of the amount of women who have blatantly batted their lashes at him tonight, but I've had my fair share of male admirers too. This dress is definitely drawing some attention. Every time a man compliments me, Max pulls me a little bit closer, it's very sweet.

We take our seats for dinner and luckily, Grace and her husband are on our table. Max struggles to use his left arm because of his ribs and shoulder injuries, so I help to cut his meat while he rests his hand on my thigh, the slit in my gown giving him full access to my stocking tops. Once dinner is over, I make my excuses to visit the ladies room. It's empty when I walk in, so after I've checked my hair and makeup, I pop into one of the cubicles. I hear the door open and several giggling voices enter the room.

"Who is she anyway? I heard she's only after him for his money."

"He won't stay with her, apparently her oven's bun-less. No future heirs to the Foxx Empire."

"Really? He seems pretty keen on her though, he hasn't

let go of her since they arrived. Did you see them walking in together?"

"It's all for show. He just wants the publicity."

"He is gorgeous though."

"Yeah, I wouldn't say no. I'll bet he's great in bed."

I feel trapped. Their snide comments and laughter at my expense, make me feel like shit. *Oh, fuck it! I'm fed up with this.* I open the door and look them all in the eye one at a time, then I push past one of them to get to the hand basin. The room immediately goes silent as I wash then dry my hands. Their blushes please me as I turn to face them at the door. "You're right about one thing, ladies," I smirk. "He is great in bed." I smile at their stunned faces, then I leave them to digest that little nugget.

My bravado has chickened out by the time I make it back to the main hall. I suspect every woman in this room is thinking the same as those spiteful girls in the ladies room. *Ladies room? Pff. Bitches room. They don't even know me.*

Max isn't at the table when I return. Only one couple is still sitting there, everyone else is either dancing or standing at the bar. I reach for the bottle of wine and pour myself a glass, I need one after that. Max takes the seat beside me and reaches for my hand.

"What's the matter, baby? You look upset," he asks, resting his hand on my thigh, and giving it a squeeze. I take a drink and look him squarely in the eyes.

"I've just met some of your fan club in the ladies room. It turns out they don't think much of me," I huff. He smiles and leans forward for a kiss, wincing at the pain in his ribs.

"Baby, they're just jealous because you're the most beautiful woman in the room." I'm just about to protest against that remark, when a man walks up behind me. Max looks up above my head and smiles up at him. "Greg." Standing up, Max reaches out to shake his hand as I turn to face whoever it is. There's something very familiar about him, but I've met so many people tonight. He's tall, stocky, and well dressed, and he has a faint white scar across the bridge of his nose. His familiar eyes swing down to mine as Max introduces me.

"Greg, this is Vivienne, my fiancé. Vivienne, this is Greg Taylor, Parker's friend and one of my new clients."

Why is that name so familiar? I reach up to shake his hand. He smiles and bends down to kiss the back of it.

"Lovely to meet you, Vivienne. You're so pretty, like a little doll."

WHAT? I blink up at him, feeling hot and cold all at once. Slowly pulling my hand away, my stomach rolls and goosebumps crawl over my flesh. His eyes return to Max as they talk business, but suddenly I can't hear a thing, and I can't tear my eyes away from his face. The face I hoped I'd never see again.

He doesn't recognise me, he's completely oblivious, and I'm grateful for that. Here he stands in his expensive suit, the facade of a wealthy businessman covering the soul of the rapist within. After all this time, all the pain and the heartache this bastard has caused me, he's here shaking hands with Max. I had hoped that I'd never have the misfortune to see him again. As I stare up at the man who raped me as a child, I feel physically sick. Standing abruptly, I grab my bag and leave the table. Pushing through the crowd, I make my way to the ladies room.

I'm relieved to find it empty and I burst into one of the cubicles just in time. When I'm sure there's nothing left to evacuate, I pull the lid down and sit for a while to compose myself.

How can I tell Max? He'll kill him. *And what about Vinnie?* There's no way he could've known his friend's vile history. He'd probably want to kill him too. *I want to kill him!*

My hands shake with adrenaline and my heart is racing in my chest. I know it's only a matter of time before someone else comes in to the ladies room so I take some deep calming breaths and grab some tissue paper.

Rinsing my mouth out, I open my bag to get some mints

and find my lipstick. Once I've blotted the tears from my cheeks and repaired my makeup, I stare into the mirror. "Come on, Viv. Don't let him win." I lift my chin and straighten my back, then I make my way back to the function room.

Before entering the main hall, I take a look around the room for Greg, but I don't see him anywhere. The sense of relief does little to stop my belly from churning as I release the breath I was anxiously holding. My hands are still shaking, and as I approach our table I see Fiona handing something to Max, he slips whatever it is into his pocket, then they laugh. I almost stop and turn around, but I've had it up to my eyeballs with the Monica's, Greg's, and Fiona's of this world. It's about time I stood up for myself. They can all fuck off.

When I take my seat at our table, Max places his hand on my thigh. "Everything okay?" he asks with concern. I smile and take his face in my hands, then I lean in and kiss him on the lips. I love kissing him, but my aim is to piss Fiona off. When I glance over at her, she definitely looks uncomfortable. "Perfect," I smile.

Fiona leaves us alone, then Max informs me that he'll be back in a minute, kisses me, and leaves the table. My head is on a swivel looking for Greg. I don't know what I'd do if I saw him again, but thankfully he's nowhere to be seen.

"Can I have this dance, Miss Banks?"

I look up at the young man. "Er, sorry, two left feet."

He laughs. "That's great. I've got two right ones, we can make a set." He reaches down for my hand.

"Oh, no, really, I'm not much of a dancer," I mumble, resisting his attempt to pull me from my seat.

"Oh, come on, it's just a dance, it's not like we're entering the final of Strictly Come Dancing," he smiles, persistently tugging on my hand.

"The lady said no!" I turn around to see Max scowling at the young man, who apologises, smiles, and backs away with his hands up. "I leave you for five minutes," he grumbles, watching the man walk away. Max reaches down for my hand and pulls me to my feet. His scorching eyes blaze down at me with love and possession oozing out of them. Kissing me tenderly on the lips, he takes my hand and pulls me to the dance floor. Leaving me standing in the middle, he walks to the stage and talks to the DJ.

I start to panic, Max doesn't know what a crap dancer I am. I glance around at all the people staring at me. Suddenly, the dance floor becomes static as the music stops and I hear Max's voice on the microphone.

"I'm sorry to interrupt the proceedings ladies and gentlemen, but I have a very special announcement to make, if you'll just bear with me." He hands the microphone back to the DJ, then he walks toward me, his scorching eyes never leaving mine. The room is now silent, all eyes on us. As he stands before me, smiling that bone-melting smile and looking into my soul with burning pools of love, he tilts my world off its axis when he leans in and speaks in a soft voice for my ears only. "I was going to wait until we were in a nice romantic location, just the two of us, but I can't watch anymore men thinking they have a chance with you. You're mine, Vivienne. All mine, and I want the world to know it."

He steps back and throws me his heart-stopping smile. Blinking up at him in a daze, I watch him take a small red object from his pocket, and then he sinks to one knee. As he opens the small, red velvet box, my heart flutters and an audible gasp resonates around the room. *Oh, my God!* I see him stifling a wince as his ribs protest when he holds the ring forward and delivers his speech, never removing his eyes from mine.

"I vow to fiercely love you, for every moment of every day, until forever. I promise I'll do whatever it takes to make you always look at me with the love you have in your eyes right now. I'm yours, baby... Heart, mind, body and soul. And you, Vivienne. You are my once in a lifetime love, my crazy-good love. Forever with you will never be long enough. Will you do me the extraordinary honour of being mine forever… Marry me?"

Suddenly, the only two people in the room are Max and I. There's not a sound, not a movement, and I couldn't feel more loved than I do right now. His eyes burn into mine with heartfelt emotion as I choke back the lump in my throat, and let the tears roll down my cheeks. Reaching out with both hands, I gently hold his handsome face between my palms, then I slowly sink to my knees in front of him. His eyes follow mine and flicker with trepidation for just a moment, until I finally have the voice to speak.

"Yes… With all my heart, and forever, yes."

His eyes blaze with love then he folds me in his arms and crushes his lips to mine. The whole room erupts around us. Breaking the kiss, he leans his forehead against mine. "You had me worried there for a minute," he whispers. I tearfully laugh and shake my head, then I kiss him tenderly on the lips.

"I love you, Max. So much. You make me so happy."

He pulls back and places the enormous diamond engagement ring on my finger, his smile stretching out across his handsome face. "This is it, baby. You're mine. You're stuck with me now," he smirks.

I smile and reach up to trace my fingers down his flawless cheek, gazing into his scorching blue eyes. "Until forever."

We're helped to our feet by well-wishers and then Max nods up to the DJ. Nathan Sykes' 'Over And Over Again' begins to play, and we dance gazing into each other's eyes, oblivious to anyone else around us. The lyrics are perfect.

"I can't believe you went down on one knee, in front of all these people. It's very romantic," I sigh, as a tear drips off my lower lashes and rolls down my cheek. "Your poor ribs, that must have hurt like hell."

He just smiles his heart-stopping smile, then he leans his forehead against mine tightening his arms around me. "It would have if you'd said no."

BITTERSWEET

Since Max proposed to me, the last eleven weeks have been incredible and chaotic. The press went wild the next morning after the charity ball. The story of our engagement ran in all the papers, and video of Max's proposal went viral on the Internet. Someone had leaked the story to the press. It could only have come from someone attending the event, and all the reports were from 'a source close to the couple.'

My money's on Fiona. I'm sure she'd love to see me buckle under the pressure, but with Max, Vinnie, and John's help, I've managed to handle the press with dignity and a certain amount of distance. I should be grateful to her really. It's done wonders for my business profile. The increase in demand has made it possible for me to pay off my debt to Max, and my company's finally in profit. Happy days.

The night of our engagement was bitter sweet. The bitter side, which still plays on my mind, was coming face to face with Greg Taylor again. That came as a massive shock. I've had many sleepless nights since then. I thought I'd come to terms with what he'd done to me, but seeing him again stirred all the long hidden memories, bringing all the fear and pain back into focus. Part of me wanted to expose him for the child molesting rapist he's hidden so well, but if Max knew what he'd done to me as a child, if he knew his new client had anything to do with me not being able to give him children, I know he'd kill him, and I'm not prepared to lose Max over a man I loathe and despise. I've survived this long without seeking revenge, it would be futile to drag up the past now.

And Vinnie? He treats me like I'm family. How can I tell him that his old friend and the man he's brought back into our lives, was once capable of such a heinous act. No, some burdens must never be shared. Some skeletons need to remain buried deep in the past. To unleash this one could destroy all our lives.

Once the news of our engagement was out, I was touched by the amount of love and best wishes we'd received. I even got an email from Frank. I thought he was going to tell me off for not allowing him to have the exclusive on our engagement, but to my surprise he just wanted to send me his congratulations, and he wished us both every happiness.

Of course, I wanted to tell my mum the good news too. It's funny, our strained relationship isn't the traditional mother, daughter variety, but I still wanted her to know I was getting married in the hope that it may bring us closer together.

The day I'd called her, she was a little worse for wear. I couldn't understand her words, they just slurred into each other. I don't even know if she'd understood what I'd told her.

I couldn't have been happier when Max presented me with a beautiful diamond engagement ring, but more importantly, he'd given me his heart, completely and unconditionally. I'll cherish that, and him, for the rest of my life. How could I be so lucky? To love, and be loved by this incredible man.

TAKE IT EASY ON THE WOO-HOO!

With only two weeks until Lucy and Dan's wedding there's much to do. Max and I have been working all hours to free up some time so we can spend a couple of weeks in France after the wedding. Max's yacht manager Sasha and I, have been talking almost daily finalising the details, and today Lucy and I are off to the bridal shop to have our last fitting.

On my way to meet Lucy, Sasha calls. "Vivienne. I'm sorry to call you again but I've got a little problem."

"What is it?" I ask, hoping it's nothing drastic.

"Four of the waiting staff have cancelled," she huffs. "They didn't have the right work visas or something."

"Do we really need them?"

"You do if you want your guests to be fed and watered." I can hear the panic in her voice.

"Can't the agency just replace them?"

"No. They've tried to draft in more staff from their northern branch, but it's such a busy time of the year for functions, they don't have anyone free for that date."

"Can't you advertise locally?"

"Actually, two men approached me looking for work a few days ago. Four would be ideal, but we can manage with just two more. I've still got their numbers, shall I call them for an interview?"

As I approach the shop, I see Lucy waiting for me at the

door. I don't want her to know there's anything wrong so I slow down. "Yes. If you think they're suitable, just hire them." I end the call and relax my worried frown before meeting Lucy.

We chat and giggle with Linda our dressmaker as she and her assistant help us into our dresses. My laughter soon fades when I realise Linda is struggling to do my zip up.

"Oh, dear," she says, huffing and puffing.

"What do you mean, 'oh dear'."

"You've put weight on. This zip is never going to close," she says, looking at me through the mirror.

I stare down at myself in a panic. "But it has to." I try to breathe in, sucking my stomach in, but she just shakes her head.

"I can let it out an inch, maybe two, but that's all," she says, shrugging.

Oh, no! I know I was very skinny the last time we came for a fitting, but I hadn't realised I'd put that much weight on.

"I'll let it out as much as I can, but if you could lose a few pounds before the wedding, that would help," Linda says, helping me out of the dress, but she didn't sound very convinced.

"What's the matter?" Lucy asks, poking her head around my door.

"I've put weight on, I'm too bloody fat for the dress."

Lucy looks nervous for a moment, then she tries to make me feel better. "Don't worry, I'm sure it'll fit once Linda's let it out a bit." She smiles, but I can see the worry and disappointment in her eyes. How could I have let myself balloon before her wedding? It's my responsibility to be her bridesmaid, I can't let her down, or myself for that matter. I'm going to have to take drastic action to get rid of this weight.

"Don't worry, Luce, I'll get back to the gym and I'll start running again. I'll get that dress on if it kills me." She laughs and gives me a strange look. "What?" I ask, putting my clothes back on.

"Nothing…" She disappears, and once I'm fully clothed I follow her.

As I see her standing in her full bridal gown, my eyes begin to water. She looks stunning. "Oh, Luce. You look beautiful. Dan's going to be so proud."

She faces me with glowing cheeks and glistening eyes. "It's perfect," she whispers.

After my very disappointing fitting, I skip lunch with Lucy and I decide to go straight home and get changed for a run on the treadmill. I knew my clothes were starting to feel tighter, but I hadn't really paid much attention to my weight, and I've been eating for England since our engagement. Blissful contentment and way too many business lunches have certainly taken their toll. I run upstairs, ignoring the delicious smells coming from the kitchen. Jan calls out after me but I don't stop and talk to her, she'll only offer me something to eat and I know I'll eat it. I've always had a good appetite, but now I'm on a mission. I must stay focused.

I quickly change into my running gear and head to Max's gym. After less than a mile, I'm exhausted. I haven't run for ages. My lungs are burning, the sweat is dripping off of me, and my cheeks are bright red. It's not a good look. I try the bike for a while, but my muscles are screaming out so I abandon the gym and head for the shower.

Dragging my aching body downstairs, I collapse onto the sofa.

"Vivienne, are you okay?" Jan asks. She's got her coat on and is ready to leave.

"Yeah, just really unfit. I've turned into a human blimp."

"Hardly," she smiles. "You've got a lovely figure." Her kind words are very nice, but if I can't get my bridesmaid's dress on in two weeks, I'll be letting Lucy down. I can't do that. "Vincent's taking me out to buy a hat for the wedding. It's so exciting, isn't it?" she grins walking to the front door. "Oh, and Mr. Foxx said he won't be home until after seven. See you tonight."

"Bye, Jan." I haven't even got the energy to wave.

After a while, I drag my aching limbs out of the sofa and walk to the study to check my emails. My phone rings. "Hey, Luce. I promise, I haven't eaten a thing and I've started running again too. I won't let you down." I feel terrible.

"Viv, don't worry about it," she laughs. "The reason I called is because I just wondered if you'd heard from Mike. He's gone missing. No one's seen him at the rugby club and Dan hasn't heard from him in ages. He was going to invite him to his stag-do, but he's not answering his phone."

"Really? The last time I spoke to him was the day Max's plane went down. He called to offer his help, but I haven't heard from him since."

"Okay, I just wondered that was all. Anyway, I'll see you tonight at the hen party."

"Yeah, looking forward to it." *Crap. More food and drink to avoid.*

"It's my own stupid fault," I mutter, standing in my dressing room trying on various dresses and skirts that are now straining at the seams. "How could I have let myself go like this?" I grumble, staring into the mirror. I still have a good shape but my boobs and belly have definitely expanded. I settle on the short purple dress for tonight, it's the only one that doesn't feel too tight.

Once I've finished styling my hair, and applied the finishing touches to my makeup, I grab the bag with all the hen party stuff, and check I've got everything I need. "Camera, L-plates, plastic willies, headbands, sashes." I take one last look in the mirror, then I head downstairs. I won't see Max before I go out, so I quickly send him a text;

```
I'm off to Lucy's Hen party.
Woo-Hoo!
No idea what time I'll be home.
```

It could be a late one.
Enjoy yourself at Dan's Stag
(not too much!)
And don't let them do anything
too embarrassing to him.
Love you
Xx:-)

His reply is almost instantaneous;

Hey, beautiful.
Don't worry I'll take care of him.
John will wait for you outside the
club to bring you home when
you're ready.
Enjoy yourself, but be careful.
Take it easy on the Woo-Hoo!
Love you more.
X;-)

I smile at his text, he's always so protective. I'd already made my mind up that I won't be drinking tonight. I can't afford the extra calories if I'm to get that bloody dress on. Lucy won't like it, but it's important to me that everything goes perfectly on her wedding day, and if that means I have to drink water all night, then so be it. *Water? Eeuuww.*

John is waiting for me downstairs. He drives me to Lucy's house, where I dress her in the L-plates, a sash that reads; 'Bride-to-be Hen Party! - Please don't judge me until I've had the chance to sober up,' and a short, white veil. She looks great, and has already started on the wine.

"I can't believe I'm getting married in two weeks. And I wouldn't be having such a wonderful wedding day without you and Max giving us such a wonderful wedding gift. I love you, Viv. You're my bestest mate in the whole wide world." She lurches forward and hugs me tightly. I can hear her sniffling in my ear.

"Now come on, Luce. I won't have any tears on your hen night. That's just not going to happen. Tonight we're going to have fun and laughter all the way."

"Yeah, we are," she giggles, tearfully.

John drives us to the pub to meet the other girls. I

cleverly took on the responsibility of holding the kitty and ordering the drinks. That means I can order myself an apple juice in a wine glass so that Lucy thinks I'm drinking.

After everyone has arrived and had a couple of drinks at the bar, we move on to the Lexus club at the Hexagon. It's not quite as plush as the Velvet Lounge, but it doesn't require a small loan to buy the drinks here and the music is great. I'm still on the apple juice and hating every mouthful, but I know if I start drinking, I'll keep drinking. Besides, I haven't eaten today and if I get drunk I'll want to raid the fridge when I get home.

After an hour or so of dancing and laughter, we're still on the dance floor when the DJ pulls the music down and makes an announcement.

Good, they're here. I'd already cleared it with the manager for us to have some male strippers perform for Lucy's hen night. The club has set up a make shift stage area, which is blacked out. I turn Lucy to face it.

"What's going on?"

"You'll see," I giggle.

"In case you hadn't noticed, we've got a hen party in the house tonight," the DJ says, over the Mic. We all cheer and whistle as Lucy jumps up and down giggling. "Your friends have organised a little treat for you tonight, Lucy, and I'm sure all the women in the house will be delighted. For one night only, please give it up and make some noise, for the 'Six-Pack Sexpots.'

The music begins, the lights flash, and smoke fills the stage, then five hot, bare chested men slink out, causing the women to go wild. It's like a scene from 'Magic Mike.'

"Oh, my God. Thank you!" Lucy grins, squealing in delight.

"You're welcome," I grin back.

With their ripped bodies and good looks, they're very easy on the eye, but they're not a patch on my man. I suddenly wish he was here. I haven't seen him since very early this morning and I'm getting withdrawal symptoms.

As Lucy and the rest of the girls huddle to the front of the stage, I walk off the dance floor to go and find Jan. Maybe you have to be drunk to fully appreciate watching male strippers at work.

"Not your thing?" I ask, when I find Jan sitting alone at our table. She smiles with a glint in her eye.

"Oh, I wouldn't say that," she grins. "But I'm old enough to be their mother."

I glance over my shoulder. "Well, Lucy's mum doesn't seem to worry about that too much," I giggle, watching her salacious grin as one of the half-naked guys cavorts in front of her.

"Are you not drinking?" Jan asks.

"Oh, ah, no. I'm on a strict diet for Lucy's wedding," I sigh, trying to ignore my growling stomach. I'm starving.

"Oh, yes," she smiles. "I'm so looking forward to that. I bought a lovely hat today."

"Yes, it's exciting, isn't it?"

"Have you and Mr. Foxx made any plans for your wedding yet?"

"Not really. Apart from my mum, I haven't got any family so there's not much to organise."

"Oh, that's a shame. Still, Vincent and I couldn't be happier for you. You make such a wonderful couple, you're just perfect for each other, and Mr. Foxx…well, I've never seen him this happy."

I feel so close to this woman, she's been like a mum to me. I lean over and give her a big hug, then she tells me all about her outfit for Lucy's wedding.

"Euww. What's this?" I turn to see Lucy drinking my juice. She screws her face up when she realises it's not alcohol. "This wine's off," she slurs. I pour her another glass of wine and hand it to her.

"Here you are, you big lush." She smiles and swipes it out of my hand.

"Viv, those guys were great! I think my mum's in love with one of them," she giggles, plonking herself down in the chair.

As everyone filters back to the table, some bright spark yells, “Shots! We need Tequila!” I check that we still have enough money in the kitty, and then I head off to the bar. The barman lines up some glasses and a bottle of Tequila on a tray. I’m not sure how to get out of drinking one of these, especially now everyone else is pissed. Once Lucy realises I’m still sober she’ll make a big fuss about it and insist I drink. *That’s my diet out the bloody window!*

I line up the shot glasses and pour the Tequila. Jan declines so I leave her out. The others all lean in to grab a glass.

“You haven’t poured one for yourself,” Lucy’s mum says, loud enough that everyone stops and looks at me, making me blush.

“Oh, ah, no, I’m not keen on Tequila,” I say, wishing they’d all stop staring at me like I’m some kind of freak.

“Since when?”

“No, mum,” Lucy says, interrupting her mother, “if she doesn’t want one, she doesn’t have to have one. Right! Bottoms up girls,” she slurs, before tipping her head back and swallowing the shot. I’m gob-smacked. I thought Lucy would’ve made a big deal out of me not drinking, but maybe she’s as keen for me to fit into the dress as I am.

It’s strange, I’ve spent many nights on the razzle getting pissed with Lucy, but tonight, as the night has worn on and the alcohol has been consumed by the bucket-load, I’m seeing for the first time what the effects of it are. No one has made any sense for the last half an hour. Drunk people laugh at the most ridiculous things, and repeat themselves over and over again.

Lucy’s mum decided to drag some of the girls back to the dance floor. How she made it there I’ll never know, her legs certainly didn’t look like they were working as a team. The rest of the girls are slumped on the sofas and chairs, trying to focus on each other, and Lucy is already nodding off.

Jan looks down at her watch. “Vincent should be waiting for me outside by now. I think I’ll say goodnight,” she smiles. I get up to walk her to the exit. Sure enough, Vinnie is waiting at the kerb. I look down the street, but John’s car isn’t there.

“Vinnie, do you know where John went?” I ask, kissing him on the cheek.

“Yeah, I noticed he had a puncture in the back tyre so he’s gone to get it fixed, he’ll be back soon.”

“Oh, okay.”

“You still sober, Miss?” he asks, with a cheeky smirk.

I raise an eyebrow. “Yeah. It turns out drinking is only fun when you’re doing it too.”

He laughs and closes Jan’s door. “At least you won’t have a stonking headache in the morning.”

“Yeah, see you tomorrow.” I watch them drive away, then I head back into the club. The chilly night air is starting to bite.

WHO'D HAVE THOUGHT

I climb the stairs to the club checking my watch. We've been here for at least three hours, if I get back in the club and Lucy's spark out, then we might as well go home. She's had a great evening, and I'll be glad to get home and get these shoes off.

Just as I reach the door to the club, a hand lands on my shoulder and makes me jump. I turn around sharply. "Mike! What are you doing here?"

He takes a step backward with a sheepish expression on his face. "I was downstairs in the bar. I saw you, and I just wanted to… I just wanted to apologise for everything."

I notice that he looks a hell of a lot better than the last time I'd seen him. "Where have you been? We were worried about you. Dan's been trying to get hold of you."

He looks down at his shoes, and then back up to my face. "I know. I needed to sort myself out. I was such a dick, I acted like a total moron and I'm sorry," he says, with a shrug and an apologetic smile.

We're standing in the way of people trying to enter the club so I move us away from the door. Mike suggests going down to the bar he was in downstairs, it's less noisy and easier to talk. I hesitate for a moment, but I really want to clear the air between us.

We find a quiet corner and I order a coffee. Mike doesn't order anything.

"What happened to you? The last time I saw you, you

looked really unhappy."

He sighs and runs a hand through his hair. "I was. I'm sorry about that. I'd lost you, and my job… It all got a bit too much for me." I feel sorry for him. Remembering the last time we'd met, he certainly seemed to have hit rock bottom. He reaches across the table and takes my hand in his, but the intimacy feels uncomfortable and awkward.

"I know I fucked up with Michelle. I never meant to hurt you, Viv, and I'm so sorry for that," he sighs. "I always thought I'd get you back. I thought you'd want me back…" He huffs out a sarcastic laugh then his eyes land on mine and he squeezes my hand. "I know you're happy with Max, and I heard about your engagement. I just wanted to tell you that I'm really happy for you. I wish it was me you were in love with, but… I want you to be happy, you deserve it." The sincerity in his eyes stuns me. "I don't want to lose you as a friend, Viv. And if I ever get to meet your fiancé again, I'd like to think I'm man enough to shake his hand. He makes you happy, and that's good enough for me."

I stare at Mike unable to string any words together. A lump jumps into my throat, and I feel relieved that he's being so mature about this. In spite of how it ended, I owe Mike a lot. His patience and understanding at the beginning of our relationship made it possible for me to learn to trust again, and his friendship means the world to me. It's funny how things turn out, I never thought I'd see the day when Mike would accept Max, especially after Max had beaten him to a pulp not so long ago.

"I appreciate that, Mike. I mean it. And I'm glad that we can move on and still be friends."

He smiles and pats my hands, then he rises from the table. "Yeah, me too." I walk with him out of the bar and we stop at the foot of the stairs. "I want to apologise to Lucy too. We've never really got on very well, but I think that's mostly my fault," he smirks.

"Well she's in no fit state at the moment. But I'm sure if

you spoke to her the way you've just spoken to me, she'd see you in a different light."

"Maybe," he smiles. Suddenly his expression becomes tight and concerned. "Take care of yourself, Viv." The intensity in his eyes throws me a little.

"Yeah, you too."

He kisses me on the cheek and pulls me into a tight hug, which surprises me at first. Then he pulls away abruptly. Without looking back, he walks out onto the pavement, pulling his collar up, and then he's gone.

Wow! Who'd have thought?

Once he's out of sight, I turn on my heel to head back upstairs. It pleases me that we can still be friends. Mike was, and is, an important part of my life. He was my first boyfriend, my first love. He loved me regardless of my deep rooted inhibitions. It's so ironic, our relationship ended because he betrayed my trust, but without his patience in the beginning, I may never have learned to trust at all.

When I wander back into the club, I find most of the girls have passed out on the sofas. Another bottle of Tequila had been drunk while I was talking to Mike. I must have been gone longer than I thought.

As I search the room, I see Lucy's dancing, but it's her mother who is busting all the moves. I watch her, giggling to myself. Her mum's a game old bird and never one to leave the party early, but Lucy looks like she's going to collapse any moment. She's completely shit-faced.

Lucy spots me and comes staggering over. "Viv. My feet are friggin' killing me," she slurs, "but I've had a fab-mazing night." I help her over to the table and sit her on the arm of one of the chairs. She wobbles a bit and begins to slide off, so I prop her up and dial John.

"Ma'am? I'm right outside."

"Great, but I think I'm going to need your help. Lucy's been drinking bendy-juice."

He laughs. "Copy that. I'm on my way."

I round everybody up and tell them that I'm taking Lucy home. They're all so pissed that most of them are happy to leave too, and most are discussing the merits of finding a kebab shop before getting a cab home. My grumbling empty stomach would love a kebab or a curry right now, but my plan is to get Lucy home and then go straight to bed, avoiding the kitchen at all costs.

John helps me get Lucy and her mum in the car. He has to fight off the amorous attentions of Lucy's mother more than once, which makes me chuckle.

"I love you, Viv-ninen," Lucy slurs as I help her into her flat.

"Yeah, I know. Love you too."

"Did you have a good time tonight Ma'am?" John asks, pulling away from the kerb.

"John, I'm not the queen, please, just call me Vivienne," I smirk. "And yes, Lucy seemed to enjoy herself very much. Although, I think her mother enjoyed it even more."

He chuckles. "Yeah, she's got a lot of spunk."

I wince at his comment. Our British slang has totally ruined that word for me.

COLD SHOULDER

When I get home, I race past the kitchen and head upstairs. One look in the fridge and I'm a goner. It's after one in the morning and Max isn't home yet so I get undressed and take a shower. As I pad over to the bed in my short, silky nightgown, Max walks into the bedroom.

"Did you have a good time?" he asks, but I can tell by the tone of his voice and his expression that he's in a mood. I walk over to him and run my hands up his chest, then I rise up on my toes to kiss him. I've missed him. I've been looking forward to getting my fix of the hottest man on the planet all night. They don't refer to him as 'Sexy M.F.' for nothing. But he doesn't bend down to make it easier for me like he usually does, and his deepening frown tells me something's up.

I drop back down to my heels and tilt my head, trying to read his mood. "What's the matter?" I ask, resting my palms on his chest. He stares down at me for a moment, then he brushes me aside and walks to the bathroom pulling his top over his head and throwing it on the floor. *What the hell's wrong with him?*

I follow him to the bathroom and stand in the open doorway. He removes the rest of his clothes and takes a shower. He never looks at me once, and his angry scowl is still firmly in place. I brush out my hair and get into bed. It can't be me who's upset him, I'm not even drunk.

I watch Max walk back into the bedroom, completely

naked. My eyes trail over his sexy nakedness, and my body responds in its usual way. I've waited all day to see him, I've missed him. I always do when we're apart. The butterflies stir in my belly, and the thud of arousal hits my sex, causing my firm erect nipples to stand to attention under my silk sheath. The anticipation of his touch has an arousing effect, he always makes me feel this way.

He still hasn't looked at me, and when he pulls the covers back and slides into bed, he turns his light off and lays on his side with his back to me. Something's obviously happened to put him in a bad mood, and I know exactly how to get him out of it.

I slide over and press my body into his back. Rubbing my hand over his chest, and sliding my leg over his hip, I softly bite and kiss his shoulder. I'm totally turned on, and ready for one of our famous all-nighters.

"Go to sleep," he says, in a flat tone. He could have slapped me in the face and it wouldn't have hurt more than those three words. He's shutting me out and I don't know why?

"Max—"

"Go to sleep." He doesn't say anything else, and I'm left feeling humiliated and hurt without knowing what I've done wrong?

I pull away from him and lie on my back staring up at the ceiling. What the fuck could I have done to warrant his cold shoulder? It's not like I got drunk and embarrassed myself in public. Well, not tonight anyway.

I feel the bed move, and then his bedside light goes on. He sits up with his back against the headboard folding his arms across his chest. He puffs out a heavy, aggravated sigh, and I can feel his eyes burning into me so I look up at him. His body is tense and his angry scowl glares down at me.

Here it comes.

"Anything you want to tell me?" he growls, clenching his jaw.

I turn on my side and prop myself up on my elbow. "What do you mean?"

His glare intensifies, and if he keeps clenching that jaw of his he's going to wear his teeth out. "I'll ask you again, Vivienne," he says, through gritted teeth. "And don't even *think* about lying to me."

Oh, my God! He knows about Greg Taylor. A hot flush prickles over my skin and I sit up in a rush of panic. For a moment, I'm completely lost for words. *How did he find out?*

His stormy eyes narrow on me while he shakes his head and curls his lips into a snarl. "Yeah! You thought I wouldn't find out about it, didn't you?" he grates. "How many cosy little meetings have you two had behind my back?"

What the…? I screw my eyes closed and shake my head. I can't believe what he's just said. How could he possibly think I'd ever want to see that man again after what he did to me? His next sentence immediately clears the fog.

"Answer me! How many times have you met Mike behind my back?"

I feel instant relief that Max is still oblivious to Greg Taylor. But now I'm wondering how the hell he found out about me talking to Mike? And now *I'm* angry that *he's* angry. I try to dial down my tone before answering him, but the irritated sigh just couldn't be avoided. I look him right in the eyes.

"I don't meet Mike behind your back. I bumped into him tonight at the club. He wanted to apologise to me, he wanted to—"

"Steal you away from me!" he snaps, still glaring at me, clenching his jaw. I can't believe he'd even think that was possible. I take another moment to diffuse my anger.

"Max. Don't you think this is all a bit childish," I sigh, "I mean the guy just wants to be friends, he's happy for me, for us."

"Like fuck!" he snarls, looking away. I don't mind being told off for something legitimate, but he knows I'd never cheat on him, especially not with Mike. In fact the way he's acting right now is exactly what Mike used to do.

"How did you know? I mean, if you'd taken the time to ask me, I'd have told you all about my evening, but you didn't. You just assumed the worst, and now we're having a row about it!" I tried not to yell, but I'm so angry with him. The fact that I'm completely sober and I've done nothing wrong, makes it worse.

His narrowed, angry eyes swing over to mine. I can tell by his expression that he's not going to back down any time soon, and when he utters his next sentence, I flip.

"Fiona was at the bar you and Mike snuck off to. She saw you two looking very cosy together."

Oh, great! That's just perfect. Bitch-face Fiona. Of all people! "Of course she did!" I yell. "I'll bet she couldn't wait to tell you!" I grab my pillow and get out of bed, seething with anger and frustration. "You know, Max, if anyone should be angry, it's me!" I yell, turning to face him. "I'm sure it was that two-faced cow who leaked our engagement to the press. She looks at me like I'm in her way. She wants you, and she hates the fact that you're with me. She'd love to split us up. It's like Monica all over again, and you fall for it every time!" I begin to stomp out of the room, but I stop before I get to the door. Max is staring at me like I've totally lost the plot. "And you!... You have the cheek to accuse me of hiding things from you, when all this time you've been doing just that! You must think I'm an idiot. Huh! Maybe I am! Why don't you tell me about those yellow letters you've been hiding?" His guilty eyes widen and slide away from mine. Confirmation that I'm right if ever I saw it. "Yeah... didn't think so!" I leave the bedroom in a huff, slamming the door behind me.

THE ONE THING

I wake in the guest room feeling like shit. I hadn't got much sleep last night. After our fight, my emotions were all over the place. Max had hurt me, and I wasn't prepared to let him talk his way out of it that easily so I locked the bedroom door. But he didn't come to find me, or apologise, and I heard him slamming doors this morning on his way out.

My empty stomach groans as I glance at my watch. It's eight o'clock. Jan will have prepared breakfast, but even though my stomach is groaning with hunger, I couldn't eat, I'm still too upset.

I haul myself out of bed and cross the hall to our room. Dressing in my running gear, I head for the gym. Setting the course on the treadmill, I pop the earphones in, then I brace myself for a gruelling run.

"Vivienne! Oh, goodness me. Vivienne!"

What the… I hear a whirring noise. I open my eyes to see Jan staring down at me with a worried frown.

"Oh, thank goodness. Lie still. Mr. Foxx is on his way." I'm damp with sweat, lying flat on my back. The treadmill is still whirring at high speed beside me. Jan is kneeling at my head, her upside down face is anxiously peering down at me.

"What happened?" I try to sit up, but Jan pushes me back down.

"No! Just stay where you are. Mr. Foxx will be here in a moment."

"Vivienne! Jesus!" Max's worried voice has Jan's head turning to face him.

"She's okay, Sir. She's conscious now. I've called the doctor, he's sending an ambulance."

Max arrives at my side, his worried eyes search my body for anything obvious. "Does anything hurt?" I make a mental check of my body. Apart from my shoulder, nothing else appears to be causing any pain. And for once, my head feels fine.

"Just my shoulder, but I'm okay." I try to sit up again but the sharp pain in my shoulder makes me cry out.

"No. You're not. You've dislocated your shoulder." Max runs his eyes over me again, then he looks over at the treadmill. "And why weren't you wearing the safety cord?" I don't answer him. He's right, I should have clipped myself on, but I forgot. I glance down at myself. My right foot is resting up on the bottom edge of the treadmill, I must have fallen off it, but I can't remember how. I try to push myself up, but both Max and Jan refuse to let me move.

"Baby, just wait for the ambulance, you need to go to the hospital." I cringe at the thought of seeing Doctor Alexander again. He must think I'm some sort of morphine addict.

"Max, I'm fine, I just slipped."

Jan brings her face into my line of sight, shaking her head. "Vivienne, you were out cold when I found you. Do as you're told." She arches her brow at me, then she looks over to Max. "She hasn't eaten since breakfast yesterday." I hear him sigh, and I can see him shaking his head in my peripheral vision. Jan leaves to wait for the paramedics downstairs.

"What happened?" His tone is softer, more mellow.

"I don't know. I must have slipped or something." Max gives me that mildly sarcastic look of his. You know, the one that makes you feel like you've done something really dumb. Which for me, is often.

"You are the most accident prone person I have ever met," he mutters, shaking his head. "Baby, you can't do a ten mile run on those settings without any fuel. It's just crazy." He leans over to switch the treadmill off, and then he takes my hand in his.

He's right. I should have eaten something before attempting the hardest course on the treadmill. "How far did I get?" I ask out of interest.

He smirks and shakes his head. "A mile and a half."

Is that all! Now I'm really miffed. Max strokes the back of my hand, his eyes softening as he gazes down at me.

"Baby, I'm sorry about last night… I was an asshole." He's surprised me. After storming off this morning, I hadn't expected him to back down. "And you're right about the letters, but we'll talk about them later. Right now, I just want to know that you're going to be okay." His eyes lift from my face as Jan comes barging into the gym with two guys in green uniforms.

Once they've thoroughly checked me over and asked me a ton of questions, they distract me as one of them pops my shoulder back into the socket. It felt uncomfortable, but the gas and air they gave me made it much more bearable than I thought it would be. They load me onto a stretcher securing my head and neck, and then they take me down to the ambulance. A warm blush heats my cheeks when one of the paramedics tells me he remembers me from the last time he'd stretchered me out of the building. At least this time it wasn't my head.

Max follows the ambulance to the hospital and waits for me while I'm carted off for tests and a scan. Once everything has been done and I'm wheeled into a private room, Max arrives and takes a seat next to my bed. He looks nervous and he almost crushes my hand in his firm grip. I smile up at him to reassure him, but inside I'm nervous too.

Apart from the dislocation nothing appears to be broken, but that doesn't explain why I had the blackout. The nausea and headaches I have been experiencing for the last few weeks have been worrying, and any blackout is a concern, especially with my history of head injuries. I'd begun to worry that a clot could've formed in my brain or something. You hear stories about things like that every day.

The door creaks open and Doctor Alexander walks in staring down at some papers in his hand. I immediately fear the worst.

"Good morning, Vivienne. I had hoped not to see you quite so soon," he says, with an arched brow and a certain amount of jovial sarcasm. I cringe and blush, I'm becoming somewhat of a regular to this establishment. Max's grip tightens on my hand as he frowns at Doctor Alexander, unable to see the humour through his apprehension.

"What is it, Doc? Is it serious?" he blurts, clenching his jaw and shifting in his seat.

Doctor Alexander's eyebrows raise and a smile seeps across his face. "I'm afraid so. In fact, it's double trouble," he smirks.

Max and I glance at each other in confusion, then we look back at him, neither of us understanding why he's looking so smug. His smiling eyes ping-pong between us. "Don't look so worried …Congratulations! You're pregnant."

"What!?" I hear the utter shock and surprise in Max's voice, but I'm speechless. Anger courses through me that the doctor could make such a horrible mistake. Tears prick my eyes, and I wrench my hand free from Max's hold, clenching my fist against my thigh.

"No! You're wrong. I can't…. I can't get pregnant." The words choke me.

Just then, the door opens and a nurse wheels in some

apparatus. She walks it over to the side of my bed and plugs it in to the socket behind me. "I'm Jean," she smiles. "I'm going to do your ultra sound." She hasn't seemed to notice my stunned expression as she begins to roll my sheet down so I quickly grab her arm to stop her, glaring up at her in disbelief.

"What is this, some kind of sick joke?" The room falls awkwardly silent, all eyes on me. Jean's startled face swings over to Doctor Alexander, then back to mine. Realising my fingers are digging into her flesh, I release her arm.

"Vivienne, your blood and urine tests confirm your pregnancy," Doctor Alexander says, nodding at the confused nurse to continue with the scan.

No! It's not possible. "But… I can't get pregnant."

The doctor's eyes flick to Max, like he needs to assess his reaction before continuing. When his eyes return to mine, there's something soothing within them. "Medical science still has a long way to go, Vivienne. Sometimes the body just needs the right elements at the right time." Something about his expression indicates that he knows more about my medical history than I'd given him credit for. He must have seen my records, and I'm eternally grateful to him for upholding the ethics of his Hippocratic Oath. I look over to Max who's staring at me open mouthed. He's white as a sheet, and judging by his vacant expression, he's as baffled as I am.

Jean gives me a harried smile before pulling my gown up to expose my belly, then she squirts on a freezing cold gel. "Sorry, it'll soon warm up." Still speechless, Max takes my hand and squeezes it, almost crushing my knuckles as we stare wide eyed at the screen together, both of us gob-smacked. "Just breathe, Vivienne," Jean says, softly, as she glides the scanner over my belly. I think I'd stopped breathing when I'd heard the words 'you're pregnant!' My mind is scattered. This can't be true, it's impossible. It's all just a big mistake. All I see on the monitor is static. My heart sinks, and tears burn my eyes.

"Oh, wait, I forgot to turn the sound on," Jean says, flicking a switch on her control panel. She presses down again and slides the scanner over the cold gel. "Here they are." I can't see anything, and then suddenly I hear it. The fast swooshing heartbeats. "Yes, it's definitely twins," Jean adds, pointing at the screen. Through my tear blurred eyes, I see them. Our babies. Our twins. Our future.

I feel Max's warm hand on my belly, and when I drag my eyes away from the screen and turn to face him, his rapt expression floors me. The sheer joy in his watery eyes as he stares at the monitor, is something I never thought I could ever be responsible for. Against all odds and any hope, I'm carrying his babies.

In a daze, I glance back at Jean, and then at the screen to check. "I can't believe it. It's… I just…" I'm literally speechless.

"You're about twelve weeks," Jean says, measuring their tiny little bodies. My head is on a swivel between the monitor, Jean, the doctor, and Max. I can't believe this is happening.

"Baby, I…." Emotion chokes Max's words. He rises to his feet and holds my face in his hands. His eyes burning with love and awe. "Thank you, baby. Thank you… I love you, Vivienne. So much. More than you'll ever know." His tender kiss, and the tears that fall from his lashes onto my cheeks, are my undoing.

Jean prints off a scan for us to keep, and then she and the doctor leave us. We sit in silence, staring in shock and disbelief at our little miracles captured in the scan. Max holds me in his arms, both of us speechless and tearful.

"I can't believe it," I whisper, staring down at our babies. Max lifts my chin and searches my eyes with two watery, blue pools of love.

"You never told me why you thought you'd never be able to have children." His raspy voice breaks a little. I've been dreading this question. I knew it was only a matter of time before he'd ask it. I reach up and cup his face, brushing my thumb across his cheek.

"It's not important now." I can see in his eyes that he needs more, but I'm not ready to tell him about my past, about Greg. He doesn't need to hear it, any more than I need to relive it. "Max, take us home."

NUGGETS OF JOY

On our way home from the hospital, Max didn't stop talking or smiling. He immediately called his parents and Vinnie, to give them the happy news, and he quite literally beamed with joy. He's super excited about becoming a father, and although I'm nervous about this new responsibility, I feel an overwhelming sense of pride that I can give the love of my life the one thing I never thought possible. A family.

We decide to keep the news to our nearest and dearest. Anyone outside our immediate circle, including the press, will find out soon enough, but while we still can, we want to keep it as private as possible.

Jean and Doctor Alexander assured us that the babies were healthy, and as long as I eat and exercise correctly, I can carry on as normal. Although, I'm becoming acutely aware that Max's normal differs greatly from everybody else's. As he rattles off a list of changes we'll need to make, I can feel the bubble-wrap and cotton wool descending as he tries to talk me out of going to work. I quietly let him think I'm paying attention to his over protective plans, but in my mind I'm reliving the moment when I saw them, and heard our babies heartbeats for the first time. And the look on Max's face when he realised he was going to become a father, will be a memory I'll cherish forever.

As the lift arrives at F1, Jan is already at the penthouse door with a big beaming smile, and tears in her eyes. "Congratulations to you both," she gushes, pulling me into a tearful hug.

Vinnie appears and shakes Max's hand with glistening eyes and a big cheesy grin expanding his rugged face. "Twins eh? I'm chuffed to bits for you Guv'." Max, who hasn't stopped smiling since we found out, pulls him in to a hug as they slap each other on the back.

"I've prepared some food, and John is bringing your parents over shortly, Sir," Jan says, walking me into the kitchen. She sits me down at the island and pours me a cup of tea.

"I thought it was strange when you began to crave fish. Knowing you were allergic to it, I did wonder if maybe you were pregnant, but of course I didn't want to say anything," she says, smiling.

I'd never given it a thought. I've lived so long with the notion that I could never conceive, that it didn't even occur to me, but now everything makes sense.

"Oh crap. I'd better call Lucy," I cringe. "I'll never get that bloody bridesmaid dress on now."

Jan laughs. "I don't think she'll worry too much about that when she knows why."

I reach into my bag and pull out the scan to show Jan, and then I grab my phone. Dialling Lucy, I stand up to pace the kitchen. Butterflies invade my belly at the thought of telling her, it still doesn't feel real, and yet, I'm looking at our two little peanuts in the scan.

"Luce…are you at work?" I ask cagily.

"No, I'm at home trimming Dan's hair. Why?… You sound weird."

"Erm, just put your scissors down for a moment, Luce. I don't want you hacking off an ear. I've got something to tell you."

"What have you done now?" Her weary tone tells me she's expecting bad news. "Please don't tell me you've tripped over a sunbeam and broken your leg. I'll still drag you to my wedding, you know. I'm not doing this without you," she grumbles.

I laugh at her assumption that I've done something stupid. She does have a point though. I did dislocate my shoulder when I fell off the treadmill this morning.

"Are you sitting down?"

Lucy exhales loudly. "Viv, just get on with it. What have you done? And what ward do I have to visit this time."

"Well, actually, it's not just me…it's we."

"Spit it out, Viv. You know I'm crap at cryptic clues," she huffs impatiently.

I take a deep breath. "…We're pregnant." The line goes silent for a moment, then I hear Dan yelping in the background. She obviously hadn't put her scissors down. "Luce?…Luce? Are you there?"

"Oh shit. Sorry Dan. Oh my God, I knew it! I knew it when I saw you at the fitting. That's why I didn't force you to drink with me last night. I'd hoped but… I just didn't think it was possible."

"Me neither, but I've just been to the hospital for a scan, and I'm looking at the babies now." The emotion in Lucy's voice brought tears to my eyes, blurring the scan and choking me up a little.

"I'm so happy for you, I— Wait! Hang on a minute …Babies? Like, more than one?"

"Yeah," I chuckle. "Twins."

All I can hear now is Lucy's whoops of laughter. I suspect she's jumping up and down too. I can only hope she still hasn't got the scissors in her hand.

"I've just got to put a band aid on Dan's ear, then we're coming over. This calls for a celebration."

"Great. I'll see you soon."

Sylvie and William arrive, followed by Lucy and Dan. The pride and joy in all their faces overwhelms me, but William is the one who surprises me the most. He looks physically moved, overcome with emotion at the good news as he hugs his son, unashamed of the tears that follow. When he finally lets him go and reaches out to take my hand, he puts a lump in my throat. "All my prayers have been answered. I'm so happy for you both," he says, laughing and crying at the same time. Sylvie tells him off for being such a big old softy, but her tears are flowing too.

Jan makes sure everyone has something to eat and drink, and Vinnie keeps us all amused with his witty banter. As I sit back and absorb the love from my friends and family, I find myself resting my hands on my belly. It must be an instinctual reaction, and I'm still finding it hard to take in the fact that inside me are two of the most important and precious people I'll ever know. Max hasn't left my side, and I've never seen his eyes sparkle as much as they do right now.

I wish my mum was here. And I wish there was some way to let my dad know how happy I am. *I miss you dad.*

"So, do you know what sex the babies are yet?" Dan asks.

Max and I glance at each other briefly. "No," we answer together, laughing at our synchronised response.

"I don't mind what we have as long as their healthy," Max smiles, placing his hand on my very small baby bump. I lay mine on top of it feeling utterly content.

As Max enthusiastically describes the moment we found out that we were pregnant, my eyes drift up to his gorgeously handsome profile. My heart swells with love and pride. He's everything I could ever want and more. So much more. I'm so lucky to have his heart, and I feel truly blessed to be carrying his babies. Secretly, I hope one will be a boy, just like Charlie. That would be the icing on the cake.

Max slides his hand out from under mine. "I'll be back in a minute." Kissing me on the cheek, he rises from the sofa. He and Vinnie exchange a look, and then I watch them disappear into the study. Dan's in conversation with

William, so Lucy comes over to sit in Max's seat.

"Viv, I've been thinking. You don't have to take the photographs at the wedding, we can get someone else to do that."

"Why? I'm pregnant, I'm not ill." I suddenly burst out laughing. "Wow. Pregnant. That still sounds so weird," I giggle, "but I'm afraid I'll never fit into that dress now."

"Oh, don't worry about that. Who gives a shit about a bloody bridesmaid's dress when your best friend is pregnant," she beams.

"I'll find something else to wear. I won't let you down, Luce, I promise."

"I know." She leans over to give me a hug. "Oh, I forgot to tell you. I got a call from Mike. He said he'd spoken to you already and he wanted to apologise to me and Dan." She rolls her eyes, she's never liked Mike.

"Did you accept his apology?"

She pulls a face. "I felt I had to, for Dan's sake. The silly idiot still wants to be his friend. And he's invited him to the bloody wedding," she huffs, giving the back of Dan's head the death stare.

"Well, I'm glad. Mike's not a bad person, and I think he really meant his apology. Life's too short to hold grudges." *I don't know how Max will take it if Mike turns up?*

"You're probably right," she smirks. "Anyway, Mike said he couldn't come to the wedding, he's helping his cousin Daryl to set up his new restaurant or something."

Problem solved.

As Max leaves the study and walks toward me, Lucy gets up and sits in Dan's lap. "Not long now, mister," she says, kissing him on the nose. He wraps his arms around her and gives her a loving smile.

"Can't wait."

Max sits beside me and takes my hand, placing it under his own on his thigh. "Lucy, your guests are flying out on the Friday morning, aren't they?" She nods in agreement. "Good, I thought maybe the four of us could fly out a few days before, so we can stay on the yacht and relax before the big day. I've organised a pre-wedding party at the hotel for Friday night. I thought you and Vivienne could share a room at the hotel after the party, and Dan could stay with me on the yacht. You don't want to bump into each other before the wedding."

Dan and Lucy look surprised and delighted. "Oh, my God, that would be amazing. We'd really appreciate that, thanks," Dan splutters, a little stunned. Lucy looks gob-smacked and tearful, just nodding her excited approval.

Dan leans forward with a serious frown. "Max, I know we've said it before, but we really can't thank you enough for everything you've done for us."

"Yes! And we'll think of some way to pay you back. I promise," Lucy adds, quickly.

I can feel Max tensing up beside me. "Oh, no, that's not necessary." He squeezes my hand and glances down at me for help. I know he doesn't accept praise or compliments very easily. I just smile at him in total awe. He's organised all that on his own, I had no idea he'd given it so much thought.

"Oh, that reminds me," Lucy says, turning to Sylvie and Jan, "Maggie and Trevor will be doing our hair and makeup, so you won't have to worry about booking an appointment at the hotel salon."

"Oh, that's wonderful, Lucy, thank you," Sylvie says.

"Yes, and how thoughtful of you," Jan adds.

Lucy's cheeks redden with a blush. "It's the least I can do."

"Hey, what about us fellas?" William asks, pretending to be feeling left out.

Sylvie smiles and pats his knee. "Sweetheart, you've got three hairs on your head, just comb one to the left, one to the right, and leave the other one scruffy." We all burst out laughing, even William.

When all our happy guests take their leave, Max checks his phone, then we lay on the sofa. His head is resting on my chest as he circles his fingers over my belly, and then he releases a long contented sigh. "I didn't think it was possible to love you more…but I do."

I run my fingers through his hair and watch him gently circling my belly, he seems in a world of his own. "Are you talking to me or the peanuts?" I chuckle.

He raises his head to look at me. "Peanuts?"

"Well, they look like peanuts, or jelly beans," I shrug.

He raises an eyebrow. "You may think of our babies as bar snacks, I prefer to think of them as little nuggets of joy," he smirks, with his roguish grin.

"Okay," I chuckle. "Nuggets it is, then."

He crawls up and plants a soft lingering kiss on my lips. Pulling back, he gazes down at me with his scorching blue eyes, shaking his head.

"What?" I frown.

"Nothing. You just…. You take my breath away. I can't believe how lucky I am to have found you. And now you're giving me two beautiful babies… You blow me away… You make me so happy, baby."

I reach up and run my hands through his hair. "Ditto, Mr. Foxx." Holding his face between my palms I pull him down for a kiss. A kiss that stirs our passion and ignites the ever present fire between us.

NO MORE SECRETS

As I lay naked and sprawled across his chest, totally content and happy, I realise something is missing. "I want to tell my mum."

"I know. You should."

"But I can't trust her to keep it to herself, what if she sells the story?"

Max sighs deeply. "It's too late to worry about that."

I lift my head and rest my chin on his chest. "What do you mean?"

He opens his eyes and runs his hand up and down my arm. "They already know. I got a text from Trencher an hour ago. The news of our babies is all over Twitter."

I'm instantly pissed off, and I sit up in a rush. "How the hell did they find out?"

"Someone talked. Trencher's looking into it," he sighs, trying to pull me back down to his chest, but I'm starting to feel panicky.

Oh, God! That will definitely bring her out of the woodwork.

"Baby? What's wrong?" he asks, picking up on my mood.

"Monica… She's still out there somewhere. If she finds out I'm pregnant with your babies…" Our eyes meet. We stare at each other contemplating the same thing.

An angry frown creases his brow as he clenches his jaw. "I won't let her anywhere near you."

"And what about you? Who will… Wait! Those letters. They were from her, weren't they." His eyes slide away from mine. "Max. You promised me, no secrets. Now more than ever we need to protect each other. I can't do that if I don't know the whole story."

Reluctantly, Max rises and hands me his shirt, then he pulls the blanket from the back of the sofa and wraps it around his hips. "Come, I need to show you something." I pull on his shirt, then I take his hand and follow him to the study.

He takes a book from the bookcase and removes five crumpled yellow letters from inside it, then he pulls me over to his desk and sits me in his lap. A frown levels in his brow, and his lips form a hard line. "These have been arriving every few weeks. We think they're all made by the same person, but there's absolutely nothing traceable on them. It's like they've been handled in a lab or something. The paper is available from thousands of outlets, there are no fingerprints or DNA on any of them, and they all say the same thing." He hands them to me, carefully watching my reaction. I read the first, and then the second, and on and on, they're all the same.

WHEN YOU LEAST EXPECT IT…

"I don't understand? Expect what? Is it Monica?" It's been a long time since I've felt Monica's cold, bony fingers around my throat, but the memories are only buried in a shallow grave waiting for something like this to bring them to the fore. A cold shudder spirals up my spine. "How do they arrive? I mean, are they posted? Hand delivered?"

"They're posted. Addressed to me at Foxx-Tech, each one posted from a different location."

"Can't you trace them back?" I ask, clutching at straws. I know Trencher will be doing everything he can to find out where they've come from, and more importantly, *who* they've come from.

"Baby, they could be from anyone. Anyone with a grudge. It could be Monica, but it could also be from a disgruntled journalist trying to whip up a story. Who knows?" He wraps his arms around me and kisses me softly on the lips. "The important thing, is that we don't allow this to affect our lives, and we don't give anyone the opportunity to hurt us. That means you keep John close, wherever you go. Understand?" I nod. Now more than ever, I understand the importance of our security.

"And what about you?"

He smiles and pecks me on the nose. "Vinnie's got my back. I don't have to worry." I lean back and tilt my head at him, searching his eyes. "What?"

"You called him Vinnie. I've never heard you call him Vinnie before, it's always been Parker."

A warm smile spreads across his lips. "He's always had my back, since the first day I met him. And he's going to be my best man when we get married, I think I owe him a little more respect." Max kisses the tip of my nose, he stands up and places me on my feet. Gathering the letters together, he puts them all in his safe. "I'll give you some privacy while you call your mom." I watch him leave the room, then I take a seat in his big leather chair and call my mum. The phone rings for ages. I'm just about to end the call when I suddenly hear it answer.

"Mum? …Mum can you hear me? It's Viv." I can hear her making noises, but I don't know what she's saying. She's drunk, or worse. "Mum, if you can hear me, I just wanted to… I just… I love you, Mum." I wait for her to respond but she doesn't. I expect she's passed out. I can't remember the last time I spoke to my mother when she was actually sober. I hear two other voices in the background, and then I hear a scuffling noise.

"Hello?" It's a man's voice, he sounds drunk. I stay silent. "Hello? …No one there." Then he hangs up.

Oh, Mum. Why won't you let me help you?

Max and I have both tried to get her some help. Even Lucy's tried to talk her into rehab, but she's not ready to admit that her life is ruled by alcohol and drugs. At this rate, she'll die before she even gets the chance to see her grandchildren.

NEVER IN A MILLION

Since Max opened up to me about the letters, my attitude to our security has changed dramatically. I've kept John close whenever I'm away from Max. Ed, Casper, and I, have upped the security protocol at my office too. Now I'm carrying our little nuggets, I'm taking no chances.

The press have run countless stories. All of them allegedly from; 'a source close to the couple.' I've adopted Max's approach to the press, and I try to ignore them like he does. It's hard, and I worry about how it will affect us in the future. Will we always be hunted by them? I hope not.

Because of the papers and social media, I know my mother must have knowledge of my pregnancy by now, but she hasn't called me, and every time I've tried to call her, I either get no response or she answers in gibberish.

Fiona called to congratulate us, at least I assume that's why she called. I avoided speaking to her. I've never liked the woman, I'm not going to start pretending any different now. I do feel slightly guilty about my feelings toward her, but not enough to make friends. Apparently she'd helped Max find my beautiful engagement ring. Her uncle is a diamond merchant and she'd been helping Max with the design, which is why he'd met and spoken with her so often. But even so, there's something about that woman that gets my back up. It could just be my irrational jealousy tainting her character, but after dealing with Monica, I've learned to listen to my instincts a little more, and my instincts tell me Fiona's a wrong'un.

Since finding out that we were going to be parents, Max has been even more protective than usual. When he first found out I was pregnant, I practically had to force him to have sex with me. It took some convincing for him to understand that our little nuggets wouldn't come to any harm. I've been super-horny recently too, so I've really been putting him through his paces. I'm happy to say he's holding up his end very well.

He's been so loving and attentive, and he's practically bursting with pride. He's already designed the nursery, and we've spent many an evening snuggled up on the sofa reading up on pregnancy and childbirth together. The morning sickness seems to have stopped, so now I feel great. I can't get enough of Max, but then, I've always felt like that, he's quite literally irresistible.

Max had once promised me that we'd have sex on every surface of every house he owns. God knows he's kept that promise. At least at the penthouse and both our offices. Oh, and in the lift. On the flight over to France, he promised me we'd christen every surface in his chateau, and on board the yacht too. We would have christened the jet, but once Dan got Max talking about planes, fast cars, and jet skis, I couldn't get a word in edge-ways.

We've been in the South of France for four days now. Just Lucy, Dan, Max and I. 'La Raposa' is more like a floating palace than a yacht, and I'm not ashamed to admit, that we've christened every surface we could find, without being caught.

Apart from the press invasion before we left the U.K., life couldn't be better. My sexy, gorgeous fiancé, has not only made me the happiest woman on the planet, he's also given Lucy and Dan, my best friends in all the world, an amazing pre-wedding holiday. He had his captain sail us out to deep water, away from the hustle and bustle of the marina, so we could sunbathe, jet ski, and swim in peace. We also sailed around to Monte Carlo and spent an evening at the casino. It's been heaven.

Max has never looked happier, and I've never felt more content than I do right now. His kind heart has always been so generous, and I had always hoped that one day I would be able to do something equally amazing for him in return. Never in a million years did I ever think it would be the one thing he wanted the most, a family.

LOVE YOU MORE

Everything is set for the party at the hotel tonight, and Sasha assures me that all the preparations for the wedding tomorrow are complete. She'd managed to secure the two extra waiters, so she's happy.

We sail back to the marina after a late lunch, and John drives us to the hotel to get ready for the party tonight. I leave Max and Dan in the hotel bar talking about Top Gear, while me and Lucy head up to her room to do our hair and makeup.

"Viv, I can't believe I'm actually here in the South of France on the eve of my wedding. It's like a fairy-tale," she smiles, her eyes glistening with tears.

"Oh, no. No tears, you promised." I have to look away or I'll start crying too. "Hey, do you want to see something funny?" I ask, trying to lighten the moment. I don't want her crying, not tonight.

"What is it?"

"Wait here, I brought something to show you. You're going to laugh your socks off when you see this." I grab my suit-bag and scoot into the bathroom. A few moments later, I walk out and strike a pose. "Tah-dah!"

Lucy bursts out laughing. "Oh, Viv, I dare you to wear that tonight."

"Are you mad? Look at the back." I turn around and show her the back view of the bridesmaid dress that's pulling at the seams even before it's zipped up. "The zip wouldn't close if you covered me in chip fat and shoe-horned me in."

"Oh, shit. That's funny," she giggles. "Well, to be fair, I was only expecting one person to be wearing it, not three."

I look at myself in the mirror, my belly is starting to show now, and my boobs have definitely filled out. It's a good thing Davis came to my rescue.

Watching Lucy and Dan with their family and friends, laughing and joking and enjoying the evening as they should, really pleases me. They look so happy together. I feel blessed to have such wonderful people in my life. My life… Who would have thought I'd end up with the man of my dreams and two perfect little people growing inside me. My life is perfect.

"What are you smiling at?" Max asks, handing me a cool drink. I gaze up into his handsome face. His warm smile and seductive eyes alert my butterflies. Even after all this time, he still affects me this way.

"Everything is perfect, isn't it?" I sigh.

He smiles and kisses me softly on the lips, then he moves behind me, wrapping his arm around so that his hand is resting on my bump. Nuzzling my neck, he nips at my earlobe. "You've never looked more beautiful," he whispers against my skin. I tilt my head to accommodate him as he trails his lush lips along my neck and shoulder. My body reacts in its usual way. His lips brushing against my skin sends a throb of arousal to my sex, and my skin heats with desire.

"Do you think they'd notice if we slipped away for an hour or so?" I ask, reaching up to ruffle my hand through his hair.

"Are you trying to take advantage of me, Miss Banks?" he asks, in his sexy, raspy, seductive voice, still nipping at my shoulder.

"Mmm-hmm." I'm totally intoxicated by him. My eyes

close and my head falls back against his shoulder as his lips trail a seductive path up my throat. He's turning me on, the thud of arousal pulses in my sex and my breathing deepens. I want him. Right now.

He takes the glass out of my hand and slides it onto the bar without removing his lips from my throat.

"And how exactly would you do that?" he asks, as his lips brush over my jaw and hover over mine. His hot breath blowing into my open mouth. I open my eyes and see his hooded pools of blue gazing down at me. He's got that roguish grin on his face which always turns me on. I turn my body into his, pressing myself against him. His arms tighten around my waist, as I wrap mine around his neck. "You want to kiss me now, don't you?" he asks, with a seductive smile.

"Yes… I always want to kiss you," I whisper, lowering my eyes to his lush, very kissable lips, "and then I want to take you somewhere quiet and strip you naked, so I can run my tongue over every perfect inch of your delicious body." I rise up to kiss him but he pulls back, just out of reach. I drag my eyes back up to his. They burn me with scorching sensuality, full of hunger and desire. "Stop teasing me, Mr. Foxx."

"And what then?" he whispers.

I curl my fingers into his hair as my eyes dance between his eyes and his sexy crooked smile. My heart flutters, and my skin heats and tingles in anticipation of his touch. Everything about him turns me on. And I know he's feeling the same way, I can feel his solid erection against my lower belly.

"Then I'm going to take you in my mouth and suck, hard." I watch his eyes close briefly as his erection pulses against me. His chest rises and falls as he takes a deep breath. I can see in his eyes that he's ready, they blaze and scorch me with desire. If he doesn't take me right now I'm going to come anyway, just his expression alone is making me wet. I know he's playing with me, teasing me, but I'm just too horny to wait any longer.

He leans down to me, his lips achingly close to mine. "What about your friends?" he whispers against my lips, then he pulls away again. If he doesn't let me kiss him soon I'm going to die from over stimulation. It's really frustrating.

"Max, please! They won't even notice we're gone." I rise up on my toes as he begins to lower enough that our lips almost meet, but he stops short again.

"What about… The Vicar—"

"Oh, fuck the Vicar!" I snap, in frustration. "He's not even here until tomorrow. Max, take me to bed. I need you inside me. Right now." The look on his face makes me freeze and blink up at him repeatedly. A flutter of panic hits me as I notice Max's eyes are trained on something over my shoulder. *Oh, shit!* "He's right behind me, isn't he?"

Max smiles, nods, and then straightens pulling my arms down from his neck. With a stifled smirk, he quickly spins me around to face the man standing behind me. The Vicar looks a little shocked.

"Oh, God. Shit! I mean, Vicar. …Erm, Monsieur Penis, I mean, Monsieur Pinez. I didn't realise you were coming tonight… I mean, I didn't realise that you would be here tonight, ah… Hi. I'm Vivienne. We spoke on the phone." I stumble my way through the lamest greeting ever, blushing my arse off, without any help whatsoever from Max. The look on the vicar's face just makes it worse. And did I just call him Mr. Penis? *Jeez.*

Lucy and Dan walk over and release me from the vicar's withering glare. As they move away from us toward the bar, I turn to see Max grinning at me.

"That was awesome," he smirks.

"You could have warned me?"

"I thought I did," he chuckles.

"So, are you going to take me to bed or not?" I grumble, arching a brow.

"Baby, you've given me a woody. I can't walk through all those people just yet." He smirks down at me, keeping me in front of his bulging erection.

I scowl at him, then raise an eyebrow. "Mr. Foxx, I've just embarrassed myself in front of the vicar. I'm sure you can handle a few fainting women, and a few jealous men. Your hormonal girlfriend wants you to make love to her, please don't make me beg."

He wraps his arms around me and pulls me into him. His roguish grin and blazing eyes scorch me to my core. "You know I love it when you're bossy," he grins. Before I have the chance to make a comment, he takes my hand and marches me out of the room and over to the lift.

We didn't make it up to the room for my first orgasm. Even before the lift doors closed we were all over each other, and he'd satisfied my aching need by the time we hit our floor. I can't even be sure there weren't any other people in there with us. When Max hits me with that look, all I can see is him.

Sex with Max has never been anything less than amazing. I don't know if it's my hormones, or just the effect he has on me, but I couldn't wait to get him to our room so we could continue at a less frantic pace.

I could have stayed in his arms all night, but we'd run out of surfaces and the chilly evening air out on the balcony was beginning to make me shiver.

"Where have you two been?" Lucy grins, as we walk back into the party.

I blow a stray strand of hair away from my face. "Oh, we just… I needed… Erm, he was… Sex. We just went and had sex," I sigh. There's no point in pussy footing around. I can tell by her expression that she knew that already.

"Good. Hold the fort would you? Me and Dan are just going to nip upstairs for one last shag before the wedding." She's off before I even have time to say anything.

Max and I mingle with the guests while we wait for Lucy and Dan to return. Everyone is genuinely happy for them, and both Lucy and Dan's parents make a point of thanking Max for everything he's done for their kids. They try to offer to pay something toward the costs, but Max won't allow it and shuts the conversation down immediately. I marvel at his generosity, he has such a kind heart.

As the evening finally draws to a close, Max and Dan walk us up to the room Lucy and I will be sharing tonight.

"I don't want to leave you," Max sighs, nibbling my ear.

"I know, me neither. But I'll call you first thing in the morning." I rise up and pull him down to me for a kiss. "Miss me," I whisper against his lips.

"Always do, baby." He kisses me again, then he leans his forehead against mine. "If I don't go now, I'll stay." He pulls away and places his hand on my bump. "Take care of our nuggets," he smirks. "And don't forget, Vinnie's on the floor below, and John will be right next door as soon as he's dropped us off at the yacht. Any problems, you call me, okay?"

"I will. I love you."

"I love you more."

I watch him walk away with Dan, then me and Lucy change for bed.

"How come you're still sober?" I ask, suddenly realising she's not in the least bit drunk. That's not normal for her.

"I didn't want to drink tonight. I want to see, hear, and feel everything that happens to me tomorrow," she sighs.

"Oh, Luce," I sniffle, giving her a big hug.

"Hey, no tears," she giggles. "Tomorrow is going to be a happy day, for everyone. Especially me."

WHEN YOU LEAST EXPECT IT…

Lucy and I wake early to a light, room service breakfast. I call Max, but I can hardly hear him above the noise of the jet skis. Apparently, Dan was feeling a little nervous about having to stand up in front of so many people today to deliver his vows, so Max decided to keep him busy. After the jet skis, they're going para-gliding. It's like an action-man convention.

Max laughed when I asked him not to break the groom before the wedding. But I could also hear the smile in his voice, he's enjoying himself. It's nice to hear his boyish laugh. The tragedy of his parents' death at such a young and vulnerable age, and the fact that he'd blamed himself for their deaths, had robbed him of the ability to laugh and truly enjoy himself for many years. And with the pressures of work left in the capable hands of Grace and his second in command, these last few days have been a pleasure to watch him relax and have fun.

As Maggie and Trevor add the finishing touches to our hair and makeup, Lucy's parents arrive. They look very smart, she in her pastel dress and hat, and he in his grey morning suit. They're beaming with pride.

"No crying," Maggie says, wagging her finger at Lucy. "I don't want you to ruin my masterpiece. And we can't have panda eyes when you meet your groom," she adds, packing up her kit.

I've been taking photographs all morning. Lucy's crumpled just-got-out-of-bed look has been magically transformed by Maggie and Trevor into her now glowing and luminously radiant, bride-to-be. Although Lucy's not yet in her bridal gown, she looks amazing.

I slip into my dress, an off the shoulder, floor length, burgundy sheath with a small train. As the original dress had to be abandoned, I'd gone back to see Davis who not only found this wonderful dress, he had it fitted to me in two days.

"I'll be back to dress you in forty five minutes," I say, heading for the door. "Our flowers should be here soon, too."

I leave Lucy with her parents to go and check on the other guests. They will be taken to the marina by the hotel shuttle bus, and I want to make sure everybody knows what they're doing. I speak to a girl on reception who assures me all the guests have been informed of the timetable, and the bus will be here waiting for them in an hour. She also informs me that our bouquets have arrived and she's sending them up to our room.

I make a quick call to Sasha. All the flowers are in place, the tables have been set, the staff are all present, and the cake has just arrived. I can hear the band sound-checking in the background so all seems to be going to plan.

Vinnie and Jan are having tea in the lounge so I join them for a moment.

"Jan, you look fantastic, I love your hat. And Vinnie, wow, you look so handsome." He smirks and pulls out a chair for me, then he kisses me on the cheek.

"You look beautiful, Miss."

"Vinnie, are you ever going to call me Vivienne?"

He chuckles and slurps his tea. "Yes, Miss Vivienne, I will if you want me to." I shake my head and smile.

"Would you like some tea?" Jan offers.

"No, I'm fine. I need to go and dress Lucy in a little while. I hope I haven't forgotten anything," I smirk.

"We're all set, Miss. John's going to take you, Jan, and Lucy's mum to the yacht with all your luggage, and I'll be taking Lucy and her dad in the roller."

"The roller?" I ask, confused.

"Yeah, the white Rolls Royce. The hotel have one for hire and apparently, Mike hired it out as a wedding gift," he says, taking a sip of his tea with his pinkie sticking out.

"Did he?" *Nobody said anything?*

"He was here earlier, Miss." He reaches into his inside pocket. "He left this for Lucy, and he told me he'd booked the car." He hands me a white envelope. It looks like a card.

"Oh. Right…" I'm stunned. I didn't think Mike was coming.

After a while, I leave Vinnie and Jan and head back up to our room. While I'm in the lift I check the envelope but it's sealed so I'll have to wait until Lucy opens it to find out what's inside.

When I get back to the room, I can smell the fragrant bouquets as soon as I open the door. "Oh good, they're here."

Lucy's parents hug her one last time. "We'll be down in the lobby when you're ready, darling."

I walk up to Lucy and hand her the card. "Luce, Mike left this for you." She takes it and opens the envelope, inside is a lovely card. As she opens it, I read it over her shoulder.

Dear Lucy

I've hired a white Rolls Royce for you and your dad to travel in style. My wedding gift to you, and hopefully my way of making amends.

I wish you and Dan every happiness.

Thank you for the invite, it means a lot, but as you know, I can't come to the wedding as I'm helping my cousin set up his new restaurant. But if you find the time before you fly back to London, you'll find me at 'Coeur du Mer.'

All the best, Love, Mike

"Fuck me," she sighs. "I never thought I'd ever like that guy, but this is such a lovely gift, so thoughtful."

"Vinnie said he was here. Why would he come all the way to France to deliver this?" I pull the card out of her hands to read it again.

"He didn't," she says, walking toward the long white suit bag hanging off the wardrobe door. "His cousin lives out here, not far from Dan's grandmother. He's got restaurants and bars all over the place. I thought you knew that?" she adds, unzipping the bag.

A hot flush travels over my skin. "Shit! Dan's grandmother! I forgot all about her. Someone needs to pick her up. Shit! Shit! Shit!"

"Don't panic," she laughs. "Jamie's already done it. Now, come and help me into this fabulous dress."

I puff out a sigh of relief. I knew I'd forget something.

So far, everything has gone as planned with military precision. Apart from the near-miss with Dan's grandmother. All the guests have been taken to the yacht, Max has called to tell me that Dan is calm and ready, and Lucy looks beautiful in her gown. I take a few more photographs before we leave the room, and I struggle to hold back the tears. She looks so happy, and so radiant, and unbelievably calm.

As we enter the lobby, her dad and Vinnie turn to look at her. The love in her dad's eyes is so touching, it puts a lump in my throat. I give her one last hug.

"I'll see you there, give us ten minutes before you leave and don't fall off the gangway," I smirk.

She gives me such a knowing look. "Viv—"

"No. Don't. You'll make me cry. Save it until after the ceremony." I refuse to give her eye contact. I'm feeling too emotional right now, the threat of tears prick my eyes. I wink at Vinnie, and then John takes my elbow and walks me to the car.

When we arrive at the yacht, butterflies fill my belly and my eyes eagerly seek him out. I haven't seen Max since last night, and I can't wait to see him. As I walk up the beautifully decorated gangway, my eyes find his as he holds out his hand to help me aboard. My heart flutters. He looks mouth-wateringly handsome in his impeccably tailored suit, and his golden tan makes the blue of his eyes shimmer like the shallows of the Caribbean.

He takes my hand and kisses me softly on the lips. "I've missed you. You look beautiful," he whispers, then he wraps his arm around my waist and leads me down to our cabin.

There's not much time, so I quickly check my hair and makeup after our brief but passionate embrace. Before we head back upstairs, I remove the scan of our babies from my bag and I place it on our bedside table. It comes with me everywhere I go. I like to look at it every morning when I open my eyes, and last thing at night before I go to sleep.

When we arrive on the rear deck, I'm blown away by the amazing transformation. Sasha and her team have turned it into a magical fairyland with white chairs, billowing organza drapes, flowers everywhere, and a beautiful canopy of white gardenias, where Lucy and Dan will give and receive their vows. It's stunning.

"Where's Ed? I thought he was—"

"I'm here," he says, tapping me on the shoulder. "It's all under control, Viv, just relax," he grins. I sag with relief. I think I'm more stressed out about this wedding than Lucy and Dan are.

Everyone is already seated, and I see Dan and his brother standing at the end of the petal covered isle, talking to the vicar. Max squeezes my hand and raises it to his lips to plant a soft kiss, then he throws me his mega-watt smile and we walk up to Dan, nodding our hellos along the way. I smile sheepishly at the vicar, hoping he's forgotten all about last night, and when we reach Dan, who looks remarkably calm, Max shakes his hand and Dan's face literally beams. "This is it!" he grins.

I give him a hug, then I turn my attention to his brother, Josh. "You've got the rings, haven't you?" I ask, on an arched brow. He just smirks and rolls his eyes.

Everything is ready. Max kisses me softly on the lips, runs his hand over my bump, then he leaves me to take his seat and I walk nervously back to the gangway to wait for Lucy.

The elegant white Rolls Royce glides to a stop at the foot of the gangway. Vinnie opens their door and passers-by stop to look as her father helps her out of the car and straightens her dress, then they share a few private words and a hug. She looks radiant. I take a few more shots of them as they walk up the gangway, then Ed takes my camera and hands me my bouquet. Raking my eyes all over her, I blink back the threat of tears. Happy tears.

"How do I look?" Lucy asks, when she arrives at the top.

"Calm. Beautiful. Serene… What have you done with my best friend?" She laughs, gives me a hug, then she takes a deep breath. The music begins. I quickly check her veil and train, and then I follow Lucy and her father up the aisle, in awe of her confidence and grace. Once her father has handed her over to Dan, I take her bouquet and sit down next to Max as the ceremony begins.

Max looks down at me with soft loving eyes as he leans in to kiss me tenderly on the cheek, then he hands me his handkerchief and squeezes my thigh. "This will be you and me soon," he whispers.

I lay my hand over his and squeeze it gently. "Until forever."

The ceremony was beautiful and yes, I did cry.

Once the formalities have been completed, and Ed and I have taken all the photographs of the happy couple with their friends and family, I finally relax. We move through to the front deck, where the dining tables and dance floor are situated. Sasha has done an amazing job with all the decorations, and the waiters are weaving through the guests busily serving celebratory Champagne.

The band starts with a few slow songs while everyone mingles and chats. And when John Legend's 'All of me' begins, Max pulls me onto the dance floor.

"I like this song, dance with me." He nuzzles his face in my neck. I feel his lips trail along my bare shoulder, then back up to that soft spot just under my ear, where he nips and kisses me softly. He knows I'm defenceless to that and I roll my head to give him better access. In each other's arms, we gently sway to the music in a room full of people, and yet when he romances me like this, I see only him.

"You, Mr. Foxx, are an amazing man," I say, pulling back to gaze at him in awe. He lowers his eyes, embarrassed by my comment. "You are…You have such a big, wonderful heart, and I'm so lucky that you've given it to me."

He searches my eyes, smiling that sexy smile of his, then he pulls me back into his chest and rests his cheek against mine. "Baby, I'm the lucky one. My heart only beats because of you." Every word, every gesture, floors me. As we sway to the music, he suddenly pulls back and hits me with his scorching eyes. "I need to marry you, woman. The sooner the better. I can't wait any longer and it's not up for negotiation."

I smile up at his serious, handsome face. "You won't get any argument from me, Mr. Foxx. I can't wait to marry you. Until forever, remember?"

He smiles, his mega-watt, knee-trembler. "Good. We fly out tomorrow."

"What?" Butterflies suddenly fill my stomach as I stare up at him incredulously. "But how?…Where?" His blazing eyes burn into mine as a serious expression comes over his face.

"Do you love me?"

"With all my heart."

"Do you trust me?"

"You know I do."

"Then that's all you need. Until forever."

I reach up and smooth my fingers down his flawless cheek. "I love you, Max." He smiles down at me, melting my heart and stirring my butterflies. "Love you more, baby." Kissing me tenderly on the lips, he ignites my senses, then he pulls me back into his chest and wraps me in his loving arms.

Swaying to the music, with his warm breath against my cheek, I feel safe, loved, incredibly happy, and now, complete. He's the love of my life. Wherever he takes me, whatever he has planned for us, I know it will be perfect. My whirlwind romance with the man of my dreams now has the fairy-tale ending I never thought possible. *How could I be so lucky?*

As the song ends, the band leader makes an announcement for Lucy and Dan's first dance. He warns everyone to clear a space for the couple, as their first dance is going to be a fast one. *Oh, no! They really are going to attempt the jive.* Max and I are jostled and suddenly, Max moves away from me, looking down at his trousers.

"I'm so sorry, Sir," the young waiter says, looking horrified at what he's done. A large empty water jug lies on its side on his tray. Poor Max is drenched.

"I'm sorry, baby, I'll have to go and change," he sighs, shaking his head.

"Okay, but don't be long, they're doing their first dance and I'm sure it'll be a doozy," I chuckle. He kisses me softly on the lips, and runs his hand over my belly.

"I'll be back in a minute." Then he walks away with the young waiter following after him, mumbling an apology.

Ed strides up, handing me my camera. "I'm going to

video this, but could you take some shots from the other side?"

"Yeah, okay." *This should be fun.*

Everyone crowds in around the dance floor. Lucy hitches her skirt up and I can see that she's changed out of her heels, and into her white sneakers. Dan looks petrified, but when the music starts they throw themselves into the dance with such enthusiasm, it's impossible not enjoy it. They couldn't have picked a faster song, and my cheeks ache with laughter. How Lucy thought she could perform such a challenging dance in that dress I'll never know.

Once they've finished, I congratulate them both on not breaking anything vital, and then I sit with Lucy and her mum while she cools off.

"Where's Max?" Lucy asks, still out of breath.

I look around the deck, but I can't see him. "Oh, one of the waiters spilt some water down his trousers, he's gone to change."

"What did you think of our jive?"

"Do you really want me to answer that?" I smirk. We burst into laughter as I show her some of the photographs on my camera.

Sasha walks over to me and leans down to whisper in my ear. "The buffet is ready, but I wasn't sure when you wanted the cake cutting to take place?"

I look up at Lucy, her cheeks are still flushed from all the exertion. She'll need to cool down before we photograph her again. "Give her another half an hour." Sasha nods and starts to walk off, but I pull her back. "Oh, Sasha, have you seen Mr. Foxx?"

"No, but there are a few people in the bar on the back deck, maybe he's in there." She smiles and walks away. I leave Lucy and her mum to go in search of my fiancé.

"Vivienne! Sweetie!" I glance up and see Clive and Luke sitting with Dan, so I wander over to say hello.

"Hi guys. I'm sorry I haven't had chance to talk to you yet, it's been pretty hectic today, and I'm missing a fiancé.

You haven't seen him have you?" They all look up at me with blank expressions.

"No, sorry," Clive says, pulling a chair out for me. "Oh, and congratulations on the babies," he grins. "I've got first dibs on babysitting duties," he adds, smoothing his brow.

"You know we're having twins, right?" I ask, on a frown.

He just shrugs and smiles. "Sure, how hard can it be?"

Luke, Dan and I, roll our eyes simultaneously.

"Right. I'm going to find my husband-to-be. I'll talk to you later." I leave them and make my way to the back deck. When I find the bar, I poke my head around the doorway. Vinnie and Jan are standing at the bar talking to William and Sylvie, but Max isn't here.

"Have any of you seen Max?" They all shake their heads so before I get drawn into another conversation, I head down to our cabin.

When I reach the cabin, I poke my head around the door, but he's not here. *We must have passed each other.* I start to leave, but then I decide to have a pee before I head back upstairs. I throw my bag on the bed and I walk into the en-suite. When I lift the lid on the toilet seat, something catches my eye in the toilet bowl. Several black items are floating in the water. I stare down at them, but I can't figure out what I'm looking at. *What is that?* I tilt my head trying to work it out. *Oh, no! …No, it can't be!*

I reach down and scoop the floating fragments of paper out of the water. I can't believe it, but as I move them around in my hand, I realise the torn pieces of paper are my baby scan. My heart stops. *No! …Why?*

I clutch them to my chest and rush out to the bedroom. The blood chills in my veins when I see the baby scan is missing from my bedside table, and in its place lies a piece of yellow paper.

AS I SAID… WHEN YOU LEAST EXPECT IT!

And then I see the blood.

"No! …Max! … Please God. Nooooooo!" I hear my garbled scream, as my tear blurred eyes stare at the blood smear on the back of the cabin door. My head spins, my stomach rolls, and it feels like all the oxygen has been sucked out of the room. I can't breathe, and the overwhelming pain in my heart slowly crushes me. I collapse down to my knees, still clutching the fragments of our babies to my chest, as the realisation hits me like a wrecking ball. *Monica!*

I quickly grab my bag and fumble in it for my phone. I call Max's phone, but a cold shiver spirals up my spine when I hear it ringing in the cabin. I frantically look all around me. Scrambling on my hands and knees, I find it on the floor underneath the bed. With shaking hands I quickly dial Vinnie.

"Alright, Miss?"

"Come quickly!" I scream, sobbing. "I'm in the cabin. Hurry!" I throw the phone on the bed and wipe the stinging tears from my eyes.

After a few moments, Vinnie bursts through the door with John right behind him. Vinnie comes to a shuddering stop as his wide eyes stare down at the yellow letter in my left hand. Slowly, I uncurl my right arm from my chest and open up my trembling fingers, revealing the damp, shredded scan of our babies.

My body jerks with uncontrollable sobbing. "She's taken him."

"Fuck!" Vinnie pulls a gun from inside his jacket. With nervous, angry eyes he turns to John, then he notices the blood on the cabin door. "Stay with Vivienne!" he barks. "And call Trencher. Now!"

John grabs Vinnie's arm before he leaves the room. "What's going on?" John's wide, confused eyes flick between the gun, me, and the letter in my hand.

Vinnie's face contorts into a mask of outright rage. "It's Monica …The fucking bitch is back!"

My thanks for following Max and Vivienne's story and deepest gratitude to all those who took the time to review my books.
See you in Book III of the Sexy M.F. Series…

Mine Forever

No me without you

Vivienne has everything she could ever wish for, including the heart of her sexy, gorgeous paramour. Max has proposed, vowing to fiercely love her for every moment of every day, until forever.

Against all odds and any hope, she's also pregnant with his babies. Finding out that he's secretly planned a romantic wedding, just completes her fairy-tale romance. Life just couldn't get any better than this…

But as the festivities of her best friend's wedding are in full swing up on deck, Vivienne soon realises to her horror, that Monica has returned to claim her prize!

Max is gone, taken by force, and without a trace.

Having suffered the wrath of Monica more than once, Vivienne knows only too well how evil and twisted her heart really is. Vivienne must face the heart breaking possibility that Max could be lost to her forever.

But how could Monica have engineered his abduction with such stealth? She must have had help! If so, who can Vivienne trust? And what will Monica do with him?

Only moments ago, Vivienne's future looked so bright and full of promise, but now it seems so empty and hopeless. '*No me without you.*'

Max is the love of her life. He promised her forever, and Vivienne won't rest until she finds him…even if it takes forever.

www.lisamackay.uk
@lisamackayuk
www.facebook.com/lisamackayauthor1/

69526839R00320

Made in the USA
Columbia, SC
23 April 2017